Lovers and Friends

Lovers and Friends

Camille Marchetta

ARBOR HOUSE
WILLIAM MORROW
New York

Library of Congress Cataloging-in-Publication Data

Marchetta, Camille.
  Lovers and friends / Camille Marchetta.
    p.   cm.
  ISBN 1-55710-049-7
  I. Title.
PS3563.A6346L68   1989
813'.54—dc19   89-30845
                                                                                CIP

Printed in the United States of America

First Edition

1 2 3 4 5 6 7 8 9 10

BOOK DESIGN BY KARIN BATTEN

Lovers and Friends

New York

October 1987

✣ Chapter 1 ✣

An advance copy of the Walton biography was sent to me yesterday and I have been up all night reading it. An editor at the publishing company, a friend of mine, knowing I was a friend of theirs, thought I might be interested. Interested? Outraged is more like it.

The biography isn't merely inept. It is a conscious attempt to grab the largest number of readers by appealing to what is universal in humanity: a vulgar, insatiable interest in the prurient. There are so many lies in it, not lies of fact, which are for the most part correct, but distortions of meanings, of intentions. Events are falsified by interpretation and the Waltons diminished in the process, the whole of their lives painted squalid and ugly.

None of us who knew David and Sarah saw them in that way. They had too much intelligence, too much charm, too much style, really. They had a vitality, an energy, that electrified the air around them and made them obsessively interesting to those who knew them, and those who wanted to. They were often infuriating, frequently destructive, but never tawdry.

No one will dispute the biography; not David and Sarah certainly, not their children, not their friends. It will be ignored by us like the many fabrications that came before: a good thing, perhaps, since the "truth" we would tell, in all its various forms, would be no more flattering to David and Sarah than the distortions of the eminent Mr. Philip Keating,

9

unauthorized biographer to the stars. And in a little while, those of us who don't keep diaries or journals, those of us who don't record facts as a hedge against delusion, will no doubt begin to believe the Keating version. Memory is like that, fickle, as attracted to glitter as a magpie.

The covering note, from my former friend, the editor, said the publishers expect the book to top the nonfiction best-seller list.

On the jacket of the book is a photograph of David and Sarah taken, Mr. Keating claims, during a weekend they spent in Vienna while each was married to someone else. This information is provided in a coyly salacious tone veneered with brisk journalese, the tone of the entire biography. David and Sarah did in fact go to Vienna together, but the photograph was not taken then. It was taken two years later, in London, the morning of their wedding, by me.

What difference does such a small discrepancy make? Can it matter? Yes, because photographs tell their own, their very powerful story. And this one tells of two people who don't give a damn for anyone else in the world but themselves, an appropriate enough feeling for a wedding day, I think, but a bit callous, a bit heartless, during a dirty weekend of betrayal. They were miserable in Vienna, as it happens, which fact will certainly alter no one's preconceived notions of such weekends, not even mine. But though they weren't unhappy for appropriately "moral" reasons, doesn't knowing they were give us a different attitude towards them, towards their characters, than believing them blithely unconcerned?

In the photograph, the background is out of focus, but I remember it was a lovely spring day, the first day of sunshine in the weeks I had been in England. David and Sarah saw it as an omen, a blessing. I'd come armed with my Olympus, and though we were already late for the registry office, we went into the garden and I posed them against the pale pink rose climbing the brick wall at the far end. It was morning, and the sunshine was brilliant, broken intermittently by clouds like white scarves waving against the blue sky. I moved in close. I wanted their faces. They stood in profile, looking at each other, smiling broadly, radiantly.

Watching them through the lens of my camera, shooting frame after frame, freezing them in that moment, I knew I was as much in love with them as they were with each other, with the idea of them. The cynic in me lay crouched in a corner, ready to spring, but held by a whip and a chair, by the sunshine and the smiles and the fragile beauty of the roses against the brick wall.

Their love for each other vibrated in the air like a held note in music. It didn't, at that moment, seem too much to ask that it should enrich and expand their lives; that it continue knocking obstacles out of its path with the ruthlessness of a Mafia don; that it triumph over time and familiarity, boredom and contempt. It didn't seem at all too much to ask that it should last forever.

London

June 1970

❧ *Chapter 2* ❧

We were sitting in a small Polish restaurant near the South Kensington Tube station when David told me about Sarah. I was in London doing a photo essay on English potters for *The Craftsman*. It was, by my standards, a major assignment, and I had meant to start work immediately and keep at it in my usual compulsive way until finished, but David insisted that a visit to the Victoria and Albert was essential to my research and that his accompanying me would be more of a help than a distraction. Because I'd missed him a lot since he and Caroline had left New York, because his insight was always invaluable, and because (more to the point) David could usually get me to do anything he wanted, I gave in and spent the day with him roaming the halls of the V&A, looking at Greek oenochoe and Roman amphora, arguing the merits of Persian versus Turkish pottery, admiring the delicate Chinese porcelain, laughing at the gaudy Italian with its florid gods and chubby goddesses, until intercepted by a guard who, uninformed and fierce, delivered a defense of his charges with the passion of the converted. David, of course, plunged into conversation. As I looked on with my usual blend of impatience and admiration, he barraged the guard with questions— about the museum, about the curator, about the collection—eliciting a wealth of historical information and personal anecdote, delighting the old man with his perspicacity, leaving him beaming after us with satisfaction and approval. David's instinct to seduce was irrepressible; his success, as notes Mr. Keating, biographer, was impressive. "Did you catch those cadences?" said David admiringly, as we went. "A museum guard, and he talks like a Pentecostal preacher. What a country! What a language!"

We crossed the Brompton Road, headed towards the South Kensington Tube station, and entered the Daquise, where David was greeted like visiting royalty by an elegant gray-haired cashier and a pretty young waitress, pink-cheeked and plump, who smiled at him expectantly, as if hoping the caress in his "hello" would deliver as much as it promised. The older woman apparently knew better, but saw no reason not to take the interest in David's eyes as a compliment. That brief, speculative glance was one of the things women found most attractive about him.

The Daquise was one of David's favorite retreats, a place he often came to read papers, write letters, to think, and make notes, chain-smoking the Gauloises which had recently replaced his Marlboroughs. The room is long and narrow, the lighting dim, the rectangular tables faced with beige linoleum left uncovered until the dinner hour, when a white cloth is added. The menu is hearty and cheap, kasha featuring largely in the cuisine. David liked the food well enough, but he went there really for the atmosphere.

A rendezvous for Polish émigrés, the Daquise is a remnant of a time when violent feeling could still be cloaked with good manners. As we sat there, an elderly man entered. He was tall, with the bearing of a prince. He had luxurious silver hair, covered by a felt fedora. Around his neck was a foulard, in his hand a cane. He crossed to a couple at the table near us. At his approach, the woman raised her head and tilted it charmingly. A smile further crumpled her lined face. She extended a hand. With a neat click of his heels, he took it in his, and raised it to his lips. It was 1970.

Thanks probably to the intercession of a trendy academic who admired him, David had won a Ford Foundation grant and had moved his wife and daughter to London the previous year. He had thought he would be able to write better away from the distractions of New York, the noise and the dirt, the street life and the drugs, the constant clamoring for his attention. Though he thought of himself as an artist, a solitary, he was in fact never alone except when working. Overlooking his temper, ignoring his arrogance, the frequent contempt in his eyes their confirmation that he was lit by divine fire, people flocked to David, drawn by his energy and intelligence, by the force of his talent, by the healing power of the charm he sometimes dispensed, suspecting that he could be (as he often was) a very good friend. He knew no one in England. At least, he hadn't when he'd arrived.

We sat in the Daquise over tea and strawberry tarts, surrounded by a haze of smoke, catching each other up with our lives, filling in the details our letters had left out. I'd missed our talking in the months we'd been apart. David not only listened, he heard.

I hadn't done much, a few photo essays that had given me the sensation of moving sideways in my career rather than forward. David had done better. He'd written a short play currently on at the Royal Court's Theatre Upstairs. One afternoon at a squash club in the Finchley Road, he had taken on the local champion and beaten him, by one point. The former champion had turned out to be a codirector at the Court. One thing had led to another and ultimately to a production of the play, *Dreams in F Minor*. The story hadn't surprised me. Luck frequently dogged David's footsteps.

David, however, didn't see himself as lucky. My story of a relatively unknown young playwright achieving almost instant success in a foreign country was translated in his version to a tale of great talent recognized too late and not with sufficient fervor. The play had received mixed reviews and was drawing only a small audience. And David minded. He was hurt and bewildered and frightened, but what he was feeling, more forcefully than any other emotion, was rage. "Those fucking cretins," he complained, meaning the critics, "would try to give *Sophocles* a lesson in playwrighting, for chrissake. Can't you hear them? 'The excessive use of a chorus,' he mimicked, 'to relay details of what has usually and tediously happened offstage shows a remarkable lack of imagination and an even greater deficiency of stagecraft.' Idiots!" Only an absolute belief in his own genius made it possible for David to write. When that was challenged, by critics, by friends, by himself in black moments, he was crippled, unable to work at all. His only weapon against doubt was fury.

He ran out of cigarettes and went to buy some from the tobacconist in the Tube station. When he returned, he stopped for a moment to flirt with the waitress and order more pastries, then slid his long body into the banquette beside me and told me he was in love.

It was a claim I'd heard David make before, once even about me, and I wasn't any more inclined than usual to take it seriously. "Presumably not with your wife," I said.

"Don't be a cunt," he replied. "I'm fond of Caroline. You know that. But I never should have married her."

Trying hard not to let my agreement show, I kept my face impassive. Though David was my friend, my best friend, and I loved him in a way

I never have and never will love anyone else, I was hardly blind to his faults. But Caroline, like her or not, was a woman, a frequently wronged woman. Some loyalty of sex often put me in a position of having to defend her.

"If it wasn't for Lissie," continued David, referring to his daughter, Melissa, "I'd have left her years ago." My eyebrows lifted at that. He looked at me querulously. "Well, what's the matter?"

"I'm not used to hearing you talk in clichés."

"That's the trouble with the truth," he replied, with a grin. "It always sounds like a cliché."

"Are you going to leave them now? Now that you're 'in love'?"

I couldn't seem to help the tone, but this time he let it go. His smile vanished. He shook his head "I don't know what I'm going to do."

More curious than sympathetic, I studied his face, trying to read its signs. David, despite all protestations of confusion, always knew exactly what he was going to do. He was relentless in pursuit of a goal, whether it was winning at table tennis, having a new play produced, or getting a woman to bed. Now, his face, that stunning face I had photographed over and over again, that face I knew as well as my own, was more gaunt than usual, its planes and angles more pronounced. His nose, broken, in a fight when he was ten, seemed bigger, as did his eyes. In person, those eyes were even more astounding than on film, so dark a brown they glowed black and reflected light as if they were opaque. Now they were shadowed. He looked as if he hadn't been sleeping well.

"I'm in love with Sarah Cope," he said, and for the first time in a long time, I registered surprise, something I didn't like to do with David. He liked the effect too much. It encouraged him, I thought, to go on relentlessly (much like his three-year-old daughter, Melissa, pleading "Again, again!" as soon as you'd finished playing one of her favorite games), trying to repeat it, his efforts frequently resulting in pain and tears.

I knew who Sarah Cope was, of course. By that time, she was a household name in England, and her fame had filtered through to the more sophisticated urban areas of the United States, where the local Sunday supplements carried knowing articles on the English theater. She had appeared in a number of films that had played to capacity in those cities' art houses. I had seen her in one, in New York, only a few weeks before, *The Folly*, which was selling out at the Carnegie Hall Cinema.

It's an extraordinary film. In it, Sarah plays a nineteenth-century English duchess married to a man years older than herself. At first, the marriage is tranquil, even happy; but as her young stepson matures, the duchess becomes more and more attracted to him until, finally, unable to resist her obsession, she lures him into an affair. They meet in an abandoned folly on an island in a Capability Brown lake, where the duke, predictably, discovers them one stormy night. The discovery doesn't, however, lead to murder, as I'd half expected, or to suicide, but to banishment, to Venice, where sins of the flesh were, if not condoned, at least ignored. For some time the lovers live there, more or less contented. But when the duke dies, his son and heir is recalled home to claim his inheritance, his sex earning him a pardon the duchess is not allowed.

I saw *The Folly* again a few months ago. Sarah's performance seems as powerful now as it did when the film was first released: subtle, intelligent, sensual, and infinitely moving. The close-up that ends it is in sharp relief, as it would be in a portrait still. The duchess has just finished reading her lover's farewell letter, and her face registers the hell of all hope abandoned. The shot is devastating.

David assured me he wasn't just starstruck. He didn't get starstruck (which was more or less true: the only talent that obsessed him was his own). "Some actors—when you meet them—are so ordinary, not only ordinary, but dull, really. Bland. You can't wait to get away from them. But on stage, in film, they're transformed. Performing, they glow. They seem more beautiful, dynamic, more charming and seductive than ordinary people. They're the 'stars.' And it isn't their success, or their money, that's at the root of their glamour. It's totally the other way around. It's that strange demonic ability of theirs that conjures the success, the wealth, that subjugates the public and keeps it in thrall."

"I saw *The Folly*. I thought she was extraordinary."

"In person, she's even more wonderful. Softer, more fragile." Her skin, he told me, had the translucence of porcelain. Her brown eyes were soft as melting chocolate. Her blond hair was a spun-gold nimbus haloing her head. She was intelligent, witty, charming. Her attraction was irresistible as a magnet's.

No woman, no matter how understanding (and I like to think of myself as *very* understanding), likes to sit and listen to a lengthy catalogue of another's virtues. Beyond a reasonable point, it begins to seem insulting. As David went on praising Sarah, I got more and more irritated. "Quite a paragon, isn't she?" I muttered. But he was so intent on his purpose, convincing me—his oldest, and best, friend—that

Sarah Cope was indeed a worthy object of his love, he didn't, to my surprise, get my point. So I added for good measure, "Her husband's a lucky guy."

He looked, for a moment, torn between a desire to hit me and a reflex to laugh. He decided on the latter. He usually did, though I've seen him take a barroom apart in a brawl. "Her husband's an ass," he appended to the laugh.

"That's not what I've heard."

"She doesn't love him."

"Of course not. She loves you."

But David didn't smile at my teasing. "I don't know," he replied. "She won't say." He looked away from me and added, his voice full of an unfamiliar anguish, "I can't make her say." He turned towards me again and slid closer along the leather banquette. Because he had after all heard what I'd said, he slid his arm around me and kissed my cheek. "You know you're one of the most important people in my life, don't you? You're my history. I couldn't stand it if I lost you."

I knew he meant it, and was appeased. David's love for me was permanent, indisputable, accepting, and—most important—platonic. As was mine for him. Our sexual interlude had been brief and, though not unimportant, ultimately irrelevant. It had been a phase we'd had to go through to get what we wanted from each other: something less, and more.

"You have to meet her. I want you to meet her," he repeated, emphasizing its importance to him. "I want you to be friends."

"You mean you want me to be your spy in the house of love. Why don't you just ask her what you want to know?"

"Do you think I haven't?" The pain in his voice again surprised me. I wasn't used to hearing it. "I can't keep badgering her. If I frighten her too much, she'll run." When I didn't reply, he looked at me warily. "You're not going to take a position on this, are you?" His voice was cold now, disapproving. "You're not going to become all proper and prim? You can turn into the most god-awful little puritan sometimes, you know?" He was angry with me in advance of what he suspected might be betrayal. "If you're worried about Caroline and Lissie, don't. I'll take care of them. They won't get hurt."

"They will," I said, keeping my voice and face as devoid as possible of emotion. I didn't want to quarrel with David. Not then. I didn't want to go back to New York with even a small rift in our friendship. It would make me feel too lonely. "They will get hurt," I insisted, knowing I had no chance of convincing him: people in love are always blind to the obvious. "If you go on like this, you won't be able to avoid hurting them."

"Goddammit, whose friend are you?"

"Yours. But that isn't the point."

A smile followed the anger. He knew he had won. "Then you'll meet her?"

"Yes," I said, surrendering. "I'll meet her."

❧ Chapter 3 ❧

I knew David Walton all my life. We were born three weeks apart at the same hospital on Manhattan's Upper West Side. Our families had similar apartments in identical houses on 86th Street, just off Central Park West. David's family was a mélange of English, German, and French stock, Protestant through and through. Mine was Irish and English Catholic. Despite the differences, we were close. Our respective parents had fled their roots and small-town prejudices with a vengeance.

We were born when World War II began, and for the first few years of our lives, we saw our fathers only when they were home on leave. They appeared in our midst unexpectedly, in a sudden burst of excitement and a downpour of tears. They were uniformed and smiling. They brought us presents and held us in their laps, the rough fabric of their uniforms scratchy against our bare legs. They laughed at our stories, joined in our games, declared our mother's bedroom suddenly off-limits. And then they were gone.

David's father was in Europe covering the war for the Associated Press, mine fighting with the Marines in the Pacific. When it was over, though David and my brother often begged him, my father never spoke of his experiences. Mr. Walton, in contrast, was full of tales and, without much coaxing, would pull out scrapbooks full of stories and photographs to show us children. There were pictures of weary, mud-splattered soldiers pausing to rest, of hollow-eyed refugee children staring blankly into the camera, of lovers kissing by a bombed-out shell of a building, shot after shot of the devastation of war. But none of those impressed me as much as the photo of Mr. Walton with his arm around Margaret Bourke-White. She was wearing a long, light scarf and a leather flight jacket, a 35mm camera (which I learned later she almost never used) slung across her shoulder. She looked very beautiful, very powerful, and very sexy. "That woman sure has guts," said Mr. Walton admiringly. As soon as I saw that picture, I knew with absolute certainty, with total conviction, when I grew up, I was going to be a photographer.

David never showed any interest in writing until he was in college. What he wanted to be when he grew up was a cowboy.

While the men were away, with no family in the neighborhood, their wives turned to each other for help with the children, with the house-keeping, with the shopping, and—most important—for moral support. When one's spirits sank, the other's rose in compensation. They took turns playing Pollyanna.

Growing up, David and his brother and sister were more like siblings than neighbors to my brother and me. We were constantly in and out of each other's apartments. We played, fought, made up, slept over, threatened never to speak to each other again, swore solemn oaths of eternal friendship. Together, we played stickball in the streets, ice-skated at Rockefeller Center, learned to ride in Central Park. We played tag in the Museum of Natural History and in the hallowed halls of the Metropolitan Museum of Art. The bond between all of us, as children, was strong; but the one between David and me turned out to be inde-structible. Our relationship survived into adulthood. With the others, we remained friendly, concerned, affectionate, but distant the way you do with people who once had parts in the same play, but now have moved on to other productions. David and I retained star status in the drama of each other's life.

For all that, we were very different. I hate confrontations. I'll do almost anything to avoid a scene. To me, negotiation through diplo-matic channels seems infinitely preferable to war. I'm quiet, rather shy, really. I'm orderly and I'm neat, about my work and my life. David was not. The only quality we shared, aside from a sense of humor, was persistence. For a long time, David never finished anything: books, model airplanes, homework assignments. His room was littered with projects begun but never completed. He would focus with such inten-sity on a subject, any subject, that he soon would solve its problems, exhaust its potential, and lose interest. That changed when he began writing. He found something that never bored him, and he stuck to it.

In the act of creating, he could devise new problems even as he solved the old.

Which was, essentially, the technique he used to retain interest in his life. His romance with Sarah Cope, I was certain, was a twist thrown in to add zest to a lagging act. Before long, it would lose its momentum and David would be forced to invent another turn to give impetus to his drama, the story of a playwright's futile attempts to create sufficient serenity in his life to make writing possible.

We left the Daquise and set off for Sloane Square, David leading us circuitously past rows of Georgian houses, through nineteenth-century squares of Corinthian columns and iron railings, the massive windows of the houses sprouting boxes of pink petunias and trailing lobelia, along a route so familiar to him he managed for once not to get us lost. It was the middle of June and the days were growing steadily longer, the light lingering until eight-thirty or nine, making the evenings pregnant with possibility. Earlier in the day it had been raining, and I was now overdressed for the late sun. Sticky and uncomfortable, I looked longingly at the pale blond ladies walking past in their Biba sundresses and Ravel sandals.

We talked about me. "If you don't marry him," said David, "you'll probably never marry anybody."

I looked at him to see if he were joking, but he wasn't. "That's ridiculous," I said.

"You love him, don't you?"

"In a way."

"In *what* way?"

"Not in a way that makes me want to marry him," I replied, irritated.

"If you don't want my opinion, don't ask for it." His voice stayed infuriatingly calm.

"It's hard to take your opinion seriously when you start making absurd generalizations."

"All right, I'll stick to specifics. I'll stick to practicalities. Ned loves *you*." David looked at me and I nodded. "He wants to marry you." I nodded again. "He's a good lawyer. He's honest, caring, shrewd. His politics are impeccable, surpassing even your high standards. He'll run for public office one of these days and end up President. Don't you want to be First Lady?"

I started to laugh, my annoyance gone. "Would I have to know which fork to use?"

"You're bright. You could learn." He put an arm around my

shoulder. "Don't be such a coward," he said, as he had when he'd coaxed me onto the horse's back before our first riding lesson. "There's nothing to be afraid of," he added, as he'd done when he convinced me we ought to make love.

In front of the Royal Court, overwhelming the one poster for David's play, were photographs of Sarah Cope and her husband, Duncan Powell, currently playing in the Court's main theater.

David had met Sarah at the play's first-night party. Sarah, the star of the evening, had paid little attention to him; but for David, it had been a good old-fashioned *coup de foudre*. He couldn't take his eyes from her face and paid little attention all evening to anything said to him, including compliments about his own play. Caroline accused him later of sulking, as he was prone to do when not the center of interest.

Sarah had worn a dress of sheer black georgette embroidered in silver. Her blond hair was swept up high on her head, held in place by black combs studded with paste diamonds. A glittering necklace circled her throat. Her skin glowed with success. "I looked at her and thought of Byron's Mrs. Wilmot," David told me, then quoted—without a trace of self-consciousness—the relevant lines. He knew I knew them, but liked the sound of the words. "'She walks in beauty, like the night/ Of cloudless climes and starry skies/ And all that's best of dark and bright/ Meet in her aspect and her eyes...'" She seemed radiant, distant, mysterious. She was infinitely desirable.

David hadn't noticed Duncan at all, though Caroline had spoken to him and reported later he was charming. David grinned at me. "I told her it must have something to do with all the tea they drink, the reason Englishmen are so charming."

"The Chinese aren't," I countered.

"They drink China tea, not India tea. And the Indians are the most charming people in the world."

The play they were appearing in was a huge hit, as the presence of Sarah Cope and Duncan Powell on the bill usually guaranteed. It was by John Massey, whose first play, two years before, had been such a phenomenon that his name was now uttered reverentially in the same breath as Pinter's. David thought this one three hours of soulless bombast, though the performances, he conceded, were brilliant. "Duncan's a fine actor," he added in that spirit of fairness that announced trouble ahead. David was always able to appreciate a rival's virtues, though the more pronounced these were, the more fiercely competitive he became. Pitting himself (the unknown playwright) against Duncan (re-

nowned star of stage and screen, the heir apparent to Olivier's crown)
was the kind of challenge he found irresistible.

We picked up my ticket at the box office, then David left to go home
to read Lissie a bedtime story, instructing me to wait for him afterwards
in the pub next door. I made my way up the crowded staircase into a
small theater, settled myself into a narrow seat, and waited for the actors
to appear.

Before *Dreams in F Minor* opened in London, David had had a total
of six plays produced, all in fringe theaters in Chicago, New York, and
San Francisco. They had received generally excellent, if confused, notices but were deemed too difficult, too special, for commercial con-
sumption, despite the fact they always sold out wherever they played.
The theaters were small, however, and David earned almost nothing
from his success. He supported Caroline and Lissie by acting when he
liked the parts, by driving a cab, by working as a night watchman, once
even as a bodyguard. Caroline, too, worked, both before she had Lissie
and afterwards. She modeled when she could get a job, worked as a
waitress, when she couldn't. Sometimes, when David was too involved
in writing to worry about finances, Caroline's erratic earnings were their
only income. And, of course, David borrowed money: from his disapproving father, his dubious brother, from his more affluent friends.
Then came the Ford Foundation grant.

I had read *Dreams*, David's interpretation of the Orpheus myth, in
draft. He had sent a copy to me in New York as soon as he'd finished
it. I don't pretend to be a disinterested judge of his work. There is
nothing David has ever written, beginning with the Christmas play he
produced for us at age eight, in which I haven't found some evidence of
what I thought was genius.

On the page, the play had seemed powerful. Onstage, it was stunning, with a vividness of imagery, a forcefulness of language, a depth of
characterization David had never before achieved. There were flaws:
sections were overwritten (he later fixed that); the character of Jimmy
still, in my opinion, doesn't work; and the first act end is weak. Still,
the play is intensely moving.

Stanley Hyde, the *New York Times* critic, and a fan, had done the
program note for the London *Playbill*. "David Walton's plays," he wrote,
"explode with energy, crackle with vitality, sparkle with mordant wit.
His language has the raw power of street argot transformed by genius
into poetry." I wasn't inclined to argue.

*   *   *

The main theater hadn't let out yet, so the pub was still fairly empty when I entered looking for David. He was at a table, talking to a small, homely girl, who was gazing at him with a combination of awe and longing. She stood when he introduced us, glared at me resentfully, and said she had to be getting on. David took her hand, pulling her toward him, so that he could kiss her cheek. "See you tomorrow," he said. Even that little made her face glow. "She works in the box office," he explained, then went and got us a couple of beers.

I told David my reaction to what I'd seen; and he listened, but didn't register my comments. His mind was on something else. Then the play's director, Simon Wroth, David's squash buddy, joined us for a while. Simon was, at that time, still unknown outside his own small and literate circle. He was a dark-haired, rumpled man, in his early thirties, bursting with energy. He flirted with me nicely, suggested dinner one night, and left. He could see David wasn't in the mood for company.

Suddenly, I knew what David was waiting for. Even before he smiled, I turned to the door and saw Sarah enter. A step behind was her husband. The bar had filled with theater evacuees, and the Powells made their way slowly through the crowd, saying hello to friends. Like the prince and princess in a fairy tale, both were blond and very beautiful.

They stopped at our table. David introduced me and I was blessed with the full glory of their smiles, incandescent and winning. Sarah's gaze was direct and her manner completely unaffected. Her voice, thick and sweet, had an edge like the honey laced with lemon my mother always gave me to ease a sore throat. Duncan, who'd by then done a number of hit films I'd seen, some of which I'd even liked, was taller than I'd expected, though not so tall as David, and broader, with a muscular, well-exercised body unusual in the English actors I had so far stumbled across. He must have spent as much time exercising it as he did his voice, the sound of which seemed to resonate somewhere deep in my stomach. I knew it was the most beautiful speaking voice I was ever likely to hear: full and rich, sexy and infinitely flexible. He had the fair, rugged handsomeness of an English sportsman, the kind who consider a two-thousand-foot climb up a sheer slope on a March afternoon a mere "hill walk." Undoubtedly, in looks, he outclassed the dark-haired, lanky David, with his broken nose and chipped front tooth. And if he didn't have David's blatant sexuality, his vitality, his intelligence, Duncan certainly had charm, and he turned the full practiced glow of it on me.

"Are you the Nikki Collier who takes those photographs in *Plays and*

Players?" he asked, and when I admitted that I was: "The ones you did of the *Hair* rehearsals in New York were extraordinary. Bizarre, interesting, full of energy."

"You made it seem such fun," added Sarah.

"Thank you." I smiled, hoping I didn't look as awkward as I felt. How could I help liking them? But I wished they would go away. I'm not a bad dissembler when prepared, but on the spur of the moment, I have a natural inclination to honesty. The longer we talked, the more afraid I became that I would somehow give away to Duncan what I had just learned. Unless he already knew, of course. I had heard stories about eccentric English theatrical folk and their strange ménages. I looked at him speculatively just as he extended a hand to me, murmured something polite about seeing one another again, and maneuvered Sarah towards a group of people in the opposite corner, one of whom I suddenly recognized: it was Mick Jagger.

"Let's go," said David, standing up.

I forced my attention back to him. "I haven't finished my beer yet. He sat again and waited, mustering as much patience as possible. "You knew she would be here?"

"They usually come in after a performance."

"You could have warned me."

"I wanted a spontaneous response."

"*You* wanted. What about me? You know how I hate being put on the spot. What if I'd given something away?"

"I trust you, Nikki, completely."

"I wish I could say the same about you." I drained my glass, then looked at him. "Don't you want to know what I think?"

"It was all over your face. You fell in love, too, only you did it with both of them."

"I thought they were very nice," I said in my primmest voice.

He laughed and stood up again. "Come on, let's get out of here." His eyes drifted across the room and for a split second caught Sarah's glance. No emotion registered on either face. He turned back to me, put his arm around my shoulder, and guided me through the packed bar. He smiled, rather smugly I thought. "We're meeting for lunch tomorrow," he said, as he led me out in to the street.

✨ *Chapter 4* ✨

The assignment from *The Craftsman* was an important one to me, in terms of space, not subject matter, which was "English Pots and Potters." I'd photographed a lot of crafts over the years for various trade and women's magazines, but never before had I been given so many pages. It was a chance to stretch, a chance to show off a little. In fact, the essay turned out well, and one photograph from it (not my favorite) still shows up in collections from time to time, the one of Anni Leigh at her wheel. She was about eighty that summer when I visited her pottery in Cornwall, but there was hardly a line in her face. Tall and still handsome, with her long gray hair pinned loosely on top of her head, she looked like a duchess in denim. Her eyes were big and startlingly blue, but her hands were the most remarkable thing about her: they were large and strong, with slender, beautifully tapered fingers. I shot over twenty rolls of film the two days I was with her, and came away with a few photographs I was proud of—the best a close-up of her hands, begrimed with clay, caressing it, molding the neck of an elegant earthenware vase she later gave me as a gift. The lighting in the photograph is crisp and clear, every detail exactly in focus. To me, it has always conveyed the deep, satisfying sensuality of the creative act.

I spent my first days in London researching my subjects at the British Museum Library, visiting the Craftsmen Potters Association, phoning to set appointments, and trying to catch all the craft and photographic exhibitions in town. There was a Bill Brandt show on at the Heywood Gallery that I remember liking despite lukewarm reviews from critics.

One morning, a few days after my arrival, my phone rang, waking me from a sound sleep. It was Caroline Walton, wanting to have lunch.

We had all had dinner together—Caroline, David, and I—the night before. I had spent an hour playing with Lissie, who, at three, was tough and funny and beautiful, with Caroline's red hair and green eyes and David's absolute self-confidence. She impressed me by reciting memorized poems (A. A. Milne's), and I won her friendship (she'd forgotten me in the year since we'd last seen one another) by teaching her how to walk with a book balanced on the crown of her head. She flung her arms around my neck, kissed me goodnight, and invited me to stay forever. "You can sleep in the other bed in my room," she said hopefully as David led her away.

Dinner with her parents was not nearly so successful. Resentful of my relationship with David, Caroline had never liked nor been comfortable with me. I could understand why and, at first, had done what I could to reassure her; but finally I'd realized that short of giving up my friendship with David (which was unthinkable), there really was nothing I could do to make her feel better about me. Wives, since marrying for love came into vogue, have come to expect that they be not only the most important woman in their husband's life but the *only* woman on any level of intimacy.

Over the years, my attitude towards Caroline's jealousy had evolved to the point where it could be expressed in one, simple word: tough. We avoided each other as much as we could. Consequently, her phone call wasn't just unexpected, it was shocking. And it wasn't just sleepiness that made me say yes. I was curious. I couldn't imagine why, now, she should want to see me alone.

We met at the Tratoo in Abingdon Road, a popular Kensington lunch place, bright and noisy and crowded. An island people, aware of limited space, the English tend to maximize its use, especially in restaurants. The tables are usually jammed so close together that deals are made and broken, relationships begun and ended, while neighboring diners pretend politely not to hear.

Caroline was there when I arrived, sitting at a corner banquette, thereby eliminating one set of neighbors. She looked gorgeous. Her beautiful red hair was unfashionably long but the cut and color of the purple Jean Muir dress she wore made her seem very stylish. Crossing the restaurant towards her, I thought (really for the first time) I might like to photograph her and wondered why she had not been more successful as a model. When I reached her, I remembered the answer. There was a bleakness about her that was oppressive. I could see behind the superb cheekbones and the sea-green eyes the face the camera would capture: one of exquisite misery—not the best kind for encouraging people to buy jewels or furs or designer clothes.

In his biography of the Waltons, Keating makes it clear that David married Caroline only because she was pregnant. That's true. What he doesn't make clear is how much David, for a long time, had wanted a child. In fact, he wanted an army of children. In contrast to most of the men of his age I knew, all painstakingly trying to minimize their responsibilities, David considered with glee the prospect of extending his. As a child, the complex family relationships portrayed in the Bible stories he heard on the radio, then traced to their source, fascinated him. Long after lights out, he sat up reading historical novels, indulging his passion for dynasties, for Plantegenets and Tudors, for Capets and Valois, for Hapsburgs and Bonapartes. *I, Claudius* was one of his favorite books. David loved the "idea" of family, be it the warm, cozy group of *Cheaper by the Dozen* or Don Corleone's sinister kin in *The Godfather*. To be a *pater familias* was what he wanted. And, more to the point, his brother Jack by then had three sons.

David had expected Lissie to be followed quickly by more children, but Caroline had said no. Perhaps denying him something he so much wanted was the only way she had of preserving her identity. It must at times have seemed threatened with extinction by the force of David's enormous ego.

The lunch was going to be even harder than anticipated, I realized as soon as I sat. First Caroline grumbled about the noise, then she questioned the waiter endlessly about the exact ingredients of the *spaghetti al vongole*, the *piccatini al limone*, the vegetables, the salads; and when he'd finally taken our order and left, she began immediately to list the shortcomings of Lissie's nursery school.

Conversation between Caroline and me was never easy. No doubt we had things in common, but the barriers had gone up too quickly between us for any exploration of what those might be. Except for Lissie, we had no neutral territory, and she kept nervously but firmly to that ground for two courses. We discussed the child's school, clothes, playmates, her vocabulary, her sense of humor. Fond as I was of the little girl, enough was still enough. When the waiter poured the coffee and left, I interrupted Caroline in midsentence. "Sorry, but I don't believe you asked me to lunch just to discuss Lissie. You don't have any problem with the child. And if you did, I'd be the last person you'd come to for advice."

She smiled feebly, then looked away as she reached for the sugar. She put three lumps into her cup, which was demitasse size. As she stirred it, she looked up, saw me watching, and smiled again. "I've given up smoking, but I can't seem to manage without sugar. I try not to let Lissie have any at all, but it seems to be in everything, breakfast foods, ketchup, fruit juices . . ."

I waited, sipping my coffee. The restaurant was emptying slowly, the business people leaving to return to their offices. Soon there would be left only a few diehards with difficult deals uncompleted, and Caroline and me on the verge of something momentous. If she didn't get to the point soon, I decided, curious or not, I'd excuse myself and go. I had work to do. Finally, she took a breath and plunged in. "What I . . ." she began hesitantly. "What I want to talk to you about does have to do with Lissie. At least, I wouldn't have noticed, or anyway not so soon, if it hadn't been for her." She paused. I could see her wavering, not wanting to go on, sorry that she'd allowed herself to involve me even this far in whatever it was bothering her. Then some other emotion intervened: fear, I thought. She rushed on, her voice carefully controlled. "David used to spend hours every day playing with her. He doesn't anymore. He's hardly ever home, and when he is he's not really there."

So that was it. Suddenly, I was furious, with myself for not having guessed what Caroline wanted, for having agreed to the lunch, with David for telling me about Sarah, for getting me involved.

There are times the truth is of no use to anyone. Trying to comfort myself with the fact I didn't even like the woman, feeling like a lying, deceitful bitch, I looked Caroline straight in the eye, and equivocated. "He's planning another play. You know how he gets when he's trying to work out an idea."

"This is different."

"I know he's worried about what to write next," I insisted. He was. He wanted to make a breakthrough to a wider audience.

"Just because I haven't known David from birth doesn't mean I don't know him at all," she sniped. "He is my husband. We do share a home, a bed, a child."

"I am not suggesting you don't understand him, Caroline." I kept my own voice neutral.

She took a breath, got herself under control again. "I'm sorry I didn't mean to snap at you. I promised myself I wouldn't."

"What I'm sorry about is that I always manage to annoy you somehow."

"It's nothing you do. It's just..." She pulled up short, leaving the sentence unfinished, hauling the conversation back to the course she'd set. "If David's told anyone what's wrong, he's told you." It was a measure of her desperation, of David's withdrawal from her, that she could make herself say that to me.

"Have you asked him?"

She nodded, then shrugged. "He says he's just tired. That the rehearsals were a strain, and the opening, that he just needs to get out of the house and unwind a little before he starts writing another play."

"That sounds reasonable."

"Does it? And if it's true, which I doubt, what do Lissie and I do while he's out having a good time, who knows where, or who with? Sit and wait? That's all?"

"David was never exactly a homebody."

"I told you. This is different. It's never been like this before."

"Maybe," I began tentatively, beginning to sense another part of the problem, a part not totally David's fault, "you're just homesick. You may just be feeling lonely without your family and friends around." I searched my mind for details of friends for Caroline. She must have some somewhere. Wasn't there a sister in Georgia? Did they speak?

"I don't need or want anyone but David," she replied, finality in her tone.

"Have you made any new friends since you've been here?" I persisted, though I knew it would do no good.

"They're all David's friends," she responded, forgetting he hadn't known anyone when they'd arrived. "They're not interested in me." There was envy in her voice as well as anger. My impatience, my irritation with her, began to mount. Caroline admired David and, in my opinion, felt smothered by him. She loved basking in the light of her husband's talent, yet resented not being seen at all outside its circle. But on no condition was she willing to move even a little distance away, find her own space, light her own candle.

She banged her cup into the rim of its saucer, sending the cup and its contents across the table in a mud-brown stain. She righted the cup and dabbed at the pink cloth with her napkin, then stopped and looked at me. "I hate this goddam city. I wish we'd never come."

ﮞ Chapter 5 ﮞ

That lunch with Caroline cost me the rest of the day. I couldn't concentrate on reading, so I left the British Museum almost as soon as I got there and wandered over to Foyle's. Never my favorite bookstore, that day it seemed particularly big and unwelcoming. I couldn't focus there either, and left without buying a book.

The sky had turned leaden and I considered returning to my hotel to sulk, but I felt restless, and instead took a taxi to a pottery in Chelsea to shoot some film. Neither did that work. My reflexes were slow, my thinking wasn't clear, and I soon realized the odds were against my getting anything worth using. I gave up and walked in the sullen evening light along the King's Road back to the hotel, window-shopping as I went, wondering how everything could look so simultaneously fashionable and seedy. The stores had already closed and the street traffic was light. I passed the Arethusa, the club where later all the smart set would dine in their chiffon midi-dresses and zebra-striped trousers. From a barrow I bought a bouquet of scarlet and purple anemones. Soon, in the distance, I could see the marquee of the Royal Court. Just before I turned into Sloane Street, I thought I saw Sarah and Duncan walking into the alley leading to the theater's stage door.

I was staying at the Austen Court, a hotel either on or near (I wasn't sure which) a site where Jane Austen used to visit. It was old and genteely shabby, full of gleaming Chippendale tables, chintz sofas, and elegant watercolor drawings of wildflowres. The lobby, when I entered, was quiet, with only a fat, waistcoated gentleman, asleep in a large armchair, a copy of the *Times* open in his lap to the crossword puzzle. A frock-coated concierge was at the desk. There were no messages, and I retreated to my room, put the anemones in a tooth glass, and contemplated them while I took a long bath. Afterwards, I went to bed without my supper (I was, in every sense, still full from lunch), curling up with a new Alison Lurie, hoping to distract myself into a good mood and read myself to a night's sound sleep. Then Ned phoned.

He was, at that time, defending a black man, Regis Boyle, accused of robbing and killing his white employer. The case, since forgotten, attracted a lot of attention then, going all the way to the Supreme Court before Ned got the guilty verdict overturned. The evidence was entirely circumstantial, the gist of it being that the hardware store had shown no signs of forced entry and that Boyle had had ample opportunity to steal a set of keys. He was a big man, six feet three inches big, very black, with dreadlocks, and a scar on his cheek his mother said he got when he fell down the tenement steps at age five. In other words, Regis Boyle looked bad, and the state went all out to nail him, ignoring in the process just a few of the rules. Ned fought hard and brilliantly and eventually won. The name Ned Conti became as familiar on the East Coast as Archie Bunker's, and Regis Boyle went free. The shopkeeper's wife later admitted killing him.

We almost got through the conversation unscathed as Ned brought me up to date on the progress of the case, which was then approaching its first trial date. My fury at the injustice of it all outdistanced his, and that somehow managed to soothe him. "God, I need you here. I need you to talk to," he said. "I miss you."

"I miss you, too." Perhaps I hadn't actually realized it until I said the words, but it was true. More than anything at that moment I wanted him to crawl into bed with me, wrap me in his arms, and remind me that David's life was not my problem. "I miss you a lot."

"Let's get married, as soon as you get back."

This was a discussion we'd had before. My defenses went up immediately. "Why? Do you think once we're married you'll miss me less when I'm away?"

He didn't laugh. "No," he replied, relentlessly serious. When Ned wants to make a point, his voice crackles with energy, his eyes blaze with righteous commitment. He is an excellent public speaker—intelligent, forceful, even witty. He's five ten, and slender. His hair—a wonderful chestnut color—is wiry and unmanageable; his face narrow, with eyes set a fraction too close together. He has a nondescript nose and a chin that recedes slightly, a defect that no doubt would have cost him the presidency had he after all, as David predicted he would, decided to run. (You can't, at this moment in history, have both that office and a beard.) In his company, you never notice the flaws: you don't notice anything but his goodness, his sincerity, the power of his concern. His concern that night was focused on me.

Although we maintained the fiction of separate apartments, he argued, we had been virtually living together for two years. It was time to "regularize our arrangement," time to make a "total commitment." He loved me and wanted me to be his wife. He *needed* me to be his wife. He was building a career, and needed my help, my advice, my support.

"I have my own career to worry about," I replied ungraciously. A proposal of marriage, I knew, demanded better manners, but some inexplicable, primordial fear had driven all thoughts of courtesy out of my head.

"I'm not asking you to give it up."

"No? I didn't hear much about me and my needs in that speech."

"I think you can be trusted to make your own case," he sniped back.

"I don't have a case." There was a knot in my stomach, a tightness in my chest. "I just don't want to get married. Not now. Not yet." Since I really didn't understand why, I couldn't explain, and frustration gave my voice a sharper edge than I intended.

"You want kids, don't you? You're almost thirty."

"Not until October."

"Didn't you ever hear of the biological clock?" Not understanding me was making him angry.

"Since when have you started reading *Cosmopolitan*?" I asked, my voice dripping with sarcasm. The biological clock was only beginning to be talked about, and all the psychological jargon was exacerbating my already acute sense of never having enough time. I told him I didn't want to discuss it, or us, not at that moment.

"You never do," he said.

"Ned, dammit, leave me alone. Please. This has not been a great day. I don't need you to make it worse."

"I'm not going to wait forever for you to make up your mind."

"Who's asking you to wait? Don't wait! Do what you want. You're free. That's the point of not being married. You can do what the fuck you want. We can both do what the fuck we want."

"Why can't you just come right out and say it? Why can't you just *admit* you don't love me?"

"Because I do love you. A lot. Just not enough to give up everything to make you happy."

"Give up what? I'm asking you to marry me, not enter a convent. Have I ever interfered with your life?"

"Yes."

"You're out of your mind!"

"You asked me not to come to England on this assignment."

"I asked you. Once. I wanted you here this week. I knew it would be a rough week. Was that a crime?"

"You shouldn't have asked."

"But you went."

"Goddam right I did."

"And did I whimper or shout? Did I accuse you of running out on me? No! I took you to the goddam airport."

"You tried to make me feel guilty the whole time for deserting you."

There was a silence, both of us overwhelmed by our inability to make the other understand. "I won't phone again," he said finally, his voice again quiet. "Call me when you know what day you're coming home."

And we hung up, angry, estranged. I turned my face into the pillow and cried.

At six in the morning, I was awakened by the phone ringing. It could only be David, I knew. No one else would have the nerve to telephone me so early. My skull felt stuffed with cotton, and my eyes felt swollen and sore. "Couldn't you have waited for a reasonable hour?" I snapped into the phone.

"Good morning to you, too," he replied cheerfully. "What's the matter? Have a fight with Ned?"

"What do you want?"

"I'm about to start work," he said, certain that excused all. "I was afraid you'd disappear by the time I finished for the day."

"Oh, I understand. Perfectly. God forbid your Muse should be interrupted for the convenience of your friends and family."

"Don't be a bitch. I called to invite you to a picnic."

"When?" I asked, my voice still grudging.

"What day is best for you?"

"Sunday. I'll be back by then." I was visiting some potters in Gloucestershire and Somerset. Later I would go to Cornwall.

"Monday would be better," he countered, attempting to wheedle.

"I work on Mondays. So do you, as far as I remember."

"I work every day, when I'm working. All right, Sunday. I'll fix it somehow."

"If it doesn't rain."

"It won't rain. What's wrong with you, anyhow? It's not like you, Nikki, to be such a cunt, even this early in the morning." Having got what he wanted, he could afford to be interested in my problems.

"What's wrong with me is I had lunch with your wife yesterday."

"She told me. She said you had a nice time."

"A nice time was had only by the masochists in the group."

"If she bores you that much, don't see her. Don't take it out on me." Now he was starting to get angry. Good, I thought. I felt like another argument, preferably with David. My mood, after all, was essentially his fault.

"I wasn't bored. Far from it," I replied, my voice rife with sarcasm. "I was fascinated watching the oh-so-proud Caroline stoop to asking my help. She knows you're up to something and she wants to know what."

"Oh, Jesus."

"I don't like being in the middle, David."

"You're not in the middle."

"I had to sit there and lie to her. Do you know how I felt?"

"Yes, my little angel. You felt as if your halo was askew and you'd got dirt on your flowing white robe."

"Don't be sarcastic. You shouldn't have told me. About Sarah, I mean."

"This is not my fault, you know, whatever you think. How was I supposed to know Caroline would ask you to lunch? How was I supposed to know you'd go if she did? In all the years we've been married, the two of you have never been more than barely polite to one another."

"Not your fault? Who's screwing around then? Who's playing with three lives? No, make that four. Let's not leave Duncan Powell, wronged husband, off the list."

"We'll talk Sunday."

"David . . ."

"I really have a hard time dealing with you when you turn prissy on me."

"Don't hang up."

"What you're feeling now is the price of friendship. See you Sunday. At eleven." I heard the click at the other end of the line.

I knew what he'd do now. He'd light a Gauloise and smoke it, drink his black coffee, and think over what I'd said, weighing the possible pleasure against the balance of possible pain. But soon his attention would begin to wander. The typewriter on his desk would begin to exert a polar force, pulling at him, and irresistibly he would move closer to it. And the closer he got, the more the sound of my words would be drowned by the sound of words yet to be written. He would begin to type, trying to capture those fleeting rhythms, those elusive melodies, and soon nothing would exist for him but that. Sarah, Caroline, Lissie, Duncan, me, everyone would vanish from his mind. The only reality for him would become the one he was creating as he wrote.

✳ *Chapter 6* ✳

David was not my only friend in London. Five years before I had met
Cassandra Blake, then a relatively unknown designer. Honeybee had
bought her collection, it was her first American sale, and Cassandra was
determined to oversee every aspect of its presentation. She was there
when I photographed the catalogue, irritating the editor, reducing the
coordinator to tears, driving the models berserk. I liked her. Eventually
liked her, that is.

Cassandra is six feet tall and seems larger. She is broad and blond
with a booming voice that erupts from her with the force of a fire hose.
I have seen people coming forward to greet her pushed backwards invol-
untarily by a simple, "Hello. So *good* to see you again." Like a giant
wave, she threatens to overwhelm and obliterate.

Cassandra occupies so much space, uses so much air, there is little
left for anyone else. In a normal-sized room, with no more than eight
guests present, she can cause instant claustrophobia. Yet after a few
obligatory business meetings, I found, to my surprise, that I was growing
fond of her. She was intelligent as well as flamboyant. And she was
generous. She picked up tabs, overtipped, invited everyone to dinner at
her place, where she cooked bounteous and delicious meals, running a
nonstop commentary the whole time. And there was no denying her
talent. Her designs are stunning, with long, clean lines that are deceptively simple and extremely elegant. We became friends.

When I returned to the hotel that day, after a repeat session at the pottery in Chelsea, I found a message to phone her.

"Darling," she boomed into my ear, "I'm so glad you rang. Are you free this evening? Charles has got some sort of beastly meeting and can't make it to the theater. I know it's awful asking at the last minute like this, but I thought if you were on your tod and feeling low, you might like to join me."

"What are you going to see?" I was leaving the next day for Somerset, and had equipment to check and routes to plan, but I was willing to be coaxed provided it wasn't into anything terrible.

"Oh, you'll love it. Everyone does. It's the new play at the Court, with Sarah Cope and Duncan Powell. And if it's awful, we can always leave at the interval and I'll buy us a smashing meal at the Caprice." Of course I said yes.

Cassandra met me in the hotel lobby, and we walked through the suddenly brilliant sunshine down Sloane Street to the Court. Heads turned as we passed, Cassandra's size and bright clothes catching every eye.

"Who's Charles?" I asked.

"A merchant banker. Yummy. He's giving me all sorts of very good financial advice. Amongst other things. I met him at the Tynans' a few weeks ago. A pity about this evening." She threw me a thousand-kilowatt smile. "Not that I'm not thrilled to see you again, darling. I was afraid you'd be so buried in your work I'd never dig you out." She linked her arm through mine. "Now, give me all the latest gen on that yummy David Walton. I quite fancy him, you know. It's his eyes, I think. So *black*. Every time he looks at me, all my thoughts turn dirty. Is it true what I heard?" she continued confidentially, her face alight with that combined look of interest and speculation that even David's most minor actions seem to provoke. "That he beat Duncan at golf, and then wouldn't take his money? The story is they'd bet a hundred pounds." When I told her I knew nothing about it, she shook her head. "The English take their betting seriously," she said. "David really should have let him pay."

I'd have bet a hundred pounds of my own that it wasn't ignorance of local betting customs that had made David refuse to take Duncan's money. He'd protest, of course, that he was merely being a magnami-mous winner, when in fact what he was going for was a double put-down, attacking Duncan on two fronts (skill and honor), demonstrating to all careful observers that he was indeed the better man. It was the kind of game David loved playing.

Preoccupied, I stepped heedlessly out into the Sloane Square traffic.

"Watch that bus," Cassandra yelled, pulling me out of the way of a hurtling double-decker. "Really, darling, you must remember which way to look when you cross."

The Royal Court Theatre—home of Wilde and Shaw, Osborne and Pinter—is relentlessly small and cramped. Our seats, in the first row of the circle, were the best in the house in terms of seeing, but as uncomfortable to sit in as the rest. My knees were a millimeter away from the balcony railing, and Cassandra had no choice but to arrange herself at an angle that inevitably caused collision with her neighbor, obviously an old Court hand who smiled sympathetically at the disturbance.

The play, *Sky Burial*, was John Massey's second London hit and had all his trademarks of macabre humor and dense texture. Sarah Cope and Duncan Powell played Agatha and Gerald, a brother and sister who'd returned home for their mother's funeral. Their performances were superbly modulated, moving from the icy control of dislike in the first act to the searing venom of love betrayed in the last. Sarah radiated the energy of frustrated passion. Duncan paced the stage like a tiger, angry, hungry, wanting to kill. They worked brilliantly together. Later, I realized that the enormous let-down at the end came from the play's refusal to deal with the incest which was its real subject, so that ultimately, as David had said, it seemed a lot of sound and fury over nothing. But sitting there, mesmerized by the performances, I hardly cared.

When it was over, Cassandra and I, like the rest of the audience, were speechless for a few moments. Then she gathered her great self together and stood. "Bloody marvelous, wasn't he, old Duncan?"

"They both were."

"We'd better go back and tell him so, or he'll never forgive me."

"You know him?" I don't know why I was surprised. Everyone in London always seems to know everyone else.

"Know him, darling?" Her smile had a dash of smugness in it. "I've had him." Her voice boomed out into the auditorium. I looked nervously around, but happily no one had overheard. Or, at least, those left pretended they hadn't.

I hate going backstage. Compliments there, even when sincere, sound false. My voice becomes tight, my smile fixed. I feel like an idiot. But that time I didn't refuse. I was too curious.

Duncan's dressing room was minuscule, cramped, and dowdy, not at all the expected setting for one of England's leading stage and film stars.

He greeted Cassandra with what seemed real pleasure, enfolding her in a hug (Duncan was one of the few men I've ever seen who made Cassandra seem almost delicate), giving her a friendly kiss on the mouth. He responded with humor to all her compliments, which were delivered in a voice so false it had to be sincere: no one would dare to lie so outrageously to your face. Then he turned his attention to me.

"This is my dear, *dear* friend, Nikki Collier," offered Cassandra, "visiting from New York. She's a first-rate photographer, darling. She did those catalogue photos I showed you. Remember? You really ought to get her to do a few snaps."

"We met the other night," he responded, as Cassandra shot me a surprised look for not having mentioned it. His reply was simple enough, but his voice, his eyes, conveyed the message that never, under any circumstances, could he possibly forget a face as wonderful as mine. He was a charmer, all right. Mustering as much presence as I could, trying to keep the superlatives within reasonable bounds, I told him I'd enjoyed his performance. "And the play?" he asked. "What did you think of that?" his voice again setting up that peculiar vibration in me. I gave him my reaction and he nodded. "David Walton said very much the same thing. I didn't agree at first, but now I've rather changed my mind." His mention of David's name was easy, totally devoid of innuendo.

"The play was fabulous, I thought," said Cassandra. "Why must everyone carp all the time? Such a waste, really. Enjoy. That's my philosophy. Whatever you can, whenever you can."

"And don't you just?" Duncan grinned, leaning forward and running his hand fondly over her hair.

The door opened and Sarah entered, saw Cassandra, and smiled. "Cassandra, love, how good to see you. It's been ages." Her voice, like warm honey, flowed into the room. She came forward in one equally fluid motion, then reached to kiss Cassandra's cheek, and managed somehow to eclipse all Cassandra's extravagant appeal with the radiance of her own. She turned to me, extending a hand. "How nice to see you again, so soon." If there was total acceptance and genuine affection in her greeting of Cassandra, in mine there was the desire to have me like her. "For David's sake," she seemed to say with her smile, "let's be friends." He'd told her, I knew. A wave or irritation rose, and passed. She was irresistible. I smiled in return and clasped her hand.

"Have you eaten yet?" she asked. "We're meeting a few friends at Daphne's. Why don't you come?" She had removed all her stage makeup and had piled her platinum hair in a cluster of curls on top of her head. In the bright light of the dressing room I could see the few faint lines around her eyes. She was twenty-eight that year and, except for those lines, could have passed for nineteen.

I declined quickly before Cassandra could leap in and accept for us both, as I knew she would. Her face betrayed just a hint of annoyance as she seconded my refusal. Cassandra never said no to an invitation. She'd been known to accept as many as six for the same evening.

"I have to be up early in the morning," I said lamely, "and I can never sleep on a full stomach."

"You don't have to eat," responded Duncan. "You could just sit and listen as I coaxed you into taking up Cassandra's suggestion." I looked at him blankly. "To take some photographs of me. In fact of both of us." He looked to Sarah for confirmation. "It's time we had some new ones, don't you think, darling?"

Sarah seemed startled, but she recovered quickly and agreed. "That would be lovely. If you have the time," she added, giving me an out.

"Of course she has the time. It's a smashing idea," interjected Cassandra. "'Powell and Cope: Hot Ticket to Happiness,'" she captioned. "I *love* it. I know a dozen editors who'd kill for photos of you two at home."

"At home?" queried Sarah. She glanced quickly at me, then away again.

"Cassandra's absolutely right," said Duncan. "At home. What a brilliant idea."

"Marvelous pubicity," pressured Cassandra.

"I'm sure you don't need publicity," I said, thinking how strange I must sound trying to talk myself out of a job.

"Every actor needs publicity," asserted Duncan. "The more the better."

Still, I hesitated. Duncan looked at Sarah, and Sarah again looked at me. "We'd love you to do it. Really."

Here they were, two of London's biggest stars, darlings of the tabloids, and Duncan was offering me—not Bailey or Snowden—a chance to photograph them. But why? My relationship with David had to be one of the reasons, but to what purpose? I knew I should keep well away from the situation, but an outright refusal seemed impossible. "I'll certainly try," I said. "Let's talk next week when my schedule will be more certain." With any luck, by that time, Duncan would have forgotten whatever impulse had prompted him to make the suggestion. We exchanged phone numbers, and, repeating bravos for their performances, I hurried Cassandra out before I could get myself into more trouble.

As I closed the door behind me, I sneaked a quick look and saw

Duncan take Sarah's hand. "You really were brilliant tonight."

"I have you to thank for that, haven't I?" she responded, her voice full of warmth and . . . what? gratitude? appreciation? love?

Cassandra agreed to room-service, sandwiches and coffee at my hotel. "You're mad, you know," she complained. "The food is smashing at Daphne's." She sprawled in the one armchair, discontentedly eating smoked salmon on soggy brown bread, while I lay comfortably on the bed, shoes off, knowing I would later regret the crumbs.

"Sorry. I don't feel sociable tonight."

"You wouldn't have had to say a word. One can always count on Duncan to take up the slack." She took another bite of sandwich, then said, her mouth still full, "What did you think of him?" I told her I thought he was charming. "Oh, very," agreed Cassandra.

"And attractive."

"The face is heaven, but that voice is the killer. So rich and . . . thrilling. When we were together, I would beg him to tell me stories, then close my eyes and listen. It was very sexy. And they weren't even dirty most of the time. Just theater lore. Really, he should write them down. I know heaps of publishers who'd leap at them. Super stories, like the one about Sir Ralph and the fireworks. You must get him to tell it you the next time you're with him. Of course, every actor in the country has a Ralph Richardson story. Still, Duncan does tell them very well."

"How long have you known him?"

"Ages and ages. We met in the late fifties at a party somewhere. For me, it was love at first sight."

"At first sound, you mean."

"Exactly. He said hello and I was lost. I pursued him rather relentlessly, I'm afraid. It took me years to get him. He had such a lot of groupies around him. And, of course, he was married."

"To Sarah?"

"Oh, no, not then. He was still married to the first Mrs. Powell when I met him, a funny pale little creature, an artist. She had just graduated from the Slade, I remember. She did these rather hideous abstract paintings in the most revolting shades of brown and yellow. They all looked like vomit to me. I don't know what's become of her. She's probably starved to death by now if she tried to live off her painting. No eye for color at all."

"Did he leave her for Sarah?"

"No. Duncan didn't meet Sarah until a year or two after the divorce. They did a play together, and by the end of the run they were married. That was about eight years ago."

"He certainly seems to be crazy about her."

"Do you think so?" She put down her sandwich with a disgusted grunt. "This really is revolting. Don't you care anything about food?"

"Not much," I confessed.

She got laboriously out of the chair and walked to the writing desk, which held the ice bucket and its bottle of wine, and poured us each another glass. "If only the food were edible, I'd be having a marvelous time. I love evenings like this: wine and girl talk." She sprawled again. "You know, I do think Duncan loves Sarah, as much as he can love anyone. He's just constitutionally incapable of fidelity. He hadn't been married to Sarah for more than three months when we finally went to bed together."

"Just because he slept with you . . . ."

"Oh, darling, I am but one of a multitude." She leaned forward confidentially. "The interesting thing is that he really isn't very good at it. At fucking, I mean. At infidelity, he's a master."

I looked at her dubiously. Disparaging remarks about the physical prowess of former lovers should always be taken with a pinch of disbelief.

She read my face. "I am *not* being bitter," she continued. "We parted amicably, though not, I admit, by mutual agreement; but we've remained good friends. I'm still mad about him. Ultimately, sex just isn't that important, is it?"

"I'm not sure. My jury is still out on that one."

"Well, I prefer a good laugh any day. And Duncan's tops in that department."

"Who's he sleeping with now?"

"Actually, no one. As far as I know. He's been sticking rather close to home of late. It's hard to be certain about that sort of thing, but one does seem eventually to find out everything. In this town, the chat never stops."

I tried to stop myself from asking the next question. It was definitely "beneath me," the product of a low and vulgarly curious mind, the sort of mind I detest in other people, the sort of mind I loathe in Mr. Keating, biographer. "Do all his lovers have the same complaint?"

Cassandra stiffened slightly. "I don't make a habit of discussing this." Then she giggled. "But one can't help hearing." She nodded confirmation; and added, smiling suggestively: "I bet David Walton fucks beautifully." I said nothing. Cassandra tilted her head and sniffed the air, as if on the faint scent of scandal. "One would think Sarah might take a lover, but she adores Duncan. He's just that much older than she, and was already so successful when they met. She just idolized him. I suppose some of that has rubbed off. She's older now and a star herself, but it's obvious she still admires him, don't you think?" I nodded. "In the years they've been married, I've never heard a thing about her and anyone else. Still, it's a bit strange Duncan's changing his spots after all this time. He's turned into quite a doting husband. It does make one think."

"Maybe he's just older and wiser. Or tired of screwing around," I said, throwing a red herring into the conversation.

"Not bloody likely," boomed Cassandra. She stood again, seeming to fill the tiny room, tossed the dying anemones into a wastebasket, muttering, "Very squalid, darling," gathered her things, and swooped over the bed to kiss my cheek. "Call me when you get back from Somerset," she said, and went, leaving behind, floating in the winy air, enough speculations to preoccupy me the length of the long night ahead.

✦ Chapter 7 ✦

True to his word, Ned didn't call me again, nor did I phone him. Once I got to New York, I knew, he'd resume his pressure for a decision. He felt we'd been treading water long enough; now was the time to decide whether to sink or swim. Under that liberal veneer beat a middle-class Italian heart as committed to traditional values as his father's. Ned wanted equal justice and equal opportunity under the law for all people. He wanted an end to poverty, ignorance, hunger. He wanted us out of Vietnam and Nixon out of the White House. But he also wanted a home and family, a wife and two point five children, and there was no reason why he shouldn't. I wished I wanted the same.

By not telephoning, I was testing what it would be like to live without him. Not very good, I had so far decided, though I kept reminding myself it was too soon to make a decision. Ned's progress to the center of my life had been gradual. How could I expect his removal to be quick?

Then, as another test, a more complex and dangerous test, though of course I didn't think of it that way at the time, I went to bed with Simon Wroth.

I had just returned from my trip to Gloucestershire and Somerset, where I'd photographed Nicholas Carey and Craig Gills at their respective potteries. I'd had a rough time. My rented car had decided to break down on a country lane, and by the time I walked to the nearest house, across miles of deceptively serene-looking hills mined with rocks and fallen trees and murmuring brooks that required wading, and called the Automobile Association to my rescue, I was hours late for my first appointment. Luckily, it was with Nicholas Carey, who not only put me up for the night but canceled his plans for the next day so I could stay and get the shots I needed, which turned out to be among the best of the whole assignment. With Gillis, I didn't fare so well. I'd been warned about his temperament, and perhaps that set up one of those negative fields of energy which cause everything to go wrong. To start with, he dropped one of his earthenware plates, a beauty, with a red-brown trailed slip decoration under a galena glaze. It made him furious, probably from fear of the incipient arthritis that was later to cripple him, but at the time I wasn't sympathetic. To make matters worse, the weather that day was so changeable, rain clouds and brilliant sun playing tag through the sky, it took even more time than usual to get the light effects I wanted, which tried his patience severely. And then the lens of my Rolleiflex jammed. We were delighted to see the last of each other.

When I got back to London, the faded grandeur of the Austen Court seemed very welcoming, and my tiny room, with its chintz curtains and Georgian prints, a haven. There were messages from Cassandra and David, but I decided not to call them until morning when my mood would be better. I collapsed exhausted onto the bed, turned on the radio, and listened contentedly to Bach's A Minor Concerto reduced to tinny insignificance on Radio Three.

Within the hour, I had an attack of incredible restlessness. I had finished the Alison Lurie, couldn't get into the Dashiell Hammett, and drew a complete blank on the Henry James. Nothing caught my interest. The phone rang; and, gratefully, I answered, hoping it was Ned.

"It's Simon here, Simon Wroth. Do you remember me?" I did. After David had introduced us in the pub the night I'd seen *Dreams in F Minor*, I'd run into him one day as I came out of the Crafts Council in the Haymarket. We'd had a sandwich and a pint of beer together. "I thought if you were free, you might like to grab a bite to eat."

I searched for something unwrinkled to wear, settled on one of Cassandra's jersey skirts and flowered print blouses, slipped into a pair of trendy plastic boots, threw on a raincoat, and walked through the drizzle to Knightsbridge, where I was to meet Simon. The rain on my face felt wonderful. I imagined it coating my bleak New York skin with the translucent patina of English porcelain. What must it be like, I wondered, to be as beautiful as Sarah Cope? Not that I think myself homely, but no heads turn when I enter a room.

Simon stood waiting for me outside Mr. Chow's. He kissed my cheek, then led me inside, smiling at the maître d', who greeted him by name, took our macs, and sat us upstairs in a long, elegant room faced with mirrors.

Simon looked, as always, a mess. His shoes were scuffed, his tie pulled loose from his neck, his linen jacket rumpled and fitting awkwardly across the shoulders. He was just under six feet tall, with straight dark hair badly in need of a cut and round hazel eyes. Stubble shadowed his face. In profile, his nose was a pronounced beak, and his smile revealed uneven teeth. His hands were large and powerful, looking capable, like a carpenter's. The nails were bitten to the quick.

When the waiter had taken our drink order, Simon leaned towards me and smiled. It was a warm, friendly smile. He really should have been homely, yet he wasn't. He emanated humor and warmth, vitality and sex appeal. "I hope you didn't mind me phoning like that on the spur of the moment, but when I thought of it, I couldn't see why not. For all I knew, you might be lonely and languishing for a meal. Hotel living can be the devil."

"You saved my life. I was about to go out of my mind with boredom."

"And I imagined your dance card always filled. To tell the truth, I was stunned when you answered the phone. I might not have had the courage to ring if I'd known you would be there."

"I'm glad you did. I wanted a quiet night, but . . ." I shrugged. "It's funny, isn't it, the way when you're busy you can't wait for a free evening and then, when you finally get it, there's no way you can relax?"

"It's the adrenaline," he replied. "I'm the same when I'm directing. And David's a bit mad when he's writing, isn't he? Have you known him long?"

As usual, the question didn't seem to me to be just a conversational gambit, or, in this case, a sexual one. Simon wasn't probing to find out if I were then or ever had been David Walton's lover. He was not trying to discover if the amatory coast was clear prior to making his own attempt at a landing. He found me attractive enough, but it was David who interested, who really intrigued, him.

Looking back over my life (as I have been doing a lot lately), it seems to me I have spent most of it, when not talking *to* David Walton, talking about him. For as long as I can remember, from anyone he encountered, David elicited curiosity and comment. It was as if people imagined his life was lived on some level different from theirs, a level more meaningful and more dramatic, and hoped, by discovering the details, either to invest their own lives with a vicarious thrill or learn how to live themselves at the same pitch of intensity. His words were quoted, his actions recounted. They were weighed in the palm of the hand, tested against the teeth, held up to the light to be studied. He was undressed, X-rayed, fluoroscoped, and dissected over and over, and yet the feeling remained that something was hidden, that something not yet seen lurked beneath the surface.

Even I, who knew him as well as anyone, remained always as fascinated by him as the grossest starfucker on the fringe of his life.

"Since we were children," I replied. "We grew up together."

"He's a brilliant playwright."

"I think so." It was somehow even more irritating to have Simon praise David to me than to have David wax eloquent over Sarah. It's not that I like being regarded as a sex object; but I'm not fond either of being overlooked as a woman.

"When I read *Dreams in F Minor,* I was knocked out by it. I'd never heard of David Walton. And here was this stunning play, powerful and bitingly funny. English playwrights have a real gift for coruscating humor, I think, for dizzying verbal gymnastics, but *Dreams* has poetry in it, vulgar, earthy poetry, like Chaucer's or Shakespeare's. It's a wonderful play. I find something new in it every time I see it. There's talk it may go to New York. Did David tell you?"

I nodded. There had been no definite offer as yet, just a few queries from producers.

"They'll probably use an American director," he said gloomily, but then immediately smiled. "And why not? It's an American play, isn't it? And I'm damned lucky to have had the chance to do it at all. Do you know how David and I met?"

"Playing squash?"

He laughed and picked up the dish the waiter had just deposited on the table, offering it to me. "Try this," he said. "It's marvelous. Fried seaweed." I began to eat, and he continued: "David was having a drink with Geoff Beane, the actor who plays Jimmy, at the bar in the squash club we all use. David was trying to talk him into a game, but Geoff was exhausted. He'd been up late filming, finishing one of those historical sagas for the BBC, and in no fit condition to play. He wasn't going to hand David a victory without putting up some sort of reasonable fight. But David kept insisting. That's when I appeared. I went over to say hello to Geoff, whom I knew. We'd done a telly together the year before. He introduced me to David, then said to him, 'If you want a game, here's your man. He beat me last week, three times straight.'

David got rather a funny look in his eye and suggested we play. By the time we reached the court, he'd stopped smiling, and I knew I was in for a rough time. It was a fierce game. I don't remember ever playing harder. David won. By a point. There was a moment when I got tired and thought, Who gives a damn? That was the moment I lost. He beat me with sheer determination. When we went back to meet Geoff at the bar, David was all smiles again. 'Why don't you let Simon read that play of yours?' suggested Geoff. 'He's a fantastic director.' David's smile got even bigger. 'If you're willing,' he said to me. 'You're just the kind of director I like working with.' I couldn't have been more shocked. Up to that point, I was convinced he disliked me. 'What kind?' I asked. "You fight hard and lose gracefully," he said. He didn't make it sound like a compliment."

It hadn't been. The only emotion losing produces in David is rage. He doesn't understand any other reaction.

Simon stopped talking, suddenly, as if embarrassed. "I am sorry. I didn't mean to talk about David, or me. I wanted to find out more about you."

I told him, in response to his questions, a little of what I'd done in the past and what I was doing in England at the moment. His questions were intelligent and occasionally penetrating, too penetrating. "Are you happy with what you're doing? Is your career going the way you want? the way you imagined it would?"

I shrugged. "Does that ever happen?"

"Sometimes. To some people." Then, sensing my reluctance to discuss that particular issue, he let me change the subject and we began trading bits of information about ourselves, my childhood during the war in New York, his infinitely worse one in London during the Blitz and, after his mother was killed, at his uncle's farm in the Lake District. "I thought I'd died myself and gone to heaven it was so lovely, clear blue lakes for boating, endless mountains to climb, and wide green fields full of sheep to eat. My uncle was exempted from service, because of the farm, so he kept me busy after school helping out around the place. It was a hard life, I suppose, for a little bloke like me, but after the hell of London it was paradise. Not to be awakened in the middle of the night by the sound of the sirens, pulled out of bed, and rushed to the shelter. I didn't even miss my mother at first. I was in shock, I suppose; but then I started having dreams about her. That was when I took sick, came down with some sort of pneumonia. Thanks to Dr. Cope, I pulled through."

The name, dropped so casually into the narrative, was startling. "Cope?" I repeated.

"Ralph Cope." He looked at me, startled himself by my tone. "Do you know him?"

"No. It's just an unusual name. And I met an actress the other night..."

"His daughter. Sarah. She's in the play at the Court. If you haven't seen it yet, you should. She's marvelous in it. And so's Duncan. Duncan Powell, her husband."

"I've seen it," I replied. "You know her?"

He nodded. "She was younger than I, just a little bit of a thing, and a girl. I pretty much ignored her then. It was her dad I thought a lot of. He was the local GP. Cured me of my pneumonia and a lot else besides. He let me talk, something my aunt discouraged. She thought I should put the whole bloody business out of my mind. After the war, I went back to London, with my dad. I didn't see Sarah again until she came down to go to RADA. Her father was dead set against it, her becoming an actress, but eventually he gave in."

"I bet you found her a lot more interesting by that time," I teased.

He smiled. "She'd turned into a raving beauty. We went around a bit together for a while. Just pals, you know. She didn't seem to give a damn about anything but her career. She was on fire with ambition. And a bit full of herself, I thought at the time. We'd go to see someone like Vivien Merchant in *Othello*, and Sara would lecture me for hours afterwards on the way she would have played Desdemona." He smiled ruefully. "She was bloody marvelous when she did it last year at Chichester," he said, then emptied the wine bottle into our glasses. "Right after she finished at RADA, she got a part in a play in the West End, playing opposite Duncan."

"Were you in love with her?"

"Everyone was in love with Sarah. She was the most radiant creature alive." Again he stopped. Aware of being impolitic, he smiled and shrugged. "But that was a long time ago. Calf love. Serious enough at the time, but over quickly and with no lasting ill effects."

"Like your pneumonia."

"No. The pneumonia nearly killed me. Sarah didn't."

We left the pub and walked back towards my hotel. It was just past eleven. The rain had stopped, leaving the night fresh and cool. Neither of us yet wanting to end the evening, we continued past the hotel, down Sloane Street, past the square, still noisy with people leaving the pubs, and on to the quiet of the river. The moon was full and the water glinted like silver in its light. A barge went past with its load of tourists returning from a river trip. We walked along the Embankment to Albert Bridge, strung with white lights, leading like a path in a fairy tale across the gleaming Thames to the Fun Park at Battersea. I told him about the war photographs in Mr. Walton's album and how I knew, even then, one day I would be a photographer. When we reached the bridge, Simon put his arms around me and we kissed.

The mist from the river, the silvery light, the fantasy bridge, Simon's arms, all wrapped me in magic. The moment felt unreal, but it was happening, and I wanted it to go on happening for as long as it could. Behind me, I heard the rattle of a taxi. Simon lifted his face from mine, hailed it, and we got inside. He gave the driver the name of my hotel, then gathered me again into his arms.

Crossing the lobby, we didn't speak, each of us afraid the wrong word would shatter the spell. There were two white-haired ladies in the elevator, so we stood away from each other, trying to achieve that air of effortless indifference married couples frequently have. In the room, we still didn't speak. The only sounds were of breathing and of occasional laughter at the inevitable awkwardness. We took our time, giving the pleasure a chance to build, savoring it, until—finally—I stopped thinking of Ned, and felt only the power of the waves, catching me up, carrying me unresistingly forward, hurling me safely onto the shore.

❧ Chapter 8 ❧

On the appointed Sunday morning, amid the murmur of determined tourists making logistical decisions over tattered street maps, I sat in the hotel lobby, reading the papers, waiting for David. They were full of hijackings, assassination attempts, the closing of the Lyons Piccadilly Corner House, and predictions about the general election the following Thursday. "It's easier reading newspapers abroad, isn't it?" said David when he arrived. He seemed, I thought, in a state of barely repressed excitement. "The news somehow doesn't belong to you, so you don't have to get into such a rage about it." He looked at me critically. "You're obviously over your encounter with the terrible Craig Gillis," he added, smiling. "You look terrific. Or has something else happened to put you in a good mood?" There was suddenly a faint edge of suspicion in his voice.

"What else could have happened?" I replied, not thinking that moment a propitious one for beginning a discussion of Simon. "Anyway, I'm not in a good mood." I wasn't. My mood was as changeable as the cloud patterns in the London sky. "I borrowed a darkroom yesterday and developed the pictures from my trip. The ones of Gillis are the worst I've taken in my life."

"Serves the bastard right," said David succinctly.

Outside, the sun shone in that golden haze of pollution which accompanies still, fair weather. David headed for an ancient blue Bentley, waiting empty at the curb. "Where are Caroline and Lissie?" I asked, surprised not to see them. Over the years, David and I had evolved an unspoken agreement never to let our meetings impinge on time others had a right to expect devoted to them. It was one of the ways we kept the peace. Sunday afternoons, if he wasn't working, David usually reserved for his wife and child.

"Lissie was invited to a birthday party. A friend from nursery school. The presence of one parent was required, and Caroline was more than happy to go. The mother is one of the few people she's met in London she likes. Do you suppose the fact her name is *Lady* Antonia something-or-other has anything to do with it?"

"Caroline's no snob," I said, though in fact I had no idea whether she was or not. "Or at least not as big a snob as you are."

He grinned at me. "I'm not a snob," he said. "I'm discerning."

Saving me in the process from a taxi and a number 22 bus, David helped me into the Bentley and then settled himself behind the wheel. The car, which he had bought used, was polished to a high gleam. The interior was of beige leather, the matching carpet clean and luxuriously thick, the dashboard of mottled walnut. "Smell that," said David. He took a deep breath.

"Leather," I said, catching the scent.

"Money," he replied. He told me the car's history, endowing it—as he did any of his personal possessions—with a personality verging on the mythic. The Duke of Bedford had owned it, then sold it to a dealer, from whom T. S. Eliot had bought it. After Eliot, Lester Pigott—the jockey—had used it as a second car. David had found it at a dealer's in Chelsea. I looked at him dubiously. "It's the truth." He grinned. "Can't you tell? The car has all the qualities of its former owners: it's aristocratic, poetic, and fast."

"And what's it going to inherit from you?"

"Determination," he said.

"No," I countered, "sheer pigheadedness."

Though David was afraid of heights, and would gladly turn the wheel over to anyone rather than risk maneuvering a car up a mountain, on reasonably level terrain he loved to drive. As we started around Hyde Park Corner, he smiled with pleasure. Even on Sunday, a relatively quiet day, that maneuver requires nerves of steel. In 1970, the traffic lights had not yet been installed, and it was pure mayhem: five lanes of traffic feeding in and out of roads converging at the corner; buses, taxis, trucks, intrepid Jaguars, and daredevil minis battling for the right of way. To me it ranked with rapids-shooting as a fun pastime. David, of course, made it even worse by considering the problem of getting from Grosvenor Street to Park Lane a challenge not only to his ingenuity, but to his courage. He played chicken with buses, accelerated past taxis, forced Rolls-Royces to give way. When the Bentley passed Wellington's house and entered the Park, David smiled as triumphantly as if he had just personally won the battle of Waterloo. "It's a great car," he murmured, modestly, magnanimously determined to give credit where it was due. He patted the steering wheel fondly with his right hand. "A great car."

In the back was an enormous picnic hamper, packed, David told me, at Justin Le Blank's. "What's the occasion?" I asked. He didn't usually go to so much trouble for me. He didn't have to. That was the point of being old friends.

"Afraid you'll have to sing for your supper?"

"Will I?"

"How did I ever get to have such a suspicious friend?"

"You acquired me at birth."

"I acquired parents and siblings, too. I've managed to push them from center stage."

"But in me you've got what everyone wants, someone who knows him completely and loves him despite what she knows."

"Lots of people love me," replied David, grinning.

"Lucky you," I jeered, though without rancor. There was never any rancor in our teasing.

He reached over, took my hand, and squeezed it. "You're right. Nobody knows me the way you do. You know all my weaknesses, and you never take advantage of them. Of course, you don't have to. You have everything from me you want."

"What about you? Do you have everything from me *you* want?"

He looked at me a moment, then away again. We had reached Wellington Road, and he pointed out Lord's Cricket Ground. "I'll take you to see a game."

I shook my head. "I've watched some on television. I'd rather have my teeth drilled, thank you."

"It's a great sport."

"For people with long lives and nothing much to do with them."

He smiled again. "I never have everything I want," he told me. "I'd prefer it if you were mad with lust for me."

"No, you wouldn't. You hated it when I was."

"You've got that wrong. It was the other way round."

* * *

Actually, it had been both ways. In the fall of 1958, David left for Northwestern University, and I went off to Cornell. Except for the couple of weeks over summer vacations that David spent on his grandfather's ranch, or I went traveling with my parents and brother, that was the first time we'd ever been separated. We hadn't expected it, but being apart was hard, for both of us. Though we wrote constantly, and phoned, though we kept each other informed of the progress of our studies, the crises in our intellectual lives, the evolution of our romances, though we were both more often than not enjoying ourselves, still there was a void we couldn't quite fill. Neither of us, until then, had realized how much we depended on one another for a daily dose of appreciation, understanding, support.

In the spring of 1959, David appeared in a student production of *The School for Scandal*. "I'm playing Charles," he said, when he called to tell me he'd got the part. His voice was full of enthusiasm. "The director's not half bad. It may turn out okay. Come and see me."

"I'm flunking calculus," I said. "I've got to start studying for finals."

"Yeah," he said. "I understand. Margaret Bourke-White never would have made it without passing calculus."

Without telling my parents, paying for the trip with money I'd been saving for a car, I flew to Chicago for the weekend. David met me at the airport, lifted me off the ground, and swung me around in his arms. "God, am I glad to see you," he said. In the tiny, bruised Simca he had bought secondhand, he drove me to the Drake, where he'd booked me a room. "Don't worry, I'm paying," he told me when he saw the worried look on my face. Because he was going to be busy a lot of the time, he wanted me to stay in the city so I could keep myself occupied with the Art Institute and whatever else took my fancy. "Take a cab tonight. I'll pay for that, too," he added, and left me to go to a run-through. David was always magnanimous when he was getting what he wanted.

The production wasn't bad. It was lively and attractive and well acted. The audience loved it. I don't think I noticed anyone, or anything, but David. I don't really know how good he was in the role, good enough, I suppose, sexy, attractive, vital, certainly. But sitting in the audience, watching him on that stage playing Charles Surface, charming wastrel with a heart of gold, I saw David for the first time as separate from me, as having an identity distinct from my own. He was no longer just my childhood friend, my alter ego, my playmate, my pal; he was, confusingly, disturbingly, a man.

We went out to celebrate afterwards with the cast and crew. I tried to enjoy myself, but each time David turned away from me to talk to the girl who'd played Maria, I felt sick to my stomach. He put his arm around my shoulder, stroked the back of my neck. Were they lovers? I wondered.

Before going back to my hotel, we took a walk along the shore. We'd both had too much to drink. David was high. I was depressed. He took my arm, and, self-consciously, I pulled away. "What's the matter?" he said.

"I don't know. You seem different. That's all."

"You're the one who's different."

I turned to face him. "Am I? How?"

He looked at me, hard, studying my face as if trying to remember where he'd seen it before. He ran a finger over my eyebrows, down my cheek, down the bridge of my nose, across my lips. My breathing quickened. Over his shoulder, I could see the crescent moon and the bright dot of Venus in the sky. "You've grown up," he said, and kissed me. He never had before. No one ever had before, not really. My boyfriends had been few and timid. I felt his tongue tracing my lips, searching for a way into my mouth. "Don't you even know how to kiss?" he said.

We went back to the hotel, and up to my room. "This never crossed my mind," he said, and I believed him because it had never crossed mine. Not in connection with David, anyway. At Cornell, there was a boy named Bob to whom I'd been planning to make a gift of my virginity.

I let David take off my clothes. He seemed to know how to go about it so much better than I. I watched him take off his, thinking all the time how beautiful he was, wondering why I'd never noticed it before. He took a condom from a pocket and put it on the bedside table. "You're so beautiful," he said, pulling me down beside him. His body was long and cool and a surprising blend of textures against mine. I opened my mouth for his tongue, and parted my legs for his fingers. Then, suddenly, I panicked. I pulled away. He stopped and held me quietly against him. "There's nothing to be afraid of," he whispered, then licked my ear.

I didn't feel anything that night, or the next, except glee at holding David in my arms, at having him inside me. But there came a time he had only to touch me to start small tremors of bliss building relentlessly until they pitched me into oblivion. When he made love to me, I came so fiercely I felt as if I'd been shot into the sky where I exploded into a million brightly colored pieces.

I failed calculus and told Bob I couldn't see him anymore. When the semester ended, I returned to New York and took up my usual summer job typing and answering phones in my father's office (he was a lawyer). I got constantly reprimanded for being forgetful. All I could think of was David: when I would see him, how he we would contrive to make love. We took enormous risks. David worked in a stable in Central Park, tending the horses and giving riding lessons. Sometimes I met him there and we made love in the stable, in the hay, when we thought everyone had gone home. Once we were discovered by another hand, who fortunately kept his mouth shut. After that, David got the key to an apartment of a friend whose family was spending the summer in Maine. And once when the Waltons were away with Claudia for the weekend and Jack was visiting a girlfriend in New Jersey, we made love in David's bed, in his parents' bed, even on the couch in the sitting room. We said we'd never felt this way about anyone before. "I love you," we said to each other.

When I got back to Cornell, I couldn't concentrate on my studies. I was barely passing even the easy courses. What was David doing? Who was he seeing? Was he making love to anyone else? There wasn't room in my mind for anything but him.

By Christmas I had lost ten pounds. "God, you look awful," he said when he saw me. "What's wrong?" I told him, and instead of being contrite, he got angry. "I don't know what the fuck you want from me," he said.

I went back to school and forced myself to date other men. I forced myself to sleep with one. It wasn't bad, but I didn't explode into brightly colored bits. When I saw David at spring break, I confessed I'd "been unfaithful." So did he.

We fought, and didn't speak for months, the worst few months of my life. I returned home for the summer, and my mother told me David had already been by, asking for me. "I miss you," he said, when I phoned him. He'd just finished his first play and wanted to read it to me. It took a while, and it wasn't easy, but we got our friendship back.

"I was afraid you'd use me up," I explained. "I was afraid there wouldn't be anything left for anyone else, not even for me."

"So you threw me over, and I fell in love with Gail Simpson."

"Rachel Weber," I corrected.

He laughed again. "Do you remember everything?"

"Yes. About you, about me." We drove in silence for a few moments, then I began speaking again, wanting to tell David a little of what had been occupying my mind since he'd left New York. "This past year," I said, "I've spent a lot of time thinking, about us, about Ned and me, about the nature of love, of friendship, about how inexplicable it is that someone should love one person and not another. Why Guinevere loved Lancelot instead of Arthur. Why Juliet took one look at Romeo and fell in love, when Paris was every bit as attractive and a lot more eligible. And why I love you, and not your brother, whom I've known as long, and as well, and who—in every way—is much nicer."

"Why?" asked David.

"The first conclusion I came to, and don't laugh, is that it's not possible to explain love. Not rationally, anyway. Really profound links between people don't seem ultimately to have anything to do with sex, or society, personality, or character, or any of the reasons usually supposed to be the cornerstones of relationships."

"And your second conclusion?"

"No conclusion, just speculation." I was a little embarrassed to tell him, but I did. Eventually, I always told him everything. "When I stopped trying to be logical, I began thinking about time, and levels of reality, about the possibility of reincarnation. It began to seem plausible that the instant attraction that sometimes happens between people is really an unremembered bond from a past life. People feel the pull of familiarity and resume the relationship, sometimes in a different mode. Twins in one lifetime, for example, might become best friends in the next. Thwarted lovers get the chance to marry and live happily ever after. Old enemies resume their battle, sometimes as husband and wife."

"That's one explanation," said David when I'd finished. I asked him for another. He thought for a moment, then smiled. "Smell." I looked at him blankly. "You've seen the way dogs sniff at each other before deciding whether to fight or be friends."

"So?"

"Someday an ingenious young scientist searching for something profoundly important, like the reason chimpanzees prefer bananas to apples, will discover that certain smells trigger certain chemical reactions in the brain, and it's those reactions that cause us to like or dislike, to love or hate, to fuck or make war."

I laughed. "That would certainly explain perfume."

"Deodorants, mouthwashes, vaginal sprays, strawberry foam contraceptives," added David.

"And the prevalence of divorce in modern society," I continued, picking up the theme, "the failure of most relationships."

"Exactly," he replied, warming to the subject. "You can fool part of the brain all of the time..."

"But not all of the brain all of the time," we chanted in unison. By then, we were both laughing, hard. We had always made each other profoundly silly.

"No matter how camouflaged by perfumes or deodorants, eventually the real smell gets through and the brain throws up its—so to speak—hands in horror, and cries: "No, no. This isn't someone I love. It's someone I hate. This person is the wrong person.' And off it will send the nose in pursuit of the right one." When the laughter finally subsided, David said, "I've been reading Nadezhda Mandelstam's autobiography, and she describes Osip Mandelstam's writing not as creation, but discovery. He would repeat phrases over and over, as if in some kind of trance, trying and discarding words, certain he would know the right one when he heard it because, somewhere, the poem already existed and his job as poet was to find it."

"Yes," I said. "I understand that. When I see a picture of mine printed, sometimes I feel it isn't the one I took, the actual physical representation of what I saw, but a photograph of something I was looking for."

"And the people we're going to love, they seem familiar from the moment we meet? Is that what you're saying? Because it's not true."

"No. Sometimes they seem, at first, very alien, very frightening. But the recognition is there: the recognition that we are in the presence of someone who matters, maybe not in general, but to us."

"'I have known your face from the first day/My soul has loved yours forever,'" he quoted.

"What's that?" I asked.

"Lines from Billy's new poem." Billy Siedler had been a friend of David's since they'd roomed together at college. The poem later was collected in a volume that won the Pulitzer Prize. "That's the Hampstead Theatre Club," he said, pointing at a small building, resembling a Quonset hut, just the other side of what looked like a fake Swiss cottage and was in fact a pub. "We're talking about doing one of my plays there."

We continued up a hill into the village of Hampstead, its narrow main street thronged with lazy Sunday people, window-shopping, buying pastries from the French patisserie, standing in chatty groups outside pubs, drinking ale and shandies. Romney had lived nearby, and Constable. Galsworthy, too, David told me, and Keats. "Let's park the car and explore," I suggested.

"We'll be late."

"What for?"

"We'll come back another time," he promised.

We continued up past the pond and waited our turn to pass single-file through the narrow gap in the Spaniards Road, flanked by its inn and tollhouse. "In the 1780s," said David, indicating the inn, "some rioters out to get the Earl of Mansfield dropped by there to ask directions to his house, and the wily publican kept them all drinking until the militia arrived. Another example of greed subverting ideals. The men had every reason to riot."

We drove through the gates of Kenwood House, former home of the Earls of Mansfield, parked in the gravel-strewn lot, and, leaving the picnic hamper behind, walked along the lanes of enormous flowering pink rhododendrons to the house. When I saw it, I smiled. It reminded me of a gracious eighteenth-century woman, a Jane Austen heroine, welcoming any weary traveler, irrespective of wealth or breeding, religion or politics. Only bad manners would not be tolerated.

Kenwood is the pleasantest kind of museum, small and absorbable, never overwhelming or bewildering or oppressive like the Metropolitan or the Louvre. I often imagine a headline in the *International Herald Tribune:* "Tourist Found Dead at Uffizi. Art Overdose Suspected."

As I walked with David through the house, I felt more and more content. The proportion of the rooms and their colors were perfect. The Adam library and a few of the paintings—Vermeer's *Guitar Player* and a Rembrandt self-portrait—were magnificent. I fell in love with the orangery, not for the Gainsboroughs, which I didn't like, or the powerful Stubbs painting *Whistlejacket* that dominated the long room, but for its wall of paned glass overlooking a view of soft green lawn tapering gently to a tree-fringed lake and beyond to Hampstead Heath. In the Victoria and Albert, I had seen paintings of the Heath by Constable, but those were of a wild and somber landscape. This was tamed, and as elegant and unpretentious as the house itself.

We walked outside, then turned around to admire the facade. "It's too bad all the world's great art can't be housed in buildings this size," said David, "where people can not only look at it, but *see* it."

The aura of excitement I had noticed earlier was even more pronounced now. David glanced at his watch, then smiled at me. "Wait here," he told me as he turned away. "I'll go get the picnic basket."

What's he up to now? I wondered, watching him disappear out of sight along the path that led back around the house to the parking lot. I sat on the grass to wait.

✄ *Chapter 9* ✄

Kenwood House was obviously not a popular spot with foreign tourists. Despite the lovely day, the grounds weren't crowded; and the snatches of conversation I heard going past, the voices calling in the distance, all were in English. The skins were bisque tinged lobster by the sun, the hair blond, the favored dress skimpy print minis for women and, for men, low-slung tan pants with colorful cotton shirts. Many of the shirts lay heaped in bright patterns on the grass as the men lay sunbathing, pathetic white chests exposed, their heads in the laps of their women. There were babies in prams, children playing ball, dogs chasing sticks. Beyond the low fence that separated Kenwood from the Heath, some people were picnicking. On the far side of the pond was a stage and a white acoustic shell. There were concerts every Saturday night in summer; every Saturday night, that is, when it didn't rain.

Slowly, I was lulled into optimism. The ordered tranquillity of the scene contradicted concepts of the fallibility of human nature and the disruptive persistence of passion. Firmness of purpose combined with a reasonable approach, a good plan with good instincts, could resolve all conflicts into harmony. Whatever problems I had, I was suddenly sure I could solve.

I didn't notice David's approach and looked up only when he called my name. With him was a woman it took me a full thirty seconds to recognize. Her hair was tucked into a straw hat with a low brim, her

64

eyes concealed by sunglasses. A knee-length cotton batik dress, layered and flounced—one of Cassandra's—effectively concealed the shape of her body and, of course, I hadn't been expecting her, though in retrospect I realized I should have known she was the purpose of the day.

"Look who I found in the parking lot." Complacency coated David's voice.

"Hello, Sarah. What a nice surprise," I said, I swear without a hint of sarcasm. This wasn't, after all, her fault. She probably hadn't realized, any more than I had, what David was up to.

"I hope you don't mind my intruding on your picnic." If she was embarrassed, it didn't show. Her voice was easy, sweet with genuine apology.

"Of course not," I said, standing to shake hands with her, "though I suspect it was your picnic to start with."

"David's picnic," she corrected. "I wondered why it had to be today."

"That's my fault," I explained. "It's the only day I had free."

She turned to David. "You could have warned me."

"Warned us," I corrected.

"I was afraid you wouldn't come." The reply covered both. "Let's go there," he said, pointing to a spot beyond the pond. "Fewer people." Carrying the blanket and hamper, he set off, leaving Sarah and me to follow in his wake.

"He's awfully determined to get his own way, isn't he?" said Sarah, annoyance and admiration mixed in her voice.

"Awfully," I repeated, keeping my own voice as neutral as possible.

"It's not that he's childish, or spoiled, really, do you think? Just determined." She had the English manner of ending statements interrogatively, which didn't come from any lack of conviction about what was said, but a desire to be polite to the hearer, not to bully into submission but lure into agreement. "He says, in fact, his parents never spoiled him." She looked at me inquisitively. She wanted to know everything possible about him.

"No," I corroborated. "It was his brother they spoiled, and his sister. Jack was older, well-behaved, a better student, even a better athlete to start with. Claudia was younger, and the only girl. It was easy to give them what they wanted. David was wild. They tried to take a firmer stand with him."

"He said having an older brother made him absolutely determined never to settle for second place again."

"He never settled for it. He kicked and hollered until he got everything Jack got, and more."

She laughed, and her laugh had the same sweet rasp as her voice.

"He told me you're his best friend. I hope we're going to be friends, too."

Before I could answer, David stopped short and set down the picnic hamper. "Grab the other end of this," he ordered, shaking out the blanket. Sarah and I took the edges and smoothed them down, then sat, Sarah leaving her hat and sunglasses in place, presumably to prevent her being recognized by a passing fan. Duncan's face and hers were frequently splashed across the pages of the tabloids.

David opened the picnic basket. "How lovely," murmured Sarah.

There were pâtés and salads, chicken and cheese, bread and wine. David uncorked the bottle and poured us each a glass, but left the lunch for Sarah to serve. She did it with so much dexterity, preparing the three paper plates with such artfully arranged samplings of food, that I wondered if perhaps she'd once worked as a shop assistant in a gourmet food store; or, better, perfected the technique for a part she'd had to play on stage. I would have dropped a quarter of the food on the blanket.

Through the smoke of his Gauloises, David watched her appreciatively, admiring her gestures—the cock of her head as she served the chicken, the movement of her wrist as she spooned the salad, the extension of her arm as the knife cut through the pâté. And though she glanced at us only casually as she worked, joining easily in the conversation, she was conscious of his scrutiny and was playing to it. They were still at that stage of heightened awareness where no word, look, movement, or feeling goes unregistered. A vibration in one sent up a matching tremor in the other. Though they didn't touch that entire afternoon, except briefly when plates were passed, the atmosphere was charged with sex. How can anyone not know they're lovers? I wondered. And considered what Cassandra had told me about Duncan and how model a husband he had become in recent months. What had he observed? What did he suspect? What did he *know*?

"I finally got to see *Hedda Gabler*," Sarah said, handing David his plate. "I caught the matinee last week." She was talking about the Ingmar Bergman production which had just opened in the West End with Maggie Smith and her then husband, Robert Stephens. She turned to me. "One of the great problems being in a play is finding the time, and the energy, to see anything else. Luckily, the matinee is on a different day to ours."

"What did you think?" David never sounded, when he asked a question, as if he were being merely polite. Politeness was not a virtue that appealed to him. It wasted too much time. If he asked an opinion (and he didn't often), it was because he was genuinely interested in the reply.

"I know you loathed it," said Sarah, "but really it was marvelous. It looked stunning. And the line of the play, the shape of it, was so clear, so controlled." I didn't listen to her words so much as watch her delivery. She spoke fluently, intelligently, unaware of the seductive power of her voice, making slight, graceful gestures with her hands, taking an occasional small mouthful of food that in no way hampered her speech, another acquired stage technique. "And Maggie's performance is really extraordinary, don't you think? Hedda isn't only proud and passionate, she's intelligent and self-aware." She went on, praising the performances. Sarah was always very generous in her praise.

"I didn't loathe it," corrected David. "In fact, I enjoyed it more than I do most Ibsen plays."

"How can any playwright dislike Ibsen?" asked Sarah, surprise vying with disapproval in her voice.

"Easily," said David, with a grin.

"Have *you* seen the play?" Seeking an ally, she turned to me. She didn't find one.

"Can't stand Ibsen," I responded. I took a sip of wine and deadpanned, "All that fuss over a dead duck."

Sarah looked stunned, and David rocked with laughter. "She's a photographer," he explained. Sarah had finished her wine, and David poured her another glass. "She likes pictures. Ibsen's got too many words."

"Well, I can see perhaps not liking *The Wild Duck*, but *A Doll's House?*"

David didn't only want Sarah's love, he wanted her admiration. He used what he knew about Ibsen (which was considerable) to do party tricks. Taking his little colored balls of unpopular opinion, he threw them up in the air and juggled them, tossing them higher and faster, knowledge and wit moving quicker than the eye could follow. I'd seen him do it any number of times, and the act never failed to impress. Sarah, who may herself have seen it a few times before, still was dazzled. Not that she changed her opinion of Ibsen then, or ever. But David got from her the response he wanted: awe unmixed with resentment. It was part of his appeal (at least when he made the effort, as he did that afternoon), this being able to present a position forcefully, yet without threat, without making a person feel like an idiot for disagreeing with him. He did not devastate Sarah with superior logic or flay her with heavy sarcasm as he could do when inclined. Instead, he gave ample credit to her intelligence, her knowledge, while all the time expounding and consolidating his own position with humor and charm. It was a superb technique for winning friends and influencing lovers, nor was it in this case solely a ploy. David did admire Sarah, at least as much for her talent as for her beauty. What he thought of her mind, I wasn't yet sure. Nor did I think it mattered. As long as she had enough intelligence to admire his, it was sufficient.

"I would love to play Nora," insisted Sarah, an odd note of longing in her voice. "It's a marvelous part."

"Of course it is," countered David. "I'm not arguing the quality of the roles, just the quality of the plays, which is totally different. Why don't you play it, if you want to?"

"Every management in town must be clamoring to have you do something for them," I added.

"To do something they want," she said. "Usually some silly little comedy." Then she shrugged and smiled wryly. "Don't get me started on that, or I'll sound just like any other ungrateful actor you've ever heard. Actually, I'm very lucky. I have a lot of competition. There are some terrific women around, all about my age. Still, I get a good shot at most things being produced. You can't ask better than that, can you?"

"You can ask for better plays," replied David.

"Will you write one for me?"

"I don't think so." She had asked it lightly, teasingly, but was clearly surprised by his answer. "It might throw everything out of balance," he added.

"Well, when I play Nora, will you come see me?"

He threw the last of the paper plates into the plastic sack he had brought, then stopped and looked at her. "I'd watch you in anything," he said. She blushed with pleasure. "Except, possibly, *Rosmersholm*," he added, grinning. "That would take more generosity of spirit than I've got."

She laughed, and there was no hint of annoyance in it. How could there be? Everything about him now delighted her.

David looked across to me, his face reflecting Sarah's. Isn't she wonderful? he asked silently. Isn't she as good as I told you she'd be? Isn't she the best?

He got no argument from me, or any further words of advice. Choice for them was no longer possible. Wherever that frontier is between lust and love, they'd crossed it. Both were beyond the point where sense holds some sway over passion. Though they might wish to avoid hurting each other, or anyone else, they were too far gone to take the steps necessary to ensure that they wouldn't.

I doubted the intensity would last. It never did. But I knew better than to be the one to remind David of that.

Sarah glanced at her watch and said that she had to go. We gathered up the remains of the picnic and went with her back to the parking lot, walking three abreast, David and Sarah carefully not touching.

At her car, a tiny red Austin Mini, she shook my hand and said she hoped she'd be seeing me again. "Duncan's determined to have you take our photographs. I hope you can." She smiled at David and climbed into her small box.

"Call me tomorrow," ordered David.

"I'll try," she said, leaving David frowning after her as she drove away. He didn't like not being sure of getting his own way.

"What was that about?" he snapped. I looked at him blankly. "Your taking their photographs," he added.

"When Cassandra and I went backstage after the play to see Duncan—"

"Is Cassandra still fucking him?"

"No. In fact, she says he's being very faithful at the moment." David snorted in disbelief. "I am only telling you what Cassandra said. Anyway, Sarah came in, and somewhere in the course of conversation, Duncan suggested I take some photographs of them."

"Did you tell him you were only interested in potters at the moment?"

"I told him I was busy, but would try to find the time."

"Are you going to do it?"

"It's tempting. It would mean pages in the kind of magazine I don't generally get access to."

"I wouldn't want to interfere with your career," he sniped, his voice laden with malice.

"How nice of you," I returned in kind.

"I can't stand seeing them together, thinking of them together." There was pain in his voice, as well as fury, but I was too angry at that moment to care. Anyone, even David, trying to dictate what I should do with my life, with my work, made me furious.

"Then don't buy the magazine. If and when I sell the photographs," I added.

David got into the Bentley and slammed the door. I followed suit. He started the car and drove slowly along the lane, turning into the Spaniards Road. It was about five o'clock and the air was still and hazy, heavy with summer and various pollutants, including anger. Where was that west wind, fresh or strong, promised by the BBC to blow it all away?

"I'm sorry," said David finally. "I'm not very reasonable lately."

"So I've noticed."

"I'm in love."

"So I've noticed," I repeated.

He grinned. "I'd rather you didn't take those photographs." He knew he was poking at a nerve, but he couldn't help himself. Neither could I. When I didn't answer, he went on, "Are you angry with me because of today? Because I didn't tell you Sarah was meeting us?"

"Not anymore, though I suppose I should be."

"Would you have come if I'd told you?"

"Probably. I keep meaning not to aid and abet you, but I can't seem to help myself. If only because I'm so nosy. I have to know what's going on."

"You did like her?"

"How could I help it? 'Everyone's in love with Sarah,'" I quoted.

"Who said that? Not me. Not to you."

"Simon Wroth."

"When did you see him? And why were you talking about Sarah?" he asked, as inveterately curious as I am. I told him about Simon and the war, about Dr. Cope and little Sarah. "I didn't now," he said, surprised there should be anything about his new love he had not yet discovered.

"You and Sarah have probably had more important things to talk about than Simon. More important people to discuss."

But David didn't want to be lured into a conversation about Duncan, or Caroline; and he certainly didn't want to think about the possible repercussions of his affair on Lissie. "Then what happened?" he asked.

"When? What do you mean?"

"You know what I mean. What happened between you and Simon after you left the restaurant?"

David always had the ability, even as a child, even despite a stubbornly self-centered streak, to forget his own problems and devote himself entirely, for the moment at least, to those of a friend. It was why people flocked to him. He seemed so genuinely interested; and if the interest was momentary, it was—at the same time—profound. When he listened, he listened completely, giving the impression that no one else could ever understand so well, sympathize so fully, give such considered and valuable advice.

So I told him about Simon, about my confusion and my guilt. And having confessed to him, I felt immediately better. What I had done, after all, was not so terrible. David didn't look at me reproachfully, condemning me. He stopped the Bentley in front of my hotel and took my hand.

"If you need Simon, you need him. But if your long-range plan is to use him as a weapon against Ned, I'd reconsider."

"It's not," I replied, outraged at the thought. "I don't want Ned to know. I never want him to know. He'd be so hurt."

"Remember that when you're back in New York and in the middle of a fight."

"I don't fight dirty anymore."

"We all fight dirty sometimes. But I know Ned. If you use Simon against him, you'll kill whatever there is between you. And I'm not sure you really want to do that."

"I don't know what I'm doing with Simon. I really don't know."

"Maybe just scratching an itch. There are worse things in the world. Don't be so hard on yourself." He kissed my nose. "You'll be all right. And if you're not, don't worry," he promised, as solemnly as if he alone had command of his fate. "I'll be there to pick up the pieces."

❧ *Chapter 10* ❧

First, Cassandra called to tell me she'd had lunch with Evie Johnson, one of the editors at *Vogue*, and just happened to mention the photographs I was going to take of the Powells.

"I'm not sure yet I can," I told her. I'd got over my bad temper by then and had begun to have second thoughts.

"Don't be a fool, darling," said Cassandra, in what was, for her, quite a reasonable tone of voice. "You've been moaning for ages about wanting to break into the big time."

"I have not been moaning."

"All right, not moaning. Let us just say salivating. Which is exactly what Evie Johnson is doing at the thought of those pictures." Apparently, though Duncan and Sarah gave the usual separate interviews whenever either had a film about to be released or a play due to open, to keep their private lives private they'd never before consented to do one together. Cassandra had indeed engineered me a coup. "I really don't understand what's got into you, Nikki," she added, showing signs of acute exasperation. "You're not usually so coy." She gave me Evie Johnson's number and hung up.

Then Duncan phoned. "Sarah tells me she ran into you and David at Kenwood on Sunday."

"Yes," I replied, hoping my voice didn't betray my surprise. It hadn't occurred to me she would tell him; though, of course, the classic way to allay suspicion is always to admit half the truth.

"She loves Kenwood," he confided. "She runs off there whenever she has a free afternoon."

"It's a lovely place," I responded neutrally. Sarah and David met at a flat in Highgate. A friend of Sarah's, so David had told me, was abroad on tour with one of the repertory theater companies and Sarah had promised to feed his cats and water his plants. It was a comfortable, airy flat, with a view out over the Heath, about a ten-minute walk from Kenwood.

"It's the Vermeer," continued Duncan. *"The Guitar Player,* I think it's called." I told him I'd seen it. "It's one of Sarah's favorite paintings." He laughed. "I prefer cricket. I spent Sunday afternoon at Lord's." I remembered the stadium David had pointed out to me as we drove past. So the endless cricket matches, after all, did serve a purpose. "I hear I missed a splendid lunch."

"As splendid as cold chicken can get."

"Sarah did mention, didn't she," he continued, his voice modulating to another key, "that we really do want you to take our photographs?"

"Yes, she did." I took a deep breath. "I'd love to."

We set a date for the following week and agreed to talk the day before to confirm the time. I hung up, settled back into the pillows of the bed, and, ignoring the spread of contact sheets around me, tried to figure out again just why Duncan was so determined to have me take those pictures.

But the only advantage that seemed clear was my own. Every attempt I'd made over the past few years to broaden my pigeonhole, to climb out of my comfortable niche in prestigious little magazines, had resulted in failure. I'd begun to feel frustrated, sometimes even hopeless. And here, unexpectedly, serendipitously, was not only my chance at more money and wider recognition, but an opportunity to try my hand at a different type of photograph entirely. David be damned, I thought. He'd never sacrifice his work for anyone, including me. I picked up the phone again and called Evie Johnson at *Vogue.*

I spent the rest of the day at a pottery in Fulham, returned to the hotel to leave my equipment, then set off, earlier than necessary, for dinner at David and Caroline's. They had rented a mews house in South Kensington, behind the Brompton Oratory, not far from the Victoria and Albert, and I was determined to find my way without a map, through the always baffling, endlessly surprising, side streets of London.

It was a Wednesday night, the Knightsbridge stores were open late, and the streets were crowded with blond women and fair-skinned men carrying green plastic shopping bags from Harrods. I walked along Pont Street, past St. Columba's Church, and crossed into Beauchamp Place. The smart shops were full of expensive clothes that didn't interest me; but at Deliss I stopped and bought a pair of outrageously expensive boots. After all, I had just sold some pictures to *Vogue*.

Compared to its neighbors, which looked like toy houses set in a row, the Waltons' was large, with a loft built over its second storey which David used as an office. It had white-painted brick, potted orange trees framing an apple-green door, and windows trimmed in the same color with boxes trailing lobelia and petunias in pink and white.

Lissie was standing right behind her mother when Caroline opened the door. She smiled up at me. "Its about time you got here," she said, mimicking the grown-up phrase she must recently have heard very often.

"She's been driving me crazy all afternoon, waiting for you," said Caroline, as close to welcoming as she could manage.

"Hello, sweetheart," I said, scooping the child up into my arms, burying my nose in her neck. As often happened when I was around Lissie, all my ambivalence about motherhood was temporarily dispelled. "Hmmm, you smell good. Have you just had a bath?"

"Uh huh. Will you read me a story?"

"Let Nikki put her packages down, Lissie."

"Are they for me?" At her mother's warning glance, she continued, "I thought maybe you brought me a present. But it's okay if you didn't. I would never be mad at you."

But the packages were indeed for her, and when she turned away to open them, Caroline said, her voice devoid of emotion, "David's not home yet. But I don't think he'll be much later. He usually gets back in time to put Lissie to bed." Our conversation at lunch might never have taken place.

I was sitting in a chair in Lissie's bedroom, with her on my lap, reading for the second time a story from the book I'd brought, when David came in. At the sight of her father, Lissie lost interest in both me and the story. She turned and buried her head in my shoulder, concealing her face. It wasn't shyness, but the first act of a ritual.

"Hello, Nikki," said David, leaning over to kiss me. "Have you seen Lissie?" he asked, ignoring the plump bundle I was holding.

"She was here a minute ago," I replied, "but I have no idea where she's gone." Lissie sat very still in my lap. Was she really convinced, little ostrich, that she couldn't be seen? Funny little creatures, children. So sweet. Why did my stomach knot when Ned mentioned marriage and a family?

"Hmmm," said David. "I wonder where she could be. Do you think she went out?" We played the question-and-answer game for a few minutes, until Lissie began to squirm with mingled pleasure and impatience. "Well, as long as she's not here," said David confidentially, "why don't I sit in your lap and you can read *me* a story." He lowered himself gently while I squealed, and Lissie squealed. "What's this?" he said, grabbing her.

"It's me, Daddy! It's me!" Her face was a study in glee. And so was David's. He swung her up into his arms, kissing her. "Again!" she cried. And the scene was repeated twice more, until David could see my pleasure wearing decidedly thin.

"Why don't you go get yourself some wine," he suggested, "and talk to Caroline. Lissie is going to read her daddy a story now."

"The cat story," announced Lissie.

I kissed her and left her happily sitting in David's lap, turning the pages of a book, pretending to read, inventing as she went along the adventures of Crispin, the Naughty Cat. David's face wore the same expression as when he looked at Sarah, as if what he was seeing was infinitely precious, infinitely pleasurable.

Caroline was in the kitchen, in the last stages of preparing dinner. The room was small but bright and well equipped, even to a dishwasher. The cabinets were pine, the walls cream-colored, the only decoration hanging pots with copper bases and a large plant of trailing ivy. Their apartment on Bank Street hadn't been nearly so nice.

"The house is okay to look at," she admitted grudgingly, as she added water to the scrubbed new potatoes and put them on to boil. "But there's always something going wrong, with the electricity, or the plumbing, or the heating. If you can call it heating." They had had to buy extra heaters for every room the previous winter or they would have frozen to death, and what that did to their electricity bill wasn't to be believed. To add insult to injury, appliances didn't even come equipped with plugs, so it was necessary to pay extra for that, then have all the trouble of putting the plugs on before the damn appliances could be used. The landlords, of course, weren't responsible for a thing. Whatever needed to be fixed, the tenant had all the trouble of arranging to

have it done, which—given the cavalier attitude of the British work-
man—wasn't exactly easy, then had to pay for it as well. "New York
may be a hellhole," summed up Caroline, "but at least it's an efficient
hellhole."

She didn't want any help with the dinner, so I poured us each a glass
of wine, pulled out one of the chairs to the scrubbed pine table, and
sat. Caroline went on shelling peas. "I always make fresh peas," she
confided. "People who say you can't tell the difference from frozen are
crazy. I always can."

Caroline was, so David had often told me, an excellent housekeeper,
an excellent mother, an excellent cook, qualifying her—certainly by my
mother's definition—as an excellent wife, though David stopped short
of crediting her with that. She was an avid reader of consumer magazines, knew every latest threat to the health of mind and body, and did
her best to safeguard her family from them. Caroline was the first person I knew to stop smoking, to insist on seat belts being used, to serve
natural foods, to stop using plastic wrap and aluminum foil. There was
a lot about her I admired, very little I liked. She greeted people with the
same suspicious air she wore as she picked up a can to read its label,
certain the contents were bound to be damaging to her and those she
loved.

"Did you enjoy the party on Sunday?" I asked, hoping she'd at least
been having a good time while David and I were, so to speak, betraying
her.

"It was all right," she said with a deprecating shrug. "Lissie had a
good time."

"Where was it?"

"At her friend Christabel's, in Holland Park. The house is beautiful,
five or six bedrooms, I guess, with furniture that looks as if it's been in
the family for generations, and a walled garden, you know the kind,
with roses growing over everything and not a weed in sight. Everything,
inside and out, perfectly kept. But the food!" She shook her head
disapprovingly. "Mostly chocolate biscuits and cream cakes. I let Lissie
eat them. I had to. But she was on a sugar high all night. And if you
say anything to anyone, even someone you'd think would be sensible,
like Lady Antonia . . ." She shook her head again. "She looks at you as
if you weren't there. "'We always have cream cakes,'" mimicked Caroline in a fruity upper-class accent. "'The children adore them. They'd
be so disappointed if we didn't.'"

I imagined the scene, the self-satisfied Englishwoman confronted by
the self-righteous American, and couldn't help a smile. "I suppose the

English are a little backward nutritionally," I offered, not wanting Caroline to think I was taking sides against her.

"Nutritionally, and every other way. Except culturally, I suppose," she added grudgingly. "Or so David seems to think."

"New York really isn't much better."

"I know. Which is why I keep trying to talk David into moving to California. To Los Angeles. I really hate cold winters."

"Maybe someday," said David, entering. The happy, contented look he wore for his daughter was gone from his face. "Lissie wants to say goodnight," he added. Caroline put the peas on, excused herself, and left the room. David poured himself some wine. "Want a refill?' he asked. I shook my head, and he turned away to rummage through drawers, searching for matches. I knew from the set of his shoulders that he had something to say. I waited. "Duncan Powell told me today you're going to take those pictures of him and Sarah," he said finally.

"*Duncan* told you," I echoed, surprised.

"I played golf with him this afternoon. I won," he added. Both bits of news were irritating. David really did go too far. He found the matches, took a Gauloise from the nearly empty pack, and turned to face me. Reading my thoughts, he said, "He invited me to play," as if that explained everything.

"I thought you were supposed to be working on a new play," I snapped.

"I work mornings," he replied. Then he grinned. "That leaves my afternoons free for mischief."

"You're impossible."

"So, sometimes, are you." He lit the cigarette. "I don't want you to take those pictures, Nikki."

"I've said I would."

"Then say you've changed your mind."

"I can't."

"I'm asking you a favor." His voice was low, and angry.

"One you have no right to ask. You don't allow anyone, or anything, to interfere with your work. Why do you expect me to?"

"A favor," he repeated, "as a friend."

"No!"

"I don't understand. Why does this matter so much to you?"

"Because it gives me pages in a kind of magazine I've never had access to before."

"Find another way," he said. His voice had risen. His eyes were cold with anger.

"Goddammit, David," I said, my temper rising to meet his, "I'm not one of your fucking puppets. You don't pull my strings. If I want to photograph Duncan and Sarah, I will."

"Nikki, I'm warning you. Don't take those pictures."

"Why not?" Both of us had completely forgotten Caroline's existence. She stood in the doorway, having returned from saying goodnight to Lissie, watching us with surprise, and curiosity. She wasn't used to hearing us argue, though we did, often, if not generally in front of other people. "Why shouldn't Nikki photograph Duncan and Sarah if she wants to?"

For perhaps the first time ever, I saw David speechless. "He's worried about me," I said. "He thinks I'm pushing myself too hard." It sounded pretty lame to me. David was not one to notice you were tired or sick or depressed until you fell in a heap at his feet. His skill was not diagnostic, but curative. On short notice, however, it was the best I could do.

Caroline looked, I thought, a little dubious. David took a drag on his cigarette and looked her straight in the eye. He knew better than to smile, or to pretend he wasn't angry. "She came here to take pictures of potters, she should stick to pictures of potters. It never does an artist"— was there a hint of a sneer in his use of that word, or was I being oversensitive?—"much good to go off on a tangent. Focus is what's important." Then he did smile. "So to speak."

That explanation almost satisfied her. I could see the "Oh God" gleam kindle in her eye. She was almost convinced she had stumbled into yet another discussion about the nature of creativity, complete drivel to a pragmatist like her. She drained the potatoes and peas, put them into bowls, and set them on the table. But if Nikki can sell pictures of the Powells to an important magazine, don't you think she should?" she asked. David shrugged, a tactical error, piquing the curiosity that had been on the wane. Caroline usually got a barrage of answers from David to any question asked. I could see her beginning to wonder what was wrong with him, why he was so upset. Caroline sat, and David began to serve the salmon. His anger by now was totally under control, as was mine. He handed me my plate.

"Well, shouldn't she?" pressed Caroline.

"Nikki can do whatever she wants," responded David.

"Which is exactly what I intend to do." I smiled sweetly.

The meal that followed, like most of my meals with David and Caroline, was tense and guarded. This would be my last dinner with them, I promised myself, even if it meant never seeing Lissie again, which of course it wouldn't. David would work something out.

"You really don't like Duncan Powell, do you? Is that why you don't want Nikki to take the photographs?" asked Caroline. She was like a dog with a bone.

"What makes you think I don't like him?"

"It's obvious."

"Well, you're wrong," snapped David. He stopped eating and lit another cigarette. Caroline frowned at the smoke drifting across her table, but said nothing. "I do like him. I think he's charming." And this time the sneer in his voice was unmistakable, though it wasn't entirely clear if Caroline for thinking it or Duncan for being it was its object.

"You saw how you get when his name is mentioned?"

"Goddammit," muttered David. "Can we please stop talking about the man?"

For what remained of the evening, we chose more or less neutral subjects to discuss: Olivier's over-the-top performance in *The Merchant of Venice*, what chance Edward Heath had in the general election, whether or not Thomas Berger's latest book measured up to *Reinhart in Love*. And if a silence seemed imminent, one of us always remembered a Lissie story to tell. Still, we didn't quite succeed in banishing the Powells. They remained indomitably with us, specters at the table, worrying Caroline, making her think, keeping David and me at odds.

✣ *Chapter 11* ✣

The Powells lived in Hampstead, in a pretty tree-lined street of small brown brick houses with walled gardens back and front. A few of the houses looked fairly ramshackle, but most were well tended, and the Powells' was especially lush, a velvet green lawn edged by flowering shrubs and a cutting garden of peonies, sweet peas, cornflowers, and extravagant blooms I couldn't name. A climber rose curtained the front in a shade of pink so delicate it might have passed for white.

I paid the driver, took my equipment from the taxi, and lugged it to the front door. It was opened a moment later by Sarah. Her smile obliterated the last of my qualms. "Duncan's had some trouble with his car this morning," she explained. "But he should be back any minute. Would you like a cup of tea or coffee while we wait?" She guided me to the living room, where I left my camera equipment, and then to the kitchen to keep her company as she made the coffee.

Inside, the house was as pretty and cheerful as its facade. The summer light streamed in at the windows. The walls were shades of cream and the fitted carpets only just dark enough not to show the effects of London's uncertain weather. Bright flowered fabrics covered sofas and armchairs. Matching curtains hung at the windows. On the walls were gaily colored paintings, two by Vanessa Bell. There were vases of flowers everywhere, some from the garden, Sarah explained, some gifts from admirers, some bought by herself or Duncan. They could never walk past a street barrow without indulging themselves. "That's larkspur," she told me, in response to my question, pointing to a bunch of tall blue wildflowers in an unusual blue-glazed vase I recognized as one by the terrible Craig Gillis. "David doesn't care at all about flowers, does he?" she asked, as she gracefully measured coffee into a glass Melior pot. The question clearly was meant to introduce David into the conversation, not to get my confirmation of a fact she already knew.

"We didn't see many flowers growing up in New York." We had only known the names of the obvious ones, I explained, roses and azaleas, the lilies in the pictures of the virgin martyrs, the geraniums in the window boxes, the orchids in the wrist corsages for the senior prom. A poppy was something that grew in Flanders Field and was worn as a paper pin on Armistice Day.

She shook her head in something like bewilderment. Butter had been rationed in her childhood, and meat, but never nature. It was a kind of deprivation she didn't understand. "But he spent summers on his grandfather's ranch, didn't he?"

"Yes, when he was very young. But then he was only interested in horses. He wanted to be the Lone Ranger when he grew up."

"And did you want to be Tonto?"

"No. I wanted to be the Lone Ranger, too."

She laughed, the warm sound filling the room like sunshine. "How did you ever get to be such good friends?" she asked. The question wasn't loaded. She did, absolutely, believe that's all we were, good friends.

"I could give you a lot of reasons, but I'm not sure any would be accurate."

"Yes, that sort of thing is impossible to explain, isn't it? Friendship, love, even hatred, the way it flares sometimes from what seems the most insignificant little spark. But I do know what draws people to David. He's so easy to talk to. He understands everything."

"Almost everything," I replied, thinking of our most recent argument.

She shook her head. "No, always," she insisted. "Even when he won't agree, because he doesn't want to, he still understands. That's what makes arguing with him so particularly infuriating." She plunged down the handle of the Melior pot, trapping the coffee grounds at the bottom, picked up the tray on which she had set cups and a plate of biscuits, and led the way back into the living room. What had they been arguing about? I wondered.

She sat opposite me, blooming out of the flowered couch like a daffodil, her blond hair haloing her delicate face. She picked up the pot and one of the porcelain demitasse cups. "He wants so much. Too much. He wants me to love him."

"Don't you?"

"It's obvious, isn't it? But I won't tell him. I won't say it. He wants me to leave Duncan, but how can I? Why should I? He can't leave Caroline, or Lissie. And I like Duncan. I like living with him." She handed me the cup. "I sound like such a terrible person, don't I?"

"No," I said. "You sound like a completely sensible person."

She laughed again, but this time the laugh had an edge of pain, and her soft brown eyes were shadowed with worry. "I don't know what to do. God, what a mess. I don't know how I got myself into such a mess. Everything was so easy before. It was perfect. I knew exactly what I wanted. And I was getting it. And now. . ." She put her cup down, rattling it in its saucer. There were tears in her eyes, but she stopped them before they fell. "I'm sorry. I have no right to inflict this on you. I hardly know you. There's just been no one I could talk to about this. You won't. . ."

"No. I won't say anything to David," I assured her.

"I knew I could trust you. I knew it at once."

After the first-night party where they'd met, David had returned for another look at *Sky Burial*, then had gone backstage to see the Powells. That time he made sure Sarah noticed him. "It wasn't what he said," Sarah told me. "He was brilliant and funny, of course, but he complemented Duncan far more than me, irritating me a little, really. It was his eyes. I could see the desire in them when he looked at me. I could feel it coming out of his body like heat. I couldn't understand how Duncan didn't notice, but he didn't." She felt afraid, and excited. She tried not to think of him and failed. Fragments of what he'd said, glimpses of how he'd looked, flashed into her mind repeatedly, distracting her from whatever she was doing. She dried onstage during the next performance.

A few nights later, they met again at a bash Simon Wroth (at David's instigation) threw for fifty or sixty of his closest friends in his large, bare, uncomfortable flat in Little Venice. "The place is a nightmare," said Sarah. "I don't know how he can bear it." Caroline had visited Simon's once before, and for her, once had been more than enough. She insisted David go alone. Duncan, happily, spent the evening working the room, at one point conveniently disappearing for a while with a little dark-haired waif of an actress. The coast was clear for David. By the time the night was over, he had Sarah's promise to meet him the next day for lunch. "I was mad for him, you see. I wanted him. I'd never wanted anyone that much in my life. And, well, I really didn't have a good reason not to indulge myself, did I? I loved Duncan and I'd been faithful to him, but I hardly felt I owed him any loyalty. Not anymore. But God, I never meant it to go this far."

Her pain was so palpable I wished I could say something to ease it, but what was there to say? "Don't trust David. He's capable of anything." That was just it. David *was* capable of anything: of abandoning Sarah if she threatened something he valued more; of loving her loyally forever. How could I predict what he'd do? How did I dare?

I kept quiet, and Sarah changed the subject, asking me about my photographs. Like Duncan, she had seen some that had appeared in *Plays and Players* and, it turned out, a series I had done on candlemaking for one of the crafts magazines. "But they were lovely!" she exclaimed with genuine admiration. "I remember thinking how exquisite the lighting was. It had a real painterly quality." Inevitably, whenever people praise work we admire, our estimation of their taste and judgment, not to mention their intelligence, increases appreciably. I had been proud of that series, and I was liking Sarah better every minute.

She looked up from refilling my cup. "Duncan," she murmured, her body tensing a moment, then relaxing again as he filled the doorway. She smiled. "Hello, darling," she said.

For a large man, Duncan's movements were surprisingly effortless, fluid, without seeming in the least effeminate. He was too solid for that, too bulky. He kissed Sarah, then took my outstretched hand and bent to kiss my cheek, apologizing in his deep, resonant voice for his lateness. Sarah poured him a cup of coffee, and Duncan acted out bits of his morning for us, playing the garage mechanic, the service manager, and himself, in a farce that resulted in a minor adjustment to his Jaguar taking not the ten minutes that had been estimated, but nearly two hours to complete. He was a master storyteller, and clearly his skill hadn't palled for Sarah in the years they'd been married. She listened with as much interest as I, and laughed just as hard; but the moment the story was finished, she interrupted him, suggesting we get started. "We've already kept Nikki waiting long enough, haven't we, darling?"

Duncan excused himself to change, Sarah took the tray back to the kitchen, and I began to set up my equipment: I'd brought a set of umbrella lights, a tripod, my Rollei, and a Nikon loaded with Tri-X. As we'd talked, my mind had been busy selecting just where in the room I wanted Duncan and Sarah placed, how I wanted them posed, what shots I wanted of them together, what shots of them separate.

Duncan was the first back into the room. Sarah was freshening up, he told me, and wouldn't be long. He was wearing the same brown

slacks and beige silk jacket he'd had on when he'd entered, but he'd
changed the short-sleeved striped T-shirt to a classic cream-colored silk
and added a tie. The colors suited him, burnishing his fair good looks
to a warm glow. He looked more formal than I'd seen him before, more
elegant, every inch a film star.

Without waiting for Sarah, I posed him—hands in pockets—against
the wall, using one of the Bell paintings as a backdrop; then—legs
crossed—in one of the wingback chairs. He placed his hand on the
arm, and I noticed how beautiful it was, large, with long tapered fingers.

"Your hand is out of frame. Could you move it about an inch?" I
wanted it in the shot. "No, a little more." It still didn't look right, and I
must have frowned.

"Show me." I went to him and took his hand, and when I did, he
tugged, pulled me towards him, and kissed me. It happened so quickly,
was over so fast, I felt almost as if I had fantasized the moment. But
Duncan was smiling at me, looking very pleased with himself. "Sorry.
I couldn't resist."

"Don't ever do that again," I snapped, too surprised to be smooth. I
was usually much better at fending off passes. But was this a pass?
Again, I wondered what Duncan was up to.

"You're embarrassed," he said.

"Yes. And you ought to be, too." I put his hand exactly where I
wanted it and stepped back.

"I never behave as I ought," he retorted as I got behind my Rollei for
cover.

"I can vouch for that," came Sarah's voice from the doorway. I kept
shooting, as Duncan's eyes moved to her, then away again. I wanted to
capture the fleeting expressions on his constantly changing face. What
were they? Smug satisfaction, I thought, curiosity, humor, a hint of
anger; and, perhaps, fear. "Have you been teasing Nikki?"

"Of course," replied Duncan. "How could I resist? She is so serious."

I finished the roll of film. "In New York, everyone thinks I have a
great sense of humor," I said.

"Humor, like wine," delivered Duncan, "frequently doesn't travel."
His manner was so fiercely Wildean that Sarah and I both began to
howl. He joined in immediately.

"Oh, darling, you are funny," said Sarah. Duncan might be a philan-
derer, a cheat; Sarah might know it; and that knowledge equally might
have impelled her to an affair with David; but it had not destroyed all
feeling for her husband. She liked Duncan, admired him, perhaps even
loved him. And Duncan knew it, and perhaps was counting on that

feeling to hold her. Whatever *his* reasons for philandering, not loving Sarah was excluded from the list. He was clearly crazy about her.

Not for the first time, I wondered why it had been necessary for human emotion to evolve into such a complex system of feeling. And why, since it had, people were totally unwilling to admit the fact. What is the point in pretending that feelings are simple, that love and hate, curiosity and boredom, passion and disinterest, are pure rather than alloyed, or constant instead of changeable as the tides?

Sarah was wearing a Zandra Rhodes dress in copper jersey, and as I posed her next to Duncan on the couch I pointed out how their colors complemented each other.

"We don't plan it," said Sarah.

"We've lived together for so long," added Duncan, "we do it instinctively."

As I photographed Sarah, Duncan relaxed, took off his jacket, undid his tie, and rolled up his shirt sleeves. He settled back into the couch to entertain us with tales garnered from years in the theater. He swore that once, early in his career, while appearing at Stratford as Horatio in *Hamlet* he had come upon two gardeners trimming shrubs. When he'd commented on the unsightly mess one of them was making, the man replied, "Not to worry, sir. I rough 'ews 'em, an' Bert 'ere shapes the ends." Sarah laughed. I caught her and wheeled to get Duncan.

I took some very good photographs that morning. My favorite is the one in which Sarah, leaning slightly forward, gazes intently and questioningly at the camera while Duncan looks at her, a slight smile softening his face. There is another of Sarah in the wing chair, with Duncan standing behind. The pose is formal, the perspective elongated and slightly surreal, the photograph interesting, I suppose, but it seems to me now very contrived, and I prefer the first, which manages to convey something of that morning and of the personalities and characters of the Powells.

These photographs, too, have turned up in the Keating biography, the two of Duncan and Sarah together, and one of Sarah, a portrait taken that same afternoon. It is a full head shot and she looks luminous, polished to a high finish, a difficult effect to achieve outside a studio and with limited lighting. Their inclusion implies my sanction of the book, which is infuriating. When I called my agent to shout, she told me she'd authorized their use when I was in Turkey on assignment, and only because she thought I'd be pleased.

* * *

When the session was over, we went out to the garden for lunch. "It's eleven-thirty," said Duncan. "The bar's open." I declined a drink, and Sarah made more coffee and fixed a plate of sandwiches. They had a daily woman, Sarah explained, but she was at home that day with a sick child.

"Leaving Sarah free to fuss around the house. She loves fussing around the house."

"If I don't have to do it too often," agreed Sarah.

"She's a brilliant housekeeper, and a wonderful cook."

"Sporadically brilliant," said Sarah with a laugh and a shake of her golden head. "When I'm trapped in a house for too long, I go mad, don't I, Duncan? Remember the summer after we were married? We rented a cottage in Wales." She turned to me to explain. "I was determined to be domestic: to cook and clean, do laundry, and garden, to be absolutely the quintessential wife. That lasted a week. Duncan came home from a swim one evening and found his dinner all over the kitchen walls."

"She has a frightful temper. You'd never think it to look at her."

Large windows in the kitchen overlooked the garden, and French doors gave out onto a patio. There was a wrought-iron table and matching chairs padded in flowered vinyl. Here, too, rampant flowers were in bloom: cornflowers and sweet peas, daisies and dahlias, an amazing array of blues and yellows, pinks, oranges, and reds, bright in the summer sunshine. I ate the salmon sandwiches that Sarah had prepared, drank my coffee, and watched Sarah and Duncan downing gin and tonics, while Duncan entertained us with stories from his days at Oxford. He was the sort of actor who needed the spotlight centered always firmly on him and used a seemingly endless repertoire of stories to call it back when it began to move away. He babbled as cheerfully as a brook, sparkling prettily in the play of light, moving quickly enough to forestall boredom, sounding because of some trick of topography like a torrent roaring with meaning. His voice was so deeply resonant whatever nonsense he spoke was given substance by it, much as would a nursery rhyme, "Mary Had a Little Lamb," for example, if played by the New York Philharmonic. He was engaging and amusing, someone who—once upon a time—might have been called "a merrie rattle." Next to Duncan, David seemed as silent as a Trappist.

"You didn't go to drama school then?" I asked, interrupting a pause. I had learned quite a lot about Sarah, but about Duncan I still knew almost nothing.

"Oh, no," replied Duncan in mock horror. "My father would never have approved. He'd worked too hard all his life to countenance anything so idle as an actor's life for his son. His dad was a coal miner, you see, and my dad—the youngest—got sent to school. He became an accountant and worked for the Inland Revenue. But not for long. He was too ambitious for that. He set up his own company and made a fortune by advising the greedy how to protect theirs. Not a bad man, my dad. He kept his family in comfort and sent my grandparents luxuriously to their graves. I was destined for the law. I was to be called to the bar, take silk, sit on the bench, and be addressed as 'm'lud.' That was the kind of social climbing my father believed in. But, unfortunately for him, soon after I went up to Oxford, I saw an OUDS production of *'Tis Pity She's a Whore.* That was it for me. Since then I've been very lucky. Now when I tell my father I'm having dinner with Princess Margaret, he shakes his head in disbelief and mutters, 'What can the world be coming to?'"

"He wasn't so much lucky as very good," added Sarah. "Right out of university, he got a part in a West End comedy. It failed miserably, but Duncan got some very good notices. That same producer cast him as the juvenile lead in his next play, which was a smash. I saw Duncan in it."

"She was a schoolgirl on holiday from Kendal," said Duncan.

"He was marvelous."

"And she fell in love with me, at first sight, across the footlights."

"I did have an awfully big crush. I cut his photographs out of magazines and pinned them to my walls." There was a note of deep seriousness in Sarah's voice as she said this, as if she felt it necessary to be scrupulously honest with me about her feelings for Duncan. I was not only David's best friend, I was his surrogate.

"When did you finally meet?"

"In 1961," replied Duncan. "We did Anouilh's *Time Remembered* together."

"I was right out of drama school, and terrified," said Sarah.

"She was bloody good. The most talented child I ever saw. And the most beautiful. We were married the following winter." His voice had an urgency I felt rather than heard. Sarah might be playing to me, but Duncan was playing only to her. He was asking her to remember, to feel again as she had eight years before when she'd finally met the man she'd idolized and managed to make him fall madly in love with her. "Luckily, I'd had the good sense to divorce my first wife before meeting Sarah. Do you remember, darling, how surprised you were when I asked you to dinner?"

"Surprised? Terrified is more like it."

"That I'd have feet of clay?"

"That I wouldn't know what to say to you." She offered me another dainty sandwich, and I took it. The conversation was taking an uncomfortable turn, and I knew I should excuse myself and leave. But I couldn't. I was too interested to go. "I was so young," continued Sarah. "You were so, so sure of yourself. I thought you were everything I could ever want. I was bound to be intimidated, wasn't I?"

Duncan put his drink down and leaned towards her, across the table. "And is that what I turned out to be?"

"What?" asked Sarah.

"Everything you could ever want?"

"I married you, didn't I?" She smiled at him reassuringly.

He wasn't reassured. "And you've never regretted it?" he pressed.

Their eyes locked, and for a moment they both forgot I was in the room. Then Sarah looked quickly at me and away again. "No, I've never regretted it." Again, because I was there, she was determined to be honest. She would not write off her marriage as a mistake just because, due to unforeseen circumstances, due to the arrival on the scene of someone who suddenly made her want more, it was no longer enough. Duncan might not, after all, have turned out to be everything she had ever wanted, but she understood that if David had not come along, she might have lived her whole life contented enough with what she'd got.

And now that she was no longer content, what was she to do? Even if David went away, even if Sarah never saw him again, he had changed the dynamic of her life. He had cracked its smooth finish, and no matter how it was placed to conceal the fracture, Sarah at least would always know it was there.

Duncan turned his attention from Sarah to me. His smile was intimate, confiding. "There you have it," he said, "the caption for one of your photographs: 'Duncan Powell and Sarah Cope, after eight years, as much in love as ever.' For a minute, I wasn't sure whether he was trying to convince himself, or Sarah, or me. "I know the public isn't taken in by publicity. Our fans can smell a rat as quick as a hound can scent a fox. They're capable of great discernment. Put the truth under their noses and they'll take it for what it is. I think these photos of Nikki's, of you and me, cozy in our little love nest, will put to rest any rumors—"

"Rumors?" interrupted Sarah. "What rumors?"

"Darling, when people as prominent as you and I have been married for eight years, there are bound to be rumors. No one believes in happiness anymore."

"What rumors?" she repeated, insistent, an edge of anxiety creeping into her voice.

"Oh, the usual sort of thing. That I have a lover. That you have a lover. That the marriage is on the rocks. Nothing to be taken seriously, of course. I'm sorry if I've upset you." He turned to me, as I was trying to decide how best to make my exit. "I forget what a little innocent she still is."

"Stop it," hissed Sarah. "Stop it now."

"Really, darling . . ."

"Whatever game you're playing, I want it to end."

"Sarah, if you don't sit down and calm yourself, Nikki is going to think you've gone completely mad."

She was standing, her eyes blazing. She looked fierce, not the least inhibited by the presence of a stranger, by my presence. When Sarah was angry, her voice deepened, and its huskiness became even more pronounced. "If you've got something to say to me, Duncan, then say it. If you've got something to ask, then ask. Don't play games with me."

"This time, I'm not the one playing games."

"Duncan, for pity's sake!"

"All right. All right." His voice was as loud and as fierce as hers. "Do you have a lover? Do you?"

"Lucky I've never asked you that."

"Do you?"

"Yes," she shouted, surprising both Duncan and me. "Yes. I do." Neither of us had expected her to tell the truth. She picked up her glass and flung it at Duncan. He moved slightly, and it went whizzing past, crashing into the window behind, splintering it. "Yes," she shouted again, but this time her voice broke and she turned and rushed inside.

After a moment, my presence intruded on Duncan's consciousness. He gave an apologetic shrug and trundled out his best smile. "When she gets that angry, she'll say anything," he said. "Anything at all."

❧ *Chapter 12* ❧

The next day did not begin well. First, I was awakened by a phone call from David.

"What happened yesterday? Sarah just called. She sounded upset."

Simon was beside me in bed, inhibiting conversation, though I'm not sure how much I would have told David even if I had been alone. "I'm sure she'll explain why when she sees you." Simon turned and smiled at me sleepily.

"That's just it," said David, controlling his impatience, speaking as he would to an idiot child. "She called to cancel our appointment this afternoon."

Appointment. When David used a word, he meant it. In this context, "date" was too juvenile, "assignation" or "tryst" too pretentious, I suppose. Or perhaps he was just afraid Caroline might overhear, and hoped the ambiguity of the word "appointment" might leave him room to maneuver.

"She wouldn't say why. Duncan must have been home. She couldn't talk."

"Neither can I." Simon got up and staggered into the bathroom.

"Jesus Christ, Nikki, get rid of him. I have to talk to you."

"I'll phone you when I get back from Cornwall." That would be in about three or four days. By then, I hoped, whatever crisis was now happening would be over.

"Nikki, please, I'm going nuts."

The pain in his voice was terrible, but I didn't know what, if anything, Sarah would want him to know about yesterday. I wasn't sure he had any right to know. I certainly didn't. "She'll phone you as soon as she can. You know she will." The toilet flushed, and Simon, sleep washed from his face, came back to the bed.

"I don't know that. I don't know anything. God, Nikki, this is awful. Being in love is shit."

"I've got to go. I'm sorry. I'll phone you when I get back." I hung up quickly, before he could protest.

Simon put his arms around me. He didn't ask who had called. Instead, he kissed my neck. "Good morning," he said. We hadn't reached the point in our relationship where we felt free to pry.

I hugged him for a minute, then grabbed two handfuls of his long, dark hair, kissed the top of his head, and pulled his face out of my neck. "I have to go to Cornwall," I said, and escaped to the john.

Then, as I left the hotel, the frock-coated concierge handed me a letter. It was from Ned. The guilt I had successfully been keeping at bay washed over me. A plump, smooth-faced, quite elderly couple, dressed in raincoats and walking shoes, must have said hello as I walked past, but the fact didn't register until I heard, behind me, the wife's voice: "Really! How rude!" And her husband's answering mutter about "Americans."

In the taxi, on the way to rent a car, I read Ned's letter. He said he was certain that whatever the problems in our relationship, we both cared enough to work them out.

I wished I had his confidence. I wished I had his certainty. What *was* I doing with Simon? I wondered.

Was Ned fucking anyone? Would I mind if he were? Yes, I conceded, but not much. At this point, another woman was no more a real threat to me than Simon was to Ned. The issue, whatever it was, had little to do with physical fidelity.

But perhaps I felt that way only because I knew, with absolute certainty, that Ned was faithful. I felt rotten. I felt unworthy. Ned, was, unquestionably, a good person, and one I couldn't even dismiss as boring. He wasn't. And he deserved someone much better than I.

I filled out the papers for the car rental, loaded my gear into the truck, and stopped at the nearest filling station for gas. A line of telephone kiosks caught my eye. I found one that worked and dialed David's number. There was no way I could leave London without talking to him again.

Back from taking Lissie to school, and wherever else she spent her early mornings leaving David free to conduct his affairs, Caroline answered and, without any pretense of small talk, told me to hang on while she got David. He was only reading, she informed me. The rule was that David was never to be interrupted while working.

"I thought you were going to Cornwall," he said when he picked up the receiver.

"I've just rented the car."

"How long will you be gone?"

"I'm not sure." We were stalling until we heard the decisive click of the downstairs extension. But even then, we were circumspect. "I can leave a little later if you want to meet for lunch."

"Thanks, but I can't. My appointment's been rescheduled for noon."

"Good, I'm glad." I was. I had no desire to do Sarah's dirty work. Or Duncan's. "You okay?"

"Better, anyway."

"I'll call you as soon as I get back."

"Nikki . . ."

His voice stopped me just as I was about to hang up. "Yes?"

"Thanks for phoning."

"Didn't you know I would?"

"Yeah, I knew."

Love can never be measured or explained, only accepted. Or, if you're very foolish or very frightened, fought against and destroyed.

There were four potters in Cornwall I had arranged to see: David Killiam, Glendora Brattle, Lawrence Howe, and Anni Leigh, all of whom had one time or another studied with Bernard Leach and then gone on to make their own separate and considerable contributions to English pottery. They lived nowhere near one another, so—armed with local maps—I spent the next several days happily touring the Cornish countryside, traveling from one pottery to the next. The weather was dry and sunny, the temperature mild, the azure sky interrupted by fleecy cumulus clouds of exotic shape. The landscape was not the gentle, rolling one I had seen in other parts of England, but stark and rugged, with surprising palm trees cropping up amid cornflowers and daisies. I photographed the potters, I photographed their work, I photographed the white sand beaches and the mutable skies. I shot roll after roll of film of the cobbled streets of Fowey, the rock formations in Mullion Cove, the Channel's spuming water hurling itself against the steep face of the cliffs in a frenzy to obliterate them. My problems and everyone else's seemed far away and, at that distance, minuscule. I stayed two days longer than I'd intended.

It was midday Friday when I arrived back in London. I phoned David immediately, but he was gone, Lissie told me. Doing research in Vienna, added Caroline when she took the phone from her daughter. He had just begun writing *The King of Rome*, which is set there.

All I really had left to do in London was deliver the photographs of Duncan and Sarah, say goodbye to Simon, pack my bags, and go. I could have done it in a day, but I stalled, waiting for David to return.

Evie Johnson, the editor at *Vogue* with whom I was working, was delighted with the pictures, less with their quality, I think, than the fact of their existence. "However did you get them to agree?" she asked in her prissy, breathy voice. "And at home? They normally avoid public-ity, positively shun it. It's amazing they let you," she added with some truth, and no tact. "But why look a gift horse in the mouth? The photos are fabulous. Truly. Loaded with character, teeming with origi-nality." She went on like that for quite some time, and the knot of tension I always have when delivering an assignment began slowly to unravel.

Over tea at Brown's, Cassandra confirmed I now had a toehold in the glossies. Someone at *Harper's Bazaar* had been talking to someone at Liberty's who'd been talking to Evie Johnson, and had called Cassandra to ask if she knew my work. "'Know it?' I said." Her booming voice drew startled glances from the proper couple on the neighboring chintz sofa. "'Why, I've admired it for simply ages,' I told her. 'I begged you lot to let Nikki Collier do those pages on me in the May issue, instead of that dolt Raeburn you lumbered me with, but would you listen? Of course not. Who am I? It takes some chat from Evie Johnson, the cow'—she hates my clothes: flashy, she calls them—'to open your tiny minds to a ray of artistic sunlight. Nikki is special, very special,' I told her."

"Thank you."

"Not to worry, darling. What are friends for? Anyway, it was hardly an untruth. Your pics *are* smashing."

Embarrassed into silence by her vehemence, I beamed at her and offered her the only thing I could at that moment: another cream cake from the dainty porcelain plate on the tiered server.

"Hmmm, lovely," she sighed, taking one. She picked up her cake fork and cut into the pastry as, without looking at me, she asked in what was for her a subdued voice, "Well, what did you make of them? You haven't said."

"Who?" I replied, not certain whether she meant Evie Johnson, the staff at *Vogue*, or the unknown executive at *Harper's*.

"Sarah and Duncan, of course, you dolt." I should have been prepared for the question, but I wasn't. Instead of answering, I took another forkful of cake. "Is there any truth to the rumors, do you think?"

"Rumors?" I said, thinking of Sarah's face as she had repeated that same word after Duncan. I kept my own as blank as I could manage.

"You are infuriating!" she said, loudly, but indulgently, with the kind of smile that transforms an insult into a near compliment. Again our neighbors cast anxious looks our way, eyeing Cassandra as if she were a volcano with a temperamental history.

"I'm only a visitor. You can't expect me to be up on all the local gossip. And please keep your voice down," I hissed.

"I am keeping it down," she said, in a much quieter tone. "I am virtually whispering. And I know it's disgustingly nosy of me, but I am horribly, incurably curious about them."

"You're not still in love with Duncan?" I asked, partly because I wanted to know, partly because I hoped to change the subject.

"Let's just say I'm fond of him. Very fond."

I thought for a moment about Duncan and Cassandra together, vying nonstop for control of the conversation, and smiled.

She looked at me suspiciously. "Don't you like him?"

"Of course. I think he's charming." It was always the word that came first to mind when thinking of Duncan.

"Sarah and he have always seemed so happy together, despite his screwing around. That never meant anything, not really. I always had the feeling he did it because it was expected of him, because if he'd resisted all the temptation strewn in his path people would have thought he was decidedly odd." I looked at her dubiously. "Well, people expect film stars to fuck around."

With that, our neighbors hurriedly paid their bill and left, while the maître d', in an effort to hasten our exit, came to ask if we wanted anything else.

"Yes," boomed Cassandra, giving him her brightest smile, "another pot of tea, please, and some more of those raspberry tarts." As he walked away, resigned, she turned back to me. "Impertinent ass, trying to hurry us like that. Service really isn't what it used to be." She finished her last morsel of eclair and said musingly, "Anyway, I told you, Duncan's been awfully good these past few months."

"Maybe he's not being good. Maybe he's just being discreet."

She shook her head emphatically. "No, he's been a positive angel. Which is why it's so odd for all this to be happening now." A waiter arrived with the tea and cakes, to be greeted by insincere smiles and words of thanks from both of us.

"All what?" I asked, as soon as he'd left.

Cassandra leaned towards me and, finally getting to where she'd been leading the entire conversation, said, "Duncan's been phoning all over town to see if anyone knows where Sarah is. She disappeared after the play on Saturday and he hasn't seen her since."

So, Duncan had decided to go public. Why? I wondered. Frustration? Rage? Or "to force the moment to its crisis"? "Everybody quarrels," I said lamely. "Sometimes I think it's only the quarreling that makes a relationship bearable. They're so boring otherwise."

Cassandra laughed, and I called for the check. The least I could do, after all she'd done for me, was pay.

I spent the night at Simon's. His flat was large and airy, a top-floor conversion of what had once been an enormous one-family home, with huge rooms and long windows overlooking a canal in Little Venice. Someone who cared could have made it a showplace. Simon didn't. The paint was stained with damp, the drapes faded, the covers of the sofa and armchairs worn to a sick green. Books and records lay stacked on boards supported by bricks, or heaped haphazardly on the floor. Though the sheets were clean, the bed was unmade. It was a cold, unfriendly place, shabby and uncomfortable.

Simon, too, had received a phone call from Duncan. "I don't understand Sarah anymore," he told me. "What she's doing to her marriage. What she's doing to her career. She was always so ambitious, so determined to be a success. And now, with *The Folly*, she's almost there. The film offers are starting to come in from Hollywood. And do you know what she said to me the other day? That none of it matters, that she'd give it all up in a minute."

"Do you believe her?"

"I don't know. She's been so odd lately." Then he shook his head. "No, I don't believe her. Next to David, Sarah is the most ambitious person I've ever met."

But I didn't want to talk about David. I kissed Simon.

"Has he said anything more about New York and the play?" he asked, when he came up for air.

I rolled over on top of him. "Say goodbye," I said.

Our love affair was over, we agreed: it had been fun, we'd both en-

joyed it, and we'd ended up friends. Who could ask for better than that?
   Then, for the last time, we made love.

   The next morning, in the throes of the nostalgia I always feel leaving
a place where I've stayed and been comfortable, I packed. I sorted
through papers, magazines, and books forcing myself to throw away the
ones I couldn't think of a reasonable excuse to keep. I wrapped the
pottery pieces I'd collected in paper and packed them carefully in my
carry-on. My clothes I threw haphazardly into a suitcase. When I'd
finished, I left to meet David in Kensington Gardens. There'd been a
message waiting for me at the desk to meet him there.
   The children's playground is a large, unkempt area of aging swings
and slides, sand pits and merry-go-rounds surrounded by patches of bare
earth and weedy grass. On the other side of the security fence is Kensington Palace, then the home of Princess Margaret and her husband,
Lord Snowden, eminent photographer. As I approached along the path
from Holland Park Avenue, I could see David's long, lean body moving
rhythmically forward and back as he pushed Lissie in a swing. It was
Tuesday, and he was the only father among a handful of young
mothers. He was talking to one, a pale girl still in her teens, wearing a
faded cotton sundress. She had that look of intense interest, of shy
self-awareness, of hope and hunger that women usually wore in David's
presence.
   Lissie was the first to see me. "Nikki, Nikki!" she called, as the swing
arced up and back. "Watch me! Higher, Daddy! Higher!" David
obliged for a moment, then slowed her down and lifted her off. She ran
to me for a kiss. "Did you see me?"
   "I certainly did. You're very brave. I wouldn't like to go that high."
   "I like to go as high as that," she said, pointing to a nearby plane tree.
   "She's not afraid of anything," said David proudly. Given his own
fear of heights, it was amazing he could bear even to watch Lissie on a
swing. Perhaps that's why he looks so terrible, I thought hopefully.
Perhaps he was just frightened she'd fall.
   I spent the next few minutes on the merry-go-round with Lissie as
David watched, a smile easing the tension in his face. Finally, he
pointed Lissie towards the slide. "Go play on the slide. I want to talk to
Nikki."
   "Nikki's my friend," said Lissie.
   "She's my friend, too," replied David. "And now it's my turn to play
with her."
   For a moment Lissie looked remarkably like David, her face set in the

same stubborn expression as his. Then she spotted a little girl her own size and she smiled. "Okay," she said cheerfully and ran off.

We sat on a bench which gave us a clear view of the children. The smile vanished from David's face. "God, I love her," he said. He reached into his shirt pocket and extracted a crumpled pack of Gauloises. He lit one.

"You look awful," I told him. There were dark circles under his eyes and his skin had a gray pallor.

"I haven't slept much recently." He waved at the young woman as she walked past us, smiling shyly, pushing a smaller version of herself in a pram.

"What did you do in Vienna?"

"Talk mostly." A smile flitted across David's face. "I went early in the week to do some research. Sarah flew over to meet me after the curtain on Saturday."

"I thought so," I said, then told him what Cassandra had told me. "Sarah left him a note, telling him she'd be back Monday before the performance. I don't know what he's up to. He didn't phone Caroline. At least I don't have that to deal with."

"Does he have any idea it's you?"

He shrugged. "Sarah hasn't told him. Not that, anyway."

"What happened? After I went to Cornwall, I mean."

Never taking his eyes from Lissie, he told me. After I'd left Duncan and Sarah's, the day I'd photographed them, the quarrel had continued late into the night and next morning with Duncan alternately irate and beseeching, Sarah both distraught and bewildered. Her life had got completely out of her control. When Duncan took a shower to try to calm down, Sarah phoned David to cancel their meeting; then when Duncan left to keep an appointment with his agent he decided at the last minute not to cancel, she phoned again. Sarah arrived in Highgate exhausted, with nerve ends frayed. She told David she couldn't see him again, that she couldn't stand the lying anymore, the scheming, the manipulating, the betrayal. It wasn't fair. It wasn't decent.

David, whose sense of decency centered more on his internal needs than on objective criteria, calmed Sarah down and convinced her no decision about their future should be made when she was so upset. What they needed was time and quiet, they needed to get some distance from Duncan and Caroline, literally and figuratively, before deciding what to do. He begged her to meet him in Vienna, and finally she agreed.

He told Caroline he needed to do more research (which was true) and left, promising to phone every day (which he did).

Sarah made no promises to Duncan. Knowing he would never agree to her going away, she ducked out of a late dinner on Saturday by pleading a headache and took a taxi to the airport, just making the last plane. She'd left a note at home for him, saying that she needed some time away and he wasn't to worry.

Sarah and David hoped that no one would connect their simultaneous absences, and it turns out no one did. Then. The paparazzi who snapped the photograph Mr. Keating believes is the one on the cover of his book recognized Sarah, but not David, and—since he was after bigger game (Callas and Onassis, I think)—filed the picture he took until it was worth something. It appeared in one of the tabloids a year later. In it, David and Sarah both look drained, exhausted, worried, and joyless.

For the first time in their whole relationship, David and Sarah had what seemed endless, luxurious hours together. They spent very few of them making love. The physical passion which normally obliterated any other consideration this time took second place to discussions about their future. The Vienna Boys' Choir was singing at a Sunday-morning concert and they went, leaving at the first interval. They visited the Kunsthistorisches Museum, looking at but not seeing the Rembrandts. They sat in the back of St. Stephen's Cathedral and talked. They drank coffee at Demel's and talked. Except for the few hours they pretended to sleep, they did little but talk.

The one stumbling block to their being together was Lissie, and she seemed an insurmountable one. Sarah said she understood and didn't blame David, but the fact remained she couldn't stand the way she was living anymore, and if it killed her she would stop it. When they returned to London, she wouldn't see him again. David pleaded, but Sarah was adamant. He believed her and was frightened.

A new, disturbing twist to the plot was added Monday morning when Sarah made a phone call to London, to her doctor, for the results of some tests she'd had done a week or so before. "Her doctor told her she was fine, in perfect health. The symptoms she has are perfectly normal, in the circumstances," said David. "She's pregnant." I looked at him, my shock obvious. Also obvious was the unaskable question in my mind. "The baby's mine," he said, answering it. "She hasn't slept with Duncan since . . . she hasn't slept with him in months."

That news changed everything, of course, though Sarah insisted it shouldn't. David felt both trapped and relieved: trapped into abandoning Lissie, which was wrong, and relieved that he had an acceptable (to him) excuse for doing it. There was no doubt at all in his mind that he loved Sarah completely and would forever. Slowly, the joy began to rise in him: they were meant to be together, and Sarah had found the way to make it possible. Moreover, the way seemed miraculous, fated. In her years with Duncan, Sarah had been told by more than one specialist that she would never be able to have a child.

David promised that as soon as they returned to London, he would speak to Caroline about a divorce. Except for working out custody arrangements for Lissie, he didn't think (optimistically, in my opinion) there'd be a problem.

They got back in time for David to say goodnight to Lissie. "I missed you, Daddy," she said, predictably, as she sat on his lap. "Don't go away anymore, ever."

The euphoria he'd been feeling since leaving Vienna drained away. There was no way what he was about to do could be easy. "But I still didn't think it would be impossible," he said to me. He tucked Lissie in and went downstairs to face Caroline.

"And?" I urged.

He had stopped speaking. He lit another cigarette and puffed at it as if it were giving him sustenance. I couldn't remember ever having seen him so grim, not even after the disastrous notices of his second play. He waved to Lissie, who had called to him to watch.

"What did you say to Caroline?" I asked.

"Nothing. I didn't get the chance. She had news of her own to tell me." He started to laugh, a joyless laugh, one I had never heard before. "You're never going to believe this, Nikki. I'm not sure I do. Except it's not the kind of thing Caroline would lie about. She's pregnant."

"What?"

"Caroline's pregnant."

"Oh, Christ."

He laughed and shook his head again.

"What are you going to do?"

"I wish I knew. I wish to God I knew. Fucking hell, Nikki, can you believe life? Can you fucking believe it?" And then Lissie fell, scraping her knee, and David ran to pick her up.

New York
December 1971

✤ Chapter 13 ✤

It was three weeks before Christmas and Manhattan was at its best. The weather was cold and bleak and the evenings closed in early, but the gray days were brightened by snow flurries and the nights by storms that turned the city into a wonderland, embroidering the trees with lace, carpeting the park with ermine. Shoppers hurried through the chill with reddened noses and arms laden with brightly colored parcels. On street corners, the Salvation Army singing carols alternated with jolly fat Santas ringing bells. The smell of roasting chestnuts was in the air. Christmas lights hung above the main thoroughfares, the store windows presented Victorian fantasies of family life, the tree at Rockefeller Center proclaimed its message of peace and hope. It was my favorite time of year and New York my favorite place to spend it.

Wrapped in fake fur and fleece-lined boots, I hurried under the lights, through the snow, up Fifth Avenue towards the Plaza, tossing coins to the Salvation Army as I went, smiling at the passersby who—with the quixotic seasonal friendliness of the New Yorker—smiled at me. The strains of "Hark, the Herald Angels Sing" followed me across the Grand Army Plaza and into the lobby of the hotel.

David was waiting for me in the Palm Court. He stood when he saw me, not out of politeness but for a better hold, and I rushed across the room into his arms. Though we'd written often and spoken on the phone (the recently laid direct-dial cable made Europe seem as accessible as New Jersey), we hadn't seen each other in eighteen months. "Oh, God, I've missed you," I said as we hugged.

Tail-coated musicians, set among the columns and the potted palms, played "Lara's Theme." There was a murmur of hushed voices and the tinkle of china. We sat, ordered tea, and studied each other's faces for a moment.

David was handsomer than ever. The weight he'd lost was still gone, but instead of looking gaunt as he had when I'd last seen him, the pronounced angles of his face gave him a rugged, a stoic, appearance. He looked like an illustration from *The Virginian*, the Owen Wister novel he'd read over and over the summer he was ten, a picture of the quintessential pioneer man. His dark eyes were full of light and his quirky, uneven smile full of love. "You look terrific," he said.

"So do you."

He reached over and took my hand and stroked it for a minute. "I hate it here," he said. "I wonder why I suggested it?"

"Beats me," I replied, standing. "Let's go." Sometimes I do like the Palm Court, and the music, and the tea, when I'm in the mood; but never with David. He was too vital for the room, too large for it. His energy shattered its calm, upset its equilibrium.

We walked over to Seventh Avenue, to the Carnegie Deli, sat at a corner table, and ordered coffee. This was our natural habitat, the kind of place where David and I had "hung out" since we were old enough to be turned loose in the streets. We had started with hot dogs and Cokes and progressed to pastrami and beer in neighborhood delis that were variations of the Carnegie. Their booths had witnessed an endless exchange of whispered secrets, of shouted arguments, of intellectual discussions and emotional cataclysms. Once in that period of awful puberty when David and I, on principle, refused to be civil to each other, I had—on a dare from a girlfriend—dumped one of those Cokes in his lap. He had retaliated by pouring his chocolate soda over my head. Our parents made us each apologize. We put up a good show of resistance then but afterwards confessed to each other that we'd been glad. It didn't feel right, then or later, our being angry with one another.

Neither letters nor phone calls were as satisfying as sitting across a familiar table, wreathed in cigarette smoke, sipping coffee, reading each other's faces. Lounging happily in the Carnegie, we repeated for each other much of what we already knew had happened in the time we'd been apart, adding detail for nuance and color.

Immediately after her return from Vienna, David told me, Sarah and Duncan had separated, but quietly, not making it public until after the run of the play they were in. Duncan had behaved well, better than I would have expected from the little I'd observed of his behavior. Angry and hurt, jealous and insecure, he still managed not to be vindictive. He confined his attacks on Sarah to a very few self-pitying sessions with mutual friends who could be relied on to gossip only with one another. Sarah confided in no one but David. When forced to discuss Duncan, she defended him vehemently; but the world assumed he'd abandoned a pregnant wife, and, unable to give the details, there wasn't a lot Sarah could say that would vindicate him. When the news of their separation was finally released, headlines and photographs were splashed across the front pages of the tabloids. It was the lead article in the trashier weeklies. And the story wouldn't die. Sarah's pregnancy was a continuing saga and, on a slow news day, could be relied on to pique reader interest. Only my photographs never got published. By the time that issue of *Vogue* was due to appear, the portrayal of Duncan and Sarah as the happily married sweethearts of London's West End was as relevant as yesterday's news. The story got killed. But by then I had completed one other *Vogue* assignment and two for *Harper's Bazaar*: the Powell photographs had already accomplished their purpose in my life.

What else had they accomplished? I wondered. Had my presence at their house that day somehow precipitated the argument? If I hadn't been there, would Sarah have denied she had a lover? Would Duncan even have asked? Would she have convinced him somehow the child was his? It was the subject of a short story by Julio Cortázar, David told me: a photographer happens on a couple in a car. They notice him taking their picture, and that intrusion alters the dynamic of the moment, and consequently the dynamic of the rest of their lives.

Duncan had offered to leave the Hampstead house, but it was Sarah who moved out, taking with her only the Vanessa Bell paintings and a few antique pieces that had belonged to her mother. She wanted a place of her own, somewhere she wouldn't feel guilty having a lover. She bought a house in Upper Cheyne Row in Chelsea to be nearer David. It had a garden in the back, and when she felt depression setting in she'd go outside and work in it, transforming it from an ordinary city plot into a small work of art. She gardened through the summer and the autumn, on good days in the winter, up to the day before her child was born. Sarah was one of those lucky women who even in their last month remain lithe and energetic.

Meanwhile, Caroline knew nothing. Or she pretended to know nothing. If David didn't seem as overjoyed at the news of her pregnancy as she'd hoped he'd be, she took comfort in the past. "You weren't thrilled about Lissie, either," she reminded him, "but you're crazy about her now. You have been since the moment she was born." When that memory made David's mood even blacker, she dropped the subject, retreating into her pregnancy like a princess into a tower. Only the news of the Powells' separation really disturbed her, and she didn't seem disposed to speculate about why. "They always seemed like such an ideal couple," she said to David, and let it go at that.

"She felt you slipping away," I said. "She must have thought getting pregnant was the only way to keep you." I thought it was a futile, a stupid thing to have done. But my irritation with Caroline—which seemed to have less to do with my feeling for David than with abstract principles about responsible behavior—was overlaid with sympathy. "What it must have cost her. She never wanted another child."

"Caroline doesn't care how much pain she's in as long as she knows I'm in it too, up to my ears. Sometimes I think she'd do anything, put up with anything, to keep me from having what I want." He sounded angrier, more bitter, than I'd ever heard him before.

"You betrayed her, David. I don't think you can expect her to respond with a smile and a cheery 'Anything you want, darling.'"

"I betrayed *her!* What do you call what she did to me? She got pregnant. Twice. And why? To trap me. And her excuse this time? The scare stories about the pill and the coil frightened her. She stopped using anything, without telling me. Frightened? Bullshit! She was never afraid of a diaphragm in her life."

"Why be so angry at her? You fucked her, didn't you? In every way possible!"

He looked at me as if I'd gone mad. "What did you want me to do? She was my wife. I was living with her. Did you expect me to tell her I couldn't?"

"God forbid," I said. Then I laughed. David was not my best friend, I had not loved him all my life, because we shared the same moral view. Sometimes I felt as if I loved him because I was condemned to. Sometimes I felt as if it was possible for me to love him only because I'd denied him the power to hurt me where I was most vulnerable.

David didn't behave badly to Caroline during the months of her pregnancy, or at least not badly in the usual sense of scenes and sulks, anger and recrimination. They'd never had much of a social life together. Aside from sex, and Lissie, they had few shared interests, so there was no marked change in their relationship. In fact, it went on very much as usual. Occasionally they went to a film or to the theater, infrequently out to dinner with friends of David's. They almost never entertained at home: Caroline wasn't an easy hostess.

With Lissie, David kept to the same schedule, having breakfast with her as always, making it a point to be at home with her to play before she went to bed, taking her out on the days she had no nursery school. In the mornings, he wrote in his snug little office at the top of the tiny mews house, putting aside for a few hours the intricacies of the plot of his life for the challenge in the plotting of his play. Except on matinee days, he spent the afternoons with Sarah, driving into the countryside for lunches at secluded pubs, exploring the gardens of stately homes, making love in the bright bedroom of the Chelsea house. When the play closed and advancing pregnancy made Sarah happy to stay at home, they'd light a fire in the paneled den; and, as the days closed in bleak and early, they'd lie together on the couch in front of it, drinking tea, reading to one another, talking. In many ways, it was the happiest time of their life together. And all Caroline's entreaties that the Waltons return to New York or, better yet, strike out for Los Angeles went unheeded.

At the end of December, as the days began to lengthen again, Sarah gave birth to a boy, Mark. Since Duncan and Sarah were still legally married, the baby's surname was listed as Powell. It made David furious, but didn't seem to bother Sarah at all. She smiled with what he thought was a strange and irritating contentment and told him not to be a fool when he protested.

Coincidentally, and even ludicrously, it was Duncan who took Sarah to the maternity clinic. By that time, living in the house with Sarah was a combination housekeeper, companion, and devoted slave, a widow in her mid-fifties always known as Mrs. T (for Thomas). Her instructions were to drive Sarah to the clinic, then phone David immediately. What he planned to tell Caroline at this point to explain his rushing out was never clear to me.

However, Sarah did not leave for the hospital in the middle of the night as everyone must have expected she would. She left at ten-thirty in the morning when Duncan happened to be with her.

Being forced to spend hours together every day performing in *Sky Burial* had helped Duncan over the worst of his anger towards Sarah. She told me later that their confrontation scenes, onstage, were for a while so violent they terrified her. The final reconciliation scene was at the same time constrained. That shifted the whole balance of the play, making its resolution unsatisfying, leaving the audience at the end unsettled and uneasy through a tepid curtain call. But, gradually, the emphasis changed again. The onstage arguments retained their violent edge, but the last scene, the one in which the brother and sister at last make peace, became almost beatific. The night that first happened, shortly after the play transferred to the West End, Duncan complimented Sarah on her performance when they met leaving the theater, the only time he'd spoken to her offstage since their separation.

When they left the play, they still met occasionally, to discuss the divorce and the sale of the house. Duncan was by that time involved again with Cassandra and spending most of his time at her place in Holland Park. Neither wanted to be reminded more than necessary of Sarah, and the Hampstead house was redolent of her. "Everything, but everything, had the Sarah touch," boomed Cassandra when she phoned to tell me the news. "Not only that, the pillows in the bed, the cushions on the sofa, positively reeked of her scent. It was hideous being there."

On the morning of Mark's birth, Duncan had stopped by with some papers for Sarah to sign. Mrs. T made them coffee, then went off to the King's Road to do some grocery shopping. No sooner was she gone than Sarah's pains started. An hour later, when Mrs. T still hadn't returned, Duncan put a protesting Sarah into his car and drove her to St. John's Wood, where the maternity clinic was. When Mrs. T got back, she found the note left by Sarah and, frantic with worry, set off in pursuit. Both she and Duncan were there when Sarah gave birth. David wasn't. Neither had remembered to phone him until a groggy Sarah asked where he was. Apparently over Mrs. T's protests, it was Duncan who finally called, another play in the game of one-upmanship he and David were to indulge in for years. David was furious.

When the time came for Sarah to leave the clinic, Duncan suggested he be the one to pick her up. The press, who were sure to be there, would then get photographs of the smiling couple and their new son to grace the front pages of the tabloids the following day. That would put to rest any rumors about his malicious treatment of Sarah, explained Duncan, and their divorce would be seen as mutually agreeable. The suggestion may have come out of a real concern for his image or out of a continuing desire to needle David. Either way, David didn't like it. It was Mrs. T who brought Sarah home. Because of the press, David thought it wiser for him not to be there. He waited for them in Chelsea.

A month later, Caroline gave birth, in the same clinic, to a baby girl, Katherine. If the staff thought it strange that David should be such an attentive visitor twice in so short a period of time, nobody said anything.

*   *   *

"They're beautiful. Both of them. Wait until you see them," he said to me that day in the Carnegie. He had said it before, but this time he could see my face. "What's the matter? You have that look I hate."

"You remind me of a sultan discussing the children of his harem."

"They're my children, and I love them. How do you expect me to sound?"

"Guilty?"

"Sometimes I do. You just caught me at the wrong moment. I felt like bragging." He smiled at me, and finally I smiled back. "They *are* beautiful," he repeated.

"What are you going to do now? I asked. Caroline was refusing to see him. She was refusing to see anyone connected with David but his father and Trudi, Jack's wife.

David shrugged and shook his head. "They won't tell me where she is. Apparently they spend a lot of time discussing what a son of a bitch I am. They keep telling me how glad they are my mother isn't alive to witness what I've turned into. On the other hand they claim she knew all along I was no good." He laughed, not a happy sound. He lit another Gauloise. The ashtray in front of him was overflowing with butts.

"Your mother adored you," I said.

"I know. But that doesn't mean she liked me, or liked the things I did. You and she have a lot in common, you know, at least where I'm concerned."

"I can't help judging you, David. I judge everybody, even myself. Especially myself. But I try to understand. And I do love you, no matter what you get up to. I can't imagine anything you could do to make me stop loving you, except maybe to stop loving *me*."

"Fat chance." He took my hand again. "God, what a mess I'm in." Which was putting it mildly.

David had waited until his daughter was four months old before he told Caroline he was leaving her. "Kate's a rough baby," he told me in a phone call soon after she was born. "She's got colic and cries all the time. She's sick a lot. I can't walk out and leave Caroline alone with that." He told Sarah the same thing, and, presumably because her own son was an angel and Mrs. T always there to help, Sarah didn't issue any ultimatums, at least not for a long time. But finally, insisting the baby was sick because of the rotten English weather, Caroline started lobbying for a move to Los Angeles, just as Sarah began resenting the uncertainty of her position and demanding David do something about it. Left to himself, he would have let his double life continue forever. When, full of self-pity, pleading pain and exhaustion, he turned to me during those months for sympathy, I gave it but knew he had more than enough energy to cope with the stress of juggling time. The complexity of the situation intrigued him. He thrived on the challenge it presented. He admitted he'd never written better. He thought his new play, *The King of Rome*, was more vital, more exciting, than anything he'd done before.

Over dinner in a Chinese restaurant in the Brompton Road, not far from their house, David told Caroline he was leaving her. He thought he had more of a chance there of getting her to listen quietly to what he had to say. He also couldn't bear to tell her in the house where his daughters were asleep. She did listen, but she didn't believe him. "You'll never leave your children," she said when he'd finished. "You'll never leave Lissie. I know you." David moved out the next morning.

His life after that was really not much different. He now wrote in a study at the top of Sarah's house, business associates came there for meetings, and they entertained small groups of friends. Occasionally, he and Sarah left the baby with Mrs. T and went away for a few days, to Paris, to Rome, back to Vienna. But he spent as much time with Lissie and Kate as ever, occasionally had lunch with Caroline or took her out to dinner. She was convinced that his decision wasn't final, that he would be unable to stick to it, and she alternately raged and pleaded with him to return. It was six months before she allowed herself to believe that he wouldn't. He left for Vienna in late November to do a few days more research on his play, and in his absence, Caroline packed up her kids and fled.

Now Caroline was holed up in an apartment somewhere in Manhattan with her two daughters. She was refusing to see David or to let David see his children. His sister-in-law, Trudi, was acting as go-between, trying to negotiate a peace settlement, but not getting very far, since Caroline kept changing the terms. Or perhaps it was Trudi, as David suspected, who kept changing the terms. More than once she'd said that boiling in oil was too good for him for what he'd done, which (in her mind) was to set a rotten example for his brother. She wanted Jack to witness, so David's theory went, the high cost (emotional and financial) of deserting a family to discourage a similar move on his part.

In fact, Caroline's flight from London had been timed very conveniently for David. Production meetings had long been scheduled to start at the beginning of December in preparation for a March opening of *Dreams in F Minor*. His new play, *The King of Rome*, was finished, and his agent was eager to open discussions with several interested producers. Plus which, though Sarah paid all the expenses for her household, the devaluation of the dollar had made England too expensive for him to live comfortably on his grant. So David would have had to leave London, even if Caroline hadn't bolted for New York. Had she realized that, I wondered, and counted on it?

He arrived no more than three days after her, moved into a borrowed apartment on Central Park West, and divided his days between business meetings and trying to find his children. Sarah's divorce from Duncan would be final soon, and David wanted to marry her as soon as possible afterwards. "I feel her moving away from me," he said. "Sometimes I feel she's very far away. It's not that she doesn't love me. I know she does. She just can't take the strain of this sort of thing the way I can."

"You love it. You thrive on it. The more entangled the strands of your life, the happier you are."

"I didn't make this mess deliberately," said David impatiently. "I couldn't help it. I had to have Sarah. I love her." He laughed again, ruefully this time, shaking his head in bewilderment. "I didn't know I could love anyone so much. I can't lose her. Christ, Nikki, how could you think I'm enjoying any of this? Do you know what it's like for me not seeing my children? I'm going nuts not seeing them. I don't even know where they are. That cunt Trudi won't tell me. Lissie has started to stutter. Did you know that?" I shook my head. "It's not good for her to be kept away from me. Why can't Caroline understand that?"

"Because she's hurt, and she's angry."

"Don't start defending her. I'm not in the mood right now."

"I'm not defending her. I answered a question you asked, that's all."

"I've got to see my kids!" he said, ignoring me. He was silent as the waiter stopped at the table to ask if we wanted anything else. "More coffee," said David, then he looked at me, a speculative gleam in his dark eyes. "You talk to Caroline," he said.

"You must be crazy. She doesn't like me."

"I can't leave this to Trudi. She'll fuck me if she can."

"Trudi won't tell me where Caroline is."

"My father will."

"Make him tell *you.*"

"He won't. His belief in punishment is too strong. He thinks I'm getting what I deserve."

"David, my talking to Caroline would make everything worse. She really can't stand me."

"Nothing could be worse. Try, please."

"All right," I said. "I'll try."

❧ *Chapter 14* ❧

It was still at least an hour before the dinner rush would start, but the Carnegie was starting to fill up. There were shoppers getting sustenance before the trip home, a couple of students on their way to see *Raga*, which was playing at the nearby Carnegie Hall Cinema, two men arguing business, an attractive woman somewhere in her fifties eating matzoh-ball soup and reading a paperback edition of the collected works of Stephen Crane.

"'The Open Boat' is the best American short story ever written," said David. Though the woman couldn't possibly have heard him, she glanced over at us, then blushed as she noticed how handsome David was, and how intensely he seemed to be studying her. She returned his smile shyly, then looked away, burying her nose again in her book.

"I prefer 'The Short Happy Life of Francis Macomber.'"

"That's because you don't know as much as I do," he replied, grinning his most ingenuous grin. I returned it. When we'd been apart so long, I found even David's arrogance endearing.

We finished discussing his life, and started on mine. I told him about my parents and brother, about Ned and my booming career. "Right now, I feel as if I could do anything. I feel as if I'm sitting on top of the world," I told him. "Do you think I should start worrying about getting knocked off?"

112

It was very flattering, very sustaining, the intensity with which David could listen. After all, if someone as intelligent, as keenly critical as he could find you interesting, then of course you must be. "No," he said. "Don't worry. It uses up the energy you need for your work. Just make sure the mattress is in place to break the fall."

When we left the Carnegie, I walked with David to the corner of 57th Street, assured him I would phone his father the next morning, and got on a crosstown bus. I wanted to do some Christmas shopping at Bloomingdale's.

Two hours later, exhausted from fighting for the attention of overworked sales assistants, I emerged from the store into a snow flurry driven by gusting winds. There wasn't a taxi in sight.

Instead of attempting the long walk home to the West Side, I struggled with my two shopping bags the few blocks to Ned's apartment and rang his doorbell. It was exactly the kind of thing I hated, and I would have been furious if he'd pulled on me; but he'd be furious, I told myself, if I played the martyr and trekked the long miles home in the cold. And I'd be a fool. There is such a thing as carrying a principle too far.

Each of us had a key to the other's apartment, exchanged on the understanding it would be used only when arranged beforehand. I'd rung the bell twice and was just about to use the key when he opened the door.

He looked surprised, and not precisely thrilled to see me. "I thought you were meeting David," he said, pulling his sweater into place. I'd obviously caught him changing.

"I did. I went to Bloomingdale's afterwards. And now it's snowing and I can't get a taxi. May I come in?"

"Oh, sure. Of course. Come in." He stepped out of the way and I entered.

Ned lived then in a floor-through on East 69th Street between Lexington and Park. I had helped him furnish it, and I loved the place. There was a lot of leather and Lucite, softened by some really fine nineteenth-century French tables and chests. It had a sturdy, masculine, comfortable feel, the same as Ned did.

I dropped my bags, struggled with Ned's help out of my coat and left it to drip in the hall, then went into the front sitting room. It had French doors that opened onto a small iron balcony overlooking the street, giving wonderful access to burglars. Despite the elaborate alarm system Ned had installed, I would never spend the night there alone.

I crossed to the Lucite bar and picked out the bottle of Grand Marnier. My fingers and toes were numb from walking those few blocks, the chill had settled in my bones. "Want some?" I asked.

"No. Thanks." He seemed impatient, restless, as if I were interrupting something he very much wanted to do.

I walked over to the couch and sat down. "I'm sorry, barging in like this. I know it's against the rules, but there really were no taxis and I couldn't face either a bus or the walk home."

"It's your rule," he said. "I never had any objection to our behaving like normal people in love. How's David?"

Ned is one of the few people who were interested in David without being fascinated by him, the only man whom David couldn't lure into a competitive relationship. Ned played pool or darts with David, golf or Ping-Pong, never giving a damn whether he won or lost, which amused David as much as it frustrated him. Much to my relief, they liked each other.

I filled Ned in on the details he was missing and he whistled. "I actually feel sorry for the son of a bitch."

"So do I. But I feel sorrier for Sarah. And Caroline." He knew better than to tell me not to get involved, so he didn't. "Are you going out?" I asked. Not only was Ned fidgeting, but I had suddenly realized that he never wore at home either those slacks or the sweater he'd been pulling on as he opened the door.

"What?"

"You seem a little impatient, and I thought maybe it's because you're on your way somewhere."

"I was just surprised."

"You're not going out?"

"Well, in fact, I am."

My coming to Ned's had clearly been a big mistake. "That's all right," I said. "I'll wait till the rush is over and grab a cab. Or," and I smiled benignly, "I'll get into bed and wait for you."

He did something resembling a shuffle. He seemed to be searching for the right words. Ned, the articulate master of the art of legal cut and thrust, at a loss for words: it was hard to believe. I waited, because I couldn't think of anything to say that didn't sound bitchy, or accusatory, or both.

"I'm having dinner with Mary Kenny," he said finally.

I had met Mary Kenny once or twice at political dinners I had gone to with Ned. Recently, I remembered, her name had been cropping up with increasing frequency in his conversation. She was a pretty woman in her late twenties, with a trim, petite figure and luxurious dark hair she usually wore in a discreet bun. I ignored the stab of pain I felt, tried to push the demeaning jealousy out of my mind and out of my face. Mary Kenny was also a lawyer and a political activist. Ned was then deep into the Regis Boyle case and probably just wanted to pick her brain on some aspect of his defense. It was a business dinner, I consoled myself.

"Where?" I asked. "I hope it's nearby. You'll never get a taxi."

"Where?" He sounded really irritated now. "That's the only question it occurs to you to ask me? *Where!*"

The problem with trying to suppress feelings and avoid quarrels is, you can't. No matter how hard the conscious you tries, the subconscious you tucks in its chin, sticks up its dukes, and says, "Come on, big boy, try and take me."

"You have a right to have dinner with anyone you want," I said, hoping I didn't sound as petulant as I felt.

"I know I have."

"Then why do you sound so guilty?"

"Because I should have told you about it. You shouldn't have had to catch me at it. I feel like a shit."

The face of Simon Wroth swam into my mind. I had never told Ned about him, and I was very careful not to leak the news: no diaries left nonchalantly open, no letters strewn indiscreetly about, no mysterious phone calls in the middle of the night. Honesty is a much overrated virtue.

When I'd returned from London, I'd explained away my residual guilt as jet lag, convinced a reluctant Ned to let our relationship continue at least for a while as it was, and gradually forgot the tensions and the problems as my career began to build. Why hadn't I noticed he was getting fed up? How stupid, how unperceptive, how unrealistic I'd been. "This isn't a business dinner, I take it."

"No. Not exactly."

"Are you fucking her?" I asked, letting the anger I felt at myself out at him.

"Of course not." He sounded genuinely shocked I would even suggest it.

"But you want to. Is that what you're trying to tell me?"

"Would you care if I did?"

"Certainly I'd care. But I'd understand. I'd try to understand. You're not ready for canonization yet."

"And you'd expect me to understand if the situation were reversed?"

"Yes. I'd hope you would."

He had been standing, hands in pockets, towering over me as I sat on the couch looking up at him. Now, flinging his hands into the air in exasperation, he turned away. "We just don't think alike, do we?"

"No, we don't." It was amazing really we'd managed to stay together for as long as we had.

He looked at his watch. "I better get going, or I'll be late." He came back to the couch, stooped, and kissed my cheek. "Wait for me. I won't be long."

I felt the ugly jealousy rising inside. It was a loathsome feeling. I turned on the television. There was a Bette Davis movie on Channel 5, *Deception*, one of my favorites. In it, Claude Rains plays an egoist whose one unselfish, loving gesture is misunderstood by Davis. She's convinced his motives must be sinister and, driven by suspicion and fear, kills him.

When Ned came home, I was asleep on the couch. I pulled him into my arms when he woke me and began to make love to him. I made love to him as artfully, as imaginatively, as passionately as I knew how. I didn't want to lose him. Not yet.

Ned had to leave early the next morning for a meeting, and instead of sleeping through to my usual wake-up time, I struggled out of bed to have breakfast with him. I needed to talk. I'd had awful dreams. In one, I was lying drugged in a hospital bed. A doctor came in and stood over me. He looked solemn. "I'm sorry, Miss Collier," he said. "Your baby is dead."

The windows of the dining room overlooked a small courtyard, and I could see the remnants of last night's snow, thin patches of dirty white glinting in the frail light. Ned looked at me uneasily as I sat opposite him at the table. "What are you doing up?" he asked as he poured me a cup of coffee.

"I didn't sleep very well. Thanks." I took a sip of coffee. "How was your dinner last night?" I asked.

"Interesting," he said. I cocked an eyebrow. "Mary's a smart girl." That was in the days before men as fine as Ned had stopped calling girls "girls" and started referring to them as "women." "She's organizing some antiwar protests, and wants me involved."

I bet she does, I thought. He told me more about what Mary Kenny had said, none of which I heard, trying to give me the impression the dinner had after all been strictly business. It hadn't been. He liked her. He was attracted to her. Fine. I understood. I really did. But what if it developed into more? And it might. In the first place, Ned wasn't really capable of a casual physical relationship. In the second, he wanted so much more than I was willing to give him. What if he could get it from Mary Kenny?

"I hope you don't like her too much," I said.

"Are you jealous?" He sounded more hopeful than worried.

"I hate to admit it, but I am."

"I thought you might be. That was quite a performance last night." I think I blushed. "I'll have to try making you jealous more often."

"No. Don't."

He got up from his seat and came around behind me. He leaned over me, wrapping his arms around me, burying his face in my neck. "I love you."

"I know."

"Marry me, Nikki." I didn't answer. "I want to buy a house, in the suburbs, and live there with you. I want to have children, your children. I want to spend Christmas with our parents, and watch them enjoy their grandchildren opening presents around the Christmas tree. I want to mow lawns and trim hedges. I want to worry about leaky roofs and faulty boilers. I want a normal life."

What I wanted to say was, this is a normal life, normal for me, but I didn't. I turned and faced him. "I love you" was all I said.

"I know," he replied in his turn, "that's why I can't understand..."

"Let's talk about this again in January, all right? Let's go through Christmas with everything just the way it is."

"And in January, you'll say, 'Let's wait until Easter.' And at Easter..."

"One of these days you'll give up on me."

"I hope not. I hope you'll be the first to change your mind."

"But not between now and Christmas."

He laughed. "No. Not between now and Christmas." He kissed me. "I won't spoil your holiday, I promise."

He wouldn't, not deliberately. He would not, I knew, phone Mary Kenny. I wondered how attracted she was, how hard she meant to pursue. I wondered what the chances were of Ned's "accidentally" running into her. I imagined her waiting in ambush to catch him unawares as he left his office, or this apartment. That kind of tracking was hard to do in winter, I decided. I was probably safe until spring.

I kissed him. Between us instantly was residual passion from the night before. "Oh, God," he murmured into my ear, "this fucking meeting. I can't cancel it."

"There's always tonight," I said. "My place or yours?"

He left, and I made another pot of coffee and sat drinking it. There was trouble ahead, I knew, but in the best Scarlett O'Hara tradition, I decided not to think about it until I had to. Instead, I thought about work. I had a *Vogue* cover to shoot that day. A *Vogue* cover. My career had certainly taken off in the past eighteen months, thanks to Duncan Powell, really. When I saw him again, I'd have to say thanks.

Finally, unable to delay any longer, I picked up the phone and called Mr. Walton.

❧ *Chapter 15* ❧

My apartment was on West End Avenue and 78th Street, just a few blocks from where I'd lived as a child. Columbus Avenue hadn't turned as yet into a self-conscious copy of the Boulevard St. Germain, and there was nothing chic about the neighborhood, but it was familiar, Zabar's was nearby, and my apartment was enormous by New York standards with its two bedrooms, two baths (one of which I used as a dark-room), an impressive foyer, and large sitting room. It was also cheap. The common wisdom was that most of New York's muggings took place on the Upper West Side, and that belief kept property values in the area—temporarily at least—within the range of employed academics and junior executives (Central Park West excluded, of course).

Given my improved circumstances over the past year, I could have afforded to move, but I didn't. I liked the apartment. I was comfortable there. And if I'd started looking for a new place it would have provoked another argument with Ned about moving in together.

Not having Ned's money to work with, I had furnished it sparsely and cheaply with early American furniture I'd picked up in my photographic travels around the country. There were naive paintings on the walls, rag rugs on the floors, and a collection of brightly colored quilts. A few thrown pots and vases and earthenware plates stood on Shaker tables and pine dressers. I like things people have made with love by hand.

The phone was ringing when I entered. It was David. "I've been calling you for hours," he said.

"I was at Ned's."

"I don't know why the two of you just don't move in together and save everyone a lot of trouble."

"Because it wouldn't save me a lot of trouble."

"It would, you know, in the long run."

"I'm seeing your father tonight, if that's what you're phoning about," I said, to change the subject.

"I was phoning to talk to you," he replied, aggrieved. "Did you and Ned have a fight?"

"How did you know?"

He didn't bother to reply. "The same fight?"

"More or less."

"When a man doesn't get what he wants in one place, he goes looking for it somewhere else, Nikki." What is it, I wonder, that makes people close to each other able to respond to unspoken messages, to hear unspoken thoughts, to surmise untold events? "A woman does, too," he added.

"Ned had dinner with a lawyer last night, a very pretty lawyer, a very smart lawyer."

"Are you worried?"

"She's perfect for him."

"Nikki . . ." There was exasperation in his voice.

"I know. I know. But I can only do what I can. I've got to run. I'll phone you tonight, after I've seen your father."

"He told me this morning Kate has bronchitis. Imagine the old bastard telling me that when he won't tell me where she is, or how I can see her. He's really trying to punish me. He was always trying to punish me. This is the first time he's ever succeeded."

"You know I can't tell you where she is, Nikki," said Mr. Walton to me that evening. "I gave her my word. I promised her I wouldn't tell anyone." It was a reply I'd been expecting, and dreading. I was in no mood for a power struggle. Another power struggle. It had been one of those days. The model, Vanessa Calhoun, arrived and threw a tantrum when she saw the fashion assistant assigned by the magazine: apparently they'd had a fight the last time they'd worked together. The hairdresser, who'd awakened that morning feeling sick, passed out in the middle of the session, was diagnosed as having flu, and was sent home, leaving the rest of us convinced we'd come down with it at any moment, ruining the job and the holidays. Someone knocked a light over and it fell, breaking a stylist's toe. Et cetera. It had taken a lot of energy for me to keep control, calm everyone down, and get the work done. I wasn't sure I had any left for dealing with Mr. Walton.

We were in the living room of the Walton apartment on West 86th Street. It was the same room I had known as a child, and everything about it was familiar to me: the rugged square-cut sofa and chairs that had remained the same under their changing flowered covers; the battered upright piano in the corner; the family photographs on the mantel; the Aubusson carpet on the floor. Five years before, two years before Mrs. Walton had died, the building had gone co-op, the apartment had come up for sale, and the Waltons had bought it. Faced with the same decision at about the same time, my parents had moved to Florida. Mr. Walton visited them once a year, in winter, when the Dodgers were at Vero Beach. In June or September, he went to Europe for a month. On weekends, he visited Jack and Trudi in Bronxville, or his daughter, Claudia, and her husband on Long Island. Nearing sixty-five, he refused to retire and continued doing free-lance articles for newspapers and magazines. An older version of David, tall and lean, with vivid dark eyes and thick silver hair, he still had a lot of contacts, a lot of friends, and an active social life. Women had always found him attractive, and now when I passed him in the street he'd stop to introduce me to his "dates," who ranged in age from mid-twenties to late fifties. Mrs. Walton hadn't had an easy time with him. Really, it was ridiculous that he should choose to take such a high moral tone with David.

"You make a great cup of coffee," I said from the same sofa where David and I had sat to play checkers, where we'd once made love.

"It's decaffeinated. I get the beans at a little store on Columbus Avenue. I grind them myself. It makes all the difference. Caroline gave me a coffee grinder for my birthday."

Caroline, I noticed, as I was probably meant to, not David. Mr. Walton was the only one in the family who actually liked David's wife. Trudi didn't. Her present moral position was more an indication of animosity towards David than of affection for her sister-in-law. I had always thought Trudi was attracted to David and so resented his essentially fraternal indifference. Not that she would have welcomed anything so crude as a pass. She was far too righteous for that.

"Have you seen the children?" I asked Mr. Walton.

"Certainly I've seen them. We have dinner every couple of weeks. Either I go there, or Caroline brings them here to me." He looked at me suspiciously. "And don't ask me when, because I won't tell you. And don't you tell David. I won't have him camping on my doorstep."

"Are they all right?"

"As well as can be expected when their father's deserted them."

"David told me Kate's got bronchitis."

"Poor little thing."

"And Lissie's developed a stutter."

"It's all the emotional strain. Caroline's taken her to see a child psychologist."

"And did the psychologist say Lissie's better off not seeing her father?" A look of annoyance crossed Mr. Walton's face. He didn't reply immediately. Instead, he took another sip of coffee. "I can't believe any psychologist would say that," I insisted.

"David ran out on Caroline. He has no right to make any demands on her."

"I'm not talking about what's right for Caroline. I'm talking about what's right for your grandchildren."

"He should have thought about that before he left them."

How many times over how many centuries had the same argument raged? Who had said those same, or similar, words to Mark Antony when he left Octavia, I wondered, or to George Sand when she finally escaped her husband?

"You aren't making what he did any easier for the children by siding with Caroline."

"I'm not siding with her. Neither is Trudi. We're respecting her wishes. Someone in this family has to do it, if her husband won't."

"David has another child now. He has a responsibility to that child, too."

"He had no business—"

"I'm not defending David, Mr. Walton. I'm just concerned about the children, all the children. Give me Caroline's number so I can call her, so I can talk to her. I promise not to give it to David. You know I'll keep my promise. Maybe I can persuade her to see him, to let him see the children. You know that would be best for everyone. They can't make peace if they don't talk." I paused a minute, for effect, and looked him square in the eye. "You do want them to make peace, don't you?"

I'd caught him and he knew it. His eyes shifted beyond me to the landscape on the wall. It was one Mrs. Walton had done, of Trudi and Jack's garden, with their dog, Muffin, playing in the foreground. She had been quite a good amateur painter.

"Of course I want them to make peace. Do you think I don't care about those children? Do you think I like to see my son suffer, even when he deserves it?" He was going to give me the number.

Over the next few days, I kept calling Caroline. Each time she answered, she hung up when she heard my voice. "I don't want to talk to you. Leave me alone," she'd say, and bang would go the receiver before I got a chance to argue. I didn't blame her. She knew everything I had to say and didn't want to hear it.

"Give me the number," bullied David, when I spoke to him. "Don't be a cunt. Give it to me."

"I can't. I promised I wouldn't."

"Jesus Christ," he yelped, "don't be such a sanctimonious, tight-assed . . ."

And I'd hang up on him.

"Keep out of it," advised Ned, in his reasonable lawyerly way. "It's none of your business."

"I know."

"David got into this mess himself, he can get out of it the same way." I nodded sagely in agreement. "If he wants to," continued Ned. "As far as I can see, the more complicated his life is, the more he likes it." Again, I nodded. "There's no point your being upset if he's enjoying himself."

"He's not. This time he's gone too far."

"It's his problem."

"I thought you liked him."

"I do. But so what? I like you better. I don't want you upset."

"Maybe I can help. I keep thinking of the children."

"If you had children of your own . . . Nikki, you can't go on living your life through other people."

"I don't. How can you say that? David is my friend. And I want to help him, just as I would you, if you were in trouble."

"I am in trouble. I love someone I want to marry, and she won't marry me. Will you help? Will you?"

Oh, Christ, would he never understand? He saw the look on my face and pulled me into his arms.

"All right. I'm sorry. I did promise. I'll leave you alone till after Christmas."

As he kissed me, into my head swam the face of Mary Kenny. I felt tears begin to trickle down my cheeks. "I'm so stupid," I said.

He nodded. "The prosecution rests," he said, and kissed me again.

❧ *Chapter 16* ❧

The day she arrived in New York, Sarah phoned to invite Ned and me to dinner.

"There's a risk David might strangle me before the hors d'oeuvres," I pointed out.

"No, he'll behave," she promised. "Come tomorrow. David's desperate for you to see Mark. And so am I. Really, he is the most marvelous baby." Her voice was thick and sweet as ever, with that dash of lemon which kept it from cloying. All the tension I'd heard in it the last time we'd spoken had been replaced by the sound of contentment. "I'm completely besotted with him. I can't imagine how I ever thought I could live without having a child."

"You sound very happy," I said, repressing a slight, uncomfortable twinge of envy.

"I am. Incredibly happy. All I want now is for David to be as peaceful and contented as I am. But everything will work out. I know it will." That time she didn't finish her speech with an interrogative. She didn't tack a little "don't you?" onto its end. She had thrown away her old life and wasn't quite sure yet exactly what she had got in its place. Her uncertainty couldn't be revealed, not even to herself, or panic might result. "We just have to be patient," she said.

* * *

Ned came directly from his office on Park Avenue to my apartment, and we walked together to Central Park West. Christmas and Chanukah lights shone cheerfully from the windows of the brownstones in the side streets. Broadway was crowded with shoppers, and the few recently opened boutiques low on Columbus Avenue were still open and doing a booming business.

It was a beautiful night, clear and cold, with almost no wind. We held hands, deep in the pocket of Ned's sheepskin coat, and made plans for Christmas, carving up the holiday between his family and mine. To Connecticut for Christmas Eve with the Contis, we decided, and across the Sound on the ferry to Long Island for Christmas dinner with my brother, his family, and my parents, who had flown in from Florida the week before.

I felt happy, I felt expectant and excited as I always do as Christmas draws near, the way I have always felt since I was a child. My apartment would have its own tree, strung with lights and popcorn and hand-painted wooden ornaments. In Ned's there would be an-other, much more chic, decorated in blue and silver. On Christmas Eve, at the Contis', after Ned's nephews and nieces had gone to bed, before leaving for Midnight Mass, we would put up their tree, a fantasy of bubbling lights and golden tinsel, of glass apples and shiny pears, of dangling candy cane and satin bows. At my brother's would be the largest tree of all, a tall Douglas fir, under which would be the same manger we had had as children: a stable of wood with a real straw roof; large painted clay figures of the Virgin and child; a bearded Saint Joseph; an alert and knowing cow; shepherds in plain tunics, holding lambs in their arms; the Magi in richly decorated robes, car-rying gifts of gold and frankincense and myrrh; and, off in the corners, the angels, all still brightly colored if slightly chipped.

I was talking to Ned and thinking of all that when, for no good rea-son, my mood changed. "We could just skip it all," I said. "We could go to . . . to Switzerland. We could go skiing." Ned loved to ski.

He looked at me as if I'd gone mad. "Skiing?"

"Why not? Lots of people go skiing at Christmas."

"People who hate holidays. People the holidays depress."

"And sometimes people who just want a change."

Ned stopped talking and turned to face me. He looked very cute, I thought, in his sheepskin coat and red wool hat, not at all like a dedi-cated lawyer and potential President, but very young, like a student. He was thirty-five years old then, four years older than I. "Are you seri-ous?" he asked.

"It might be fun."

"You really want to go to Switzerland for Christmas?"

"Maybe. I don't know." I didn't. I didn't even know what had made me think of it, why I had suggested it. "Would you like to go?"

He didn't answer immediately. He started walking again. Hand still in his pocket, I followed after him. "There are peace marches over the holidays. I'd like to be around for them."

Suddenly the idea of getting away was very appealing. "It would be fun to forget all that, forget everything."

"I gave my word," he said. "I'm sorry. The marches are important."

I was about to get angry when I imagined my mother's face as I told her I'd be going. My father would be hurt, and my brother, too, though he'd try not to show it. I thought of Christmas morning without the hoopla of my nephews opening gifts. That's the problem with loving people: there's no way to hurt them without hurting yourself. "Forget I mentioned it," I said. "It was a crazy idea."

"Maybe next year," said Ned.

"Sure," I replied, without much conviction. "Next year."

David and Sarah were staying in one of those splendid old buildings on Central Park West with a view across the same park as its far more expensive counterparts on Fifth Avenue. A doorman stopped us as we entered, and while he announced us, Ned looked appreciatively around the Art Deco lobby. It had soaring walls of beige marble, mirrors of beveled glass, and elevators decorated with brass fretwork. "This looks like Rockefeller Center," he said. "I thought David was broke."

"The apartment's borrowed from a friend of Sarah's. An actor. He's in Rome making a movie."

"It really is something," he said. Although he was definitely a West Side sort of person, Ned was then convinced the only place possible to live in Manhattan was on the Upper East Side.

Sarah answered the doorbell, and Ned was even more impressed with her than he'd been with the lobby. "Come in," she murmured. "How nice to meet you, Ned. I've been so looking forward to it. You're positively the only man David says nice things about." Her hair was swept up high in a pile of golden curls. She wore a full print skirt and a sweater of peach cashmere cut in a deep V. The color made her eyes melt into pools of chocolate and polished her skin to a porcelain sheen.

Ned had seen her on film, but he hadn't expected her presence to be so powerful: he had attributed all the magic to the camera. "What Nikki's told me about you doesn't come close to the truth," said Ned, returning the compliment. "You're a knockout."

Some women accept compliments greedily, seeming to grab them with both hands, storing them like a miser's coins to count over again later in private. Others accept them with embarrassment, as if it were a case of mistaken identity; or with mock humility, pretending the expected gift is undeserved. To Sarah, a compliment was a soap bubble: pretty but insubstantial, to be admired as it floated by, but not touched for fear of destroying it. And once it was out of sight, she never thought of it again. There were only a few people whose praise Sarah took seriously. Duncan was one of them. David was another.

"Thank you." She smiled at Ned, accepting the compliment and letting it go. Then she turned to me. "It's lovely to see you again," she said. "Sit down. David will be here in a moment. He's bathing the baby. What can I get you to drink? I'm having gin."

She led us into an enormous sitting room, with deep comfortable sofas in worn leather and a luxuriously thick carpet. There was a large fireplace and walls lined with shelves holding books, stereo, television, a few pieces of African sculpture, and a multitude of photographs. Bouquets of fresh flowers decorated the mantel and end tables, stood in large vases on the floor. Near the windows which overlooked the park was a pool table.

I sat in one of the sofas and picked up a book from the coffee table. It was Robert Sencourt's biography of T. S. Eliot. Inside were scrawled notes in David's writing.

"He got home late," said Sarah, as she fixed Ned a scotch and me a spritzer, "so we're running a bit behind. Apparently there was quite a battle about casting this afternoon. The producer was insisting on someone David didn't want to play Jimmy."

"Who?" I asked.

"Sean Lazar," said Sarah.

"You're joking!" Lazar's last three Broadway shows had been hits. But not only was he years too old for Jimmy, David loathed him. He thought he was a bad actor, mannered and shallow, who got by on looks and hype.

"Don't look so worried." I turned and saw David in the doorway, carrying Mark. The baby's head was still damp from the bath, and his face glowed clean and rosy over the top of his sleep suit. "He didn't get the part," said David. Then he grinned. "I yelled louder than everyone else."

"For an unknown playwright," I said, "you sure have a helluva lot of chutzpah."

"That's when you need it most. That's when the people with the biggest feet try walking all over you. This is Mark," he said. "My son."

Ned and I smiled at the baby, and said hello in that mock-polite tone adults assume with children.

"Hello, darling," said Sarah. "Are you all lovely and clean?" She gazed at him with unmitigated delight.

David put the child down. He looked at Ned and me assessingly with David's dark eyes, then toddled to his mother. He was almost a year old, and all David, dark and intense and handsome, with none of his mother's fragile beauty.

"Look at that balance," said David. "Look at how he carries himself. A natural athelete. Hello, Ned." He extended a hand.

"Congratulations," said Ned, looking warily at Mark. He wanted children, desperately, but he had none of David's natural ease with them.

David kissed me hello. "Let's call a truce for tonight," he said softly. "I won't ask any questions you don't want to answer."

"That's fine with me," I said.

"Aren't you going to say hello?" coaxed Sarah. She touched Mark caressingly, and her face as she looked at him expressed astonishment that she could have produced anything so wonderful. "You do know how to say it, darling, don't you? Hello," she prompted.

"'uhlo," repeated Mark dutifully. Then he smiled, and reminded me of Lissie.

For a few moments, the attention of the entire room focused on Mark, but then it began to splinter. I coaxed the child onto my lap by my usual method (I'd brought him a book and bribed him with it); and while I read, Mark attempted to repeat some of the more familiar words, with David listening delightedly and urging him on. "He's just like Lissie," David said to me. "He loves words."

Ned and Sarah, meanwhile, had started discussing movies. They had both admired Dominique Sanda in Bertolucci's first international success, *The Conformist*, and were eagerly waiting to see her in de Sica's *The Garden of the Finzi-Continis*, which was just about to open in New York.

"She was marvelous, wasn't she?" I heard Sarah say. "That first shot of her, standing at the top of the stairs, took my breath away, she was so beautiful. And her performance!" As she continued praising the actress, I could see in Ned's face what he was thinking: not so beautiful as you, not so talented as you, not anywhere near so wonderful as you are.

David and she sat next to each other on the couch, their hands loosely clasped, maintaining a physical link despite the split in attention. If a hand had to free itself to gesture, it would return to its mate immediately after. And occasionally one would stroke the other, rubbing a finger along the tender inside of a palm.

Finally, Sarah stood. "Mrs. T's gone out to a movie tonight," said Sarah. "And we've let Mark stay up far too late. She'll be furious with us if she finds out." She picked him up out of my lap. "Time for bed, darling. Mummy's good little boy." Whereupon Mummy's good little boy began screaming. He was enjoying himself too much to want to go to sleep. "You can play with Nikki another time," she said soothingly, to no avail. Ned began to look uncomfortable, and so, surprisingly, did Sarah. The flailing bundle in her arms clearly dismayed her.

David, like Dr. Spock, came to the rescue. He took the crying child from Sarah. "Of course you don't want to go to bed. I wouldn't want to either." Some quality in his voice calmed the child. The sobbing subsided. "We'll just go inside and sit together, until maybe you'll want to go to sleep, okay?" David kissed the soft cheek. The baby's frame gave a convulsive shake, but the crying dwindled to a murmur. "I won't be long," said David. "He's so jet-lagged, he'll drop right off."

"Jet-bag," repeated Mark.

"He's so good with children, isn't he?" said Sarah, a faint note of envy in her voice. "So patient. I'm not at all patient."

"He's had practice," said Ned consolingly, as much to himself as to Sarah. He hoped that's all it took, practice.

Sarah shook her head. "I don't think it's that," she said. "I think it's a talent, and either you have it or you don't."

As soon as David came back into the room, the telephone rang, a call for Sarah, from her agent in London. She had been offered the female lead in a film with Steve McQueen that was to start shooting in February in the Seychelles, explained David as Sarah murmured into the phone in the background. She'd turned it down twice, and each time the film company, Twentieth Century–Fox, had come back with more money. It wasn't that they knew her work so well, or admired her so much, jibed David with a laugh; it was just that they assumed since she'd said no she must be good.

"Is the script that bad?" I asked.

"No," replied David, with unusual magnanimity. "It's an excellent script. And it's a good part for her. But she doesn't want to be away from Mark right now, or from me, and the play is opening in March, so I can't go with her."

"That's ridiculous," I said. "Sarah can take the baby with her to the

Seychelles. And Mrs. T. You can go visit when you have the time. That's what other people do." It hadn't occurred to me that Sarah would ever let her personal life interfere to such an extent with her career. She took it and her talent very seriously, I knew: as well she should. And she hadn't worked since the close of *Sky Burial*, except for one BBC television play which Simon Wroth had directed.

"Maybe her home and family matter more to her than her career," said Ned. "They do to some people." He carefully avoided looking at me.

"Do they to you?" I shot back.

"It's having a baby," said David, in the surprising role of peacekeeper. "It seems to knock the ambition out of a woman. It changes the priorities."

When her phone call finished, Sarah and I went into the kitchen to get dinner ready, leaving David and Ned to shoot pool, at which Ned was good, though not so good as David.

"You don't take it seriously enough," said David, as he chalked his cue. "That's your problem. You can't expect to win if you don't give it all you've got."

"I can't take games seriously. I never could. I was a lousy athelete at school. It's life I try to win."

"It's all the same thing," said David, incomprehension and irritation both in his voice. It still sometimes surprised me that two men so different could like each other as much as those two did, though I understood that's exactly why it was possible. Each admired in the other the virtues he had no desire to possess.

"Ned's awfully nice," said Sarah as soon as we were out of earshot of the two men. "And interesting."

I don't know why, but I had expected her to say "attractive." "I'm glad you like him."

"David says he could be President someday, if he wanted to."

I shook my head dubiously. "Not unless politics in this country changes significantly for the better. Ned has a habit of saying things people really don't want to hear. It's hard to get elected doing that."

"But things are changing. People all over are getting out to protest. Look at all the antiwar demonstrations. It's a very exciting time, isn't it?"

"It's a rotten time," I said. I couldn't share her optimism about the future, and I didn't want to talk about the war. It depressed me. "My

God, what have you done?" I said as we entered the kitchen. It was a shambles.

"When I cook, I use every pan in sight, I'm afraid. And I've been cooking a lot lately. I'm feeling awfully domestic at the moment. Poor Mrs. T. I do clean up as best I can, but it's never good enough to suit her. She says I double her work when I try to help." I thought of the look of mingled disgust and disbelief that would certainly appear on Caroline's face if she could see this kitchen. Her own was always meticulous.

"I don't know why you do try," I said. Sarah began to make the salad dressing, while I tried to restore some semblance of order, stacking the dirty dishes in the dishwasher, putting the used pots to soak. Like Caroline, I am almost obsessively neat. "You have Mrs. T. Leave it to her."

"And what would I do with myself all day? Have facials? Get my nails manicured?"

"You could go back to work. David says you've just turned down a good part in a good film."

"Work doesn't seem to interest me at the moment."

"Why?" I asked with more curiosity than belligerence. I stopped rattling the pots so I could hear her answer.

"I'm not sure. I only know that right now I don't want to be away from Mark and David."

"You could take Mark with you. And Mrs. T," I said, repeating my argument. "David would visit you."

She shook her head emphatically. "That's what he said. But I can't leave him, not just yet." She took a sip of gin, then poured the dressing over the salad and tossed it.

"He won't go back to Caroline, if that's what you're afraid of."

"I'm not afraid of that," she said sharply. She walked to the oven and yanked it open. Then, carefully, she slid the Beef Wellington from its rack and carried it to the counter. "Are you so sure?" she asked.

"Positive," I replied. I had never been more certain of anything in my life. He might fall out of love with Sarah, but he would never leave her, because of Mark, because—if he did—he would never then be able to justify what he had done to Lissie, and Kate.

"I'd die if he left me," she said. "I love him so much. I thought I loved Duncan, but I' didn't know. I had absolutely no idea." Tears welled in her eyes but didn't fall. "All I want is to keep him and Mark near me, always. Nothing else matters to me."

* * *

Not in the mood for David's pyrotechnics, I only half listened to the conversation over dinner. It consisted, as I remember, mainly of David's impression of the state of the New York theater scene, why he detested *Jesus Christ, Superstar* and admired *The Basic Training of Pavlo Humel*.

"He's seen everything," said Sarah. "Have you?" I shook my head. "Would you like to go with me? *Mary Stuart*'s on at the Vivian Beaumont. I'd love to see it."

"It's closing," said David. And the conversation shifted to the John Chamberlain exhibition at the Guggenheim.

"They're not sculpture," I said. "They're scrap metal."

"They're totems," replied David. "They're beautiful."

"This food is beautiful," interrupted Ned. It was. It was superb. There was salmon mousse to start, followed by Beef Wellington with roast potatoes and four vegetables, each perfectly cooked, a green salad with lemon dressing, a cheese board, and Poire Belle Hélène for dessert. Ned's admiration for Sarah increased moment by moment. David radiated love and pride. I just sat there thinking how much more I would rather watch Sarah act than eat a marvelous meal which she'd taken too much time, too much energy to prepare.

❧ *Chapter 17* ❧

The next day I had lunch at Bradley's on University Place with Carl Weiss, a friend of mine who ran a small publishing company. He wanted to do a calendar featuring the stars of the American ballet. Since the film *The Turning Point* had not as yet appeared, reviving once again the public's flagging interest in ballet, there wasn't a lot of money in it. Carl had the choice of using existing photographs or, if I was interested and my price was right, having me shoot the calendar.

I was interested. Eighteen months of fashion photography had been exacting, exciting, and most definitely lucrative; but though I'd hardly reached the second or third rung of the ladder, let alone joined Penn or Avedon or Bailey at the top, I was, as always anxious for the next experience, the new challenge. I had never done a calendar before, so I agreed to his proposition of a small fee and large royalty, which, in hindsight, was absurd. As Carl and I both could have predicted, if we'd cared to think about it, the calendar didn't sell. Carl did a beautiful production job: the paper, the printing, the quality of the color reproduction were all superb. The quality of the photographs was good, too, I think, though there's one of Makarova that I gimmicked too much with light instead of letting her innate dramatic quality speak for itself. But people just weren't interested. We had much better luck with our second calendar, the one we did on the same subject in 1978. That was, as those things go, a runaway best-seller.

Carl and I left the restaurant together and I was just about to accept his offer of a lift uptown when I spotted Caroline turning into 9th Street. It was a bleak, cold day, and the collar of her sheepskin coat was raised around her ears and a woolen cap pulled low on her head. A shopping bag dangled from her arm and she was pushing a stroller, in which, presumably, Kate lay buried under a layer of blankets. Lissie, snug in a bright pink snowsuit, was walking at her side. I refused Carl's invitation, waved him on his way, and dodged cars as I crossed the street in pursuit.

After days of trying to make her listen to me on the phone, I had serendipitously caught Caroline out shopping. Why, I asked myself, hadn't David been the lucky one? Instead of badgering his father and Trudi, instead of spending hours on the phone bullying Caroline's sister and trying to track down former friends, why hadn't he simply walked out of a Village restaurant and stumbled into her? Then, lucky devil, he could have been the one about to have the conversation I was dreading.

I called her name. She turned, and for a second looked at me blankly; then her face paled with anger.

I think I may have expected to find a frail faded shadow of a woman, diminished by the loss of her man. Caroline certainly wasn't that. Her last pregnancy had left a few extra pounds, so the lines of misery were softened by the added weight. She seemed more substantial, more solid. Her eyes had a fierce and determined look. She reminded me of a calico cat protecting her litter of kittens. "Have you been following me?" she said.

"No. I had lunch across the street. I just happened to see you walk by."

"I don't want to talk to you."

Lissie was looking at me shyly, curiously. "Hello, sweetheart," I said. "Do you remember me?"

"I th-think so," she answered, with that faint trace of a stutter David was so worried about.

"I'm Nikki."

"Why don't you leave us alone? Haven't you done enough?" hissed her mother.

Lissie looked worriedly at Caroline, shifting her weight from one foot to another. The anger in her mother's voice disturbed her. Then Kate began to cry.

"I have to get her home," said Caroline. "It's too cold. I've had her out too long."

"May I see her?" Grudgingly, Caroline stooped over the stroller and adjusted the bundle so I could have a better view. Looking back at me, face crumpled with grief, was a smaller, wanner version of Lissie.

"Hello there," I said, offering her a finger, which she grasped. "She looks like you," I said to Lissie.

"Sh-she's smaller," replied Lissie gravely.

"Much," I said. I looked up at Caroline. "Please, let me come by to see you. I really want to talk." She hesitated. "I won't tell David, if you don't want me to. I promise."

"D-David is my daddy," offered Lissie, smiling for the first time.

"I know."

"He's g-gone far away, on b-bithness. But h-he's coming h-home soon."

"Please," I repeated.

Caroline's mouth was a thin line in a grim face. She nodded. "Come tomorrow night," she said, "after eight. The children will be asleep by then." She gave me her address, then walked away.

I took the subway uptown and was so preoccupied thinking about Caroline that it must have been a full ten minutes before I realized the man sitting next to me had his hand on my thigh. Even then I might not have noticed if he hadn't squeezed. Since I'd not moved or complained, he no doubt had thought I liked it. His timing was impeccable. The train had stopped at Columbus Circle and its doors were open. As I shot him a filthy look and delivered a few expletives, he exited, leaving me behind feeling sick to my stomach with rage and fear. He was a nice-looking, well-dressed man, too, in a chesterfield coat, carrying a copy of the *Times*.

Between him and Caroline, work that afternoon was impossible. I almost ruined a roll of Tri-X by forgetting it in the developer, and as soon as I made certain I hadn't, I called it a day and curled up on the couch with a cup of coffee and a novel, Luke Rhinehart's *The Dice Man*, which kept me feeling off-balance and uneasy. What if, like the book's protagonist, I should roll dice to decide my fate? What if I tossed a coin, heads I marry Ned, tails I don't? So much of life is decided anyway by luck—why not embrace it rather than try constantly to minimize its effect?

The phone rang and I was tempted not to answer. If it was David, I'd end up telling him about Caroline, and I preferred to do that after I'd seen her. On the other hand it could be Ned, or *Vogue*.

It was, in fact, Cassandra. "We arrived this morning, darling," she boomed at me down the telephone line. "I have a meeting tomorrow with the Martex people about designing some bed linen for them. My own label. It's all very exciting. Then we go to Los Angeles. Duncan's about to begin a new film. Won't it be bizarre spending Christmas there? Do you suppose all I've heard about pink Christmas trees is true? What are you doing this moment? This very moment?"

"Reading."

"Then I'll be right over. Duncan's gone to a meeting with some theatrical-type person and we'll be able to talk. I have absolutely loads to tell you. Do you have anything there to eat?" she added, as an afterthought. "I seem to be always famished these days."

Not trusting my taste in food, she arrived carrying bags from Zabar's. She looked like a yeti, in a fabulous coat of fake mongolian lamb. "Isn't it wonderful," she agreed when I complimented her. "I'm doing all sorts of things these days in fake fur. I got co-opted into an antivivisectionist group a few months ago, and really it is disgusting what people will do to poor little animals just to look good."

"I saw coats made of rat in the Galeries Lafayette the last time I was in Paris. I couldn't even try one on. The idea of it made my flesh crawl."

"When you feel the same way about mink, you'll be considered enlightened," she replied from the high moral plane on which she was currently residing. She had brought bread and cheese and fruit. I opened some wine and we settled ourselves around the coffee table in the living room. We'd had a few telephone conversations since I'd left London, but not what we considered a real talk.

"Your David Walton really is a crafty devil, isn't he?" said Cassandra, with both fascination and admiration in her voice. "I should have known if anyone could lure Sarah away from Duncan, he would be the one. He's so intense, almost frightening really, but sexy. There's something animal about him. He reminds me of a panther. Those eyes! I'll never forgive you for not telling me," she said.

"It was a secret," I replied.

"Secrets always do make the best gossip, don't they?" She took a bite of cheese, and the pleasure of its taste irradiated her face. "This is glorious cheese. Explorateur. Try some," she said, as she settled back to provide me with Duncan's version of events.

Though Duncan was at the time heavily involved in an affair of his own and Sarah was being very discreet, she was only two weeks into her affair with David when Duncan sensed something was wrong. At first he wasn't quite sure what. Sarah's habits remained essentially unchanged. She was always home when she was supposed to be. There were none of those abruptly ended phone conversations when he entered a room, no mad dashes to intercept letters when the mail arrived, no evasive answers when he asked what she'd been up to in his absence. What he noticed were the subtle differences, an aloofness, a remoteness about Sarah: the fact that she no longer took his arm in the street, never reached for his hand, never touched him unless she had to. Their lovemaking, which for some time had been infrequent, stopped altogether.

At first, Duncan thought she had found out about his affair and was finally fed up with his infidelities. That frightened him. His sexual needs were a mystery to him. He didn't know why he always found it necessary to move from one willing female to the next. He often didn't like or really enjoy the women he was with. But he did love Sarah. He ended his affair, became as attentive to his wife as he had been in the days of their courtship, and waited for her to love him again.

But when he was home so much, he noticed that she was in fact out a great deal. She returned from her excursions flushed and happy, and though her explanations were more than reasonable (a visit to the Tate, to Kenwood, tea with a friend, shopping in Bond Street), she still didn't touch him. And when he asked her, she refused outright to have sex.

It was more instinct than evidence that convinced him her lover was David. He saw them together only a few times, backstage, in a pub, at a party, that sort of thing. And then they never exchanged more than polite commonplaces in his hearing, never maneuvered to have time alone together. But he sensed between them the same connection I had thought so palpable that afternoon at Kenwood. He felt the waves of sex, of love, passing back and forth, from one to the other.

Duncan had always assumed Sarah knew about his love affairs but did and said nothing because her common sense told her there was no point, that the women meant nothing to him, that accusations might end a particular relationship but they would also somehow damage the fabric of their marriage. There would never be that same ease between them again. So Duncan decided to follow Sarah's example and keep quiet.

His resolution didn't last long. Sarah may not have felt threatened by Duncan's women, but Duncan felt definitely threatened by David. Duncan not only wanted Sarah back for her own sake, he wanted her back so that David couldn't have her.

Perversely, he insisted that Sarah and he spend more time with David and Caroline. He asked them, over Sarah's protests, home to dinner. He invited David to play golf. He asked me to take photographs. All in an attempt to prove to David that while Sarah might be willing to dally, she and Duncan as a unit were indestructible. He expected David to take the hint and back off.

But David didn't, and Sarah seemed to fall more in love with him all the time. Finally, Duncan lost control and made a scene.

"But why in front of me?" I asked Cassandra. "I don't understand."

"I don't think he does either. I suppose he might have thought if Sarah would just tell him not to be silly, if she would tell him she loved him in front of you, you could be relied on to convince David his case was hopeless. Or he might finally have just lost control."

When Sarah disappeared to Vienna, Duncan was frantic. He didn't want to lose Sarah, but he didn't know how to keep her. He had already exhausted his repertoire: he'd been faithful, he'd been patient, he'd been understanding, and finally he'd been violent. Nothing he did seemed to make any impression on her. She'd respond appropriately to the emotions of the moment, much as she did to a cue onstage, but after the scene she'd retreat unmoved into her self. She was out of his reach.

The day Sarah returned from Vienna she went immediately from the airport to the theater. Duncan only knew of her return when the porter brought him a note from her. He saw her for the first time from the wings, just before he made his entrance. "So," he said, delivering his line, "you've decided to come." In a triumph of professionalism, they performed the play without a hitch.

At home that night, Sarah told him everything. They drank as they talked, and they erupted finally into violence. Duncan smashed up a lot of the furniture and Sarah sent a ceramic vase crashing into a mirror. Then she ran from the house, got into her car, and drove to the flat in Highgate to spend the night. Duncan, with no idea where she'd gone, was terrified.

The next morning, Sarah returned home and they continued the discussion, this time more calmly. There were fewer accusations and counteraccusations. Sarah was determined to leave, and Duncan knew there was nothing he could do then to stop her. His prime concern became finding a way to win her back. He was convinced he could. Her relationship with David seemed too fraught with problems to survive. For a while early on it seemed certain that Caroline's pregnancy would do it in. Duncan insisted they continue together in the play until the end of their contract. He wanted access to her. He wanted to be near and ready when the affair ended.

Each night Sarah and Duncan met onstage and argued out their problems through the medium of the play, but though that may have kept them friends it didn't save their marriage. Sarah accepted Duncan's offers of help and friendship gratefully; but even when she was most despairing about her future with David, she refused to return to the Hampstead house. All Duncan's promises that he would raise her child as his own, would love it like his own, went unheeded. Sarah, hurt and bewildered as she was, still was only waiting to see what David would do.

David eventually calmed Sarah down and got her to promise to wait, patiently, until after both children were born. He gave his word that he would leave Caroline then and marry her. She believed him, and they settled into the idyllic last months of her pregnancy in a happiness so profound that Duncan found it not only incomprehensible but impenetrable. By the time Mark was born, Duncan—though he couldn't resist one last salvo at David—was resigned to his loss of Sarah. And by then he had found his compensation. After a few months of indiscriminate fucking, he had rediscovered Cassandra, who was the best ego balm of all: she absolutely adored him.

"We were at a party at the Tynans', oh, a couple of months after Sarah moved out, I suppose, and all these little dolly birds were fluttering around him. It was inhibiting, let me tell you. They were all a lot younger than I am."

"You're just thirty," I protested.

"They had these incredibly smooth skins, not a trace of a line anywhere, and these gorgeous bodies, most of which were showing. And there I was in one of my tents—"

"Looking sexy as hell, I bet."

"And I kept remembering how fantastically beautiful Sarah is. I almost lost my nerve. 'Come on, old girl,' I told myself. 'Nothing ventured, nothing gained.' And I crossed the room, sat at his feet, laughed at his stories, took him home, fucked his brains out, and told him what a fabulous lover he is." We both remembered what she had once told me about Duncan's lack of prowess. She blushed slightly, and looked away. "I do love him. And I have made him happy. I'm the best thing that could have happened to him. The very best."

"I'm sure you are. Nothing makes a person feel better than being loved." She looked at me with surprise. "Unless it makes them feel worse," I added, more in my usual style.

The doorbell rang, interrupting what boded to be a lecture on the virtues of marriage. "That's Duncan," said Cassandra. "We're going to the theater tonight, to see Robert and Mary in *Old Times*. I told him to meet me here." She meant Robert Shaw and Mary Ure, then appearing in Pinter's play on Broadway. "I hope you don't mind."

"Of course not. I'd like to see him."

A moment later and Duncan was in my apartment, filling it. The lines in his face were deeper, there were a few strands of gray in his blond hair, but his smile was as devastating and his voice as affecting as I remembered. "Nikki, how good to see you," he said, kissing my cheek and enfolding me in a hug. I felt a small tug in the pit of my stomach and a faint desire to hang on.

"Would you like something to drink?" I asked as I disposed of his wet sheepskin coat. It had begun to snow.

"A whiskey, please, if you have it."

"Darling, how was the meeting?" asked Cassandra.

Duncan leaned over her to kiss her mouth, then sat next to her on the couch, letting his arm rest along the top of the cushions. Occasionally, as he talked, his hand would fondle her neck. "It was a wank," he said. "We spent hours discussing the 'concept,' and more woolly-headed ideas I don't think I've ever heard in my life." His voice dripped sarcasm. "They want me to do *Macbeth*," he explained, "after I finish my next film, but they can't decide whether it should be set in nineteenth-century Chicago with Macbeth as a robber baron or in twentieth-century Hollywood with him as a film mogul. It didn't seem to occur to anyone that in either case an American might be better in the role, so I suggested it. They looked at me as if I were mad, then asked if I thought Sarah might be interested in playing Lady Macbeth. 'Who?' I asked in my best Dame Edith manner. 'Lady Macbeth, the lead,' said one, and 'Sarah Cope, your wife,' replied the other. By now they were convinced I was demented. 'We're divorced,' I told them. 'But she's in town, too,' they insisted, as if somehow I'd got the facts of my life wrong. 'That was part of the divorce settlement,' I said and smiled at them benignly. They were ready to have me committed."

Cassandra whooped with laughter, and so did I. The producer and director Duncan had spent the afternoon with were then the city's intellectual darlings and the most pretentious asses ever to have graced the cover of *Rolling Stone*. "They're not all like that," I said. "If you're serious about doing a play in New York, there are serious people you should be talking to."

"He's not really serious, are you, darling? It just flatters his ego to think he's wanted."

"I haven't done a play on Broadway in ten years, and then it wasn't a hit," contradicted Duncan. "*Coriolanus*. Not a wise choice, I suppose. I wouldn't mind being the toast of New York. It must be very exciting."

"But you're the toast of the world," said Cassandra. "Do you know," she said, turning to me, "Duncan has just been voted the world's top box-office star? Isn't that fantastic?"

A film he had done just after appearing in *Sky Burial* had been released in June and was an enormous hit, breaking box-office records everywhere. This was Duncan's third or fourth big international success, *Special Envoy*. He played an English diplomat on a special mission to Washington who is saved from a life of profound stuffiness by falling in love with a madcap tour guide played by Jessica Field. The plot didn't bear too close an investigation, but the film was, to quote the newspaper ads, "delightful, charming, outrageously funny." It wasn't the sort of film I would have expected to be a hit in that political climate, but it turns out that even a country fighting an undeclared civil war isn't impervious to charm and now and then is in need of a good laugh. And there was, I think, something about Jessica Field's performance that appealed to the collective unconscious. She seemed to embody the American ideal. We all then wanted so much to believe the country was still inhabited by intelligent, straightforward, honest men and women, attractive without being shallow, idealistic without being naive, and funny without appearing stupid.

"You were wonderful in it," I said to Duncan.

"It was fun to do. May I have another?" he asked, handing me his whiskey glass. "They were a terrific lot of people to work with, Jim Dreiser, the director, and Jessica."

I saw a shadow flit across Cassandra's face. "She's lovely," said Cassandra, a little too emphatically. "Of course, she hasn't any dress sense at all. Her clothes are diabolical."

"We had a first-rate crew," said Duncan, ignoring the interruption. "The camera operator was a bloody fool, but there's always got to be one in the group, hasn't there?"

"We saw the film at a preview in London with all those dreadful studio people," said Cassandra, regaining the conversational ball, "and they were convinced it would be a disaster. It was the wrong time to release it, they thought. Hmmph," she snorted scornfully, "a lot *they* knew. 'Nonsense,' I told them, 'anyone with sense can see it's the best comedy in ages, since *Some Like It Hot*, though totally different, of course. More like *Ninotchka*, but much funnier,' I was terrified they were going to shelve it."

The conversation ping-ponged for a while, as they filled me in on Duncan's next film, a psychological thriller destined, insisted Cassandra, to be an even bigger hit than *Special Envoy*. They shared the spotlight better than I'd expected. They didn't seem at all like competing acts but a well-rehearsed double with an established routine. The relationship might last longer than I'd cynically surmised.

Cassandra excused herself to go to the bathroom, and as soon as we were alone, Duncan asked if I'd seen Sarah.

"Yes," I said cautiously.

"How did she seem to you?"

"Fine. Very good, in fact. She seemed happy."

"I'm worried about her." I didn't say anything because, as before, I couldn't understand what he was up to. On the one hand, there was no trace of bitterness in his voice, no suppressed anger, no hint of the discarded ex-husband nursing a grievance, determined to make trouble. There was only genuine concern. On the other, he was a very fine actor. "I'm not up to anything this time," he said. "When I asked you to take those photographs, I was a little mad, I think. I don't know what I hoped to accomplish." He had arrived a little drunk from his meeting, and the two whiskeys he'd had since his arrival had further blurred his edges. He looked at me fondly. "I apologize for dragging you into a rather sordid scene. If not for kissing you." Congenitally incapable of not flirting, he once again bestowed his smile on me.

"There's nothing to apologize for," I replied coolly. "Those photographs were an enormous boost to my career. I thank you for letting me take them."

"They never appeared," he said.

"It didn't matter."

He took a sip of whiskey. "No," he said. "I suppose not." Then he leaned forward and looked at me intently. "Sarah's not working. The only thing she's done in the past year is one television play. And that only because Simon Wroth badgered her into it."

"I'm no expert in these matters," I said reassuringly, "but I understand it's difficult for a mother to leave a new baby."

"All that talent going to waste."

"It's not going to waste," I said, playing devil's advocate. "It's taking a vacation."

"She's turned down a lot of parts, good parts. People are getting tired of asking and hearing no in reply. Some have already stopped asking. It took a lot of time, and talent, and energy to build her career. I hate to see her throwing it away like this."

"Why tell me? Tell her!"

"Do you think I haven't? She smiles and says she's perfectly happy. That's a load of bollocks, if you ask me. I think she's playing a role, the role she thinks David wants her to play. And if he does, he's making a mistake. Sarah is as ambitious as she is talented. If she doesn't work..." He didn't finish the sentence, but his words hung in the air like a threat. "Why don't you have a word with her? With David?"

What is it, I wondered, that made people view me as some sort of Mercury? It wasn't a role I liked, playing messenger to the gods, though

I found myself cast in it fairly often. Maybe Ned was right: maybe people, believing I had no life of my own, felt it possible to burden me with theirs. Was it only a family, a spouse and children, that bestowed legitimacy? My sense of irritation was suddenly overwhelming, my sense of being impinged upon. Duncan wasn't anyone who had any right to make a demand of me. "It's Sarah's life," I said, "and she has a right to ruin it any way she likes."

He was about to protest when Cassandra reappeared, hair recombed, makeup renewed. "We can call the theater and try to get an extra ticket," she offered. I shook my head. "Well, then join us afterwards. You and Ned. We're having dinner with the Shaws at the Russian Tea Room. Don't say no, Nikki. We're not in New York for long, and it might be ages before we see you again."

But I did say no. I felt exhausted. I ushered them out the door and retired to my couch with a glass of wine. I had no right, I thought, to be worried on Sarah's behalf, no right to judge what would or would not make her happy. She was a beautiful, talented, intelligent woman. If she didn't know what was best for her, who did?

❧ *Chapter 18* ❧

My mood of determined Christmas cheer was taking a severe beating.

Shortly after Duncan and Cassandra left, David arrived. The collar of his sheepskin coat was raised and a woolen scarf was wrapped around his neck. He wore no hat, and his dark hair was flecked with snow. The tips of his ears and his nose were red from the cold.

"What are you doing here?" I asked.

"I was at my father's," he said, "negotiating. We're having Christmas together. I finally convinced him it was his Christian duty, and in keeping with the spirit of the season, to meet Sarah and Mark." He reached into his pocket and extracted a small brown-wrapped parcel. "I saw these in a store window." He handed the parcel to me, took off his coat, hung it on the rack in the hall, then searched his pockets for cigarettes, lit one, and sat. "The whole family will be together. Except for my girls," he continued as I opened the package. "The old bastard still won't tell me where they are. I don't know why I bother with him."

"Because you love him."

"Not *that* much," he said, with a smile.

Inside the package were two hand-painted Victorian Christmas ornaments, a toy soldier and a choirboy. They were so lovely that for a moment I was speechless with pleasure. Finally, I leaned over and kissed his ice-cold cheek. "Thank you they're beautiful. Where did you find them?"

"In that junk store down the street."

"I was in there yesterday. I didn't see them."

"That's not my fault," he said, responding to the slightly aggrieved tone of my voice. I still hated it when David outdid me in my own arena. "You should have looked harder."

David didn't want anything to drink, so we had tea instead. "I'm drinking too much lately. I can't take it. I don't think straight when I do. And that's all I need with what's going on in my life right now, to lose concentration and drop one of the balls I'm juggling."

Not only was he racing around Manhattan trying to find Caroline while making sure that Sarah felt happy and secure; but every day he went to long, argumentative casting sessions for *Dreams in F Minor*; spent hours revising the play for the start of rehearsals in January; and, in his spare time, met with producers about *The King of Rome*, trying to winnow out one who, though successful and intelligent, would yet have the wisdom to bow to David's will in a fight. In pursuit of that goal, a few days before he'd had to fire his agent for trying to maneuver him into a deal with an off-Broadway producer (presumably because said producer knew in which closet the agent kept his skeletons hidden) short on money, taste, and power. His new agent was Rob Maxwell, without whom (so they said) no worthwhile play ever saw the light of Broadway's neon. They were, apparently, close to a deal. "Rob suggested Sarah for Marie Louise. What do you think?"

"She'd be perfect."

He looked dubious. "I'm not sure I want her in it," he said. I don't like what happens when lovers work together."

"What happens?"

"The reality of the relationship overwhelms the truth of the work. People are miscast, parts rewritten, structures readjusted, the work gets distorted."

"That didn't happen to Duncan and Sarah onstage. They were wonderful together."

"Perhaps it did happen. Perhaps no one ever noticed. I'd notice."

"Does Sarah want the part?"

"Probably. We haven't talked about it," he said. "Is there something wrong?" he asked then, changing the subject. "You seem strange." I hesitated, considering my reply, but I never even got the chance to lie. "You've seen Caroline, haven't you?" Accusation, irritation, and a smattering of satisfaction blended in his voice.

I told him that I'd run into her, and that she'd agreed to see me. He stubbed out his cigarette and sat looking at me. Then he said, very quietly, "I'll leave it to you, for now, Nikki. But if you can't change her mind, you're going to have to tell me where she is, or I'm going to have to take my father apart bone by bone." He dropped his head into his hands. "God, Nikki, you don't know how much I miss those kids."

I got up, walked around the table, and put my arms around him, burying my face in his thick black hair.

"What could I have done?" he asked no one in particular. "What else could I have done?"

I didn't answer. What was the point?

Ned arrived about then, and we discussed for a while the various legal maneuvers open to David. The conversation clearly made Ned uncomfortable. He liked David, he liked Sarah, he didn't like Caroline, but the situation was one he heartily disapproved of, and though disinclined to moralize, at rock bottom he thought David had behaved like a shit from beginning to end and had no one but himself to blame for the mess he was in. "This is the sort of thing friends should stay out of," he replied, when David asked Ned to represent him. "Everybody stays calmer when the lawyers are perceived as emotionally neutral, as not having any personal ax to grind. I'll put you in touch with someone really good, if and when the time comes."

"Whoever it is had better be good. I may be in the wrong," said David, "but I don't intend to pay in blood for my sins."

We left the apartment together, David heading back to Central Park West and Ned and I to a Cuban restaurant on Columbus Avenue. We were just about to be seated when Mary Kenny came in with one of the mayor's aides whom Ned also knew. Of course he asked them to join us.

She was less pretty than I remembered. Her face was round, with no bones to speak of, with a full mouth and narrow pointed chin. But her coloring was spectacular, jet-black hair falling in soft crinkles to her shoulders, pale white skin, and blue eyes, lapis lazuli eyes, brimming with intelligence and interest, the latter mostly in me. She was surveying me with the same critical eye that I had turned on her, and what she saw was disturbing. Had I been five years older or less interestingly dressed or employed as a saleswoman in Alexander's, she would have been happier, I suppose. But I was too young, too attractive, and too successful to be dismissed. She saw what Ned saw in me and didn't like it. What she couldn't know was that I saw the same in her and felt frightened. I put my hand on Ned's arm and called him "darling" a little more often than I normally did, not so often that he thought it strange, just enough so that he was aware of it and pleased.

What the young man with her looked like, I can't remember. But when the conversation turned to the war in Vietnam, as it inevitably did in those years, he was the only hawk in the group, and I watched as Ned demolished his position with peculiar relish, using all the verbal agility he normally reserved for particularly odious prosecuting attorneys. He was showing off, and certainly not for me. As Mary's head nodded more vigorously in agreement, as her eyes sparkled more with admiration, as she jumped in with increasing enthusiasm to support his attack, Ned grew visibly plumper with satisfaction. I was tempted to toss the victim a little help, but decided against it. Let him look after his own ego. I had mine to protect.

Walking home, despite the bracing night air, I could feel the exhaustion numbing my body. It takes so much energy to be thoughtful and intelligent, cogent yet charming, all the while suppressing fear and rage.

"Are you all right?" asked Ned.

"Great," I chirped.

And when we got home I proved it by making love to him until he collapsed with satisfaction and fatigue. I didn't sleep all night. I knew sex was a weapon of unreliable value. Love was far more potent, and a congruence of need perhaps more powerful than all.

Despite everything, the next day I was ebullient. One of those inexplicable waves of euphoria swept over me, flooding me with optimism and goodwill. Ned had made coffee and scribbled me a love note as sloppily sentimental as he was capable of. The sun was shining and lacy cirrus clouds waved happily against the sky. I could hear Christmas carols coming from somewhere, and as I reached the curb humming "O Little Town of Bethlehem," an empty taxi was passing and the driver stopped to pick me up. I felt like a Robert Browning poem.

Consequently, I got through the day without a hitch. Nanouchka Fevel (then one of the top international models), a woman who normally hated my guts, behaved much like a pet borzoi. A usually disorganized assistant managed to have everything in place, on time. And when one of the beautiful young boys I was using as props for Nanouchka made a not too subtle pass at me, I chalked it up to good taste rather than ambition. The last thing I wanted to do was see Caroline and spoil the mood.

She was living in an apartment building on lower Fifth Avenue, a block from Washington Square. I arrived at exactly eight-thirty and was greeted with the usual blend of good manners and cool hostility.

"Would you like something to eat?" she inquired politely.

"No, thank you. I stopped for a hamburger on the way."

"Coffee? Wine?"

"Coffee," I replied, feeling I needed all my wits about me for the ensuing conversation.

The apartment was small but spotlessly clean and cozy, filled with the shabby furniture I remembered from Bank Street. It had a view looking east to the river and one bedroom—for the children. Caroline slept on the convertible couch in the living room.

"Trudi got it for us," she told me. "A friend of hers owns the building. David's father wanted us to stay there, he has plenty of room, but Trudi didn't think that was a good idea." She looked unhappily around. "It's awfully small, but considering how tough it is to find a place in Manhattan, I guess we're lucky. I can't take the kids near the park, though. It's full of druggies. It's disgusting." I felt my hold on my good mood loosening moment by moment. Any second now and it would slip over the edge into the abyss.

She ground decaffeinated coffee beans and spooned them into a filter, poured boiling water over them, and let it drip, as she filled a pitcher with cream. "I've finally managed to give up sugar," she said, with the hint of a smile.

Our conversation, which used to be limited to Lissie, now expanded to embrace Kate. The baby was basically healthy, Caroline assured me. She was just one of those children who caught cold easily, and the colds sometimes turned to bronchitis. "It's nothing to be concerned about," she said, a little defensively. "She'll outgrow it, the doctors tell me."

"I'm sure she will. I did," I replied. The last thing in the world I wanted was for her to feel I was in any way critical of her. I sat on the couch and faced her in the armchair opposite. There were tension lines in her face I hadn't noticed in the street. Her hands moved anxiously, playing in her hair, tugging at her skirt, refilling my coffee cup before it was necessary. She was wondering why in the hell she had let me come and what she was going to do with me now that I was there. I wondered the same thing.

"And Lissie?" I asked.

"She's fine."

"I know it's none of my business, but what are you doing for money? Do you need any?" She didn't have any of her own, I knew, and since David couldn't find her, she wasn't getting any of the little he had. David assumed she must have borrowed some from his father.

"I wouldn't take a nickel from you," she said.

"Caroline, I'm only trying to help." The words sounded feeble even in my own ears.

"Why didn't you help me when I asked you? I begged you to tell me what David was up to. But you wouldn't. If I'd known, maybe I could have done something to stop him. Why didn't *you* do something to stop him? If not for my sake, then for Lissie's? He would have listened to you. He always listens to you."

"David only listens to what he wants to hear. It's not fair to blame me, Caroline. I did and said what I could."

"You didn't tell me. You didn't warn me."

"I couldn't. I couldn't break my word to David."

"David!" Her voice was full of anger, of hatred. "He doesn't deserve loyalty, anybody's loyalty. The way I loved him! Do you know what this past year's been like for me?" she wailed. "Do you know what I've been through?"

Over the next few hours, over endless cups of coffee, in a voice changing constantly, like music played first in one key than another, in fast rhythms and slow, *con brio* and *molto doloroso*, Caroline told me the story of her life. She took what before had been a mere melodic sketch in my mind and turned it into a full symphonic work. This woman, who had kept me at arm's length for years with her silence, was suddenly trying to lure me to her with a song. Perhaps to her, David's mind and mine seemed so attuned that she felt by gaining my sympathy she would automatically get his. Or perhaps she only wanted me to join Trudi and Jack and Mr. Walton in the camp, leaving David in isolation and confirmed in his guilt. If she could convince everyone else he was totally at fault, maybe then she could convince herself. Whatever her reason, she talked.

Caroline had been an army brat, and for her the life had been torment. She didn't have the personality for it. She didn't make friends or adjust to change easily, and—time after time—when she failed to do both, she was crushed by her parents' disappointment. Each move for her was wrenching emotionally, psychologically, and physically, far beyond her ability to cope. She was ill a lot. Her schoolwork suffered. Gradually, she accepted the others' assessment of her: she was unhealthy, unlovable, and dumb. But, instead of humble, this verdict left her resentful and angry, which of course added to the list of reasons people found it hard to befriend her. Dale, her more amiable older sister, one Christmas gave Caroline a copy of *How to Win Friends and Influence People* and her parents insisted she would be fine if only she could learn to enjoy all the advantages she'd been given. She didn't spend much time with any of them anymore.

When she got to college, life improved significantly for Caroline.

For one thing, staying at or leaving UCLA was totally within her own power, and that made her feel for the first time in control of her fate; and, to her parents' amazement, she ran a B+ average. Secondly, a health-food store in Westwood, near the campus, introduced her to a new way of life. She became convinced that illness was not a necessity, at least not for her; and that notion combined with good eating habits, swimming, tennis, and southern California sunshine turned her from a potential hypochondriac into a healthy keep-fit enthusiast. Finally, she had become a beauty, with flame-red hair, green eyes, and bones that encouraged top modeling agents to hand her cards in restaurants and ask her to call. She dropped out of college and began modeling, took a few acting classes, and occasionally got small parts in television shows. She wasn't very successful, but the attention she got was balm to a sore ego. And if she still didn't make friends easily, it seemed less important. Her social calendar was filled with men who were flatteringly attentive, at least for a while. Caroline had also discovered the currency of sex.

While it isn't true, as Mr. Keating suggests, that Caroline was on the verge of a big success when she met David, it is possible that if she hadn't married so young, or if she had married a different man, someone less egocentric, less ambitious, less determined than David, the positive qualities that were beginning to take root in Caroline might have flowered. She might have turned into a reasonably secure, reasonably contented woman. But she didn't. She married David and instead of the stable home life she needed, she found herself tied to a gypsy; instead of someone to feed her ego, she got a man who never had enough fuel for his own.

They met at a theater. An agent she was dating flew her up to San Francisco with him for the weekend to see one of David's plays. They all went out to dinner afterwards, and Caroline's notable lack of interest in his work, and in him, intrigued David. What he didn't understand then, and never did until it was too late, was that insecurity rather than self-assurance accounted for Caroline's intriguing, enigmatic aura. Captivated by her face, like a Hemingway hero dreaming of Garbo, David imagined her aloofness to conceal, instead of self-doubt and fear, wisdom and an arcane eroticism.

He pursued her to Los Angeles, asked her out, got her to bed, and still wasn't satisfied. He hadn't really touched her yet. But it wasn't easy to resist David when he had made up his mind to be irresistible. He charmed and coaxed and wheedled, he made love to her with singular attention to her pleasure, he listened to her opinions and discussed them with her seriously, he flattered her intelligence and inflamed her libido, and before long she not only loved him but she loved him more than she had ever loved anyone in her life. She loved him without understanding him, without appreciating him, without really knowing him; but she loved him as fully as she was capable of loving. Life without him was suddenly inconceivable.

Though Caroline wanted to, they didn't live together, and David traveled a lot. He sailed the Caribbean and fished in the Pacific Northwest; he journeyed to remote parts of Central America to look at ruins; he rode out with the cowboys running cattle on a friend's ranch; and he went to watch his plays wherever they were produced. Sometimes Caroline went with him, but not too often, not really because, as Keating says, David wanted to be free to pursue other women, but because at bottom she bored him. They had nothing to talk about. She had no real understanding of or interest in his work, and it infuriated him when he was deep into a production to see her totally absorbed in a magazine article on nutrition. After about a year, David stopped being jealous when other men flirted with Caroline. Slowly, he began to disentangle himself; then, with an instinct for self-preservation or self-destruction (depending on your point of view), Caroline got pregnant. Instead of leaving her, David married her, not for her sake but for his own. It was a twist of the plot he wanted to live with.

At first, Caroline was so happy to have him that she was determined to do anything he wanted to make the marriage work. Her resolution didn't last long. Soon, the anger, the bitterness, which had been in remission for a long time, returned.

Caroline knew, she confessed, that David had married her only because she was pregnant, and the thought undermined her always fragile ego. Still, once Lissie was born, she became confident she could keep him. He was crazy about the child, and he cared about her, she knew, as much as he'd ever cared for any woman, except possibly me, and that was so totally different. He didn't want me, and he did want her. That he proved often, to her satisfaction, his theory being that as long as he had made his bed, it might as well be a good one to lie in.

She followed him cheerfully enough when he insisted on living in San Francisco; but then he decided a move to New York was essential, and all the out-of-control feelings of her childhood returned. By the time the Ford grant made the year in London possible, she fought him tooth and nail on the move, but her resistance was finally defeated by the absolute implacability of his will.

As David withheld from her the kind of love he gave their daughter, she denied him what he wanted most—another child. As his always superficial interest in her ideas waned, her own lack of interest in his work reached the proportions of outright hostility. As her own modeling career faltered for reasons she could never understand, she became more and more scornful of David's growing success. Unable to make friends of her own, she treated his coolly, seeing in them both a reproach to herself and another obstacle to his affection.

In general, it is possible to say that David, in the years they were married, treated Caroline better than she treated him: he rarely lost his temper with her, he was always polite, and he observed punctiliously all the outward forms of a happy marriage. In fairness, it is necessary to say that he did, not because he was the better person, but because he didn't care about her. He cared only about Lissie, and he did everything he could to keep her. If he hadn't met Sarah, he would—I think—have gone on doing that for the rest of his life.

When David told her about Sarah, she heard him almost with relief. She wasn't fighting vague demons anymore with uncertain weapons. She knew who the enemy was: Sarah Cope. Though Caroline knew her life with David had never been good and was likely to get worse, still she couldn't believe it would in any way be better without him, and she decided to stand her ground and fight. There was a good chance of winning, she thought. "And I would have won," she said, her mouth twisting with bitterness, "if Sarah hadn't had a boy."

As she said it, I knew it was true. Those months David had traveled back and forth between Caroline in Knightsbridge and Sarah in Chelsea, he had been biding his time, making no decisions, waiting to see which woman would produce the son he wanted. A wave of anger washed over me, but all I said was, because it also was true: "David loves Lissie and Kate. You know he does."

"He doesn't care about anyone but himself. I was a fool to get pregnant."

"Why did you?"

"I felt him slipping away. I thought . . . Christ, what a fool I was . . . I thought if I had another baby, he'd never leave me. Why didn't you tell me, when I asked you?" she said, nursing her grievance against me.

"I couldn't," I repeated, hiding my impatience. How could she understand the rules of friendship when she'd never had to play by them? "Anyway," I continued, in a more conciliatory tone, "It wouldn't have made any difference. By the time I found out about Sarah, everything had gone too far to stop."

She closed her eyes for a moment, to hide her despair. When she opened them again, they held tears. I had never seen Caroline look so forlorn, so helpless. She had never allowed me to. "He's not coming back, is he?" she asked.

"No," I said.

The tears trickled down her cheeks. I understood finally that her flight from London, her hiding in New York, her determination not to see David or let him see his children, were not just her way of punishing him. They were a last-ditch effort to try to make him see the folly of his actions, to make him understand exactly what he was losing in losing her. I wanted to put my arms around her, but I knew she would resent my pity. As soon as I left, she would be sorry she had let me see her cry. By tomorrow morning, she would be furious. Anger is the only emotion the would-be strong consider suitable for public display.

From the bedroom came the sound of Kate crying. "She'll wake Lissie," said Caroline , standing, wiping the tears from her face with her hands. She reached into a pocket, extracted a Kleenex, and put it to her nose. "I'd better get her."

The coffee tray lay on the table in front of me, and I considered carrying it into the kitchen, rinsing the cups, and putting on another pot to brew. Again, I didn't. Caroline would be sure to consider the gesture a slap at her abilities as a hostess. Instead, I browsed through the books and magazines on the coffee table. There was a Jackie Susann novel and something called *The Chemicals We Eat*, copies of *Good Housekeeping* and *Vogue*. I opened the *Vogue* and looked again at the Irving Penn photographs of Morocco. They were beautiful: formal to the point of contrived, perhaps, but beautiful.

A moment later Caroline returned, carrying Kate, who looked plumper than she was in her yellow sleepsuit and very flushed. "She has a fever," said Caroline. "It's this weather. It's awful."

"Hello, sweetheart," I said and smiled. She didn't smile back with that reflex small children seem to have, wanting to mirror the reflections they see. Instead, she regarded me with eyes not only grave, but suspicious. Her little face was so like Lissie's, but she had none of her sister's frank and open manner, none of her warmth or charm. Her mother's daughter, I thought, and is it any wonder?

"She's such a good baby," said Caroline, as if responding to a criticism. "Even when she's sick, she's no trouble. She's so much quieter than Lissie was." She settled the child in her lap, covered her with a blanket she had brought, and murmured to her softly for a moment. Kate closed her eyes. "I'm not sorry I had her," said Caroline, when she looked up at me. "It's just so hard raising children alone."

"You don't have to," I said.

"I never thought David was much help," she went on, as if she hadn't heard me. "But I was wrong. Damn him!" She said it softly, so as not to disturb Kate.

"He's really upset you won't see him. I've never seen him so upset."

"Good. Now he knows how I feel."

"Caroline, I don't want to try to excuse anything that David did. It was inexcusable. I don't even want to try to convince you to forgive him. In your place, I'm not sure I could. All I want is for you to understand that David does know how much he's hurt you, and that he's sorry—"

"Not sorry enough to do anything about it," she interrupted.

"Sorry enough to do what he can, which is not to make it any worse for Lissie and Kate than necessary."

"How good can it be, when your father deserts you?"

"Caroline," I said, keeping my voice even. I didn't want to feed her emotion. I didn't want to turn it into a scene that would justify Caroline's anger. "As bad as David's leaving was, you know his not being able to see the girls is worse, for everyone, even you."

"The girls are fine."

"They're not. You know they're not."

Kate, who had drifted off into a light sleep, stirred in Caroline's lap. "I should put her back in her bed. She'll sleep now, I think." Caroline stood, adjusted the child in her arms, then carried her back to the bedroom.

I looked at the coffee tray, thought what the hell, and carried it into the kitchen, a narrow room with barely enough space to turn, but state-of-the-art from cabinets to appliances. On the counter was a copy of *The New York Times Natural Foods Cookbook*.

"Thank you," said Caroline, when she returned. She didn't mean it.

I knew I didn't have much time left, so I took a deep breath and plunged in again. "You don't have to be alone in this, Caroline. I'm willing to help, if you'll let me. I care about those children. I'd never do anything to hurt them. Not even for David," I added.

"I'm not alone. I have Mr. Walton. And Trudi. I don't know what I would have done without them."

I did. She would have seen David weeks ago. She would have had to, if only to get money. "Kate and Lissie need their father."

"I'm sorry. Could you go now? I'm tired. And I get up very early with the children."

"Let David see them."

"No!"

"I don't blame you for wanting to hurt David. But what's the point in hurting your children?" There was such anguish in her face, but still I didn't shut up. "What's the point?" She was crying again. "Let me give David your phone number. Let me tell him where you are."

She held her breath for a moment, then let it loose in a wail. "All right, tell him. Tell him."

I put my arms around her and held her. She might hate me in the morning, but she needed me then.

✣ *Chapter 19* ✣

When I left Caroline's, I went as planned to Ned's apartment. He made himself some tea, then stretched out beside me on the couch, wrapping his arms around me. "I am so glad," he said, "you chose such a big couch." We lay together quietly, looking at the fire, listening to Schubert. How I love him, I thought.

"You should go to bed," I said finally. I knew I wouldn't be able to sleep.

"I will," he said, "in a while." He tightened his hold on me and kissed the back of my neck.

"I feel so sorry for her," I said.

"She'll be all right."

"In a garden full of flowers, she only sees the weeds. How awful her future must look to her now."

"She's much better off without David, you know. She should never have married him. He's completely the wrong kind of man for her."

Having only discovered that myself a few hours before, I turned in Ned's arms and looked at him with something close to amazement on my face. "Did you always know that?"

"Not always, but for a long time."

"Why didn't you say?" I moved around to face him, sticking my feet under his bottom to keep them warm.

"I assumed you knew. Didn't you?" He began to stroke my leg.

How I would miss it, I thought, sitting and talking, just like this, with Ned, the friendliness of it, the warmth, the love. "No. I just thought *she* was the wrong kind of woman for *him* to have married. I never looked at it from her point of view. Not that I ever thought David was an ideal husband. I can't imagine many worse fates than being married to him."

"There is no such thing as an ideal husband."

"Could we stick to gossip," I pleaded, "and not get into philosophy? I've had a rough day."

"Or wife," he continued, ignoring me.

"No," I replied, preparing to hoist him on his own petard, "but you yourself just pointed out that some people really shouldn't be married to each other. Unfortunately, they are usually the last to realize it." I leaned forward and grabbed his wiry hair with my hands and pulled it. There was something very sexy, very erotic, about it. "I love your hair."

"And?"

"And your mouth." I leaned forward and kissed it. I put my hand on his crotch, lightly, just letting it rest there. "And everything else about you."

"Do you realize you've ended every conversation we've had for weeks by making love to me?"

"Does the prosecution have any serious objections?"

"Several."

I undid his belt and opened his zipper. "This isn't how my mother told me it would be," I said. "She told me there was nothing a man wouldn't do or say to get laid. And here you are, complaining."

"Your mother never told you that."

"Not in so many words. But that's what she meant."

"I just don't like being manipulated like this!"

I laughed. "And I thought you did. Shall I stop?" I asked. I licked his ear. "Shall I?"

"No," he said. "Not now."

The phone rang the next morning at six. Ned grabbed it on the first ring. "It's for you," he said sleepily, handing it to me. "Guess who."

"I was going to call you as soon as I got up," I said defensively.

"Did you see her? What happened?" David fired his questions at me like bullets, hardly waiting for a reply. "What did she say?"

"You can see the girls."

It was as if he had been holding his breath for days and now finally could breathe again. "Oh, God." I heard the long sigh of relief.
"Nikki, thanks."

I gave him Caroline's address and phone number. "But don't call her
now," I cautioned. "It's too early. She'll resent it. You'll end up having
a fight."

"You don't have to tell me how to behave," he said, but without any
real rancor in his tone. "You're not so thoughtful yourself. Why the
hell didn't you phone me last night? I called your place till one in the
morning. I didn't want to phone Ned. I was afraid I'd wake him."

"God, but your manners are impeccable."

"Why didn't you phone me?"

"Because I knew you'd call Caroline as soon as I gave you her
number. And I didn't really think she was ready to talk to you last
night."

"You don't think I have any self-restraint at all."

"None," I said.

I was wrong. He restrained himself for half an hour, and then didn't
phone, but took a taxi downtown. I discovered that from Caroline when
I called her in the afternoon to see if she was all right.

"I'm fine," she said. "He nearly frightened me to death showing up
like that so early in the morning. I was expecting him to phone first. I
should have known better. Anyway, he took Lissie to school, then came
back and spent the morning with Kate and me. We're all fine, really.
Thanks for calling."

Her voice had a peculiar note in it, a satisfied note, as if suddenly
everything that had been wrong was magically put right. Had David
been waving his little wand? I wondered. Had that bastard fucked her?

I had called Caroline from the airport on my way to Grenada for a
shoot, bathing suits for a spring issue of *Harper's Bazaar,* so I had a few
days to decide whether or not I really wanted to put the question to
him. I wasn't sure I wanted to know.

If it had been January, I would have been ecstatic to be in the Caribbean. By then, Christmas is only a vague memory and I'm more than
fed up with winter. In December, however, I never want to be anywhere but Manhattan. And compared to the Grenadians, New Yorkers
were as cheerful and merry as Santa's elves. I pointed my camera at one

old man unloading a banana barge and work came to a halt. The crew turned and stared, and I put my camera back into its case. The message was clear: they'd far rather use their machetes on me than on their cargo. The quaint charm of the city of St. George's, the beauty of the lush hillsides, the azure of the sea, the endless stretch of white sand beaches were obscured by a cloud of hostility and fear. I saw a white woman nervously remove her baby from the sea and retreat to a remote corner of the beach rather than tell a group of black adolescents to stop clowning. My sympathies lay entirely with the Grenadians. If I were one of them, my ears too would be deaf and my eyes blind to the benefits of colonization. I would hate the white exploiter with his smug sense of innate superiority. I would resent being thought picturesque. I would long to kill, especially the tourist with his loud voice, big tips, and ubiquitous camera. But I was not one of them, and the atmosphere left me uneasy and unhappy and full of guilt. I wanted to get out of there. It seemed a very long three days.

"You should have seen Lissie's face when I walked in," said David.

We were in Central Park, the afternoon of my return, watching as Lissie played in the snow with some newfound friends. The children, in their nylon snowsuits, were the only bright spots in a somber landscape. Compared to the brilliant colors of Grenada, even in sunshine Manhattan seemed monochromatically dull. After the sleek dark bodies and vivid clothes of the island, New Yorkers of every complexion seemed bleak and pale, all of us huddled under heavy coats that never seemed to keep us warm enough. A mounted policeman rode by at a canter, perhaps in pursuit of a criminal, perhaps hurrying to end his tour, the breath of his horse a low white mist against the shrubs. A jogger went past in a gray track suit, earmuffs on his ears, a woolen scarf around his neck trailing like a pennant behind him. A mother walked towards us, pushing her baby's carriage, a look of fierce determination on her face: her child was going to get its daily dose of fresh air if it killed them both. Only the decorated trees in front of the Tavern on the Green were jolly, and the dogs chasing sticks, and David.

"It was as if someone had switched a light on inside her," he said. "She threw her arms around me and just kept saying 'Daddy, Daddy' over and over. She didn't cry, though. I was the one who cried. It was all I could do to get her to let go so I could take her to school." David, too, looked as if the lights were back on inside. He looked like a man who had everything in the world he wanted. "She didn't want to go," he said. "She didn't want to leave me. God, I love that kid."

"You spent the morning with Caroline and Kate?" I asked, as innocently as I could manage.

He nodded. "We weren't reading actors till after lunch."

The children had stopped playing with the ball some obliging parent
had brought and had begun a series of extremely awkward movements,
stepping forward and back, hands over their heads and down, bowing
from their waists, trying impossibly to kick up their legs in the hamper-
ing snowsuits. Lissie seemed to be in the thick of it, issuing orders.
"What are they doing?"

David looked in the direction I was pointing and laughed. "I took her
to see *Nutcracker* yesterday. She loved it. I had to tell her the story
three times on the way home. She told it to her mother twice. Now
she's trying to get everyone to dance it. Isn't she something?"

She was, I agreed; then asked how she liked Sarah.

"They haven't seen each other yet."

He had used his "soothing" voice on me, so I knew there was a reason
for it I wouldn't like. "Why not?" I asked.

"I promised Caroline I'd take it slow. She was afraid it would upset
Lissie to see me living somewhere else, with another woman, another
child."

"It will upset her, but unless you plan to change your mind, again,
what's the point of waiting?"

"How can I change my mind?" He laughed. He reached into the
pocket of his coat, took out a package of Gauloises, lit one, and puffed at
it thoughtfully. "I'm caught this time, Nikki," he said. His incredulity
was mixed with surprise, and a little anger. "I love Sarah. Worse than
that, I need her. I can't stand to be away from her, even for a few days.
Christ, I've never felt like that about any woman before."

"How does Sarah feel, about waiting, I mean?"

"She understands." I snorted in disbelief. "Not everyone's got your
rigid little mind."

"There's nothing rigid about my mind," I snapped back. "It seems to
expand to absorb everything you're capable of doing."

"We'll all be together on Christmas. Caroline's agreed to that. Nikki,
for chrissake, you know I can't do anything now to upset her."

"All?"

"I'll pick up the kids in the morning," he explained patiently, "and
take them to my father's. Sarah and Mark will meet us there. We'll
have lunch with Jack and Trudi, my sister and her husband, we'll open
our presents, then Sarah and the baby will go. And Caroline will come

and spend the evening," he concluded, as triumphant as Nelson delivering the battle plan for Trafalgar.

"You have got to be kidding," I said, even though I knew he wasn't.

He looked at me in surprise. He couldn't imagine what I found wrong in the scheme. "What's the matter?"

"Do you go with Sarah, or stay with Caroline?"

"I'll stay, for a while." He saw the look on my face and snapped, "I couldn't walk out the minute Caroline gets there, could I? How would that make her feel?"

"I can't believe you got either of them to agree to it. I just can't believe it. Women are really idiots, aren't they?"

"Some women know how to compromise. They don't insist on making everybody miserable for a lot of inane rules, or hollow principles. I wouldn't call that idiotic."

"Some women," I sneered, "know how to eat shit."

"For chrissake, all I want is a halfway decent Christmas for my kids. A family Christmas."

"Your kids, in my humble opinion, are not a good enough excuse for what you're doing to those two women."

"What are you talking about? What am I doing?" As inconceivable as it might seem, he had no idea.

"Have you made love to Caroline?"

He looked at me, outraged. "None of your goddam business." I could see the fury blazing deep in his dark eyes. Fury, and one small flicker of guilt. "Don't you know I'll do anything, anything I have to, to keep my kids?"

Was any of this, I asked myself as Ned might, any of my business? Were either of those two women worth jeopardizing my friendship with David? On the other hand, was a friendship with someone like David worth having? I started away from him, towards Lissie.

"Where are you going?"

"To say goodbye to Lissie. I really don't want to be around you right now." It was an effort to distract Lissie from her dance for a moment, but I wanted a hug. "Bye, sweetheart," I said.

"I'm C-clara. And he," she said, pointing to a round blue bundle, "he's the p-prince." The unhappiness I had seen in her little face was gone. She beamed at me. Everything was fine, she thought, now that she had her daddy back.

I walked away without looking back. I didn't have to. I knew what David looked like—hurt and angry—and I didn't want to see it. My life without him was inconceivable. He had been in it for too long, and

I was too dependent on his letters, his phone calls, his presence, for understanding, for comfort, for amusement, and—yes—even for drama. I wasn't sure if there existed a boundary I wouldn't cross to keep his friendship. Which was why I felt such fury at those two women for allowing David to behave in a way I could only despise. Their weakness forced me to defend them, and I didn't want to. It compelled me into their corner, where I didn't want to be. I loathed them for the self-destructiveness of what they called their love, and myself for not being certain I wasn't capable of the same. I was far angrier at Caroline, and Sarah, than I was at David, and with myself for being in any way involved in their cowardice. Perhaps like Caroline and Sarah for his love, or David for his children, I would do anything to keep his friendship. But not just then.

The next day I worked at home, on the proofs of the Grenada photographs. I found them disappointing and wasn't sure whether the fault was in my mood or in the photos themselves. The compositions I had thought so interesting when viewed through the lens of my camera in proof looked contrived and trite. The choice of filters seemed to have been made by an amateur with little light or color sense. The topography of the island seemed dull, the models lifeless. I had somehow made Hila Helsin, one of the most beautiful women in the world, look like the scheming hustler she gradually became. But I didn't know her future then, and attributed the truth the camera told to a failure of my craft.

I was trying with my grease pencil to rectify some of my errors with inventive cropping when the intercom rang. "Miss Cope to see you," announced the new doorman in a clear and cheery voice.

As if I didn't have enough problems, I thought. "Thank you," I said, grudgingly. "Send her up." Fool, I kicked myself mentally as soon as I'd replaced the receiver, you could have pretended to be the cleaning lady.

"I'm sorry," said Sarah. "I didn't plan to come, I was just walking, and suddenly I found myself right outside your door. Have I arrived at an awful time?" She saw the contact sheets spread over the table. "Oh, God, you're working. I am sorry. I'll go, shall I?"

"Don't be silly. I'm grateful for the interruption," I lied. "I'm cross-eyed from looking at proofs. Stay at least and have a drink. Tea? Coffee? Wine? What would you like?" I asked as I took her coat. It was soaked. "Is it raining?" I looked towards the window. I had been so disturbed by the photographs I hadn't noticed the weather.

"Gin, if you have it," she replied. "Teeming. It's a filthy day. But I couldn't bear the thought of staying in. I left Mark with Mrs. T and went out to do some shopping. But I didn't seem to be in the mood for that, either." She looked tired, a little faded, like a spring flower the day after it's been cut.

"Where's David?" I asked, though I knew I shouldn't.

"With Rob Maxwell. A meeting about *The King of Rome*. The deal's almost set. David thinks he can work with this producer," which, euphemistically, meant David knew he would be able to stay in control. "Corey Chase, I think his name is." Chase had won a Tony two years straight, one for a production of *As You Like It*, another for *Uncle Vanya*. "They're talking about a May opening. It's all very exciting," she said, straining for enthusiasm. "Then, I suppose, he'll go to Caroline's to see the children." That time, she tried and almost succeeded in keeping her voice level. I handed her the gin and tonic. "Thank you. Aren't you having anything?"

"I'll make myself a coffee. I can't drink while I'm working."

"I never drink before a performance. The people who do insist it helps, it soothes the nerves, and gets the energy up. But I lose my concentration. Afterwards, however..." She laughed. "Oh, I do like a drink afterwards. Duncan and I used to get plastered after a performance and just fall into bed." No wonder they didn't fuck, I thought. "I'm drinking much less now," she added. "David's virtually a teetotaler, isn't he? And, of course, I'm not working, so there's less tension. Less socializing, too. I gave it up entirely when I was pregnant. David thought it was best for the baby."

That was one of Caroline's theories which she had practiced years before the effects of alcohol on a fetus were widely known or accepted. It was one to which David fully subscribed. He'd done drugs and drink indiscriminately in his teens and early twenties, but had stopped when he started believing they hurt his writing. The seduction of Coleridge's opium dreams, the nostalgia for Hemingway's drunken machismo, even the fraternal pull of the rock highs of his musician friends lost their appeal when he was confronted the day after a binge with either his inability to write or the detritus he had dropped onto paper when he thought he was creating a masterpiece. Now, he drank rarely, and in insignificant amounts.

"Anyway, it certainly didn't hurt," said Sarah. "Mark's the most wonderful little baby, isn't he?"

"He's beautiful," I agreed. "So, you think motherhood's all it's cracked up to be?" I asked, not just making conversation. It was a subject which at that time occupied a lot of my thought.

"Oh, God, yes." For a moment, a smile irradiated her somber face. "Sometimes, when I'm holding Mark, and he's absolutely quiet, and I can feel his peach-fuzz skin and smell his talcum-powder smell, a feeling of utter peacefulness comes over me. It's amazing, really. I've never felt anything like it." She gave a bemused little shrug, then leaned towards me. "I can't bear it when he cries, though. It's awful, isn't it, not being able to reason, to explain? To have to watch someone you love be so unhappy and not be able to do anything about it? David just holds him and he says that's enough, but I can never quite believe it."

"I suppose the thing is to accept that we can never do, or be, enough for the people we love."

"Can you?"

"Accept it? No. I haven't even learned yet to live with the failure. That's what most people do, I think."

"There's a third alternative, isn't there? To be like David, and not give a damn. Just to be who you are, do what you do, and let the people who love you take or leave you as they can." What surprised me most about what she said was the complete lack of bitterness in her voice. It expressed only interest, as if she were recounting an anthropological study of the mating habits of some obscure jungle tribe.

"I'm not sure you're right," I said. "It seems to me that David sometimes goes to unbelievable lengths to make the people he loves happy."

She shook her head. "No. What he tries to do is manipulate them into thinking he's doing his damnedest to make them happy when, in fact, he's only trying to please himself. That's a different thing entirely." She swallowed the last of her gin and tonic and handed me the glass. "May I have another, please? I'm just beginning to relax." She settled back into the sofa. "I won't stay much longer. I promise."

"Stay as long as you like."

"It's just that I don't have anyone here to talk to, except David. I don't really know anyone but him. And it's not always a good idea to tell the man you love what you're thinking, is it?"

"There's a lot to be said for honesty," I pussyfooted. Though actually I've always considered it a much overrated virtue, I didn't like to encourage anyone to stray from the path of righteousness. *Chacun à son péché* is my motto.

"Do you tell Ned everything?" As soon as she spoke the words, Sarah thought of Simon. I could tell by the sudden embarrassment in her eyes. Had he told her we'd been lovers, or had she guessed? "I'm sorry," she added quickly. "That's none of my business."

"No, I don't tell him everything." I grinned and handed her the drink. "But only because he wouldn't understand. I know that sounds feeble, but I believe it's true. David, on the other hand, always understands. *You* told me that."

"But I'm not sure what I mean to say to him. My mind's in such turmoil, I change it a dozen times a day. And I don't want to threaten, I don't want to bluff. I don't want to play those kinds of games with David. I really don't."

"So, you want a kind of dress-rehearsal argument with me."

"I'm going mad not being able to talk to anyone." Her voice was thicker than ever, its rasp more pronounced. She was straining to control it, fighting not to cry. "Oh, Nikki, I know I'm asking a lot of you. But there's no one else. No one."

"I'm David's best friend. I'm not exactly impartial."

"I don't want you to be impartial. I need you to be on David's side. That's why it's you I have to talk to. Otherwise I could just as well call Duncan. Can you understand that?" She looked at me beseechingly, and finally I nodded. I did understand: it is only possible to criticize the person loved to someone else who loves him. Anything else is a betrayal. She put her drink down on the table, wrapped her arms around her legs, and stared down at the floor. "I think I should leave David," she said softly. Then she looked up at me and repeated more firmly, "I think my leaving him would be best, for everyone." She didn't present it as a position she wanted to be talked out of taking, but as an option that had to be discussed. She wasn't wheedling for reassurance about David's love, but using me as a sounding board as she planned her future.

"Leave him? Now?" I had expected anger, grief. I had expected a stinging denunciation of David's character and morals. I had expected a lot of things, but not for her to have come this far so soon.

"Did he tell you about Christmas?"

"Yes."

"He really hasn't decided, has he, just with whom he wants to be?" Her face was even paler than when she'd arrived.

"Sarah, you're really putting me in an impossible position." I stood up and walked away from her, towards the window. I couldn't look at her.

"I know he loves me. But everything is just so monstrously complicated. And I've been very patient, for me. I've waited so long for him to decide."

"He's living with you."

"Since he's been seeing Caroline, and the girls, I've felt him moving away from Mark and me. It's like last year in London, only this time in reverse. I can't stand it, Nikki. If I'm going to lose him, I want to do it all at once, not gradually."

"'It's not love's going that hurts my days/But that it went in little ways,'" I said, staring down at the wet pavement. The rain had stopped as we'd talked.

"What's that?"

"It's from a poem, by Edna St. Vincent Millay."

"You agree I should go."

I turned back towards her and saw a look of anguish on her face. "No. I'm sorry. The lines came into my head. I only meant I understand how you feel."

"What should I do?"

"What do you want me to say?"

"What I *want* you to say," she responded, this time with bitterness, "is that everything will work out, that everything will be fine, if I'll just be patient. That's what David would tell me, isn't it?"

"Yes. Look, Sarah," I said, exasperation tinging my voice, "life doesn't come with guarantees, for anyone." I hated being in that position, refereeing between David and his women. I would have promised myself not to do it again, except that I knew myself too well.

She stood up and walked towards me, needing to bridge the distance between us. "If you were me, you'd refuse to go to Christmas lunch, wouldn't you? If you were me, you'd agree to do that film. You'd pack up your baby, and go wherever it was for however long it took. You wouldn't let your career go."

"I don't know what I'd do. When you love people, it's hard, it's almost impossible, not to do what they ask. That's why it's important not to love the wrong people; and even more important not to ask the wrong things."

"God, I'm trying to be sensible, but I love him so much. It frightens me how much I love him. Everything that used to seem important to me doesn't anymore. People and things I've cared about all my life I don't even think about now. I only think about him. I know I should leave, but how can I when I'm not sure anything else really matters to me, not my work, not even my baby?"

"You're beautiful, you're talented, you're successful. You're a strong woman, Sarah. You're all those things without David. I can't tell you to leave him. I won't tell you to stay. How can I? It's your life. You have to make up your own mind about how you want to live it. All I will tell you is that, either way, it would be better if you didn't love him quite so much."

"Sometimes I wish I didn't love him at all," she said. And, finally, the tears began to stream down her face. I put my arms around her to comfort her as I had Caroline just a few days before and I thought, strangely enough, about Ned. Or, rather, about Ned and me.

"You know what the problem is?" he had said to me one night before the Christmas truce, "you don't love me enough. It's that simple. You don't."

"Then I'll never love anyone enough," I retorted, hurt that he should underestimate what I felt for him.

"That's too bad," he said. "That's really too bad, not just for me, but for you."

Was it? I wondered, as I held Sarah. Was it too bad? I felt an incredible soaring of my spirit, followed immediately by an ache in my chest.

❧ *Chapter 20* ❧

On Christmas Eve, I was still working with the lab on the Grenada photographs. Finally, at about three, exhausted and bleary-eyed, Stu Richards, the technician, declared them as good as they were ever going to get. We donned our sheepskins and went across the street for a celebratory drink. Then I took a taxi crosstown to the *Vogue* offices, and delivered the photographs to Ellis Miller, who'd already had a merry lunch and was just getting into the swing of a Christmas party. He thought they were wonderful. "Trust you, Nikki," he said. "All we expected was sea and sand, asses and tits. These are fabulous. They've got a quality of danger that's almost, well, erotic." He continued in that vein for a while, as I sat there beaming, attributing his enthusiasm to alcoholic goodwill. It was only months later, when I opened a copy of *Vogue* and saw the photographs laid out, page after page of them, that I understood what he meant. By pushing the light to compensate for the flatness in the original negatives, by cropping ruthlessly to get some originality into the composition, Stu and I had managed to add an element of strangeness, of menace. The photographs showed exactly what I had felt about Grenada when I was there. Later, when the island erupted into revolution, I wasn't surprised.

By the time I left *Vogue*, it was dark. The air was cold and crisp, the atmosphere was electric. Crowds of frenzied people were buying last-minute Christmas presents before hurrying home to the evening's festivities. A bag lady, pushing a shopping cart packed with her worldly possessions, including a large red parasol strapped to its side, walked past me. I gave her my gloves because her hands were bare and chapped with cold, and put a twenty-dollar bill into the collection basket at the corner where the Salvation Army was singing "Silent Night." I called Stu to tell him the good news, bought some roasted chestnuts from a street vendor, and took the Madison Avenue bus uptown to Ned's.

When I got there, Duncan and Cassandra had already arrived. "You're late," greeted Cassandra. "We have to go soon," she added, sounding aggrieved. They were taking a plane that night to Los Angeles.

"There were no cabs. I had to take a bus. Sorry." I kissed everyone hello, said no to a drink, and sat, smiling guiltily at Ned, who smiled blandly back at me. Since Cassandra was not one of his favorite people, I really shouldn't have inflicted the afternoon on him, but she had been determined to see him before leaving town. Not that she liked him a lot either. It was just that, as my friend, she felt it her duty to try. "He's so *good*," she had explained to me once, "he positively oozes morality. I like to remind myself occasionally that men like him do exist. I should think, though, he'd be death to be married to. He has so many high principles, such a lot of rules to follow. You're not really thinking of doing it, darling, are you?"

"You're looking particularly lovely today. You're beaming, in fact," complimented Duncan, looking at me appraisingly over his glass of whiskey.

"They liked my photographs," I explained. "I never think they will. And when they do, I feel, well... I feel like the ugly ducking transformed into a swan."

"Silly girl," retorted Cassandra, her voice filling the room. "You're extremely talented, darling. Why shouldn't they love your photographs?"

"Don't you ever suffer from nerves?" I asked.

"Nerves? Oh that's different. Everyone suffers from nerves."

"David called," said Ned. "He wants you to call him immediately."

"I'm not speaking to him," I replied.

"He said you were to call him anyway," Ned said, grinning, as he handed me a glass of red wine.

There was a Christmas wreath of holly tied with plaid ribbon over the mantel, and on the glass coffee table was a white poinsettia. The Christmas tree stood against the window, its blue lights blinking a cheery message into the street. Underneath were piles of packages in motley. One had been opened, and a paperweight, elegantly simple in design, lay peeking out of tissue paper in a blue Tiffany box. "I do love Christmas," I said.

"Don't tell me David's finally gone too far," said Cassandra with unrepressed curiosity. "I thought you forgave him everything in advance."

"I saw Sarah yesterday. I thought she looked ghastly," said Duncan.

"Did you?" Cassandra's smile was firmly fixed, her voice set at casual. "Of course, I only saw her for a few seconds, before I had to leave. Duncan and she had lunch," she explained parenthetically to Ned and me. "I had a meeting, with the Martex people. She looked ravishing, I thought."

"She looked done up," insisted Duncan.

And Ned looked uncomfortable, as he always did when caught in confused emotional currents. The preceding April his parents had celebrated fifty years of marriage, all of them felicitous, so he claimed. He wasn't fool enough to believe that everyone's love life could be arranged so neatly, but what he perceived as the deliberate emotional untidiness of people like David and Sarah, Duncan and Cassandra, bewildered and angered him. I often angered him. "Would anyone like another drink?" he asked, hoping to change the subject.

"Thank you," said Duncan, giving him his glass. But he wasn't to be diverted. "In the few weeks since she's left London, Sarah's aged ten years. Haven't you noticed?" He looked at me pointedly.

"No," I lied.

"She'd be doing herself a favor," he continued, not for a minute believing me, "if she'd take that film she's been offered. They called her again, you know. I told her she was a fool to turn it down."

"I can understand her not wanting to be away from David for such a long time," said Cassandra, taking a sip of the wine Ned handed her.

"Don't talk rubbish," said Duncan impatiently. "It's a good part. And if you ask me, she needs to get away from David."

"But nobody *is* asking you, so do be quiet, darling."

"What the bloody hell," snapped Duncan, "do you mean by that?"

"I'm just pointing out," continued Cassandra, refusing to be intimidated, "that it's not your business anymore, is it, to worry about what Sarah does with her life?"

"I don't intend to stand idly by and watch her wreck it, if that's what you want."

"You know what I want. I want you to think about me for a change, worry about *me*."

Duncan laughed, harshly. "That would be as much use as worrying about a tornado instead of the town it was about to ravage."

"Are Nikki and I inhibiting you?" asked Ned. "Would you like us to leave so you could really get down to it?" Considering how irritated I knew he was, his voice was very even, very reasonable. There was even an edge of humor.

"What?" said Cassandra. She looked at Ned blankly, then reacted more to his smile than his words. "Oh, darlings, sorry. How awful of us. The trouble is both Duncan and I can never resist a good row."

She didn't seem the least embarrassed, and neither did Duncan. "It's good exercise for the mind. And the mouth," he said.

The phone rang, and Ned got up to answer it. "If it's David, I'm not here," I called after him. He went into his study to have the call privately.

"Have you and David really quarreled?" asked Cassandra. "About what?" I sidestepped the question, she pressed for a bit, then let it go. "By the way," she boomed in her equivalent of a whisper, "guess who's on his way to Los Angeles? Simon! He's just been set to direct his first Hollywood feature. Isn't that absolutely fabulous? He called last night to tell us. He's over the moon. He sends his love, darling. And an invitation to come out to Los Angeles anytime you like."

It was the first message he'd sent to me in any form. "I hate Los Angeles," I said. Has he told everyone? I wondered. I, of course, had only told David.

"It's David, again," said Ned, returning.

"You told him I was here," I said accusingly.

"There was no point in my lying. You'll talk to him eventually anyway. It might as well be now."

I got to my feet. "This won't take long," I said. I walked through the guest bedroom to the study. Behind me I could hear Cassandra and Duncan vying to keep Ned amused, determined to convince him their quarrel had just been part of the jolly good times they enjoyed together.

"David," I said into the phone, without preamble, "leave me alone."

"Ned said Duncan and Cassandra are there."

"Yes."

"That bastard's been at Sarah to take the movie."

"I really don't want to talk to you, especially not about Sarah. Or Caroline."

"Can you come to my father's on Christmas Day?" he asked, ignoring me. Back in his voice was that anxious, pained quality that had been missing the last time we spoke.

"No. Absolutely not."

"I could use your help."

"David, I'm going to hang up now."

"Sarah's going to leave me."

"If we're not careful, David, we're going to ruin this friendship along with your love life."

"Come tomorrow, please. You can help me keep the peace."

"No," I said and replaced the receiver.

Ned was much more relaxed when I returned to the living room. He was telling Duncan and Cassandra about his fight to free Regis Boyle, and they were listening with surprising interest.

"How can you be so sure he's innocent?" asked Duncan.

"Whoever killed the shopkeeper had access, that's certain. But it wasn't Regis."

"How can you *know*?" persisted Duncan. "I've played heroes and villains, murderers, innocent men wrongly accused, guilty men never suspected, and all very convincingly. How can you be certain your Mr. Boyle isn't just a very clever actor?"

"Are you as good an actor offstage as on?" Ned asked.

Duncan looked at me. Was he thinking, as I was, about that scene I'd watched him play with Sarah? He smiled. "Nearly," he said. "I'm never unself-conscious. I usually know what effect I want to achieve. Sometimes, though, I miscalculate."

"That's what liars always do," replied Ned. "They miscalculate. I don't think Regis Boyle is lying."

I sat quietly, observing the two men: Duncan large and powerful, with his wonderful sexy voice and devious playful manner; and Ned, younger, slighter, but eminently trustworthy, firmness of purpose evident in every word and gesture. I had sat next to him at a dinner party five years before and had been convinced he wasn't my type. I was still convinced of that. But I had managed somehow, against my better judgment, to fall in love with him. I could never have loved Duncan. Not just because I found him all lovely surface and no substance, but ... why? Because we weren't linked in some preternatural way? Because, as David joked, our scents were inimical? Obviously, he smelled just fine to Cassandra.

She looked at her watch. "Darling, we have to leave this minute, or we'll miss our plane." She stood, rising impressively like a massive kite, displaying the full splendor of her blue-and-black flowered jersey dress. "Do you like it?" she asked. "I'll have one sent to you. But in red-and-orange, with your coloring."

"Good luck with the movie," I said to Duncan.

"Look after Sarah," he whispered into my ear, as he kissed me goodbye.

"Come see us in Los Angeles," boomed Cassandra, as she hugged me. "You, too, of course," she added as an afterthought to Ned.

"That's a lovely paperweight," I said, as we hurriedly tidied up after Cassandra and Duncan. We were due at Ned's parents for dinner and still had to stop at my place for a change of clothes and my presents for the Contis and my brother's family. "Who's it from?" I asked.

"Mary Kenny," he replied, with just a hint of strain in his voice. "She stopped by the office today."

"And what did you give her?" I said, though I knew I shouldn't.

"A book on Florence. She's going to Italy in May."

"Italy," I repeated. "Why Italy?" I inquired snidely, as if her only interest in the country could be to inveigle herself further into Ned's esteem. His pride in the land of his forebears was notorious, and though I normally considered it an endearing trait, at the moment I thought it ludicrous. "Why doesn't she go to Ireland?"

"Because the Uffizi's not there," he replied. "Anyway, she went to Ireland last year. Who's this Simon Cassandra mentioned?" he added quickly, as much to change the subject as out of any real curiosity.

I wasn't prepared for the question. Though I knew there was only the remotest chance he hadn't heard Cassandra's whisper, I'd been sidetracked by Mary Kenny out of mustering a plausible explanation. "Just someone I met in London last year." I said it all wrong. I miscalculated the tone of my voice, and Ned was too used to cross-examining witnesses not to notice.

"Just someone?" he repeated.

"He directed David's play. They're very good friends," I supplied. "He's known Sarah forever." Annoyance was creeping into my tone. It seemed unfair to me to be interrogated now for an offense committed so long ago, for reasons I could hardly remember, for a pleasure I could barely recall. "We had dinner a few times," I added, unnecessarily. Disastrously.

"You never mentioned him before."

Mentally, I cursed Cassandra, though Ned hadn't in fact been made suspicious by anything she'd said. I'd accomplished that all on my own. "I never mentioned it because I forgot. Because it wasn't important." I carried the glasses into the kitchen, Ned hot on my heels, and began putting them into the dishwasher.

"Come off it, Nikki, please. For chrissake, do you think I don't know when you're lying?"

"I'm not lying," I replied, outraged. I hadn't been—in so many words.

"Did you sleep with him?"

"I have better sense than to ask you that about Mary Kenny," I shot back.

"You know you don't have to ask me. You know you can trust me."

The justice of that hurt far more than a wrong accusation would have done. I had too good a conscience to be proud of my deceit, though not a good enough one to be convinced it was wrong. I wasn't about to concede. I slammed the door of the dishwasher and turned to face him. "And you don't trust me!"

"Let's just say you operate on a system of principles I can't always follow."

"What about your principles?" I said. "Don't you think it's wrong to encourage that woman when you have no intention of following through? I'll give you the benefit of the doubt and assume that is your intention," I added bitchily.

"Mary? Encouraging her?" He was as amazed as he was angered by the attack. "How am I encouraging her?"

"Buying her presents, for one thing."

"A present. A book. In the same category as candy and flowers, friendly but impersonal."

"Books are *not* impersonal."

"This is ridiculous. There is nothing, absolutely nothing, going on between Mary Kenny and me."

"You want her to think there could be. You want to keep her around, admiring you, flattering your ego. That's what men do, they promise and then they don't deliver." It occurred to me, somewhere in the midst of all the rage, that I was lashing out at David as much as at Ned.

But because there was some truth in my accusation, Ned—even more furious than I—struck back. "But you, you're different. You deliver. Is that what you're trying to tell me? But what? Not fidelity, not loyalty, not commitment. Sex, that's all you deliver, as I'm sure your friend Simon discovered. And it's not enough. At least it's not enough for me."

We were both too furious to stop. Ned, hurt by my betrayal, and I, suffering the anguish of guilt, took refuge in rage and hurled accusations back and forth. We raked up old quarrels, old disappointments, we tilled every piece of dirt in our relationship. We indulged in the sort of orgy of recrimination we'd always despised others for enjoying. We reached that peak of resentment from which nothing was visible below but bleakness and devastation.

When I couldn't bear any more, I got my coat and went, leaving everything unresolved, abandoning Ned to his grievance. I didn't even have the strength to go to bed when I got home. I lay on the couch and stared at the mocking lights of the Christmas tree, weeping, waiting for the phone to ring.

It didn't.

❧ *Chapter 21* ❧

Christmas Day was barely a glimmer when I forced myself off the couch and into the bathroom to take a shower. I patched the damage to my face as best I could, drank a cup of strong black coffee, gathered the Collier presents up from under the tree, carried them to the nearby garage where I kept my car, and drove the sixty-odd miles to my brother's house on Long Island. The weather was good, there was little traffic at that hour, and so nothing along the familiar route distracted me from the contemplation of my sins. I replayed the scene between Ned and me over and over, finding each time yet something else to have said or done to have allayed his suspicions. Had my subconscious finally resorted to sheer stupidity to end the relationship? I wondered. It was hard to believe. I didn't want the relationship to end. I wanted it to go on, as it was. The cosmic unfairness of it all overwhelmed me. My sleeping with Simon had convinced me of how much I wanted Ned. How absurd, how infuriating, eighteen months later, when it was nothing but a vague memory, to have it be the thing to drive Ned and me finally apart. I knew he wouldn't forgive me.

My brother lived in St. James, in a red frame farmhouse that pre-dated the Revolutionary War. Mike had bought the old farm soon after he joined the faculty at the State University at Stony Brook. He'd sold most of the land to developers, modernized the house, converted the barn into a garage, and planted hemlock hedges and chestnut trees to

176

screen his remaining two acres from encroaching neighbors. His wife, Pam, had done the interior in a tasteful mix of contemporary sofas and chairs with early American country furniture. It was all very pretty, very comfortable, and normally I loved to visit.

As I turned from the quiet country road into the gravel drive, my nephews came riding towards me on shiny new bikes. "Where's Ned?" they asked as they kissed me hello.

"He's not coming," I replied. "We had a fight," I added in response to the same question from the rest of my family. They were in the kitchen, having breakfast. My mother's face tightened with disapproval, my father's with concern.

They had flown in from Florida a few weeks before. Ned and I had picked them up at the airport and taken them out to dinner. "Have you set a date yet?" my mother had asked when we were alone in the ladies' room. Her skin, at sixty, was virtually unlined, and she rinsed her hair a soft auburn color. She was tall and thin like me, the same height as my father. He looked like Eugene O'Neill in that famous Karsh photograph. When my father died, my mother stopped coloring her hair. She died two years later.

I shook my head. "There's plenty of time," I replied.

"He's a good man," she said as she dabbed powder on her nose. "You won't find better. I don't know what you're waiting for."

"Have you spoken to Mr. Walton?" I asked to change the subject. Immediately, I regretted it.

"He called us a few days ago. We're having dinner next week. He's heartbroken about David. And I don't blame him. Leaving two little girls like that. David always was a wild one. I'd hoped his marriage would settle him a little." She snapped her compact shut and put it in her purse.

"Don't you expect a little too much of marriage?"

"I expected a lot of mine," she said. "And I got it." She had, too, by being a model wife, a ministering angel, a supportive helpmate, a good pal, an attentive lover. She had, over the years, at every turn, sublimated her own desires and got satisfaction from satisfying my father's. She was an admirable woman, and I wasn't the least bit like her. I was like my father, selfish.

"Maybe if I talk to him?" suggested my father, as I arranged the presents I'd brought under the tree.

"I think it would be better if Ned and I both had a little time to calm down," I said.

"It's a pity for Ned to miss Christmas," added my mother, "because of some silly little fight."

"If I know my sister," said Mike, "it wasn't a little fight. She doesn't have them often, but when she does . . ." He grinned at me, wanting to cheer me up.

"Don't tease, Mike," cautioned Pam, the family peacemaker. "Nikki isn't in the mood. What would you like to drink?" she asked.

"Eggnog. Please." I was determined at least to try to have a nice day. I looked more closely at the manger, the one Mike and I had had as children. The angel was missing from the rooftop. "Where's the angel?" I asked.

"Mikie dropped it."

"Can it be fixed?"

My brother shook his head, and again, suddenly, I felt like crying.

Pam handed me the eggnog. "Mikie feels awful about it. He was lifting the angel out of its box and it just fell out of his hands. He couldn't stop crying."

My brother and I had quarreled over possession of the manger, and he looked at me guiltily. "Accidents happen," I said, with as much grace as I could muster. After all, who was I to blame my nephew for smashing only a statue?

Somehow I got through the day, even enjoying some of it. Pam's sister and her family joined us, and the children's pleasure in Christmas was so unrestrained it was contagious. But once the presents were opened and the turkey eaten, I felt the usual lassitude set in. The day wasn't over, but Christmas was. The morning's excitement had dissipated not into contentment but into boredom. The adults turned cranky. The children began to quarrel. I gave up trying to keep my mood at bay. Ignoring my parents' and brother's insistence I spend the night, I got back into my car and drove home. They thought I was too unhappy to be alone: I was, in fact, too unhappy to be with people. Most people, that is. I would have welcomed David's company. And his advice.

No sooner had I hung my coat on the rack in the hall than the buzzer shattered the quiet, and the doorman, like God answering my prayer, announced David. A spark of pleasure began to battle for life, but it was immediately snuffed by the realization that David's arrival boded no good. Unless something awful had happened, my apartment was the last place he'd appear on Christmas night.

Looking at all the unopened Conti presents under the tree, seeing Ned's big box in its shiny foil wrapping and big green bow lying there reproaching me, I grew more and more annoyed as I waited for the doorbell to ring. How dare David come and burden me with his problems when I'm so miserable, I thought. That he didn't know about my misery didn't seem a mitigating circumstance. Nor did the fact that moments before I had desperately wanted his comfort make me feel more disposed to offer him any. Preoccupied with the shambles I'd made of my own life, I wasn't in the mood to hear what further insult he'd offered to Sarah and Caroline. There seemed to be a limit to the amount of destructiveness, self or otherwise, I could tolerate at one time, and I was past it.

By the time I opened the door, I was ready to send him back to whatever woman he'd just come from without even a cup of coffee. "If you've done anything terrible, I don't want to hear about it," I said. "Not tonight."

"Let me come in, Nikki." He looked awful. I stepped back and opened the door wider. He took off his sheepskin coat and hung it next to mine. "How about a drink?"

"Red wine?"

"Do you have any brandy?" I was surprised. I hadn't seen him drink more than wine in a long time. I poured him a brandy. "Have one yourself," he said. "You look as if you could use it."

I poured one for myself and took a sip. "Let's go to a movie," I suggested. "Let's go see *Nicholas and Alexandra*. It's long." In a movie, we wouldn't have to talk. We could offer each other the comfort of our presence, without the concomitant words. For the first time in my relationship with David, silence was what I wanted from him, and what I was prepared to give.

He shook his head. He took a package of Gauloises from the pocket of his flannel shirt, extracted a cigarette, and lit it. "Nikki . . ." He stopped as if searching for the right words. That, too, was surprising. David was never at a loss for words. Whatever it is, I thought wearily, must be really awful. "Ned's been hurt. He was out in the street playing football with his sister's kids. A car skidded out of control, on a patch of ice, and hit him." It was so far from what I had expected to hear that at first I felt nothing. "He has a ruptured spleen. They're operating now."

"Are the children all right?"

David nodded. "Nobody else was hurt."

I began to cry. David put down his glass and took me in his arms. Fear and guilt and grief all combined to make the most awful ache in my chest.

"Do you know where he is? I want to go."

David didn't argue. We put our coats back on and walked the few blocks to the garage where my car was parked. If it had been in my power, I would have extinguished every Christmas light in the city, in the country, in the world. "Give me your keys," said David. I handed them to him and, without protest, let him get behind the wheel of the car. I needed him with me.

Soon after I'd left, David told me, the Contis had called my brother's house hoping to find me there. It was Mike who'd phoned David and asked him to meet me at my apartment to tell me about the accident. Everyone thought I shouldn't be alone when I heard. Everyone was right.

"Ned and I had a fight yesterday," I said to David as we hurtled up the West Side Drive towards Connecticut. I could see Christmas-tree lights blinking on and off in the windows of the apartment buildings across the river.

"Mike told me."

"It was about Simon Wroth. I was so stupid. Everything I said somehow just convinced Ned I'd been unfaithful."

"The accident wasn't your fault," said David. "Thinking it is is only melodrama."

"I know," I said, though I didn't at that moment really believe it.

Mr. and Mrs. Conti were still at the hospital when David and I arrived. They were sitting at the far end of the lounge, on an orange leatherette sofa, looking gray and small and dazed with misery. Ned was their only son, and they idolized him. As did his sister, Barbara, who sat next to her mother, holding her hand.

"They're still operating," said Barbara.

"It's been so long," said Mrs. Conti.

"One of the doctors came out a little while ago and said everything was going as well as could be expected." Although she looked terrified, for her parents' benefit, Barbara kept her voice resolutely optimistic.

"There's nothing we can do but hope for the best," added Mr. Conti softly. His grief was so overwhelming he could hardly speak. He stared at the brightly colored landscape on the wall opposite as if trying to memorize its every detail. I doubt he even saw it.

Mrs. Conti began to sob. "Mama, Mama. Shhh," soothed Barbara. "Ned will be all right."

"If you want to go," I said to David, "I'll be okay now."

He shook his head. "I'll stay."

We sat with the Contis, saying little at first, but gradually, thanks to David, some of the look of dumb despair seemed to fade from their faces. He got them talking about Ned, listened patiently to their endless stories, added a few of his own, and once even coaxed a smile from Mrs. Conti. When it wasn't blunted by self-interest, David's power to heal was impressive. He knew just what to say or do to draw the pain, leaving you peaceful and full of hope.

Finally, the operation was over and Ned was taken into the recovery room. We were allowed to see him briefly, I suppose to convince us he was still alive. He was ashen. An IV fed into his arm and oxygen into his nose. Wires ran from points of his body to monitoring machines. There was a large bandage taped over his left eye. Apparently he'd received a cut from a piece of flying glass. He was lucky he wasn't blinded. He was lucky he wasn't dead. Yet.

The surgeon who'd operated on Ned explained the situation to us. He was pale with exhaustion, his face reflecting the green of his gown. His hair stood up on end, as if he'd been running his fingers through it. He needed a shave. What a rotten Christmas he's had, I thought, and then was surprised at how many irrelevant details managed to get through the densest wall of grief. It would be hours, he told us, before we could be certain Ned would live.

Barbara persuaded the Contis to go home and try to rest. She would drop them off, she told me, stop in to check on her husband and children, and come right back. The children were very upset. I persuaded her to get some sleep herself first, and promised to call if there was any change.

David stayed with me. We sat in the lounge talking, drinking coffee from a machine, waiting for someone to appear with news.

"If he dies," I said, not sure how I meant to finish the sentence. But the idea of Ned's dying was so awful I had to say the words. David took my hand and sat quietly, holding it.

At about six in the morning, a nurse entered, but only to say that a Mary Kenny was calling and wanted to speak to a member of the family. I went to the phone and repeated what the nurse had already told her, that Ned's condition was still critical and it might be hours before we'd know anything more.

"Would you mind," she said, "if I called again later?" Her voice was tense with the effort of trying to keep her pain out of it.

"No," I said. "No, of course not. If you give me your number, I'll call you, as soon as there's any news."

"Would you? Oh, thanks."

"How did she know?" asked David when I returned to the lounge.

"Barbara must have called Ned's partners. One of the wives is a friend of hers. Apparently everyone in the world knows she's in love with him."

"Does Ned?"

"He says they're just good friends." We both grinned, the first time in all that long night. "She's so perfect for him it hurts."

"Nobody's perfect."

"She could give him exactly the kind of life he wants. If he lives," I added.

"For chrissake, Nikki. Don't start pretending to be noble. At least tell yourself the truth. You're afraid of not getting the life *you* want."

"All right," I said angrily. "That's true. But that doesn't mean I don't care about what's best for Ned. That doesn't mean I don't love him."

David wrapped his arms around me. I resisted for a moment. "Of course you do," he said. I let myself lean into him, letting him hold me. "That's why you should marry him. You know, it may not turn out to be as bad as you imagine."

"If he lives, maybe . . ." I said. "If he still wants to."

Resting against David, I fell into a light sleep, only to start awake about ten minutes later when the surgeon entered the lounge. He, too, had had a little sleep. His face had lost some of its green color. His hair lay neatly in place. As my heart seized up with terror at what he was about to say, I thought, he's shaved. But then he told us Ned was out of danger and I felt, rolling through me, the most miraculous wave of relief, of joy, which receded a moment later leaving me feeling only exhausted.

I phoned the Contis and Barbara, and my brother, Mike. Finally I phoned Mary Kenny. "Thank you," she murmured. Her voice was thick and nasal, as if she'd been crying. "It was very kind of you to call me."

Then I went in and spent a few moments alone with Ned. His color was better. I sat next to him and touched his hand. Eventually his eyes opened. He looked at me and smiled. "Hello, darling," I said. He's forgotten how angry he is with me, I thought. But he'll remember. He's certain to remember.

❧ *Chapter 22* ❧

Most of the next week I spent visiting Ned. I'd had few business appointments anyway in those days after Christmas, and those I did have
I canceled. Which in retrospect was a mistake. There's nothing so distracting as work, and I needed distracting.

Ned was polite to me, but no more. It wasn't just his weakness, or
my imagination, because his manner to his parents, to his sister and
brother-in-law, was totally different: warmer, less guarded. If he didn't
bar me from the room, it was because he didn't have the strength yet to
quarrel. And because, I liked to think, running along parallel, just
underneath his anger, was his love.

He had a steady stream of visitors: uncles, aunts, and cousins from his
voluminous Italian family; partners and associates from his law firm;
members of various peace groups; politicians from New York and Al-
bany; Mike and Pam with my nephews; my parents; David and Sarah;
Regis Boyle's mother; so many people. His room overflowed with
flowers and balloons, with baskets of fruit and boxes of candy. I had no
idea so many cared about him. I don't think he did either.

One afternoon Mary Kenny arrived, bringing with her another young
man, this one intense and bearded, involved with her in the peace
movement. I sat there, a warm smile fixed on my face, watching her as
she watched Ned, trying to reassure herself that he was indeed going to
be all right. Ned joked with her, a little self-consciously (no doubt due

to my presence), until gradually she relaxed and began to look almost happy, almost delighted, to be able to spend time with him, no matter what the pretext. They talked about the bombing of North Vietnam, about the peace marches that were going on all over the country. Her friend looked at me occasionally, a little embarrassed, I suppose wondering what I made of Mary's behavior.

That's chutzpah, I thought. If we were married, she wouldn't dare come here and behave this way.

But you're not married, I argued. And you've no one to blame for that but yourself.

Soon even Ned began to show the strain, and I suggested politely that they go. Then, before (I hoped) Ned could notice I was in a rage, I too left. Fuck him, I thought, he's welcome to her. At that moment, I hated her. I hated her single-minded devotion to him. I hated her puppy-dog appreciation of every look and word he bestowed on her. I hated her pretty face and perfect body. Most of all, I hated her willingness to make him happy.

From the hospital I drove directly to David and Sarah's apartment, parked the car illegally, and asked the doorman to keep an eye on it. Mrs. T let me in. She was a woman in her early fifties, plump and matronly, with white hair, startling blue eyes, and a northern lilt to her voice. Like Margaret Rutherford playing Miss Marples, she exuded affability and common sense. Widowed and childless, she had adopted Sarah for her own and looked after her, and David, with a fierce protectiveness. I never heard her refer to either of them by their first names. "Miss Cope's in the sitting room," she told me. "Mr. Walton's not come in yet."

The apartment was decorated with multitudinous pots of white poinsettias. A spray of mistletoe hung from a chandelier. A large fir tree with twinkling candlelights stood in the corner near the mantel. On the coffee table was a small bouquet of fragile white snowdrops.

Sarah, in white cashmere pants and sweater, looking delicate as the flowers, sat in the middle of the floor playing with Mark. She looked up and smiled as I entered. "David's casting again," she said. They were building an unsteady structure with the fabric blocks I'd given the baby for Christmas. Rather, Sarah was building it. Mark kept swinging his arms and knocking it over, laughing happily every time it toppled. Just like his father, I thought unkindly. "You look dreadful," she said. "Would you like a drink? Maybe some coffee? Mrs. T, be a dear and make us some coffee, please. Ned is all right, isn't he?" she asked.

"Ned's fine. He's being released from the hospital next week. He has remarkable powers of recovery, the doctor said."

"Mummy, more," demanded Mark.

"He's mad about these blocks," she said.

I watched her play with him, envying her his soft roundness. He toppled the blocks and chortled with delight. "Fall down," he said.

"You ungrateful little wretch," she reprimanded him fondly, "after Mummy worked so hard to build you a lovely house." She swept him up into her arms. "He thinks destruction is the point of every game we play," she said to me. She held him aloft and butted his stomach gently with her head. "Don't you, you little imp?" Mark laughed and grabbed at her hair with his hands. "I hope it's just a phase he's going through."

Mrs. T brought in the coffee, then took Mark out of Sarah's ams. "Time for bathing, lovey," she cooed. He yelled with fury as she carried him from the room.

"I don't know why he does that," said Sarah, frowning after him. "He's dotty about her, really." She poured the coffee into the china cups and offered me a cookie. "Would you like a biscuit?" she asked.

I shook my head, settled into the couch, and asked her to tell me what had happened Christmas Day. I'd asked David at some point in the past week, but he'd put me off. "Everything's fine," he assured me. "Under control. You don't have to worry about anything but Ned. And yourself." I wasn't optimistic enough, or dumb enough, to have believed him.

Sarah had decided finally, she told me, to do what David wanted and spend Christmas at the Waltons. But it wasn't, as Philip Keating says, totally missing the point, to rub Caroline 's nose in defeat, or crow over the vanquished family. It was too soon for that. She went to do battle.

By the time Sarah and Mark got to Mr. Walton's everyone else was there. "David staged-managed it beautifully," she said, a rueful admiration in her voice. He had gone earlier to pick up Lissie and Kate and was at his father's when she arrived.

Sarah's plan of action was to be reasonable. She understood that the breakup of David's marriage had come as a great shock to his family, and she knew they blamed her for it. Their opinion demeaned her, she felt, not because it wasn't—on the obvious level—warranted, but because it failed to take into account who else she was, the sacrifices she'd had to make, or the destruction that had been wrought in her own life. Neither did it reckon the fierceness of her attachment to David, the overwhelming richness of her love for him. Those were things she was certain David's family could not understand, were in fact *determined* not to understand, so she had no intention of wasting time and energy in vain attempts to vindicate herself or her actions. There was no point in letting them see how resentful she felt at being cast in the role of the Other Woman, a character without nuance, without depth or complexity. She would be content, she decided, if she could make them accept if not forgive her; though, since people had been falling at her feet since she was a child trying to win *her* approval, she would have been surprised—she confessed—if she couldn't make the Waltons like her even in her role as *femme fatale*.

It was, after all, easier than she'd anticipated.

Although David had bullied his father into meeting Sarah, Mr. Walton made no promises about how he would act when he did. And because he was upset and embarrassed, he behaved at first as could be expected: badly. He resisted the temptation to verbal abuse (which must have been very hard for him) but was cold and withdrawn, hardly speaking to Sarah and ignoring Mark. Which made David furious, of course. Several times, Sarah headed off a fight. Gradually, though, Mr. Walton began to soften. Sarah looked like an angel and acted like a lady: she was hard to resist.

Trudi was, to Sarah's surprise, even easier. Her dislike was based on the idea of Sarah as a grasping, predatory woman. But Sarah failed to live up to the image. Despite having made Jack take her to see one of Sarah's films (a fact which David had told me at some point), Trudi had still been expecting if not the physical equivalent of Jayne Mansfield, at least the moral analog of plunging neckline and heaving breasts. Against all odds, Sarah not only seemed nice, she was nice.

Jack, as honorable as David was not, went out of his way to make Sarah feel at home. So did Ken, Claudia's husband, though for different reasons. In his usual tasteless fashion, he flirted; and Claudia, David's younger sister, was so grateful for Sarah's ability to be both unresponsive and kind that she became an instant friend. She had, anyway, always loathed Caroline.

Only Lissie resisted her. Trying hard, Sarah had won a grudging smile from Kate, but Lissie kept her distance. She adored Mark and was delighted to have a little brother now as well as a little sister. But Sarah she refused even to acknowledge.

The worst moment of the day came, as expected, when Caroline was due at any moment and it was time for Sarah to leave. Sarah's condition for going to the lunch, her nonnegotiable condition, had been that David leave with her. It was that which was to demonstrate to his family (and to her) that he'd made a choice, a final choice, and it was Sarah. If he didn't, she warned, she would go immediately to the airport with Mark and take the night flight to London. It would be over between them. David believed her.

When he came out of his father's bedroom, carrying Mark bundled into a snowsuit, David was wearing his coat.

"Where are you going?" asked his father.

"Home," said David.

"But Caroline will be here any minute."

"I'll see her tomorrow." Lissie began to cry. "I'll see you first thing in the morning, sweetheart. Don't cry," soothed David. But that didn't quiet her. He looked at Sarah, silently begging her for permission to stay.

She felt as if a cold hand were slowly squeezing her heart. She felt pity for the crying child. She felt anger at David for having put her in this position. She was afraid that if she didn't force him to choose now, she'd lose him forever. She was afraid that if she did, she might anyway.

"Tell him to stay," said Mr. Walton to Sarah, assuming rightly that hers was the deciding vote.

"David knows he can go or stay as he likes." She tried to keep her voice even, but there was a tremor of emotion she couldn't control.

Trudi began, out of instinct, to offer an opinion but, catching a signal from Jack, shut up. He gathered his boys and Claudia's children and took them into another room, out of the line of fire, to play. "I'll take Sarah and Mark home, if that's what you're worried about," offered Ken.

David handed Mark to Sarah, and she began to tremble. He's going to stay, she thought. He really is going to stay. But he only knelt to kiss Kate and give Lissie a hug. "I'll be there to see you tomorrow, baby, first thing. I promise."

"He didn't keep his promise," I remembered. "He was with me, at the hospital."

Sarah nodded. "It's so awful not being able to live with your children. It really is so awful. I do understand. But there wasn't anything else I could do, was there? If I hadn't made him choose, he would have gone on forever, dithering, making us all miserable." She spread her hands beseechingly, but didn't wait for me to answer: she knew she was right. "We didn't talk all the way home, in the taxi. We couldn't talk. And when we walked in here, the phone was ringing. It was your brother, and David left immediately to tell you about Ned. When we did finally speak, the next night, when I tried to tell him how sorry I was, all he'd say was that I was right." She smiled at me. "At least he understood, didn't he, why I had to be so hard? David always understands."

We heard the door open and shut, the clatter of keys as David dropped them on the table in the hall. Sarah called to him and a moment later he entered the room. I instantly felt less tired, invigorated by the surge of energy that preceded him everywhere. The light that Sarah gave off increased in intensity as he leaned over to kiss her. "Did it go well, darling?" she asked.

"Brilliantly," he said. "Richard Drew is set to play Jimmy. And I heard this afternoon that Don Badham wants to do *The King of Rome.*" Both men were already established "names" as well as fine actors, and David had been fighting for weeks to get them. He kissed my cheek. "How's Ned?"

"Fine," I replied shortly, and he knew by my tone something was wrong. He looked at me questioningly: did I want to talk? I didn't. "I am, too," I added.

Mrs. T brought Mark in and we all fussed over the baby for a while, then David put him to bed and the three of us went out to dinner. Arms linked, like schoolchildren, we walked down Central Park West. David was in a wonderful mood, his personal problems for the moment forgotten as he allowed himself to enjoy the success his work was having.

"What are you doing tomorrow night?" he asked.

I realized, with a jolt, he meant New Year's Eve. I'd lost all track of time. "I'm not sure. I haven't decided." Ned and I had been invited to some glitzy party by one of the *Vogue* editors and to a black-tie dance by one of the partners in his law firm; Mike and Pam had asked us, as always, to their usual neighborhood bash. I wasn't in the mood for any of them. "I think this year I may just go to bed with a good book."

"Come with us," said David, who was immediately seconded by Sarah. They'd been invited to a gala evening by someone on the board at Lincoln Center.

"You just want to impress me with how important you suddenly are. You want me to witness how those theatrical types fawn all over you," I teased.

"Exactly," said David, a big grin lighting his face. "How else am I going to get you to take me seriously?" he said, knowing no one in all his life had ever taken him more seriously than I.

Since we were celebrating, we went to the Café Marmottan, on West 64th Street. We'd been eating there from the early sixties, as often as we could scrape the money together to afford it, and some old friend, waiting on tables or handling the desk, could always be relied on to find us a table. We liked its frescoed walls and gilded mirrors, all a bit shabby but cozy, like its chipped pottery plates and hearty Norman cooking.

Tessa Hoffmann, a friend of mine, a writer, came in with her husband, an actor who'd appeared off-Broadway in one of David's plays. They joined us and we ordered another bottle of wine. And another. The conversation, at first, as always, revolved around David's life and work, then almost bogged down in the morass of Vietnam until I declared that subject off-limits and David encouraged us instead to trash Philip Dow's current best-selling novel. It was the one called *Not in Vain* and like all Dow's books was trite and sentimental and successful. Some doctors, said David, insisted a chapter of Dow's books worked better for the glucose tolerance test than a dose of pure maple syrup. Hypoglycemia, then, was fast becoming the illness of choice.

Sarah watched him as he talked, her face glowing with contentment. Tessa tried flirting with him, and David, instinctively, responded, but with amusement, not real interest. Sexually, he was obsessed by Sarah. He touched her constantly, almost unconsciously, taking her hand, letting it go, putting an arm around her shoulder, running his fingers through her hair.

We were all in good spirits when we left the restaurant, all of us a little bit high, and I let David and Sarah talk me into returning to their apartment for a nightcap. I suppose the last few days had been so bleak for me, I was reluctant to let the happy mood go.

I should have quit while I was ahead.

On the table in the hall, propped against the Chinese lamp so that it was impossible to miss, was a large envelope.

"It's addressed to you," said Sarah to David. "It must have come by messenger while we were out. How curious." She smiled at me. "You Americans never stop work."

"Klein, Lefrak, Miller, and Woolf," said David. "It must be the contract for *The King of Rome*." Sarah and I followed him into the living room.

"What's everyone having to drink?" asked Sarah.

"More wine, please," I said.

"Same here," echoed David. He had ripped open the envelope and begun to read the covering letter. "Jesus Christ!" he exploded. "I saw that bitch this afternoon and she never said a word."

"What is it? What's wrong?" David went on reading. "David, for God's sake, what's the matter?" Sarah's eyes were wide and her voice afraid.

"Here." He thrust the papers at her and looked at me. His eyes were blazing with rage. "Caroline's suing me for divorce. In New York State. Naming Sarah."

"Oh, God," sighed Sarah, relieved. "Is that all?" She scanned the letter briefly.

"She was planning this all week, and she didn't tell me." David sounded outraged, betrayed.

I could imagine why not: she was afraid he'd manage to talk her out of it.

"I thought something awful had happened," said Sarah.

"Don't you understand?" said David, turning on her. "Or are you too stupid to understand? Can't you see she's about to take my children away from me?"

"I understand perfectly." She straightened her back a little, trying not to bow under the weight of the insult. "It's you who don't understand."

David didn't answer. He turned and started out of the room. Sarah went after him and stopped him.

I knew I should go. But I didn't know how to exit. I didn't know how to get past Sarah and David at the door.

"Where are you going?" she asked.

"Where do you think? To see Caroline."

"Now? At this hour?"

"If I can't sleep, why should she?"

"And what will you do when you get there? Fight with her? Make love to her? What? What will you do to change her mind?"

"I can't let her divorce me."

"Why not?"

David pushed her away. "Let me go."

Sarah clung to him. "I can't," she cried. "I can't let you go."

"Dammit, let me go!' He pushed her again, and this time she staggered back from him and fell.

"David, for chrissake," I muttered.

But Sarah was up again, lurching after him, grabbing him before he reached the door. "Think about what you're doing. Think!"

"I know what I'm doing."

I wouldn't have thought Sarah was strong enough to keep him from leaving, but she was succeeding, holding him back with a furious grip.

"You can't have both of us," she said. "You can't. If you go to Caroline, you'll lose me. And Mark. If you stay, you'll lose her. That's how it is. Can't you see that? If not tonight, then tomorrow night, or next week, or next month. David, can't you see that? You can't keep us all." He didn't answer, but he stopped struggling. "Caroline thought you made your decision on Christmas Day," continued Sarah, more softly. "So did I. Oh, God, David, don't make us keep playing the same scene over and over." She let go of him, finally, and took a couple of steps backwards. I could see her face. The anger receded, and the fear, until only a terrible weariness remained. "Don't you love me? Don't you want to be with me?" she asked.

David reached out and took hold of her. He pulled her into his arms and buried his face in her hair. "Oh Christ," he said. "Oh Christ."

They were no longer blocking the doorway. I walked past them quietly, got my coat, and left.

Vienna
August/September 1979

❧ Chapter 23 ❧

My first encounter with Vienna, "city of love and sparkling wine," was not felicitous. The air conditioning had failed on the British Airways flight; I had stomach cramps; there were no porters to be found, and I had to wrestle my luggage and camera equipment on my own past unsympathetic airline personnel and customs officers. If a woman is foolhardy enough to travel without a man, they seemed silently to opine, she should be willing to take the consequences. It was not that I was unused to hefting, I was just not in the mood: my stomach hurt. Which was why I was even happier than usual to see David, long and lean and dark, dragging on a Gauloise, towering over the broad flaxen natives in the airport lobby.

It was the summer of 1979 and *The King of Rome* was being filmed on location in Europe. Most of it was shot in Prague, a city not much ravaged by modernity, with the production moving to Vienna, where the film was set, only in August to complete a few key scenes. David had been suggesting for months, in letters and phone calls, that I take a short vacation, visit him, and watch some of the filming. I was ambivalent, the excruciating boredom of a film set weighing heavily against my desire to see him. But I'd had to go to London on business, and when he'd phoned me there, the suggestion sounded more like a plea. "Christ, Nikki, it's only a two-hour flight from London to Vienna. I'm not asking you to trek to Siberia."

I was in that energy slough between the end of one bit of work and the beginning of the next; I also had a few weeks' leeway before I absolutely had to be back in New York; I had no good reason to say no to him, and I didn't.

"That's my pal," he said, sounding suddenly very pleased.

"Don't expect me to hang around the set. If you haven't got a real job to do, it's about as much fun as a cricket match."

He laughed. "I'll fix it so that you can take pictures," he added magnanimously. "That ought to keep you happy."

The King of Rome, a little to everyone's surprise, had been a smash hit when it opened at the Village Globe in Manhattan in the spring of 1972. We had all known it was good. It was the most finished play that David had yet written, the most totally integrated, the most powerful and poetic, the most accessible; but no one expected the public to be very interested in a historical drama about an unknown young man who accomplished absolutely nothing in his short, tragic life. The producers, it was generally assumed, mounted the play not as an economic venture but as a bid for critical acclaim. Even with Don Badham, who played the lead onstage, they expected no more than a respectable, money-losing run. But when the critics raved, the audiences flocked to see it. The play transferred to Broadway and ran for close to two years, then for six months in Los Angeles. There was a national tour, a London production, a Stockholm production, a Berlin production. The film rights were bought by an important independent producer for a sum of money so large I can never remember it. The play made David rich and famous. It did the same for the play's director and its cast.

With hindsight, I can understand what it was about *The King of Rome* that made it so appealing to an audience. The production was excellent, epic in fact, and the performances almost uniformly brilliant, but it was to the play itself that the public responded, to the story of a young man of extraordinary ability condemned by his place in history to be a nonentity.

The turn-of-the-century French play *L'Aiglon* was based on the same character, Napoleon's son, and it, too, was enormously successful, primarily as a vehicle for Sarah Bernhardt. But Rostand's play was a historical drama in the romantic style, dealing with a single critical event in the young Napoleon's life. David's was both a sprawling epic and a psychological study. It was a paradigm of the struggle of Everyman against a relentless and obdurate Fate.

King of Rome at birth, and Napoleon II, Emperor of the French, when his father abdicated, Napoleon's son was stripped of both titles before he was old enough to say them. In their place, he got the fabricated title Duke of Reichstadt, which carried with it no lands, no money, and no power. Even his first given name, his father's name, was dropped in favor of Franz, in honor of his grandfather, the Austrian emperor. Forbidden to go with Napoleon into exile, the four-year-old child was soon abandoned by his mother at the imperial court in Vienna. There this handsome, charming, intelligent boy grew and worked and studied with a surprising lack of bitterness, in almost complete obscurity, waiting for his chance to enter the mainstream of history. But no sooner would an opportunity arise than it was snatched from him by his archnemesis, Prince Metternich, terrified of the destabilizing effect he feared another Napoleon would have on Europe.

In the play's last scene, the twenty-one-year old Franz, dying of tuberculosis in the room at Schönbrunn Castle in which his father had once slept, forgives Metternich for denying him the chance to live his life at its full potential, giving the drama its grand cathartic moment, the moment we all yearn for, the moment when we can give up the struggle to make something of our lives and surrender finally, peacefully, to death. "Oh, what you might have been, had I let you," pities Metternich. And yet the question niggles, how much did the King of Rome collude in his own fate? Was Metternich really his destiny, or was he perhaps poor Franz's superego?

In May of 1973, a year after the play's opening at the Village Globe, a week after his divorce from Caroline became final, David and Sarah were married. I was a witness at the wedding, as was Simon Wroth, who, since directing *Dreams in F Minor*, had become a good friend of David's, as well as Sarah's.

Although we were late for the registry office, I posed David and Sarah against the pale pink climbing rose growing against the wall at the far end of the garden in Sarah's Chelsea house. They smiled into each other's eyes, the turbulence of the past three years forgotten. From the kitchen came the sound of two-and-a-half-year-old Mark arguing with Mrs. T about whether or not he was allowed a biscuit at that time of the morning. Under Sarah's cream-colored silk skirt was the slight bulge of Olivia, who was to be born the following October.

"I love you," said Sarah, her eyes glistening with happiness.

"I love you," said David.

"I don't know why you want to get married and ruin it all," derided Simon from the doorway where he watched. But he didn't mean it. Even he was convinced these two were fated for each other.

I snapped a soft-focus filter on my lens and continued shooting. Sometimes it doesn't pay to see the details too clearly.

David took my bags and signaled to a porter who had miraculously appeared.

"Chauvinist pig," I muttered.

"You're in a great mood," observed David. "On the rag?"

"I *hate* that expression."

"I know." He grinned. "You look wonderful."

"I'm successful," I replied. "God, it's good to see you." He looked handsome and rich, confident and happy. But there was a wrong note somewhere. Why, I wondered, had he been so anxious to see me?

We followed the porter outside into the hazy August sunshine. It was hot and humid, and within seconds my cotton dress felt damp against my body. "Ugh," I said.

"You can have a swim as soon as we get to the villa." David led the way to a black Porsche and opened its trunk for the porter.

"Very nice," I admired.

"Courtesy of Paragon Films," said David. He laughed. "Paragon Films. What a name. Here's hoping they live up to it."

"How's it going?"

"They want to change the title. It's too confusing, they say. 'How can a film called *The King of Rome* be set in Vienna?'" he mimicked. "Life's confusing, I told them. I once wanted to call it *Le Fils de l'Homme*. Do you remember?" I shook my head. "It's the title of a poem some French Bonapartist wrote about young Franz. That title says everything. But it's so pretentious calling an American play by a French name. A pity I have such good taste. Put on your seat belt," he cautioned. "It's the law, and this is a very law-abiding country." When he had steered us out of the parking lot, he reached over and took my hand. "I'm glad you could come. Austria's beautiful. Incredibly beautiful. You should see it."

"I did see it," I said, "in *The Sound of Music*."

He laughed. "There's more to life than pictures," he said. He smiled at me, and, as always, his excitement was contagious. My stomach began to feel better, my mood to lighten. He reached into his pocket for the ever-present package of Gauloises.

"I'll be sick if you smoke in the car," I threatened.

He put the packet away. "Someday I'll give these up. How was London?" he asked.

"Terrific. I brought you an autographed copy of the book." I had been in London for the publication of a book on the sculptor Ronald Graves, for which I'd done the photographs and Tessa Hoffmann had written the text. "Autographed by Ronald, that is. The publishers expect it to be a big Christmas seller."

"If you were a real friend, you would have got me an autographed statue."

"Why? You can afford to buy one now."

"I can afford to buy two," he corrected, and we both laughed.

Gossiping, mostly about our families in New York, we drove for a while through a nondescript suburb, remarkable only for its bland similarity to all roads leading into and out of all major airports, then along a stretch of muddy-green Danube lined with nineteenth-century buildings in a monochromatic tan. These grew steadily more baroque until, finally, we were out of the city and into a landscape of rolling hills and gentle forests. We passed through a pretty village which seemed lifted from the pages of a travel brochure. Just beyond it, David turned into a narrow road, then into a graveled drive. He stopped the car in front of a small white stucco villa with a gabled roof and wooden shutters at every window. I use the term "small" to distinguish it from the mansions which abounded in the vicinity: in fact, it had eight bedrooms. The villa was set in a lush swell of green lawn, dotted picturesquely with shade trees, and screened from its neighbors by a towering hedge. I remember everything seeming incredibly neat, unbelievably tidy: not a blade of grass too long, not a stray leaf marring the lush perfection of the lawn, not one dying flower in the beds bordering the house.

"Enjoy the peace while you can," said David, as he took the bags from the car. "Everyone's out. They've gone to the wildlife park. 'Der Lainzer Tiergarten,'" he declaimed slowly, drawing out the syllables, delighting in their foreign sound.

"Are you learning German?" I asked, surprised. It was not a language that had much appeal for me.

"A word here and there. The Austrian accent is interesting, softer than the German. It has a lilt I like. It reminds me of Schubert." He handed me the camera equipment out of the trunk and grabbed my suitcases. "But I've been too busy this summer to study seriously."

"Have you started the new play?"

He shrugged. "I've done a few scenes. I haven't had much time. I'm rewriting as we shoot. And acting. It's harder work than you think, even doing a small part." David had not only written the film script based on his play, but was appearing in the movie as well, in a small character part, playing Count Adam Neipperg, Marie Louise's lover. "Plus, all my kids have been here." He turned and grinned, a flicker of pure joy in his eyes. "You think it's easy having a family?"

"Me? Never."

"You don't know what you're missing."

The Walton household at this point was extensive. Lissie and Kate were, as usual, spending the summer with their father. In addition to Mark and Olivia, David and Sarah had had another child, Nicholas, now four. There was Mrs. T, whose official title was still housekeeper, though, in fact, she functioned as the perfect granny: efficient, loving, and unobtrusive. Will, a reformed alcoholic whom David had collected somewhere along the way, usually lived nearby and was employed both for odd jobs by the Waltons and in some minor capacity on any production with which David was involved. On *The King of Rome*, he was a driver. The newest addition to the household was a Breton girl named Marie-Paule, whom I'd not yet met. She'd been hired at the beginning of that summer as an au pair to help Mrs. T with the children.

And Sarah was once again pregnant. When David had told me in New York in the spring just before leaving for Europe, he had seen the dismay register on my face. "But Simon told me she was going to play Marie Louise," I said.

"She wanted another baby," replied David, his eyes shuttered against me.

"Why now?"

"Goddammit, don't judge everybody by yourself," he snapped. "Not everybody's obsessed by work. Some women like children. Some women want to have them."

The interior of the house was bright and cheerful with polished wood floors, whitewashed walls, and timbered ceilings. Doorframes and chair rails, banisters and chimneypieces were all in worked wood. There were few pictures on the walls, and most of those were facile oil renderings of majestic landscapes. All the windows were open, and the hazy golden light filtered in, together with birdcalls from the garden. Vases of cut flowers, roses, daisies, dahlias, and others I didn't know the names of, all brilliantly colored, were everywhere.

"Do you want to go upstairs and change, or do you want a cold drink?" asked David.

"How about both?"

"David? Nikki?" The voice was Sarah's and it came from the back of the house. "Is that you?"

David put down the suitcases and, without looking at me, walked through the sitting room, through the French doors, and out onto a patio. I followed him.

"I thought you were going to the wildlife park," I heard him say.

"I was. But I had a headache."

"You were fine when I left." In his voice was a note of suspicion, of accusation. I had never before heard it directed at Sarah.

"And I'm fine now. I took something the doctor gave me." She closed the book she had been reading and put it aside. David picked up the drink lying on the table beside her and took a sip. "Don't do that," she snapped. "I can't bear it when you do that." She looked beyond him, to me, standing in the doorway, and smiled. "Nikki, darling, I'm so glad you've come. How good to see you."

Her voice flowed towards me like honey from a spoon, and I approached her, smiling, barely conscious that its lemon-edge was more pronounced than usual. I leaned over and kissed her cheek, which was still flawless, as smooth and cool as porcelain. She was six months pregnant and radiant with it, her belly rising like the moon out of a sundress that was the color of a sunset in summer. "Will you let me photograph you while I'm here?" I asked. "You're exquisite."

"I'm fat," she returned, shifting her weight a little, so that she rested on her left hip. She was lying on a white wicker chaise, against pillows of pale blue. A printed silk shawl was draped across the top. In the hazy golden light, she looked like a painting I had seen somewhere in my travels, by Palma Vecchio, I think, called something like *Nymph in a Landscape*.

"She's beautiful," said David, pouring us each a glass of lemonade from the pitcher on the table.

"He likes me pregnant," commented Sarah dryly, smoothing her dress over her round stomach. "That's strange, isn't it? I always thought a man would loathe his wife's being pregnant."

"You don't know anything about men," said David.

"Who does?" I asked.

"Helen Gurley Brown," he replied, deadpan. I laughed. "I've learned most of what I know about being a real man in *Cosmopolitan*."

Despite his joking, I could still hear a worried note in David's voice. And so could Sarah. "Well, I confess I don't like being pregnant, but I do like the babies," she said, trying to keep the mood light, "even if I can't frolic with them like the giant child my husband can be," she added. "Even if I do get headaches and can't go with them to the wildlife park as promised. You would like a swim, wouldn't you?" she went on, efficiently changing the subject. "Here I am, babbling on about nothing, and you both look as if you're about to drop with the heat. David, would you show Nikki where everything is? You don't mind, do you?" she said, again looking at me. "I'm feeling too lazy to move. Hurry and change. It's delicious out here." She gestured beyond the patio to the stone-edged pool that looked like a pond landscaped into the enormous garden. This was much less tidy than the front, with children's toys scattered everywhere, and a rubber raft left floating on the water. At the far end was a cutting garden, where Sarah culled the flowers to decorate the house. "I think I'd be happy just to lie here forever."

I finished my lemonade and followed David back into the house and up the polished wood stairs and along the cool white corridor to my room. It, too, was bright and cheerful, with a double bed covered in a yellow flowered print and matching curtains at the windows.

"This is lovely," I said, looking out the window, across the back garden to the hills beyond, dotted with houses resembling—from that perspective—the pretty ceramic keepsakes sold in souvenir shops. In the distance, I could see a tiny village.

"Heiligenstadt," said David, in answer to my question, savoring the sound. "Beethoven once lived there."

"It's so peaceful here."

"You won't think so when the hellions start playing water tag."

"Whose house is it?"

He told me a very long, very impressive name, which I didn't recognize. "He's a diplomat, in Washington right now. He's a member of the Courland family," added David, with glee.

I looked at him blankly. "And who are the Courlands?"

He seemed, as usual, surprised that I should be so ignorant of something so commonplace to him. "The Courland Whores," he explained. "A mother and four daughters who were variously and consecutively mistresses to Metternich, Talleryand, Czar Alexander, et cetera. An interesting family." For close to ten years, since he'd begun researching *The King of Rome*, David had spent a good deal of time living imaginatively in early-nineteenth-century Europe. Sometimes I had the feeling those people were as real to him as the cast of *General Hospital* were to my sister-in-law, as real as any of the rest of us, Sarah, his children, his friends. Or, looked at the other way, sometimes I felt that none of us were anything more to him than star players in the drama of his life.

He turned to go, but I stopped him. "Are you going to tell me why you wanted me to come?"

"What makes you think I have an ulterior motive? I missed you, that's all. I wanted to see you."

"David, I've known you for a long time . . ."

"You're my friend, dammit. I like to see you occasionally."

I remembered the times I had wanted David near me: the night Ned was hit by a car, the day he married Mary Kenny. I thought of how he'd held me when my parents died. "What's so bad you can't tell me about it?" I asked.

"I'm worried about Sarah," he said finally. He sprawled in the armchair near the window. "Something's wrong, but I don't know what."

"Have you asked her?"

"Of course I've asked her," he replied impatiently. "She says I'm imagining things. She says she's fine. She's not. She's drinking. She usually stops when she's pregnant, but this time she won't. Or can't. And her headaches? They arrive very conveniently, just in time to keep her from doing anything she doesn't want to do. The doctors can't find a thing wrong. I've been so busy, I think maybe they're a way of getting my attention. Maybe she's bored with nothing to do all day but read and pick flowers. Maybe she's lonely with no one to talk to but Mrs. T and the children. I've asked her if she wants to go home, to New York, or maybe to London, but she says anywhere would be worse without me."

"Do you want her to go?"

"Are you crazy? You know I go nuts away from her and the kids. I'd hate being here on my own. Goddammit, other women are happy with their husbands and children around, why can't she be?"

"She seems a little on edge," I conceded. "But unhappy?"

"When she's not angry, she's withdrawn. Most of the time she's so remote I can't reach her."

"That happens to pregnant women sometimes," I said reassuringly. "They become very focused on their interior life. The way writers do," I added to make my point.

"I don't want her remote. I want her here. I need her here. With me."

"Maybe she feels the same about you."

"I am here, goddammit. As here as I can be. I have work to do."

"And you want me to keep her cheerful in your absence? You want me to keep her occupied?"

"Yes."

"And to keep her from drinking?"

"I don't want you to be a watchdog, if that's what you're worried about. If I needed one, I've got Mrs. T. If Sarah's happy, she won't drink."

"I can't stay long, David. I have a job in New York I have to get back for."

"I wouldn't dream of interfering with your work."

"Don't start."

"I won't," he said, as apologetically as he could manage. "I'm worried, Nikki, and I want you here, for as long as you can stay. It's that simple. Now, hurry up and change. I bet you a hundred schillings I can beat you in a twenty-lap race."

"I won't bet real money on that. I know you can beat me."

"I'll give you a five-lap advantage," he said, smiling, and he left the room.

I looked out the window again and saw that Sarah had moved after all. A straw hat on her head, she was in the garden cutting roses. She jerked back her hand, as if in pain, then put a finger into her mouth to soothe it. A moment later, she lifted the hand and covered her eyes. I could see her shoulders shaking. Pregnant women are often moody, I told myself, with the expertise of extensive reading, with the experience of several friends in mind. Sarah's only crying because her hormones are out of kilter.

But, somehow, I didn't believe myself.

❧ *Chapter 24* ❧

Early the next morning, before any of the rest of us were awake, David left for the location. Even when he wasn't in a scene, he liked to be there as much as possible in case a problem should arise, which happens with relentless frequency during the making of a film.

Generally, writers are not welcome on a set: their presence seems to query the dogma of the absolute power of the director. But as long as they keep a low profile and do as they're told—that is, make requested alterations obediently and well—they're allowed to hang around. Should they venture an opinion, however, or (heaven forfend) object to a change, they are castigated as stubborn and obstructive, destructive and petulant, and are instantly barred from the set.

Most writers labeled with a reputation for being difficult don't deserve it. David did. When threatened with not getting his own way, he could cause enough psychic blood to flow to make Al Capone look like a nice guy. Yet, it wasn't just his charm, his "charisma" as Mr. Keating likes to call it, that made his producers and directors not only tolerate but welcome his presence. When he chose to be, David was as adept solving problems as he was creating them. With the accuracy of a laser, he could isolate the difficulty and excise it. His doubts, his fears, his insecurities he hid from all but a few of us. On a film set, in a theater, there was nothing but positive energy flowing from him, total conviction that his way was the right way. Consequently, few people were inclined to argue, and most were relieved to have someone around with sufficient balls to make a decision and take whatever fallout might result.

David was like a tornado that sucked up everything in his path. But though many were drawn to him by that power of personality, a relationship was possible in only one of two ways: either you acknowledged his intellectual, artistic, or physical superiority and so played satellite to his sun; or you declared yourself an equal and, like a Knight of the Round Table, were prepared to defend your claim in combat anytime David should throw down the gauntlet. Each way was fraught with danger. The first contained the possibility of being swamped by his gravitational pull. The second was exhausting. But to both groups, David was a loyal and benevolent and sympathetic friend. The only people he despised were the ones who challenged him and failed.

For a long time, I considered Simon Wroth safe in the second category. He was no straw man, no pushover, but he and David had seemed to evolve over the years an easy working relationship, so the set of *The King of Rome*, which Simon was directing, was relatively trouble-free when I arrived in Vienna. "He watches my ass," said Simon, accurately. "I'd pay money out of my own pocket to keep him around."

As for me, I like to think my friendship with David was also in the latter category, but can't be completely sure. I admired him too much, loved him too well. I forgave him everything. But then, David did the same for me. It wasn't his fault there was so much less to forgive me for.

As I stood knee-deep in the pool that Monday morning, in the warm August sun, with all David's children splashing around me, trying to teach young Nicholas to swim, I was pondering whether or not David's ability to solve problems was merely an extension of his will to get his own way; considering whether or not his present problem was real or manufactured for the sake of drama; and, if so, why he could not feel satisfied now that he had more success, more money, and finally even more children than his brother Jack, more than anyone else he knew, excluding an occasional Saudi Arabian prince who happened to cross his path.

"Mommy, Mommy, watch!" called Nicholas, who had spotted Sarah coming towards us from the house. "I can do it myself. Let me go," he commanded. He was wearing little inflated wings on his arms and, as soon as I released him, swam unaided the few feet to the edge of the pool and smiled up at Sarah. "I can swim," he said.

"So I see. That's wonderful, darling." She wore a flounced black bathing suit trimmed in silver, belted low on the hips like a flapper's dress.

"Did Cassandra do that?" I asked.

Sarah nodded. "She made it specially for me. She is a darling, isn't she? I do like her. I was very upset when she and Duncan were divorced." Cassandra and Duncan had married, finally, in 1974. The marriage had lasted four years, longer at least than I'd expected.

"Have you met his new wife?"

"Yes." Sarah smiled ruefully. "She's twenty," she said as if that said it all.

Lissie broke off the game of water tag she was playing with the others and swam down to us. "Do you want us to get out of the pool so you can exercise?" she asked Sarah.

"Thank you, darling, but no. I'm going to sit for a while. You go on playing." As the relieved Lissie swam off to rejoin the game, Sarah looked after her fondly. "She's the most considerate child I've ever met," she said.

Lissie that summer was twelve, tall and lean, with breasts just beginning to bud, but otherwise the same confident and loving child she'd always been. There was no trace of the stutter that had worried David and Caroline at the time of their separation. Her sister, Kate, was eight years old, and much more like their mother in temperament. She was a somber little thing, still prone to illness. Caroline had made several attempts to move herself and the girls to California, where she thought the better weather might help, but always David's will had prevailed and they had stayed on in New York to be near him. Mark was only a month older than Kate, but he towered over her, and she adored him; in fact, the only two beings in the world Kate seemed to care anything about were her half brother Mark and her father, both of whom teased and bullied but returned her love unstintingly. Olivia, at six, was a miniature of Sarah, with blond hair and large brown eyes, her emotions quick and terrible, moving from rage to laughter and back within seconds. Four-year-old Nicholas was the most like David, cocky and charming, curious about everything, with an oddly metaphysical bent to his mind. "See me!" he'd demand when he was being ignored, as if he understood that getting someone to look wasn't even half the battle. All the children, with the exception of Nicholas, who was too young, attended the Lycée Français in New York, David's theory being that he could then move to any major city in the world anytime it was necessary and his children not miss a day of school. The Lycée's curriculum was standard all over the world, the same lessons always taught on the same day. In reality, David often ended up where there was no Lycée, with only Sarah for company, the children left at home in New York with Caroline and Mrs. T to care for them. David rarely went anywhere without Sarah.

Nicholas toddling after me, I climbed out of the pool and joined Sarah on the patio. She wrapped her son in a towel and rubbed him dry, planting kisses all over his face and neck as she did. "Mommy, stop," he demanded imperiously. "I'm too big for kisses."

"Who told you that?" she asked, a little surprised by his declaration.

"Mark. He said kissing was for babies."

"Well, he's wrong, isn't he?" said Sarah, drawing me into the discussion.

"Nobody's too big for kissing," I declared solemnly.

"Not even Daddy," added Sarah, planting another kiss on the top of his nose. He looked uncertain, torn between the desire to believe his mother and an unquestioning faith in the wisdom of his older brother. He was saved from having to reach a conclusion by Olivia. Bored with the game of water tag, she arrived to claim Nicholas's attention.

"Do you want to play in the sandbox? I'll help you build a castle," she wheedled. He nodded and ran happily after her to the painted box at the side of the yard.

"Mark's at that misogynist stage," said Sarah. "I don't know what to do about it."

"Nothing," I suggested, settling myself comfortably into one of the wicker lounges. "He'll outgrow it."

"Nothing," repeated Sarah. "That's what I usually do."

Marie-Paule came out of the house carrying a tray with a pitcher of lemonade and some plastic tumblers. She was about seventeen then, plump, with round steel-rimmed glasses worn far back on a sharp nose, and lank dark hair fastened severely behind with a barrette. Her walk was awkward, as if she hadn't yet learned to coordinate arms and legs. "Is there something else you would like?" she asked in timid, heavily accented English as she put the tray on the table between us. The glance she bestowed on her employer was laden with adoration. Sarah's luminous beauty was all she aspired to and would never achieve. What would it be like, I wondered, to have that effect on people, to be able to captivate by the power of beauty alone? Not that Sarah didn't have more, much more, to recommend her, but people did usually succumb before they ever realized that.

"Not a thing, Marie-Paule, thank you. You're an angel. What are the children having for lunch?"

I watched Sarah covertly as she discussed domestic business first with the au pair, then with Mrs. T, who came bustling out of the house with vitamin pills, which she insisted Sarah take immediately. Among them, they decided the lunch menu, the dinner menu, and how to keep the children occupied during the long lazy afternoon. Sarah seemed less tense to me than she had the day before, less on edge. When the other two went back into the house, Sarah turned to me and smiled. "I am glad you're here. I adore Mrs. T but she is inclined to fuss, and Marie-Paule may be sweet but she is also incredibly dull. It's good to have someone to talk to." She poured us each a glass of lemonade.

"David hasn't been home a lot, I take it."

"Not a lot. No. And when he is, he's either locked in his study writing or totally preoccupied with the children. They take up such a lot of time, children, don't they?"

"I suppose that's why I never had any," I said. She was talking about emotional and psychological time, I knew. Since Mrs. T and Marie-Paule took care of all the commonplace chores of child-rearing, Sarah was spared that drudgery. On the other hand, she was also denied its concomitant joys and the satisfaction of knowing she was an absolute necessity to her children. And with the children taken care of and her career largely abandoned, she was left with only one real outlet for all her energy, all her talent: David.

"It's very hard," she agreed. "I love them so. And yet?" She shook her head, then changed the subject. "Are you going to watch any of the filming?"

"Later in the week. Have you seen any?"

"A little. I really don't like to watch. A film set's awfully boring, don't you think, if you're not actually working?" She looked away from me and towards the children, who were now noisily playing King of the Mountain on the rubber raft. Mark was kneeling, his dark hair plastered wetly to his scalp, his body glistening with water, trying to ward off the attempts of Lissie and Kate to topple him into the pool. "Darlings, must you be so loud?" called Sarah. "Remember we have neighbors. There's lemonade here if you want it."

"In a minute, Mommy," shouted Mark, as Lissie did a shallow dive under the raft, coming up beneath it and flipping it over.

"Ow, that hurt," wailed Kate as Mark slid into her.

"Crybaby," said Mark scornfully.

"I'm not!"

"You are too!"

"I'm king!" said Lissie, scrambling up onto the raft, causing the other two to stop squabbling and get on with trying to dethrone her.

"Did you know I was going to play Marie Louise?" asked Sarah, an edge of pain in her voice. I nodded. "But then I got pregnant. I didn't mean to, really. But I spent so many years believing I couldn't have children, I never learned to be cautious. I'm terrified of pills and coils and things. And David hates it when I wear a cap. I don't much like it either, so sometimes I don't bother. And sometimes I forget. If I've been drinking, I forget. It's easy to do, isn't it?"

"No," I said. "No, it isn't. I never forget."

"It's different for you," she replied, for the first time sounding defensive. "You're so clear about what you want. I used to think I was, too. But I'm not."

"No one is," I said apologetically, looking back over the muddle that was my life. "No matter how it seems, all of us are just stumbling around in the dark, hoping we're on a path leading to somewhere, and not just walking in circles."

"Not David," said Sarah, a grim smile curving her lips.

"No," I agreed. "Not David."

"He always knows exactly what he wants. And the most extraordinary thing is, he gets it, doesn't he?"

"I know how much David wanted this child. What I don't know is how much you did."

"When I lost my last baby," she said, referring to a miscarriage she'd had two years before, "I was very upset. It was awful, Nikki. The sense of emptiness afterwards nearly overwhelmed me."

She had been depressed for months following it, cheering up only when she was offered a small part in a film Duncan was doing. Against David's advice, she took the role. He insisted she wasn't strong enough yet, and that it wasn't a good idea for her to be away from home when she was feeling so low. Sarah claimed she needed the distraction of work.

It seemed to be an excellent idea. First of all, it was shot on location in the Bahamas, which got Sarah out of the bleak New York winter and into sunshine. And then it was the kind of film which even in preproduction was much talked about, and her being cast reminded everyone that Sarah Cope was alive and well and willing to work. Since she'd got pregnant with Olivia, the only thing she'd done was a short-lived revival of *Hay Fever* in the West End. Both the production and Sarah got terrible reviews.

The film was *Calypso Bay*, one of Duncan's bigger hits, a sociopolitical drama sugar-coated with an excellent love story and heavily seasoned with adventure. Duncan played an apolitical priest drawn into conflict when he realizes that the island tribe he is working with is less in danger from sin than from a governmental policy of genocide. Not only does the tribe control the island's one natural harbor but their burial ground is sitting on top of a fortune in zinc or tin or something. Sarah played the owner of a bar in the town, madly in love with the priest, who is himself struggling mightily against his desire for one of the women in the tribe. It was all good Humphrey Bogart stuff, tough and lean, unsentimental and exciting. And Sarah was wonderful in the movie, playing against type, a cheap embittered slattern with the morals of the proverbial alley cat, who achieves at the end a kind of nobility. It is the film's ultimate irony that the priest, by providing her at last with someone worth loving, succeeds in saving her soul as he loses his own.

Sarah's part took only three weeks to film, and David was with her most of that time. He sat in the hotel room, rewriting *The Robber Baron*, which was to open in New York the following winter; or swam in the clear turquoise water that lapped gently against the island's shore; or played golf and tennis with any of the cast not scheduled to work. He especially enjoyed playing with Duncan, who provided the kind of challenge David craved. Duncan, too, played to win, and David could beat him only two out of every three times, and only then by using every atom of skill and energy he possessed.

David rarely watched any of the filming. His presence distracted Sarah. She could feel him resenting her, she told me when they returned to New York, for keeping him from his home and his children, from his study and his favorite coffee mug, from all the props he liked around him when he was writing. He returned to New York occasionally to see the children and for meetings about *The Robber Baron*, but it was even worse there, he claimed: with Sarah not around he couldn't seem to concentrate on work at all. Which, of course, succeeded in making Sarah feel more and more guilty, since his work by then had acquired totemic proportions in her mind. It also made her feel angry, though she wasn't prepared to admit that at the time. She was furious with him for spoiling her enjoyment in *her* work with his determined, smiling air of one who is bravely enduring enormous sacrifice, and by undervaluing it with his obvious assumption that his own was more important. They quarreled a lot, about everything: whether to have an early night because Sarah was due on the set at dawn, or go out on the town because David was bored from being cooped up in the room writing all day; whether Sarah was friendlier with Duncan than she had to be, or David was spending more time than he ought with one of the actresses in the cast. Their bloodiest battle happened the night David wanted to read her a scene he had just rewritten and Sarah refused to listen because she had lines to learn for the next day's filming. She lost her temper and started throwing things, breaking two lamps and a mirror before David was able to stop her. That night, for the first time since she'd started filming, she needed a tranquilizer to sleep. Luckily, she still had a few left from the prescription the doctor had given her when she'd lost the baby.

To me, David grumbled that Sarah's work was interfering with his own; but he also expressed enormous pride. He knew from the little filming he'd watched and the rushes he'd seen that her work in the film was good. More than good: superb. And he was full of praise for it. Her talent to him was as worthy of awe as her extraordinary beauty was. And the only person to whom he couldn't convey that was Sarah, either because he couldn't, or because she wouldn't hear. "The offers are going to come pouring in," he told me. "Wait and see. She's dynamite."

The offers had come pouring in, even before the film was released, but they all involved Sarah's being away from New York again, and she turned them down. When I heard, I couldn't believe it. I couldn't understand how Sarah could betray her talent like that: and that's what it seemed to me, a betrayal. After years of waste and idleness, after small attempts at salvaging her career as abortive and as hurtful as miscarrying her child had been, she'd finally succeeded. She'd got a second chance and she was throwing it away.

When I said as much to her, she looked at me as if I were mad. "I couldn't bear to be away from David and the children for any length of time," she said. "You know that. It would be awful. And David can't come with me right now, not with a play in rehearsal. Anyway, I don't seem to care much about work anymore. It's such a strain. It's so exhausting. I'm much happier being home with my husband and my babies." She said it so convincingly, I almost believed her.

Sarah's film and David's play opened in New York on the same night. There was no discussion at all about which opening any of us would attend. It was taken for granted that we would all be at the premiere of *The Robber Baron*, and we all were. After all, who among us did not believe in the superiority of the stage over film, or the playwright over the actor? If we'd believed otherwise, we would not have been David's friends.

The next day when I stopped by their townhouse to gloat over the rave reviews *The Robber Baron* had received, I saw the only tributes Sarah had been paid: a dozen red roses from her producer, an enormous cymbidium from Duncan, and a diamond necklace from David. He was always generous when he was getting what he wanted.

Finally, Sarah was offered something she would do, *The Duchess of Malfi* at the Circle in the Square. While David did not exactly encourage her, he was by then so preoccupied with rewriting the screenplay for the long-delayed film of *The King of Rome* (all the usual problems of casting and budget etc. were exacerbated by its being a "period piece") that he didn't trouble to discourage her either, and she agreed to do it.

They continued to quarrel, both their nerves strained by David's wanting and not getting Sarah's full attention, by Sarah's being torn apart by the demands of an exhausting role and the exhausting demands of her husband and children. The production itself was a failure and didn't run long, but it was a personal triumph for Sarah. It was the first time she had been seen onstage in New York, and the critics were knocked out by her.

After seeing that performance, the head of Paragon Films allowed himself to be convinced by Simon that Sarah would be perfect in the part of Marie Louise. And then she got pregnant.

"I wanted this baby very much," she said to me that Monday morning in Vienna. "You can't imagine how much. And so did David," she added. "It was extraordinary really how delighted he was when I told him. It's a wonderful feeling, isn't it, to be able to make someone you love that happy, even if it doesn't ever last?"

It was a question I couldn't answer. I didn't think that I ever had made anyone so happy. Certainly when I thought of Ned, I saw pain in his eyes more often than I saw joy. And I'd tried as hard with him as I had with anyone.

From the back of the garden, from the sandpit, came a yell. Nicholas came running towards us, crying. "She hit me!"

"I did not, you little pig," Olivia shouted, tearing after him.

"She did. She hit me."

"He smashed my castle," conceded Olivia, close enough now to clout him again on his back.

Nicholas yelled again and raced onto the patio, throwing himself across his mother.

"Stop it! Stop it at once, the two of you," said Sarah.

"She hit me," repeated Nicholas, wailing.

"He's a little pig," insisted Olivia, also starting to cry.

"I can't bear it when you fight. Stop it this minute or go to your rooms." Sarah, as usual, was helpless in the face of her children's anger. She was shaking with distress.

Mrs. T came hurrying out of the house. She picked Nicholas from Sarah's lap as if he were a puppy. "What a carry-on," she said, soothingly. "Upsetting your mother like this. You ought to know better."

She turned to glower at Olivia. "And so ought you, madam."

The children repeated their complaints as Mrs. T took them into the house, to get them out of Sarah's way until they were calmer.

"I really can't bear it when they cry," she said to me

"All children fight," I replied, since I could think of nothing more comforting to say.

"I know. I know," she said despairingly, as if she had discovered some giant flaw in herself.

"Are you all right, Mommy?" asked Mark, dripping water from the pool as he peered into her face.

"Fine, darling." Sarah smiled reassuringly.

"They'll make it up in a minute," soothed Lissie. "They're always fighting. It doesn't mean anything."

"Are you coming back in?" demanded Kate from the pool edge where she waited.

"Time for lunch," called Mrs. T from the doorway. "And don't come in without drying off. I don't want you dripping water in my kitchen."

And Sarah and I were left alone. "I'm sorry," she said. "I'm a little on edge. I don't want to take anything because of the baby."

"That's all right," I said. "I actually enjoy watching families squabble. It's the only reassurance I get about not being married, and not having children."

She didn't smile. "David thinks I'm drinking," she said, as if she hadn't heard me. "But I'm not. Or at least not much. Did he tell you I was drinking?" She looked at me and while I searched for an answer. "He did, didn't he?"

"Sarah," I began, haltingly, "really . . . "

"Did he also tell you he's having an affair?" Her eyes filled with tears. Oh Christ, I thought, not again. Please, not again.

❧ *Chapter 25* ❧

Just then, Mrs. T appeared again in the doorway and insisted Sarah and I come in immediately for lunch. And afterwards, for a long while, we were occupied with the children.

I had raided the Victoria and Albert gift shop before leaving London and had brought the girls Victorian paper dolls, Mark a paper model of a stage set, and Nicholas a coloring book. Though I suggested they leave them for a literally rainy day, they didn't want to, so Sarah and I spent the afternoon cutting and pasting and coloring. If Sarah was hopeless at disciplining her children, she was wonderful at playing with them, and we all had a lovely time, the sort of time that used to tempt me to reassess the benefits of my solitary life. The children were on their best behavior, confining their disputes to a brief exchange of malevolent looks or muttered words of warning, and gradually Sarah relaxed. Occasionally, each would go to her for a dose of attention, leaning against her for a moment, receiving a kiss in return. Only Kate kept apart.

"Come give me a cuddle, darling," coaxed Sarah. Showing little enthusiasm, Kate went to her and submitted to a hug. "Isn't she a beauty?" said Sarah. Kate had the same good looks marred by the same vaguely petulant expression I had once so disliked in her mother. Recently Caroline had looked much happier.

"Do you miss your mother?" I asked.

"No," Kate assured me solemnly.

"She phoned us Sunday," explained Lissie. "She was supposed to go away for the weekend, but she had to work." Caroline was at the time managing a boutique in SoHo.

"It's nicer here than New York," added Kate. "There's a pool here. But the ice cream is yucky."

Later in the day, Mrs. T got the children into their clothes, and Marie-Paule with Will, the driver, took them off to a nearby playground, promising to stop on the way back at one of the local "ice saloons" for some of Kate's despised ice cream. It wasn't yucky at all, as I soon learned, just different, and Kate was a child who adjusted reluctantly to change.

When they'd gone, Sarah and I got into her car (which was much less grand than David's, since the Waltons were paying for it themselves, as they were for the Volvo station wagon used to transport the children) and drove further into the hills to the Kahlenberg Heights.

Perched right at the top of the Kahlenberg is a restaurant with a porticoed terrace. It was crowded, but quiet, with the polyglot murmur of voices carried off by the light wind. There were Americans in jeans and plaid shirts; English in Khaki walking shorts and sandals; Japanese toting large camera bags; Austrians in loden and dirndl.

Sarah and I sat at a table, laid with a bright orange cloth, and ordered coffee. While we waited, she pointed out the sights, as she had intermittently on the drive, using the scenery as a device to forestall further confidences.

As always, I was curious; yet, this time, I was reluctant to hear more, not only because I knew it was sensible to keep out of the line of fire but because, as I was slowly beginning to understand, I had a large investment in the Walton marriage. Despite all the evidence to the contrary, gathered during years in their company, I still wanted them to prove to me that two talented, intelligent people could live together in love and harmony, with neither sacrificing any of their basic needs to the selfish demands of the other. I was still rooting for them to make it.

"When the Turks were besieging Vienna in 1683, Jan Sobieski and his Polish cavalry came tearing down from here," said Sarah, "across the hills, to save the city. It must have been quite a sight."

There were views I saw later in my trip that were to surpass that one, but for the moment I thought it superb. A neatly trimmed lawn sloped down to a confining hedge, beyond which were a spray of fir trees, then rolling fields, the vineyards of Dobling, and finally Vienna. To the east were the tower blocks of Uno-City, which just the week before had been formerly handed over to the Secretary General as the international headquarters for several United Nations agencies. Across the Danube from it lay the rest of the city, dominated by the baroque dome of Karls-kirche, and—poking above it all—the Gothic steeple of St. Stephen's.

"Tomorrow," continued Sarah, "we'll go sightseeing."

"I don't want you tiring yourself out on my account."

"I won't. And we'll make David come with us. There's no real rea-son he has to be on the set all day. He doesn't have a scene." She shook her head. "I'm still not quite used to the idea of his acting." There was, I thought, just a hint of irritation in her voice.

"I can go alone," I said. "I don't need a nanny."

"Don't be silly. David's the best guide in the world, I don't have to tell you that. Anyway," she added, "he invited you here. He ought to be prepared to look after you, oughtn't he?"

The waiter brought our coffees, large glass cups foaming with cream and splashed with chocolate, and placed them in front of us with a neat flourish of his white-jacketed arm.

"*Danke*," said Sarah.

"If you want me to leave, I will," I said, as soon as he had moved off to the next table.

Sarah was instantly contrite. "I didn't mean that. Truly, I didn't. You know how fond I am of you. I'm glad you're here. I just some-times think David ought to live with the consequences of his actions, that's all, instead of making decisions and leaving the rest of us to cope with them."

"You could always refuse."

"I do. At least, I think I do. I start out vehemently saying no, and somehow end up doing exactly as David wants. I'm never precisely sure how it happens, but it does. And it's the same for all of us, even you." I must have looked startled. "Isn't it?" she added.

"David's very hard to say no to," I admitted.

"Isn't he though?" replied Sarah, irony heavy in her voice.

"But I never say yes if it means giving up anything really important to me. I'm too selfish for that."

"Caroline, to this day, does everything he wants. Everything!"

Usually, when she spoke of Caroline, there was humor in Sarah's voice, a vague tinge of condescension, perhaps impatience. Never anger, never bitterness. After all, Sarah could afford to be generous: she'd been the victor in that battle. But that day there was more than anger, there was contempt.

"Caroline?" I repeated blankly.

"She wants to move to California, to Los Angeles. Did you know that?" I nodded. "She's wanted to do that for years. But now she has an idea for a business that she thinks would do well there, better than in

New York. She's even found finance for it. For months she's been making plans. Then, when she called on Sunday to talk to the children, she told David she'd decided after all not to go."

"It's not just David," I said. "It's Lissie, and Kate. She knows how upset they'd be moving away from their father."

"It's David," insisted Sarah.

"Come on, Sarah!" Now there was impatience in my voice. "You know how important those girls are to David. How important he is to them. Whatever else David may be, he's a hell of a good father."

"Is he? I wonder." She collapsed back into her chair, all her anger expended.

I had spent most of my life studying David Walton's character, and that was one aspect of it I'd never questioned. "I don't know any better," I responded. "Do you?"

She shrugged. "Sometimes," she said, "I think the children aren't individuals to him at all, with their own peculiar needs, their own special desires. I think they're the toys he needs to play father, to live up to his image of what a father should be, which is as unlike his own as possible. Other times, I think they're just the weapons he uses to keep Caroline and me exactly where he wants us."

"You don't think he's sleeping with Caroline, do you? Is that what's bothering you?"

"No, of course not."

"Because I'm sure he's not. I know he's not," I insisted.

"Though he probably would," she added, pursuing her own train of thought, "if that's what he had to do to get his way." She shook her head. "No, he's not sleeping with Caroline. He's sleeping with Fiona Brent." The name was only vaguely familiar. "The actress playing Marie Louise in the film," explained Sarah. "The actress playing *my* part." Then, suddenly, she laughed, a worrying sound full of bewilderment and rage. "Isn't life grand?" she said.

David was home when we got there, standing in the pool with the kids around him, playing King of the Mountain. He was the king, of course. Over his head, he held Kate, giggling hysterically, terror and joy combined. "No, Daddy, no!" she shrieked.

"Say who's king," he commanded.

"You are. You're the king."

"Too late," he said, as he lowered her slightly and let her drop, screaming with pleasure, gently into the water.

"Me next," demanded Nicholas, not getting the point of the game, just wanting attention. "Me next!"

As the other children attacked him in concert, throwing themselves at his chest, diving underwater to attack his legs, David swept Nicholas up into his arms. "Say who's the king!"

Sarah had sounded so certain, so absolutely convinced. But seeing David there, surrounded by his children, so happy, so obviously contented, I found it hard to believe she was right.

Perhaps that was it, I thought. Perhaps everything had been going too well, too smoothly: his reputation was established, the money rolling in, Sarah unemployed and pregnant, his children all with him, the filming on schedule and on budget. Perhaps he'd got bored, and decided to create some excitement for himself. Perhaps he'd decided to fuck Fiona Brent and drive Sarah to drink just to relieve the relentless sameness of a contented life.

"They do adore him, don't they?" said Sarah softly, either to me, or to remind herself of something she had forgotten. "He's so good with them. He knows just how to *be* to make them happy. He takes them in stride. And when he loses his temper, which isn't that often, really, they seem to know it doesn't matter." She shook her head again, as if trying to clear it. "I've been so confused lately. I get so many strange thoughts. I don't know half the time if what I'm thinking is true, or if I've made it up. I do love him, you know."

David climbed out of the pool and came towards us, dripping water. "Where have you two been? I came home early, thinking I'd find you lazing on the patio."

"To Kahlenberg," I said. "It was spectacular."

"For coffee," added Sarah. "I wanted to take Nikki to a *Heurige*," she added, untruthfully, "but she said she'd rather have coffee than wine."

David didn't rise to the bait. He dried his head with a towel and kissed both of us hello. "We should drive to Salzburg," he said, "while Nikki's here. If she thinks the view from Kahlenberg is spectacular, I want to be there when she sees the Salzkammergut."

Sarah looked at his body appraisingly. He was then thirty-nine years old, and he looked better in his racing trunks than he had ten years before. He'd been working out regularly with weights, and his hips were as slender as they'd always been, and his legs, chest, and arms more muscular. "It's unfair, isn't it," said Sarah teasingly, "that men aren't the ones who have to get pregnant?"

There was more appreciation than resentment in her tone, and David smiled. "Very," he agreed. "But you can't blame me for that."

She laughed, and for a moment I caught a glimpse of the Sarah Cope I'd met in London nine years before: working actress, star of stage and film, secure in her beauty, in her talent, in her success. I hadn't until that moment been aware of how much she had changed, of how completely she had turned into David Walton's wife, the mother of his children. When had it happened? And why? Suddenly I no longer wanted to be with them. "Excuse me," I said. "I'm exhausted. I think I'll have a nap before dinner."

"I brought you a present," David said to Sarah, as I left them. "It's there, on the table." When I reached the doorway, I stopped and looked back. David was lighting a cigarette, watching while Sarah opened a large, flat, paper-wrapped parcel, all the while regarding it without curiosity, almost angrily, her expression saying: if you think I can be bought, you're wrong. But when she saw what it was, she gasped. David smiled. "It was in the window of a gallery and I couldn't resist. I knew you'd love it." For a moment she stared unbelievingly at what she was holding, then she too smiled. It was a small painting by Jan Brueghel: miniature white and pink roses with purple lobelia on a gold salver, a bee with transparent wings hovering nearby.

"It's beautiful," she said. "Exquisite." She turned to David and kissed him. The anger had left her body. She understood the painting wasn't a payment, wasn't a bribe. He'd bought it only because he knew it would give her pleasure.

I went to my room, lay down on my bed, and thought not of David and Sarah but of Ned and Mary Kenny. Though I'd convinced myself it was best for all concerned, I had cried all day long the day they were married. David had been with me, not even trying to cheer me up, just bundling me from one movie to another, from one coffee shop to the next, and finally just sitting with me at home until I fell asleep.

Six months after they were married, they bought a house in Rye. Two months later, Mary got pregnant. A month before their son was born, she stopped working. She hadn't worked since. Two years later, they'd had a second child, another boy. Life was going exactly the way Ned wanted it.

Because I always find it impossible to give up anyone important to me, I continued to have lunch with Ned, sometimes as often as once a week. Occasionally I would go to Rye for dinner with Mary, who had somehow come to regard me as a friend. They were among the happiest people I knew.

But for that matter, so was I.

❧ *Chapter 26* ❧

The King of Rome was on location that week at the Prater. The last film of any note that had been shot there was *The Third Man* in 1949. It, of course, had featured the giant Ferris wheel which, this time around, had so far only appeared in Simon Wroth's nightmares. The wheel hadn't been built until almost seventy years after the death of young Franz, and one of Simon's biggest problems was keeping it out of his shots. That and the airplanes, the television aerials, and the tourists.

"Goddam Ferris wheel," I heard him muttering as I arrived. He was wearing khaki shorts and worn sneakers, a madras shirt hanging loose and buttoned awry, a safari hat on his head, from which trailed long strands of dark hair. "Whose idea was shooting here anyway?"

"Yours," reminded David. "You wanted to give the film a—let me see—sense of place, I think you said."

"Next time, I stay on the back lot," he replied, taking off his hat, running an impatient hand through his hair. "I'm too old for all this."

I went up beside him and slipped my arm through his. "You don't look a day over thirty-seven," I said.

He enveloped me in a bear hug. "Whatever you do," he warned, as he kissed me, "don't get in my shot. I'm having enough trouble with the fucking Ferris wheel."

"I'm glad to see you, too." I smiled.

"Where's Sarah?" asked David.

"Over there somewhere." I gestured, vaguely, towards the spot where Sarah had left me, saying she was going to find Duncan. She hadn't wanted to come at all. Film sets, she'd said, were hell for an out-of-work actor, and she'd meet us later in the city. But David had insisted, and Sarah had given in.

David's eyes raked the crowd, looking for her. They lit for a moment with pleasure as they found her, then darkened again. She was standing, looking up at Duncan, listening to him intently. At that distance, they looked as they had nine years before when I'd first met them: perfectly in tune with each other. Was David really jealous? I wondered. Was he so competitive, so possessive? Or was he merely play-acting for dramatic effect? Not that, ultimately, such distinctions ever matter.

"Come, talk to me," said Simon, pushing me into the high canvas chair beside his own. It had the name Fiona Brent stenciled on it.

The unit was setting up for that scene in the Haupt-Allee where Franz, riding with Prince Eugène de Beauharnais, encounters Metternich. Seeing him in the company of Napoleon's stepson triggers all Metternich's paranoia, and his greeting is more arctic than usual. He tells Franz that unfortunately affairs of state prevent his granting, at any time in the foreseeable future, the interview Franz has requested.

All around was that combination of intense activity and total idleness peculiar to film sets all over the world, where apparently little or no attention is paid to the fact that each minute ticking by is calculated not in seconds, but dollars. The area had been cordoned off, and the location managers patrolled to keep the curious out of the way. The electricians were rigging lights while the director of photography and the camera operator huddled in conversation. Handlers were grooming the horses needed in the scene. Costumers raced back and forth between the various trailers with odd bits of raiment over their arm. An actor called but not yet needed lay on the grass asleep with a newspaper over his face. Extras, in and out of costume, stood talking in clusters or sitting alone with books and magazines in their laps. The script girl sat off to one side studying the pages about to be shot. An assistant director argued with the chief electrician about the amount of time the setup was taking. A woman lay resting, the skirt of her dress extending in elegant flounces, her head in the lap of a man in breeches who fanned her with a piece of paper.

"Hans," shouted Simon into a megaphone. "Tell them to stand up." He pointed, an AD repeated the command in German, and the couple leaped to their feet. "They'll get grass stains on their costumes," explained Simon.

"I don't know how you do it," I said admiringly.

"What?"

"Notice everything." The details of what I had to get right when I took a picture sometimes overwhelmed me. I couldn't imagine what it must be like to be a film director running a set with its infinite capacity for error.

"I don't," replied Simon. "That's why I have a crew. Not to mention David. How was England?"

"Rainy."

"Lovely," said Simon who was, as usual, fed up with the heat. "And the book?"

"Beautiful."

"We're ready," called an AD.

"Where's Duncan?" asked Simon. I looked around. He and Sarah had disappeared. The faces stared at him blankly. "Someone call Mr. Powell," said Simon patiently. "Tell him we're ready to go." A girl took off at a sprint towards the trailers.

"Could I talk to you a minute, Simon?" asked a beautiful young boy with black hair and eyes as dark as David's. From publicity stills I'd seen, I recognized him as Joe Vasari, the actor playing Franz, the King of Rome.

"Certainly," replied Simon. "Nikki Collier, Joe Vasari," he introduced quickly. "Dinner?" he asked, as I got up to leave him with his star. "Tonight? We'll wrap about seven."

I nodded. "Do you mind if I take some pictures?"

"Not at all. Just remember to keep out of my shot," he repeated.

Joe was too impatient to wait until I was out of hearing range. "I don't think I can do the scene," I heard him tell Simon as I walked away.

"Why not?" asked Simon, sounding to me eminently reasonable.

"I just don't get it," said Joe, a note of belligerence creeping into his voice. "I mean, why wouldn't Franz confront Metternich, right then and there? Why would he wait to do it in private?"

"Because he's not a hero in a television series, is he?" suggested Simon patiently. "He's a prince. He's schooled in the art of diplomacy."

I took my Olympus out of its bag and fixed the zoom lens. Joe was seated in the chair I had vacated, one foot on the rest, one dangling to the ground, his body swiveled to face Simon's, his hands gesturing to plead his case. Simon sat relaxed, hands in pockets, head turned slightly to look at Joe. Their attitudes reminded me of a Roman fresco I'd seen once somewhere near Naples of a supplicant entreating a reluctant god. I snapped their picture and heard Simon call for David, who'd moved away to the refreshment table while I'd been talking to Simon and now stood chatting to some of the crew, the tension not yet gone from his face. At the same time I did, he saw Sarah, with Duncan in costume, crossing the grass from his trailer. Her blond hair wisped softly in the humid air, framing the fragile loveliness of her face. In her white linen sundress, she looked like a visiting fairy. Her beauty was luminous, and despite her protruding belly, men turned to stare at her as she passed.

"Be with you in a minute," he shouted as he walked instead towards Duncan and Sarah. He kissed her, then stood with an arm around her shoulder for a moment, an instinctive gesture establishing possession, while he talked to Duncan. I got that picture, too, for my personal collection. It had no commercial value. Only a few people at that point remembered (or cared) that Sarah and Duncan had once been married, and even to them the memory came as a small shock, the way it does when the present is so vivid it makes the validity of a different past difficult to accept. In most minds, Sarah and David were such a complete entity, so totally a unit, it seemed as if they'd been together forever, despite evidence like Lissie and Kate to the contrary.

Whatever David was saying made Duncan laugh in appreciation and Sarah—all her resentment, all her unhappiness, for the moment forgotten—look at him the way she always had, as if he were the handsomest, most intelligent, most wonderful man ever to have existed. If anyone ever looked at me that way, I thought, someone I loved, someone I respected, I'd be lost. I'd hand him my heart and my life, not to mention my head, on a silver platter. But that was it, the rub as they say: adoration has to be mutual or it's intensely irritating. The unrequited lover merits not only scorn but cruelty. If there is a God, perhaps He sends troubles to plague the world not because of the few who don't do Him homage, but because of the many who do Him too much. I sometimes imagine Him sitting on a cloud tinted gold by the morning sun, saying, "Take that, you whining little wimp," as He deals out diseases and plane crashes, volcano eruptions, earthquakes, and wars.

David looked at Sarah and smiled. There was not a sign of the tension I'd seen just moments before. He kissed her again and walked away to join Simon. Sarah followed him with her eyes for a moment, then saw me, and waved. She headed Duncan in my direction.

"I'd heard you were here," he said, taking my hand, his rich voice warm and welcoming. "I can't kiss you, much as I'd like to. If I muss my makeup and cause a delay, Simon will have my head."

"You look very impressive," I said. He was in riding boots and breeches, with a superbly cut coat in green wool, a patterned waistcoat, a lace cravat, and a tall hat. I stepped back and began snapping pictures.

"I'm dying of the heat," he said and smiled, turning his best side towards the camera. "I thought we were ready to start," he added impatiently.

"It appears that Mr. Vasari has called a script conference," said Sarah, gesturing towards the group David had now joined.

"Oh, Christ," muttered Duncan. "Not again."

"He's sweet, really," said Sarah. "Just very unsure of himself."

"You wouldn't think so if you had to work with him, my darling," said Duncan. "Fiona came near to slapping him the other day."

"Well, she has got a frightfully short temper, hasn't she?"

"Not as short as yours," reminded Duncan.

"Places, everyone," called an assistant director, as the group around Simon's chair finally came out of their huddle.

"Let's have a drink, Nikki, and talk," suggested Duncan. "Did you see Cassandra when you were in London?"

"Yes. She's fine," I said, exaggerating only a little.

"Duncan's terribly interested in the welfare of all his wives," said Sarah, teasing him.

"That's the truth," replied Duncan, moving off. "I care a great deal about the lot of you. Any changes?" I heard him ask the AD as he passed. He was assured there weren't and, shaking his head, continued to where his horse was being held ready for him.

"Fiona's not here right now," said Sarah when Duncan had left us. "She doesn't have a scene until later today."

"I know her name, but I don't think I've ever seen her in anything."

"You probably have. She's been in just about everything lately." Sarah didn't even try to conceal the bitterness in her voice. "She was a year behind me at RADA." She smiled at me brightly. "Everyone who used to be behind me is just shooting right past. And the ones in front are farther ahead than ever."

"Is she any good?" I asked.

"Who?" asked David as he rejoined us.

"Fiona," replied Sarah, her voice neutral.

I watched David's face to see if it betrayed anything. It didn't. "Good enough," he said. "She's in the next scene. We can stay if you want to, but I thought we'd watch this master and leave."

Sarah smiled at me. "I knew your visit would work wonders. I haven't been able to coax him away from this production in weeks."

"What would you like to see?" asked David, ignoring Sarah's remark except to put an arm around her and pull her close to him. He was determined not to quarrel.

"She must see St. Stephen's," said Sarah. "There's the most wonderful Gothic pulpit," she explained to me, "and incredible baroque altars. The whole thing is incredible, isn't it, darling?"

"The Rembrandts," I said.

"They're in the Kunsthistorisches," said David, who used every opportunity he found to say a German word. "We'll start there, go to the Sacher for coffee, and if you have any energy left, we'll tackle the Stephansdom."

"St. Stephen's Cathedral," translated Sarah. David had somehow again managed to dispel whatever black mood had possessed her, and she looked up at him with enormous amusement on her face. It was the look a proud parent might bestow on a precocious child.

"She thinks I'm a fool," he said.

"I wish I did. But in fact I think you're wonderful."

When I saw the rose-and-black marbled splendor of the museum's baroque lobby, with its soaring arches and elegant columns, its perfect harmony of space and color, it was enough for me. I think there's a limit, a very small limit, to how much beauty it is possible to see at any one time. Beyond that limit, it begins to be expected, and therefore ordinary. Which might in fact explain why there is so much ugliness in the world. If there weren't, the human race might become totally immune to beauty, unable to recognize it at all.

But I was driven as usual by fear, fear that this might be my only time in Vienna, that what I didn't accomplish now would be an opportunity lost forever, so we looked at the Rembrandts, only the Rembrandts, until we were sated; then went to the Hotel Sacher, and sat on the terrace beneath the striped awning drinking coffee and eating Sachertorte. When we were rested, we went to St. Stephen's.

"My guidebook said the interior is 'not all that interesting,'" said Sarah, gesturing widely to embrace the zany combination of elegant Gothic and wild baroque. She pointed to a carved stone pulpit. "Look at that. Marvelous, isn't it?"

"Sixteenth-century," supplied David. "By Anton Pilgram. There he is." Under the ramp, the sculptor had portrayed himself, tools in hand, peering out a window. He looked like a homely, friendly, unpretentious craftsman, the kind who liked a good beer after a day's work. "I bet he didn't talk a lot of bullshit about art," said David.

We had a wonderful day, the three of us together. We showed off and were admired. We made speeches and uttered epigrams. We clowned for each other and laughed until we couldn't stop. It was if we were high, but we weren't, except possibly on the sugar from the Sachertorte.

I saw again between David and Sarah what it was that bound them together, what I hadn't seen since my arrival, except for brief flashes at odd moments. They had fun together. They admired one another, respected, entertained, loved each other. All of which could have been said as well about David and me, I suppose. But there was at least one essential difference: they wanted each other, so much, that the connection between them was as palpable as if they had a live electric wire running between them. They gave off sparks when they touched. They emitted light. I couldn't believe David had another lover. All his sexual energy seemed vested in Sarah. What could there possibly be left over for anyone else?

It wasn't a question I had any intention of posing to David. I wanted to know, but I wouldn't ask. There was no way I *could* ask at that point without betraying what Sarah had told me in confidence. She may have wanted me to, of course. That thought crossed my mind. Sarah may only have confided her suspicions to me in the hope that I would go to David with them. She may have wanted to put me in the middle, as either stalking horse or champion. Well, I was prepared to defend her if I had to, or David for that matter, if he needed defending, but only on my own ground, and in my own way.

When finally I had to leave them to meet Simon for dinner, I did it reluctantly, the way one leaves a warm room with a cheerful fire to go out on a rainy night.

The night was in fact very warm, and Simon and I ate on the patio of a small restaurant off the Kärntnerstrasse where the food was good and hearty and amazingly cheap. Auden had died in a house two doors away, David had pointed out when we'd walked past that afternoon. Had the restaurant existed then? I wondered. Had Auden perhaps sat at this same wooden table, in the flickering candlelight, eating a plain dinner of boiled beef and potatoes, shielded from the street by the same thick growth of vines? "'Before this loved one/Was that one and that one,'" I quoted.

"Auden?" said Simon. "Did you know he lived two doors down," he pointed, "there?" I nodded. "And," he continued, "what about you? Do you have a loved one? Someone special?"

Special? Of course he was special. By virtue of the fact he was in my bed he was special. I would wake up, turn over, and look at the man beside me, and an incredible wave of feeling would wash over me. It wasn't love, not recently anyway, not since Ned, but tenderness certainly, affection, concern. It was unimaginable to me how it could be otherwise. I'd had strong, even overpowering sexual urges, but I'd never in my life felt a *pure* one. I wasn't sure there was such a thing, no matter how many articles appeared to the contrary in *Penthouse* and *Playboy*. I've never felt an unadulterated feeling. And I tend to doubt anyone else has either. Every emotion is purchased at the cost of another: loss is frequently tinged with relief, love with fear, fear with excitement, freedom with loneliness.

That man in my bed, for the preceding two years, had been Sam Graber, investment banker, financial wizard. He was married, with children, and very few people, only a few trusted people, knew we were lovers. The one before him had been married, too. The one immediately after Ned hadn't been; he was, and is, the Africa correspondent for *The Washington Post* I met on a photographic shoot in Kenya. What all three had in common, I can see with the blinding clarity of hindsight, was their unavailability, their limited potential to upset my life. But at the time, I didn't make the connection. I thought I cared about them only because they were interesting and exciting, because they were intelligent men and good lovers.

"I'm not in love, if that's what you mean," I told Simon.

"You're amazing," he said.

"Why?" I snapped, irritated by what I knew he meant as a compliment. I felt frequently as if I were being congratulated for having two heads.

"You're so self-sufficient, so independent. I don't know anybody else like you, man or woman."

"I'm not independent. I'm a bottomless pit of need."

"You don't need anyone," he insisted.

"That's where you're wrong. I need everyone. And everything. That's why I can't make long-term commitments. I never seem able to concentrate on what I'm getting, just on what I have to give up."

"Have you ever been in love?"

"Once."

"With David?"

"Oh, twice." I grinned. "If you insist on counting David. But I wasn't even twenty."

"You never got over him, did you?"

Simon and I had by now been friends a long time. After that brief few weeks in London, we'd never been lovers again; but his working relationship with David and his friendship with both Waltons had meant that he and I over the years had chalked up a considerable amount of time spent together, a lot of it talking about David. It was a vice most of David's friends compulsively engaged in. But this was the first time Simon had ever suggested I was still carrying some kind of torch for our mutual friend. And, as always when I felt misunderstood by someone who had known me for a long time and rather well, I was annoyed. "No, " I snapped. "That's not true. At least not in the way you mean."

"In what way then?" Again, I felt Simon's interest wasn't so much in me as beyond me, centered somewhere deep in David.

"He taught me the cost of loving someone too much. It's a lesson I never forgot."

"He must have hurt you a great deal."

"No. But he would have, if I'd let him. Oh, Christ, I don't want to talk about him, Simon. Really I don't. I've been doing it for too many years."

"Aren't you jealous?" he asked, pouring me another glass of wine, paying no attention to what I'd just said.

"Aren't you having any?" I asked.

"I have to direct tomorrow, remember? Well, aren't you?"

"Jealous of Sarah?" I responded, sucked in despite myself. "I suppose I am, in a way," I conceded. "I'd love it if men were so overwhelmed at first sight by my fatal beauty they'd crumple in a heap at my feet."

"Isn't that what happened the first time I saw you?" asked Simon with a grin. "That's how I remember it."

"Thank you," I said.

"But that's not what I'm talking about," he continued, returning to his point. "When I see a marriage like theirs, like David's and Sarah's, it makes me feel as if something important, something essential, were missing from my life. Do you ever feel that?" Though the state of David and Sarah's marriage at that moment should hardly have infected anyone with orange-blossom fever, remembering the afternoon I had just spent with them, I understood exactly what Simon meant. "They make me feel lonely," mourned Simon. "I don't know anyone who has a better time together than those two."

"They don't have such a good time all the time," I pointed out.

"Nobody does," returned Simon.

"And when they don't, it's pretty awful."

"But when they do, it's bloody marvelous, isn't it?"

"Is it worth it?" I asked. The distance from the mountain peak to the bottom of the canyon always seemed frighteningly great to me.

"Damn right it is. That kind of thing is worth anything."

Simon had been married twice and divorced twice since I'd met him.

The first time had been to an actress, the second time to a set designer. Both had lasted about two years. He'd been so dazzled by his first wife's pretty face, he'd once told me, he hadn't noticed until almost a year into the marriage that she read only fashion magazines and their conversation was always about the jobs she would have got if only her hair had looked better. Since, over the years, he'd hired a lot of actresses with messy hair, aside from the excruciating boredom of the conversation, he found it increasingly difficult to take it seriously. Determined not to make the same mistake twice, the second time he married an extremely intelligent woman, very knowledgeable about literature and art. Dazzled by her brains, it took him even longer to realize that somehow their conversation had been reduced to talking about the jobs she would have got if only theatrical managers and film producers weren't so sexist. But there were too many successful women set designers in London for him to believe that. Disbelief and boredom, he insisted, had killed both his marriages. "Ultimately, I couldn't take *either* of them seriously," he confessed.

Couldn't or wouldn't, I wondered.

But, despite the failure of his two marriages, he was willing to try again. Anxious to try again. He hated "dating": the effort of it, the uncertainty, the transience, the feebleness of the emotions involved. He wanted something permanent in his life, something solid and dependable. He wanted a home to which he could return after months of filmmaking abroad. Most of all, he wanted to be desperately in love.

Simon paid the ludicrously low bill, and we walked through the dark, quiet streets back towards the hotel.

"Do you want an ice cream?" he asked as we passed the large café at the corner of the Kärntner Ring. "They have wonderful ones here."

"No, thank you. I had a Sachertorte this afternoon. Why isn't everyone in this city obese?" I asked, peering in at the tables crowded with elderly people eating giant sundaes smothered in whipped cream.

"They walk too much, and I work too hard," he replied, patting his flat stomach. "Just as well." He sighed. "I should really get to sleep. There's a five-thirty call. Unless you can think of a good reason to keep me awake?" he added.

"Not a one," I said.

He slipped his arm around me. "Why aren't you married, Nikki? You're terrific. You really are."

"Oh, Christ. Don't you start."

"I meant it as a compliment," he said, getting very frostily English.

"I'm not married because I don't want to be," I snapped. Then, because he was an old friend I was fond of, I slipped my arm through his as we crossed the Ring to the hotel. "Do you think," I asked him be-cause I'd been wanting to all evening, "that David is sleeping with Fiona Brent?"

"What?" he said, surprised by my abrupt change of conversation. "No, I don't. He'd better not be," he added, teeth clenched. I looked at him, surprised myself by the ferocity of his tone. "I am," he said.

I looked at him blankly for a moment, then I started to laugh. After a moment, he did too. We stood there on the sidewalk outside the ho-tel, watched by the doorman and two taxi drivers, laughing. I wasn't sure why.

❧ *Chapter 27* ❧

Driving Sarah's car, I got myself back to the villa without one false turn, and experienced that same inane satisfaction I always feel when my sense of direction, as it usually does, functions flawlessly. Since it is an innate sense, something I was been born with like my ear for music, I should take it for granted, I suppose. But I don't. In childhood, it had been a source of conflict between David and me. He would insist he knew the way and bully me into following, and inevitably when I did, we would end up lost and late for wherever we were going. Since it was one of the few things I was better at than he, I wanted him to acknowledge it, and finally—when the evidence was overwhelming—he did. The taste of that victory remained sweet.

I used the key I'd been given and let myself into the villa. Though it wasn't very late, I moved as quietly as I could in case everyone had already gone to bed. But they hadn't. There was a light on in the sitting room and I heard the low murmur of voices.

"No, no, no," Sarah was saying. Her voice was intense, but without anger. "She wouldn't weep, not then, not because she has to kill an animal. She knows she has to do that to survive."

"She doesn't cry because she has to kill," protested David, "but because she's alone."

They were talking, I realized, about David's new play, the one he later called *Just Until Spring*. It was about Janette Riker, a young woman who had survived alone the winter of 1849 in the Montana wilderness. Now that the *The King of Rome* was almost completed and its problems (in terms of his own work at least) virtually solved, David was starting to think ahead, creating a new puzzle whose secret even he wouldn't know until it was done.

"That's not clear," insisted Sarah. "It seems as if she's crying because she doesn't know how to handle an ax, because she's feeble. And she's not."

Sarah was lying on the couch, holding a sheaf of typewritten pages, quoting from them to make her point to David, who was sitting at the opposite end, his fingers stroking her ankle as they talked, Nicholas asleep in his lap. As clearly as if I were looking at a photograph I'd taken then, I can remember now the soft light thrown by the reading lamps, the smoke from David's cigarettes hanging in the air, his look of concentration and contentment, the curve of Nicholas's cheek repeating in the plump line of his naked thigh, the tinfoil sword he clasped loosely in his right hand, Sarah's emphatic face. They made a picture I didn't want to disturb. I started to move away, out of the doorway, towards the stairs, but David looked up and saw me. "I didn't hear the car," he said accusingly, as if it were my fault.

"I'm a very quiet driver," I replied, entering the room and sitting.

He grinned. "Find your way home all right?" he asked.

"Yes," I said, trying not to smirk. He laughed.

"It's a truck of a car to drive, isn't it?" said Sarah. "I loathe it."

"If you hate it so much," said David, "get another."

"Oh, it's not worth the bother. We're not here that much longer," she replied. "How's Simon?"

"Fine. Except for a mild case of exhaustion."

David stood. "I'd better get him to bed." Nicholas muttered a protest at being moved and buried his head in his father's shoulder.

"He had a bad dream," said Sarah, as David carried him out of the room. "He was so frightened, poor little darling. He was being chased by a dragon. David told him the story of Saint George and made him that sword so he'd have something to fight with if the dragon reappears." She shook her head and smiled. "One can get so furious with David, then he says or does just the right thing. It's hopeless, isn't it?"

"What is?"

She thought for a moment. "Trying to hold a position against him, I suppose. One can't go on eternally saying no, just for the sake of saying no. And he makes it seem so appealing, so easy, so right to say yes. It's the rightness I find particularly infuriating. I feel like a fortress constantly under siege by Love, crumbling slowly away." She straightened the papers she was holding, and put them first into a folder, then into an envelope, which she laid on the table beside the couch. "Would you like something to drink?" she asked, changing the subject. "Some iced tea or lemonade?"

"I really should go to bed. I want to leave with David in the morning. As long as everyone's agreed I can take photographs, I might as well make some serious effort to do it." But I poured myself a glass of lemonade, and sat in David's seat, facing Sarah. Through the open French doors came a light, warm breeze, and the sound of crickets.

"Do you remember," she said, "the day you came to photograph Duncan and me?" I nodded. "That day, that quarrel we had, it was the turning point. Afterwards, there was no going back, no way ever to make things the same again. I used to wonder sometimes what would have happened if you hadn't come." So had I, of course. "The same thing, no doubt. Eventually," she continued, not sounding completely convinced. "I hope so," she added quickly, with more conviction. "What a dreary, empty life I would have had without David. Not that I didn't adore Duncan. I still do. He's been a very good friend to me, always. But it was different. So different. I never knew I could love anyone the way I do David. I didn't know there was that much love in the world. When he enters a room I'm in, I switch on, just like an electric light. I glow. I can feel it."

"I envy you," I said, and at the moment I did, with all my heart. "I've never felt that, with anyone."

"You must have," she said, "some time or other." I shook my head. "Not even with Ned?" she asked. It was curious how, unlike Simon and so many others, she had no interest in my early relationship with David. But she didn't. He was too completely her own for her to fear phantoms from the past. Only the sirens of the future worried her. "I was very fond of Ned," she said.

"So was I." Against my will, my eyes filled with tears. I hoped she wouldn't misunderstand. I didn't want her to think I was still regretting Ned. I wasn't. I was regretting much more than that.

"I could never understand why you two didn't marry."

"What two?" asked David, coming back into the room.

"Ned and Nikki," replied Sarah, looking at him, the light, just as she'd said, coming on in her face.

"Because she's a fool," delivered David cheerfully.

Keating is wrong when he says David and Sarah were simply living in a state of truce those few days. They weren't. The pendulum of their relationship had swung back from the hostility and mutual distrust I'd seen on my arrival to the easy companionship, the profound intimacy that was the hallmark of their marriage in its best moments. They were in love, again, and aware of it. They were always aware of themselves, I think, and the effect they were creating. David, the playwright, seemed never able to resist stepping back to admire the drama that was his life; Sarah, the actress, seemed often to be gauging the quality of her performance in a part she'd been cast to play. Or so it seemed to me. Which is not to say that I don't believe in the reality of their joy, or in the validity of their suffering. Their happiness and their pain both went far beyond their abilities to control or admire them. David and Sarah, ultimately, transcended self-consciousness.

"Thank you for coming," said David the next morning as he drove us through the sand-colored suburbs of Vienna towards the Prater. "Sarah's been a changed person since you got here."

"I don't think that has anything to do with me."

"She hasn't had a drink since you arrived."

"You've been spending more time with her these past few days."

"If you mean I was neglecting her before, I told you, I was busy." He felt misunderstood, misjudged. His voice took on a petulant edge. "You'd think she'd be pleased instead of resentful. For chrissake, I'm keeping her like a fucking queen. She's living in a goddam palace. Do you know how much money it takes? How hard I have to work? Someone has to work to support that ménage."

"Sarah's aching to work," I said. "She would work, if you'd let her."

"Let her? Who's stopping her?"

"If you'd encourage her, I mean."

"If she wanted to work, she'd work," he said. "Nobody has to encourage me to do it."

"That is not exactly true."

"The trouble with old friends," he said, "is that they have long memories, and memories distort the present." He reached for his pack of cigarettes, remembered I'd be sick if he smoked, and put them away.

"Memories *explain* the present," I corrected. "Anyway, I'm not talking about when you were twelve."

"My father still doesn't believe I ever finish anything. You know what he said to me just before I left New York? 'It's a collaborative medium, the theater.'" He mimicked Mr. Walton with deadly accuracy. "'All the actors, the director, the set designer, everybody chipping in their two cents to get a play on. You want to know what it's like to do something really on your own, to be out there on a limb with nobody to help you climb in, try writing a newspaper article on deadline.' Not even a novel, a newspaper article, for chrissake!" I laughed and so did David, his laugh a blend of amusement and anger and frustration. "I've worked steadily, since I was twenty. I never really stop working. When I don't finish something now, it's because it isn't worth finishing. Who knows," he added, "perhaps that was true when I was twelve, too. Perhaps I understood that everything I was working on then was shit."

"Everybody encourages you," I said. "All of us, even your father. We do it by expecting you to work, by believing in your talent, by admiring what you write. If we didn't, how long do you think you'd go on?"

"Forever," he said emphatically. I looked dubious. "Schubert did," he added. "Keats did. Emily Dickinson. Vincent Van Gogh . . . "

"All right," I conceded. "But not everyone has your ego. Some of us need encouragement."

"Nothing would ever stop you," he said, turning his head to smile at me. "You'd roll over anything or anybody in your way. Like a tank."

"Watch it," I said, as a car pulled suddenly into our lane in front of us, cutting us off. David jammed on his brakes. The driver behind hooted his horn.

"That was no Austrian," said David. "That was an Italian, or a Jap. I'd put money on it."

"You're not prejudiced," I said. I was as irritated as he knew I would be. "Why do you pretend you are?"

"It's not prejudice to perceive the truth and speak it," he replied, with maddening pomposity. "Do you know my theory about kamikaze pilots?"

"I don't want to hear it."

"They weren't heroes on suicide missions," he persisted. "They were just lousy flyers."

It was exactly the sort of thing he used to say to Ned, to try to get under his liberal skin. He never succeeded. Ned always found a way to shut David up without arguing with him. "I save my anger for the real bigots," said Ned to calm me, who was always the one who got upset.

"David is a real bigot," I'd reply.

"No, he's a snob," corrected Ned. "That's a different thing entirely."

But David wasn't even a snob, not in any conventional sense. He admired intelligence and talent, grace and beauty, skill and determination, no matter what the size or color or sex of the person who possessed them. He admired success and wealth, too, but he didn't toady to them or to those who had them, and he despised the people who toadied to him when at last he'd achieved both.

He pulled into the left lane and caught up with the car that had cut us off. "Look," he said, "see who's driving." I couldn't resist, and I turned my head to the right. So did David. "Japanese," he said smugly. I frowned. "Come on, laugh," he encouraged.

"It's not funny," I replied.

He picked up my hand and carried it to his lips. "You are a completely admirable person," he said. "God, how I admire you."

Finally, I did laugh. "I hate it when you make fun of me."

"Not enough people do these days," he said, and changed the subject. "I read in the *Tribune* last week that Ned is going to run for the Senate. Did you know?"

"He told me just before I left New York. We had dinner. But all he really wanted to talk about was the antinuke rallies he's organizing with Jane Fonda and Tom Hayden. Three Mile Island really scared him."

"Him and a lot of other people."

Over the past nine years, Ned had continued in private practice but had taken on more and more public-interest cases, waiving fees when necessary, supplementing his income by judicious investments in the stock and commodities markets, thereby establishing his financial security while earning the admiration of the men who mattered in the Democratic Party. It was now time, he'd decided, to run for office. He'd worked hard to eradicate injustice, prejudice, inequality where he found them, but his successes had been limited. He thought if he could place himself at the center of power, at the heart of government in Washington, it might somehow be possible to achieve more.

"He's wrong," said David.

"Someone has to have ideals," I said. "And work for them, or there's no hope for civilization."

"Hanging out with Jane Fonda isn't going to help him get elected, if he's serious about this."

"He'll get elected," I said. "See how wrong I would have been to marry him? Can you imagine me a senator's wife?"

"Just as long as you have no regrets," said David.

"I have plenty," I said. "Who doesn't?"

We crossed the Danube Canal over the Gurtelbrücke and continued driving along the muddy green waterway to the Prater. There were a few more days' shooting scheduled at this location, then the company would move to the Spanish Riding School, then to Schönbrunn Palace. They'd already finished several street scenes in the Old City, plus the scenes at the Hofburg and the Kaisergruft, the latter the crypt where the Habsburgs are buried, where the King of Rome himself was buried until 1940, when his body was removed to Paris.

The scene filmed in the crypt is one of my favorites. Shaken by the sudden death of the Protestant Archduchess Henriette (also an outsider, though because of her religion, not her ancestry), Franz detours his mother's lover, Neipperg, from the nearby Sacher Café into the crypt. His own death less than three years away, the eighteen-year-old Franz is gripped by a sense of terrible foreboding. How awful to die before one has accomplished anything. Is that to be his fate? He can't allow it to happen, he rails. At first, Neipperg attempts to placate him with platitudes: Franz is young, healthy, and Habsburgs live forever. But he soon gives up the effort. He tells Franz that the duty of every man is to carve the fate he wants from the resistant matter of the universe and to accept with grace and dignity his inevitable failure to do it. It was David's best scene.

But that morning I had not yet seen one frame of film, nor David in costume.

"Are you scheduled to work while I'm here?" I asked as he parked his car in the section set aside for the company. "I'd like to see you."

"I'm a dream in hose and breeches." He grinned.

"I'll bet you are."

"I've got better legs than Duncan." I hooted in response. "And a better ass," he added.

"A better voice, too?" I teased.

"No," conceded David immediately. "Duncan's voice is phenomenal. It's beautiful. It's an instrument he knows how to play superbly. It's too bad he has to talk such shit all the time. Listening to him is like hearing a nursery rhyme played by the London Philharmonic."

I had thought the same thing when I'd first met Duncan, I remembered, but I'd never mentioned it to David. I was sure of it. How odd the same image should occur to him. "I like Duncan," I said.

"So do I," replied David. He reached across as I got out of the car and took some packages of Gauloises from the glove compartment and put them into the pocket of his denim shirt. "He's quite a guy," he added, getting out of the car and slamming the door. He lit a cigarette. "A good friend. Dependable. Loyal. To everyone but his wife. His current wife, that is."

"Unlike you," I replied before I could help myself. He looked at me sharply, knowing I meant something, but not quite sure what. "What are you talking about?"

"Nothing. Sorry. I didn't mean to start fencing. I just parried and thrust before I thought about it."

"Does this have anything to do with Caroline?"

"No," I said emphatically. "Absolutely not." I had let my guard slip and he could see that curiosity, my nemesis, was on the rampage. Still, I couldn't detect in him any flicker of guilt, any dawning comprehension that I was on to him. If there was, indeed, anything to be on to. All I could see in David's face was the determination to find out what was going on in my head.

Hans, one of the assistant directors, hurried over to us. "Mr. Walton," he said, "Mr. Wroth asked to see you as soon as you arrived."

"Yeah, sure," replied David. "Be right there." He turned to me. "Try and stay out of trouble," he said.

I watched him walk to where Simon sat drinking coffee, frowning over the pages of his script.

Damn, I thought. Damn, damn, damn. When are you ever going to learn to watch your mouth?

♔ *Chapter 28* ♔

"How nice to see someone smiling," said Duncan to me when I joined him at the buffet table. He was already in makeup and costume and, as usual, waiting not very patiently for filming to begin. "I think I have the wrong temperament for working in films. All this hanging about. In the theater, the curtain goes up more or less on time every night and you get out there and say your lines. Even if you're dying or drunk, you get out there and say your lines. We had a five-thirty call this morning, and we'll be lucky if we start this scene by noon."

"What is it this time?" I asked.

"The *enfant terrible* can't get out of bed."

"Can't?" I repeated.

"He apparently did coke half the night to get high, then took Valium and who knows what else the other half to come down. Frankly, I'm sick of the little bastard."

"Has this happened before?" David and Simon had both indicated Joe Vasari was a major problem; neither had mentioned cocaine as a cause.

"This is the first time he's been too drugged to work, but that's no doubt been his problem from the beginning. Amazing, isn't it, how incredibly naive we all are? All of us thought he was just temperamental."

"Mr. Powell," Hans interrupted, "could you please join Mr. Wroth in his trailer?"

"I'll be right there," said Duncan. He opened the tap of the large urn that held pride of place on the table and poured himself another cup of coffee. "That probably means we're going to try to shoot around the bugger, leaving me with a lot of new lines to learn very quickly. If someone's not careful, I'm going to show them what temperament is really about." He tapped my camera. "Don't quote me."

I grinned. "You can trust me."

"I know," he replied. "That's why I always talk more or less honestly to you." He flashed me one of his best smiles, then kissed my cheek. "As Spencer Tracy once said, 'I'm too tired and old and rich for all this, so let's do the scene.' Though I'm not in fact as rich as people think I am. Or as old. See you later, darling."

I watched Duncan cross to the trailer where Simon and David had earlier repaired for their script conference, wondering what to do with myself until the stars of the show reappeared. There wasn't one magazine I could think of that would be interested in shots of a film crew hanging around waiting for the action to begin.

Nevertheless, I got my camera ready and began walking the location. One never knows where or when a good picture, a great picture, might happen, I reminded myself, thinking of Lartigue's series in the Bois de Boulogne and Weegee's scenes of New York life. Event is not necessary in photography; only light and composition are.

I caught two of the grips playing chess, the script girl doing needle-point, the best boy and an extra necking, a prop man regilding a carriage that had been damaged the day before, the gaffer heading off a fight between two electricians about the preceding day's cricket results, all of which I used later in an essay called "Behind the Scenes" for a French film magazine. Then Fiona Brent arrived and shattered my concentration.

"Where *is* everyone?" The voice asking the question was soft but with a power that ensured it was heard. I turned to look at the speaker and recognized Fiona Brent immediately. Though I hadn't put face and name together, I had indeed seen her before, in a BBC serial on *Masterpiece Theater*. She was wearing khaki culottes, a safari shirt, sandals, and no makeup. Her skin was milky white. Her long brown hair hung clean and shining to her shoulders. Large horn-rimmed sunglasses screened the eyes I discovered later were brilliant blue. She was far from a beauty. Her features were small, sharp, ferretlike. But she had power, energy, and an erotic quality that

seemed somehow perverse. One could imagine her saying yes to anything, even the unimaginable. She was the kind of woman that men
lusted after and women didn't like.

"Oh fuck," she said when the AD finished his capsule summary of the
morning. "Someone might have phoned me at the hotel to let me
know. Why wasn't my call canceled?"

"I'm very sorry, Miss Brent. The thing is . . ." Hans started to explain, but she turned away without letting him finish.

"That fucking little sod," she muttered, walking towards the parked
trailers. "I'm going to take a nap," she called back to the dejected
Hans. "Call me when I'm needed. If I'm *ever* needed."

I snapped his picture, then smiled at him cheerfully. "What! And
give up show business?" I said, though how I expected an Austrian to get
the joke is beyond me.

He didn't, quite, but smiled anyway. "It's got to get better, yes?" he
said. "It can't get worse."

A few minutes later David and Simon, Duncan and Milos Andrejvik,
the director of photography, emerged from the trailer with a battle plan.
The master of the scene had been shot the day before, so Simon now
proposed covering it not from medium to close shots, but in reverse,
doing Duncan's close-up first, and using a body double for Vasari in the
medium if he hadn't appeared by then fit for work. That was simple
enough, though a bit risky, and hadn't taken long to decide. What had
kept everyone talking for over an hour was Simon's suggestion that they
not continue the scene at all, but go on to the next between Duncan and
Fiona, which had been on the schedule for the preceding afternoon, but
hadn't been got to because of delays with Vasari. Andrejvik eventually
convinced him that setting up the new scene, then resetting the old,
would cost too much time and, therefore, money. Which then led
Simon and David into an argument about cutting some of Joe Vasari's
lines or, worse (at least in David's opinion), giving them to other actors.

"He knows you can't hand out dialogue as if it were chocolate candy,"
fumed David to me while we stood on the sidelines watching the flurry
of activity as the crew prepared for the take. He took an angry drag of
his cigarette. "Simon's not usually so thick-headed. I don't know what
the fuck is wrong with him today."

"The same thing that's wrong with everybody: Joe Vasari."

David ran his hand through his straight, dark hair and shook his
head. In the sunlight, I noticed a few strands of gray I'd never seen
before. "It wasn't Joe. I know how he gets when he's upset about Joe.

This is different. It's me he's pissed at." David's air of outraged inno-
cence succeeded, as it always did, in making me laugh. He transferred
his anger at Simon to me. "What's the joke?"

"You, of course, are completely reasonable. You never do anything
to irritate anyone, do you?"

"I didn't this time," insisted David. "I bent over backwards to be
agreeable. For chrissake, I know we have a problem." He shook his
head again. "How was Simon last night, at dinner?"

"Fine," I said. "Absolutely fine."

"He didn't say anything about me?"

"Only that he worships the ground you walk on."

"Very funny," replied David.

"Places, everyone," called an assistant director, echoed by Hans in
German. The extras who'd been lounging at the sidelines sprang into
activity.

"Mr. Powell, we're ready for you," said Hans.

Duncan climbed into the gilded phaeton which was set at the camera mark and took the reins offered by the handler while a hairdresser
climbed up and smoothed a strand of hair back under the cover of
his hat.

"Atmosphere," shouted an AD as the extras took their positions in
carriages and awaited their cues to pass as fleeting, indistinguishable
background images behind the close shot of Duncan's head.

"Wait for the plane," called the sound man, pointing to a jet that was
just coming into view overhead.

Eventually, the hubbub died, everyone was in place, everything was
quiet.

"Everybody quiet," said the AD, echoed by Hans in German.

"Rolling" said the camera operator.

"Action," shouted Simon, and Duncan began saying his lines into the
camera.

"It must be Fiona," said David speculatively, turning back to face me.

"What must?" I asked, for a moment not understanding what he was
talking about.

"Simon's not mad at Joe. Or me. He's mad at Fiona. He probably
found her fucking someone on the crew when he got back to the hotel
last night." David seemed suddenly to be enjoying the scenario he was
creating. "She was probably furious he took you out to dinner."

"Great," I said. "Good theory. That makes Simon's mood my fault."

"Of course it's not your fault," said David, smiling again now that
he'd found a satisfactory explanation for Simon's behavior. "It's his, for
not being more diplomatic. The woman's a cunt and he knows it."

David left me to go stand by the script girl, where he could hear Duncan delivering his lines. Only then, fool that I am, did I understand the implications of what had happened. I felt a wave of apprehension, of guilt, wash over me: there was a possibility, a large possibility, that Simon's mood was indeed my fault. He may have laughed with me at the idea of David's having an affair with Fiona, but what if afterwards he had begun to suspect, during the long hours of the night when any chimera can take on the hard shape of reality, that it might be true?

My tongue was really working overtime to cause mischief. Would anyone, even me, believe for much longer that it was unintentional?

Joe Vasari, to everyone's amazement and relief, did turn up in time for Simon to complete the coverage of the scene. His boyfriend, aided by the production manager, had fed him black coffee, given him a cold shower, dressed him, and got him to the location. In costume and makeup he didn't look bad. He was still young enough to absorb most damage with little outward sign. Uncharacteristically, he apologized to Simon and to the company in tones that sounded to everyone's ears sincere. He seemed frightened, but whether it was for himself or merely for his career, it was impossible to tell. He may just have been afraid of Simon, not because he was the dictatorial director of film folklore, but because he ran his set as a good father runs a family, and there was no punishment worse than being banished from his favor. Until that morning, Joe Vasari had confined his misbehaving to the limits tolerable in a feisty son. He must have known he had gone too far.

Simon spent thirty minutes or so alone with Joe, during the tea break, talking to him, calming him, trying to figure out (he told me later) how to get a halfway decent performance out of him. Whatever Simon said, and did, worked. If Joe wasn't brilliant in the scene, he was extremely good. Franz's face on camera had a strained, a vulnerable look that belied the formality of his request to Metternich for an interview. It gave the brief, rather unimportant linking material a pathos no one really had expected.

David, surprisingly, accepted with no more than a frown Simon's dictum that he keep well out of the way of the discussions with Joe. Instead he arm-wrestled with Hans while I photographed them, then challenged Milos Andrejvik to a game of darts (a board had been hung on one of the trees), with which I soon got bored. I went off to photograph Duncan while he was still in costume, and Louis Foch, who was playing Eugène de Beauharnais.

When I finished with Louis, I headed back to the buffet table for a cup of coffee and saw David standing there with an arm around Fiona Brent. He was whispering into her ear and she was laughing as if he were the Marx Brothers and Abbott and Costello rolled into one. He raised his head, caught me watching him, and beckoned me over.

"Lovely to meet you finally," she said, when David had introduced us. "I've heard so much about you. From Simon," she added, untruthfully. I doubted he'd said anything but that we were old friends. "I was so sorry I couldn't make dinner last night, but I had such an early call this morning. Or, at least, I thought I did." She smiled at me sweetly. "I hope I'm forgiven."

He hadn't asked her to join us, he'd explained to me; but, innocently enough, only because she'd already told him she needed an early night and wouldn't see him. The temptation to have at least one of us tell the truth was overpowering, and I gave in to it. "Oh, there's nothing to forgive," I said, at my chirping best. "I was glad to have Simon to myself. We're such old friends and I hadn't seen him in a very long time." If I cause trouble, I thought, at least this time it will be deliberate.

"I'm sure Simon felt the same," she responded smoothly. "He admires you so much. He thinks you're a superb photographer." There was just the slightest emphasis on the second "he," to let me know she'd seen better.

At which point, David intervened. "Nikki's taking some photographs for us," he informed her.

"Oh?" Her eyebrows raised. "For any particular magazine?"

"I don't think I'll have any trouble placing them," I said. "I hope you'll let me photograph you while I'm here," I added, wondering if she'd have the guts to refuse.

Self-interest battled with irritation in her eyes. "Are you staying long?" she asked.

"No," said David quickly, grinning at me, delighted to head me off at the pass. "Nikki can never be kept away from her work for long."

I ignored him. "I've already photographed Duncan," I said, "and Louis," and I named a few other members of the cast. "Really I've only you and Joe Vasari left to shoot."

"Wouldn't I just love to be the one to shoot Joe?" she said, and smiled. David laughed, and so did I. "By all means, photograph me as much as you like," she continued. "What about now? God knows I've got nothing else to do at the moment, thanks to that fucking little pervert."

It was by then almost three o'clock in the afternoon and Fiona had been waiting since eight that morning to work. She wasn't yet even in costume or makeup, since Simon still wasn't confident there would be time to move on to the next scene before the light failed. Watching her, standing there, her arm linked with David's, intelligence, cynicism, and self-awareness evident in her face, her body lean and well exercised, everything about her thoroughly modern, there was no way to imagine the melting softness, the weak hesitancy, the ovarian amplitude she would put into her portrayal of Marie Louise. The only thing that remained on film of the Fiona Brent I knew and disliked was the eroticism which made Napoleon claim his second wife to be the most voracious fuck he'd ever had.

"What are they doing?" asked Fiona, turning to look at Simon and Joe, who were still deep in conversation. "Christ, what *can* they find to talk about for so long? The scene is not what one might call difficult."

"It's the subtext," said David. Fiona looked at him as if he must be kidding, which he was. "You must never underestimate the profundity of my subtext," cautioned David. "It's a wellspring of hidden meaning."

Fiona laughed. "Oh Lord. For a moment, I forgot you wrote it."

"You must never do that either," David said, grinning.

She laughed. "If I wasn't crazy about my husband..." she said, ignoring my presence, sparing a thought perhaps for the first time in weeks for her film-producer husband, who was then in Africa trying to get a film made.

Ha, I sneered silently, if you thought David could do more for your career, if you thought you had a chance at having him, if... I really didn't like her at all. She leaned closer into him and kissed his cheek, which is the exact moment Simon chose to look our way. He frowned, then realized he was, and stopped. He flashed us a strained smile and resumed his conversation with Joe.

There was not a doubt left in my mind, not a loophole large enough for my guilt to wiggle through: Simon was definitely suspicious.

Joe sailed through his work that afternoon with amazing ease. Determined not to waste anyone's time, he didn't. He was word-perfect in every take, and what time was lost was due to technical problems, not temperament. If he hoped to earn a smile from Simon in gratitude, he didn't get his wish. Despite the concerted efforts of everyone in the cast and on the crew to cheer him up, Simon's mood remained bad.

They got the last shot of that scene by five, and began setting up for the next: Fiona's scene with Duncan. It's the one where Metternich, driving in the Prater with Marie Louise, tells her she has been granted by secret treaty the Duchy of Parma but only on condition that she leave her son Franz behind in Vienna in her father's care. "In my father's care, or under your thumb?" she asks.

While they were lighting and Duncan and Fiona were having their costumes and makeup adjusted, I cornered Joe Vasari and photographed him. It seemed a sensible thing to do while his mood remained contrite and conciliatory. The following year, when the film was released, Joe was heralded as a major new talent, and it was supposed that he would have gone far if he hadn't died in a light-plane crash a few months later. I think he went as far as he could, for someone determined on self-destruction.

A photograph I took of him that day was released as a poster and collected by his fans after his death. I still can't bear to look at it.

When I'd finished, I looked around for David to see if we could leave: I'd had enough of film sets and film stars. He was talking to Simon. Arguing with Simon. They stood in a huddle, ignoring the activity around them, oblivious to the curious glances occasionally thrown their way. Everyone seemed a little surprised at the sudden crack in their formerly united front.

Bits of the argument floated on the air, enough for me to know it was Fiona they were fighting about. Or rather, Marie Louise. In an attempt to make up for some lost time, Simon wanted to cut some of her longer speeches. David was resisting. It was a usual sort of argument, typical between directors and writers, and they'd had similar ones often before. Only this one was acrimonious. Simon attacked, David defended. The director of photography, braver than most, interrupted to point at the position of the sun. "All right, have it your way," said Simon gracelessly. "I've got to make my goddam shot." And he stalked away.

During the drive home, David was unusually silent. He was mulling over Simon's behavior, trying to understand it.

"I think I know what's wrong with Simon," I said finally.

"So do I," replied David. "Fiona."

"Not exactly," I said. He took a cigarette from a pack in his pocket and lit it. "You know I get sick if you smoke in the car," I reminded him.

"Warn me when you have to vomit," he said. "I wonder just what she did to upset him."

"She didn't do anything."

He turned his head and looked at me. "He did say something to you last night."

"He thinks you're having an affair with Fiona."

"He what? Is he crazy? Where did he get an idea like that?"

"From me," I confessed.

"From you?" He stubbed out the cigarette. "I don't want to make you sick until after you explain."

I told him what had happened, exactly how, and why, omitting only that I'd got the idea from Sarah.

"But what made you think I was fucking her? Wouldn't I have told you if I was?"

"Maybe. I wasn't sure. Sarah said you were out a lot. I thought Fiona was a possible explanation."

"Jesus Christ. I've been busy. Even if I'd wanted to do her, which I don't, where the hell do you think I'd have found the time?"

"You usually manage, when you want something badly enough."

"Well, I don't want her. Christ, she's having an affair with my best friend."

"I didn't know that at the time. Sorry." He didn't say anything. "I am sorry, David. Really I am. I'll explain everything to Simon."

"Don't explain anything. Just keep out of it. All right?"

"If that's what you want."

"It's what I want."

"David . . ."

"Jesus, don't say you're sorry again."

"All right. I won't."

We drove in silence for a while, David concentrating on the hilly road, me absorbed in contemplation of my own perfidy. Then David's voice broke the quiet. "It was Sarah, wasn't it? She told you. She's the one who thinks I'm fucking Fiona. Christ, what do I have to do, how *much* do I have to do, to make that woman happy?"

❧ *Chapter 29* ❧

Like a circus performer on a tightrope, happiness is always balanced precariously over the abyss of some darker emotion. David didn't want to be the one to push it off. I suppose he wasn't sure how far down, if at all, was the safety net.

Instead of confronting Sarah with her suspicions, David decided to ignore them. For the next several days, he spent even more time at home, not only devising games and excursions to keep the children happy, but courting Sarah. He accused her of letting her golf game get rusty and challenged her to a match at a nearby club, though his solicitude stopped short of letting her win. He read to her, teased her, made love to her. Late at night I could hear the sound of laughter coming from their room.

On the pretext of wanting to show me the Salzkammergut, he planned a long weekend for all of us, which delighted (as he knew it would) not only me, but Sarah. She had been trying, unsuccessfully, to lure him away from the filming, both in Prague and in Vienna. It was as if she felt herself in competition not so much with Fiona Brent as with *The King of Rome*. Having sacrificed her part in the film to give David what he wanted (that is, another child), she required a similar sacrifice from him, albeit a token one. She wanted him to choose her over it, if only for a day or two. "All he thinks about is that movie," she had said to me shortly after my arrival. "I could slit my wrists and bleed to death in front of him and I doubt he'd notice."

That wasn't true. David noticed everything, but was very selective about what he chose to pay attention to. Usually it was his work that occupied the forefront of his mind, everything else existing in the periphery, until something happened to change the balance. And something had happened: Sarah had rocked the boat, first one way, then another, until David had been forced to pay attention to the sea of misunderstanding about to swamp him.

Sarah's delight about the trip was unmitigated. Though Caroline, placed in a similar situation, would have supposed that David's change of heart had something to do with me, Sarah didn't make that mistake. She understood I was only the device used to grant her wish, the pumpkin transformed into a coach. And if she thought his sudden agreeableness was in any way the product of a guilty conscience, she didn't let it show. Like David, she seemed for the moment caught in a cobweb of happiness and content to stay there until an ill wind should blow it away.

With Simon, David tried the reverse strategy: the low profile. Though he still went to the location a lot, writing when he had to, kibitzing with the crew when he didn't, he arrived later or left sooner than he was used to do, kept out of Fiona's way when it was possible, and censored more carefully what he said in the inevitable script meetings. And if he didn't succeed in bridging the gap between himself and Simon, he kept it from becoming an open breach. At least for a while.

"Talk to him about it," I urged one afternoon as we sat on the patio watching Sarah swim her laps. It was late in the day, the sun low in the sky, the garden shimmering in a golden haze. In a few minutes the children would come exploding into the scene, back from an afternoon's outing with Will and Marie-Paule; but for the moment it was tranquil. Even the flowers at the end of the garden seemed to be dozing in the soft light.

"And say what?" asked David. "'Listen, buddy, you've got it all wrong. I am not screwing your girl.' Do you think he'd believe me?"

"He might," I said. "It's the truth."

"Fat chance," replied David, ending our conversation with a sudden leap to his feet. He ran to the pool and dove in. Startled, Sarah stopped in midstroke and looked up. He surfaced at her side. "Wanna play?" he asked. When David didn't want to talk, he didn't talk.

During that period, a matter of just three or four days, really, I followed David's "order" not to try myself to straighten matters out with

Simon. And I was happier than usual to oblige. Considering the damage I'd managed to do by speaking, it seemed to me the better part of valor to keep quiet. But I began to notice as I wandered the locations, taking my pictures, that Simon's attitude towards me had shifted, that there was tension where before had been only easy camaraderie. That tension came finally to a head on the day before the Waltons and I were to leave for the Salzkammergut. I was, I suppose, an easier target than David.

The company had moved from the Prater to Schönbrunn Palace, which had been the home first of Marie Louise and her son after their flight from Paris, then of Franz alone when his mother abandoned him for Count Neipperg and the Duchy of Parma. They were shooting in the Small Gloriette, a frescoed pavilion set in the palace grounds, with views beyond of lush green lawn, Neptune's Fountain, and the Gloriette arcade which crowned the hill at the close of the park. Compared to similar palaces—Versailles, for example, which it was intended to surpass—it was all surprisingly shabby. On film, of course, none of the decay showed. Milos Andrejvik's photography gave Schönbrunn the rich, the opulent beauty its reality totally failed to achieve.

When I arrived, David and Fiona were rehearsing for the master of the scene in which Neipperg convinces the ambivalent Marie Louise that she must accept Metternich's offer. Away from public scrutiny in Vienna, their love has its only chance of survival, he tells her; and once secure in Parma she will have a better position from which to pressure both her father and Metternich for her son. In the rehearsal I watched, Marie Louise conceded slowly to the logic of Neipperg's view. That was what Simon wanted, to show her as an intelligent woman and caring mother, aware of the political tangle she'd have to survive to secure her own and her son's future. The scene on film, however, conveys more than the cool political savvy Simon was after, or even the undercurrent of pathos he was willing to accept. It has a powerful erotic aura: the openness of the pavilion, the presence of a servant removing the remnants of lunch, the brilliance of the sunshine, all somehow highlight the suppressed lust of the lovers, who for too many months had had to be discreet under the watchful eye of Metternich's secret police.

All of us watching knew when and how the dynamic of the scene changed, though none, I think, realized until we saw the movie in release what a powerful change it was. It's this scene which Keating uses in his biography to substantiate his claim that David and Fiona Brent were indeed lovers.

As soon as the rehearsals were over and film began to turn in the camera, Fiona's rampant eroticism, as well as her sexual curiosity about

David, folded into her performance, adding depth and color to her characterization of the deposed queen. Weak and frightened, astute but irresolute, Marie Louise may have been, but—as Fiona played her—she was also a woman in love, a woman who wanted to *make* love to the man whose advice she was seeking. And David matched her performance, combining with Neipperg's courage and determination a lust to match Marie Louise's own.

In short, what happened is that, as soon as Simon called "Action," David and Fiona began in earnest to act.

At first, aware of the watching servants, Marie Louise and Neipperg stand apart, not touching, their eyes sending secret messages, the air between them electric with meaning. Then Neipperg takes her hand, to kiss it in farewell; but instead of raising it to his lips, he stands staring at her. After a few tense seconds, he pulls her into his arms.

David and Fiona were line-perfect and there were, for once, no technical problems, so the scene ran straight through to the end as the crew watched appreciatively, and I moved closer and closer, my camera ready, wanting to capture in my lens some of what I, what everyone, was feeling. David kissed Fiona lengthily, passionately, tugging impatiently at her stiff bodice to free a breast, clutching at her hips to pull her body into his, pushing her back against a marble column as he searched for a path through the voluminous folds of her skirt, until stopped by a warning cough from a servant. I waited for Simon's shout of "Cut" so I could begin taking my pictures.

"Cut," said Simon, his voice full of anger. "Nikki, for chrissake, you're in my line of vision."

Startled, I jumped back. "Sorry," I called.

"I told you to keep out of the way. I can't have you creeping around, ruining my concentration."

I knew I hadn't been in his line of vision. Or, if I had, so had half the crew. But it didn't seem the time to argue. "It won't happen again," I said.

"Damn right it won't," he said. "Off the set." I looked at him disbelievingly, though knowing that now he'd said it, there was no way he could go back. "Off," he repeated.

"I'm going," I said.

"How was it?" asked David, I thought to change the subject, but he told me later he was still so caught up in the scene he had just played he wasn't aware yet of anything else going on. In any event, I doubt he would have thought it a good idea to come to my defense.

"Fine," muttered Simon unconvincingly, watching Fiona adjusting her gown, smoothing her hair. "Fine. Let's chat a minute, then do it again." He walked towards the Small Gloriette to talk to David and Fiona, and I walked away.

As I went past him, Milos Andrejvik shrugged as if in apology and Hans, the assistant director, smiled kindly. "It is not a good day," he said.

"No," I replied. "It certainly isn't."

That evening, at about seven-thirty, I arrived at the Imperial Hotel to meet Duncan for dinner. When I asked for him at the desk, the concierge gave me a message saying he'd been delayed and suggesting I have a drink while I waited. As I turned towards the bar, I saw Simon entering. He excused himself from the others in the group (Fiona was not among them) and came towards me, smiling apologetically. His shirt was hanging out of his khaki pants, it was buttoned askew, and there was a stain on the pocket. Tension lines were etched deep in his face. He looked exhausted. "Nikki, darling," he said, kissing my cheek, "about today. I am sorry."

"Me, too," I replied.

"It's been a bugger of a week, but I shouldn't have taken that out on you."

I might not have gone looking for him to try to settle matters, but, presented with a golden opportunity, it seemed crazy not to take advantage of it. "Simon, let's have a drink. I want to talk to you."

He looked at his watch. "I have a dinner date."

"So do I. Just one drink," I insisted.

"Just one," he conceded reluctantly.

We sat in one of the small alcoves off the main lobby and ordered white wine spritzers. As the waiter left, Simon sighed. "If it's about today. . ." he began.

"It's not," I said. "Or at least, only peripherally. You've been mad at me for days now. Why?"

"I have not," he insisted.

"And you've been angry with David.'

"That's absurd."

"You're right. It is absurd. But it's also true."

"You shouldn't take everything so personally," he replied, turning one of his better smiles on me. "I have been having rather a rough time, lately. It's not easy, you know, shooting around a Ferris wheel," he continued. "Not to mention a cocaine-addled star."

I looked across to the two middle-aged women, talking earnestly, drinking Campari and soda in the alcove across from us. One had dyed red, the other dyed blond hair. I shook my head. "It's more than that."

"Nikki, really, who needs more?" The warmth was gone now and only the irritation showed. He heaved another great sigh. "All right. Why don't you get it over with and tell me what you think is wrong, since you so clearly think you know." The waiter returned with the spritzers, placing them with a flourish in front of us. "Thank you," said Simon graciously, not really seeing him.

"I think you're jealous of David and Fiona, and I think you're angry with me for suggesting they might be lovers," I said, as soon as the waiter was gone.

"Jealous?" he repeated, as if the idea were totally new to him. Perhaps it was. The English I've met don't take first prize in the self-awareness stakes.

"Yes," I continued quickly. "Only I didn't *tell* you they were," I corrected, "I *asked*. And I certainly wouldn't have done that if I'd known you were involved with Fiona. And after I asked you, I found out the answer. They are *not* having an affair."

"I never believed they were," he said.

"That's not how you've been acting."

Simon pondered that for a minute. "How can you be so sure they're not?" he asked finally.

"David told me."

"And he wouldn't lie to you, I suppose?"

"He might, if it affected me. But this doesn't. He has no reason not to tell me the truth." Simon studied my face for a moment, then looked away again. "Simon, he's your friend. He wouldn't do anything to hurt you. Not casually. Not like this. Not without a damn good reason."

"I know," he conceded finally.

"I can't tell you how awful I feel for starting all this."

"The thing is," said Simon, "I don't trust Fiona. I love her, but I don't trust her. I don't suppose I even like her very much."

"You *do* love her?" I asked. Maybe she was a better person than I was willing to give her credit for being, but one thing I knew for certain: she didn't love Simon. I doubted Fiona Brent could love anyone but herself.

"Love her, want her. If there's a difference, I've never discovered what it is," said Simon bitterly. "She'd go to bed with David in a minute, if he asked her."

"He won't," I said.

"Christ, do you think that's much consolation?" He swallowed the last of his drink. "You know what the trouble is? David's so fucking talented, so fucking attractive. Everything, everyone, just falls into his lap. It's not easy being his friend. It's not easy telling whether one actually is a friend or merely a sycophant, a retainer, a hanger-on."

"Yes," I said. "Yes, it is easy."

"Do you know the only reason I'm directing this film? Because David insisted."

"That's not true," I denied, outraged at the suggestion. The cocky, self-assured Simon I had known for years was vanishing right before my eyes.

"He insisted," repeated Simon.

"And you think Paragon Films just rolled over nicely and gave David exactly what he wanted? Do you think I do? Or that Fiona will? Bullshit. Don't credit David with more power than he has. You're directing this film because you have three box-office successes behind you and a string of stage hits. That's it. *Finito.*"

Again, he was silent for a moment. "I don't know what's wrong with me," he said finally.

All at once, I did. And although Fiona Brent was the instigator of the present trouble, she wasn't its cause. All she had done was bring to the surface all the latent competitiveness Simon must always have felt for David. Or perhaps it wasn't so latent. Perhaps it had been more or less overt in their friendship all along, but I had never noticed because Simon had seemed always so appreciative of David's victories, so secure in his own territory.

Now I remembered how often I'd thought Simon's interest in me was predicated on my relationship with David. I remembered he had been in love with Sarah. That the few parts Sarah had taken in the years since she'd met David were usually at Simon's instigation. That it was he who had insisted she play Marie Louise in the film version of *The King of Rome*. This continuing interest, this meddling, in Sarah's career, it occurred to me, went beyond friendship. It smacked of rivalry. By courting Sarah, by championing her, perhaps Simon hoped to convince her that he was a man altogether more reasonable, more supportive, more loving than her husband. Perhaps he hoped that once she understood this, Sarah would one day leave David for him. Taking from David something he had, something he wanted, was no easy chore; the victory would be very sweet. In this context, of course, Sarah was less a woman than a symbol.

When David got Sarah pregnant, Simon had been checkmated. How furious he must have been at his plan's going awry. No wonder he was enraged now at the possibility that David might have once again taken the queen in a game he hadn't realized they were playing.

I knew I was psychologizing wildly, spinning behavioral theories out of the thinnest air, but suddenly everything seemed much clearer to me than it had before. Well, most friendships have a hidden, a dangerous, a neurotic layer, as do most love relationships. They aren't less important for that, or less necessary.

"Your friendship with David may not be perfect, Simon, but it's valuable. You matter a lot to each other. David isn't interested in Fiona. And I don't think she's interested in him. I think she likes to play. I think she likes to calculate who she could have and on what terms. It's a little ego game, maybe one we all play on some level. Don't take it seriously. Especially not if you mean to go on with her."

The women in the alcove opposite us paid their bill, and got up to leave. The older one, the one with the dyed red hair, flashed me a sympathetic smile. She must have thought Simon and I were lovers quarreling.

"You're right," said Simon. "You're very right."

"Don't be a fool, Simon. Let this go. Forget it." I took his hand and smiled. "If not for yourself, for me. Think how miserable I'd feel, how guilty, if you ended your friendship with David because of some stupid remark of mine."

"Don't worry." He smiled back, encouragingly. "It won't come to that. And if it does, believe me, it won't have anything to do with you, or anything you've said."

And leaving me with that small comfort, he called the waiter to pay the bill.

✌ *Chapter 30* ✌

Duncan and I had dinner in the hotel restaurant, which was convenient, luxurious, and with an essentially French menu. "I am sick of Wienerschnitzel," he said to me. "And if I never see another dumpling for as long as I live, I won't complain."

Duncan had not been scheduled to work that day and had spent the afternoon being entertained by a high-ranking diplomat in the British embassy. He'd been taken to lunch, plied with pastries, introduced to countless English and Austrian officials, and in general made to perform as befits an international film star. He had comported himself wonderfully well, he assured me. I was certain he had. Duncan liked being a star and thrived in the spotlight. The only time he was ever discreet was during his divorce from Sarah, which to me was the measure of how much he really did love her.

While he regaled me with stories of his afternoon's adventures, transforming the events of what must have been many dreary hours into amusing anecdotes he would continue to refine in his countless retellings, I paid as always less attention to what he said than to his voice. It had lost none of its richness, none of its power. It hadn't, as happens with a lot of English actors, become mannered.

"Do you know what I miss about him most?" Cassandra had moaned to me over what had by then become our ritual tea at Brown's. "His voice. Isn't that absurd? But it's so sexy. You can't imagine how exciting it was, always, just to have him walk in the door and say my name. Of course," she added as she bit into a chocolate eclair, "the rest of him isn't bad, either.

And it wasn't. The hours he spent every day working out, Duncan insisted, more than compensated for the amount of liquor he consumed each night. The alcohol he drank hadn't padded his body or coarsened his features; and the lines added by time to his face had sketched a depth of character he didn't in reality possess. His hair hadn't noticeably lost any of its thickness, though it was by then (unless wigged or dyed for a performance) a beautiful shade of silver-gray. He was just fifty but had the look of a distinguished elder statesman. He must have looked more the diplomat than any of the men with whom he'd spent the afternoon.

"Damn the man," boomed Cassandra, her eyes suddenly filling with tears. "When am I going to get over him?" They had been divorced for nearly two years, and there didn't seem to be any sign yet that she would. "I was such a fool," she moaned, helping herself to a strawberry meringue. Cassandra had gained a lot of weight, which only her extreme height helped her to carry. She looked more the Amazon than ever. "Such a fool," she repeated.

What she was castigating herself for was allowing Duncan to go off alone on location for a film. Busy with designing her fall collection, she was certain he could be trusted for at least half the scheduled eight weeks in the Bahamas, by which time she would be able to join him. She was wrong. Not only did he start an affair with the seventeen-year-old who played his daughter in the film, he fell in love with her, as foolishly in love as a middle-aged man can be with a woman far too young for him. Hurt and jealous, Cassandra was nevertheless willing to sit it out, to wait for the first obsessive surge of lust to dissipate and for Duncan to come to his senses—as he had before. This wasn't the first affair he'd indulged in since their marriage. But Duncan, at that point, appreciated neither Cassandra's patience nor her understanding. He wanted a divorce. He wanted to marry his Deirdre. "I've never felt like this before in my life," he assured Cassandra, who didn't doubt it was true: after all, Duncan had never before in his life been so old.

"They are revolting together," she had confided to me in her penetrating whisper. "Obscene. Is there anything in the world more grotesque than the sight of an aging lover with his child paramour? It makes my flesh positively crawl to think of them making love. I'd despise him, if I didn't love him so much."

*   *   *

When the waiter arrived with our entree, Duncan ended his tales of life among the diplomats; and as soon as we were alone again, I tucking into my *canard au poivre vert*, Duncan into his *foie de veau au lard*, he asked me again about Cassandra and I told him again she was fine, wonderful, in fact. That didn't seem at all to be what he wanted to hear. Others who had seen her recently, he told me, had said she was still in a pretty desperate state. I went on nonchalantly eating, replying that Cassandra hadn't seemed in the least desperate to me, that in fact she had been quite jolly. Since Duncan still looked dubious, I happily supplied some corroboratory evidence: the success of her latest collection (after several greeted with giant yawns), her excitement at having one of her early seventies ensembles included in the Victoria and Albert Costume Collection, a whirl of social engagements; and—for good measure—I added the name of the man she was seeing, who happened to be American and the head of a successful advertising agency. People who gloat on the psychic scars they've left on lovers make me furious.

"Oh?" said Duncan, trying not to sound as interested as in fact he was. "Really? I read about it in one of the gossip columns so assumed it wasn't true." He smiled. "Nothing ever is that they print about me."

"Oh, it's true," I said.

"Is it serious?"

"Who knows? But she was in a very good mood."

Despite my annoyance, I was willing to concede that Duncan's interest in Cassandra was, on one level, genuine concern for her welfare. But that other, totally despicable level of possessive egotism was not one I was inclined to indulge. How he would have loved to hear that Cassandra was still pining for him, that all the pleasures of her life in no way compensated for his loss. And though that was largely true, I would never have told him so. Even had Cassandra not been my friend, some sense of female solidarity would have prevented me. Not that I didn't understand and even empathize with Duncan. Contemptible or not, I would have been delighted to know that Ned spent an occasional sleepless night thinking of me.

"I treated her very badly," said Duncan, with a mixture of real regret and smug self-satisfaction.

"If only," I said, "making people happy made us feel as powerful as keeping them continually miserable, what a much better place the world would be."

Duncan looked at me blankly, not knowing what I was talking about; but then the waiter appeared to clear our plates, show us the dessert trolley, and bring us coffee. Once again Duncan changed the subject, reverting to gossip, and this time I gave him my undivided attention. Not only was he very amusing, he was also a vast bouillabaisse of information, providing me tasty little tidbits about, among others, Joe Vasari, who didn't interest me much, and Fiona Brent, who did.

She had been married first, Duncan told me, when still in her teens to an actor whom she'd left for the man who'd directed her in her first television episode. She'd then left the director for a newspaper television critic, and the critic for the head of drama at one of the television companies. The head of drama had been the one to leave that time, when he arrived home early one day because of a canceled meeting and found Fiona in bed with the wife of his best friend. The wife was in the process of writing a series of thirteen half-hours for one of the independent television companies and had been instrumental in Fiona's being cast in the lead. And so on. She was presently married to an up-and-coming English film producer, hence the quasi-discretion of her affair with Simon. "She is a woman of vast experience and catholic taste," concluded Duncan, "which is what makes her attitude to Joe rather unfathomable, don't you think? One would expect her to be a little bit more liberal, a trifle more understanding."

"No one as ambitious as she sounds can take the time to be understanding," I responded. "If she had to think about anyone but herself for a minute, who knows what golden opportunity might pass her by?"

Duncan smiled at me. "I see she's earned herself another fan."

"My dislike isn't rational," I said. "I loathed her at first sight."

"I alway reckoned you had very good instincts," he comforted.

He told me about an evening he and Deirdre had recently spent with Simon and Fiona. "You haven't met Deirdre yet, have you?" asked Duncan. I shook my head. "You'd like her. She's in London doing a telly, a new BBC sitcom," he explained parenthetically. "Anyway, there we were, the four of us, having this reasonably pleasant meal together, talking about what we planned to do when we finished filming, where we were going on holiday, that sort of thing. Then Simon mentioned he'd been sent an interesting new play, by Jeremy Hall, this year's Pinter. He'd liked it so much, he said, he was thinking about doing it in the West End as soon as he completed editing on *The King of Rome*. Fiona looked surprised. That was clearly the first she'd heard of it. Her eyes began to glitter with speculation. You could see her mind turning over endless possibilities. She began to question Simon, in general terms, about who had sent it, when he'd got it. Simon knew where she was heading and said immediately that the lead role was a wonderful part for a woman and that he'd sent it to Sarah to read. We were all, I confess, dumbfounded. 'But she's pregnant,' said Fiona, with a great deal of indignation. 'She'll have had her baby by then,' responded Simon, with amazing *sang froid*, I thought. 'The timing will be perfect.'"

"Not very politic of him mentioning it at dinner."

"Not very politic of him sending the play to Sarah," corrected Duncan, pouring us each a glass of wine from the new bottle the waiter had just brought. "But the truth is, Sarah's a much better actress than Fiona. Fiona really isn't in the same league, not nearly. And Simon's not so besotted he doesn't know it. I suppose he was hoping Fiona would take the news better if she heard it in public."

"Why does everyone always think that, when nobody ever does?"

Duncan laughed. "There was an unbelievable row. Fiona doesn't throw things the way Sarah does, but that voice of hers! It does carry. She used every expletive I've ever heard, very forcefully. Even the people who didn't understand English got the general drift. There was quite a lot of gaping. We were in a very posh restaurant, and you know what the Viennese are like: excruciatingly well-mannered. The maître d' came scurrying over. Simon told Fiona to sit down and shut up. She told him to stuff it, and stormed out. Simon apologized and finished his meal. He didn't seem in the least bothered. Deirdre was, though, poor little thing. She'd never heard anything like it in her life. That was the week before you arrived. They seemed to have patched it up," he added. "Or at least I thought they had until the past few days. Fiona's been flirting like mad with David. And Simon's been in a wicked mood."

"Did Sarah agree to do the play?" I asked. She hadn't mentioned it to me, and I hadn't heard her discuss it with David.

Duncan shrugged his shoulders. "You know Sarah," he said. "She won't agree to anything at this point. But Simon is convinced she'll say yes eventually. And these past few years he's certainly had a better track record than the rest of us getting her to work."

"If Sarah doesn't want to work," I said, for the moment playing devil's advocate, "why not leave her alone? Why don't Simon, and you, and me for that matter, just leave her alone? If she's happy being a wife and mother, why does she have to do anything else? It's a full-time job, you know."

"For one thing," responded Duncan, "Sarah has a great deal of talent, which she's wasting. For another, she isn't a full-time wife and mother. She has Mrs. T and Marie-Paule. And she needs them, don't you doubt that for a minute. She'd go mad left alone with those children. Not that she doesn't love them: she just doesn't have the temperament. For a third, I don't think Sarah is happy. Not completely happy."

"Who is?" I asked.

"Sarah was happy when she was married to me."

"If that were true, Duncan," I said, as kindly as I could, "she would never have left you."

"She was more at peace," he insisted. "Now she seems fragmented, torn, as if nothing she has is really satisfactory. She seems always to be looking for something more. She didn't use to be like that. When she was married to me, what she didn't have wasn't important to her, or at least not important enough to make her miserable."

"She was younger then," I said. "When you're young there seems to be all the time in the world to get what you want. It's only as you get older, when you realize you're not going to get it after all, that it begins to hurt."

He wasn't really listening to me. He wasn't even with me. He was caught in the past, in that golden age when he and Sarah had been young and happy. "You know," he said, "it's a pity Sarah ever got pregnant. It would have spared everyone a great deal of trouble if she hadn't." He was thinking, I knew, of that long-ago summer in London when Sarah had told him she was pregnant and was leaving him.

"The path not taken," I said. "Do you really think it would have led to somewhere so different?"

"Yes, I do." It was my turn to look dubious. "I'm not still in love with her, if that's what your look means," he said. "And it isn't just my ego, as large as you may think that is. I care about Sarah. And I don't, quite honestly, think David is good for her."

"He loves her," I said, defending David instinctively with conventional words even I knew were inadequate.

"Love," repeated Duncan. "When has that ever kept me, or anyone, from fucking someone over?"

"And he's faithful to her," I added viciously.

"He's ruining her."

"Duncan, come off it. Nobody's responsible for making, or ruining, anybody else's life. Not in the sense you mean. You know that."

"I thought you'd defend him." He sounded less angry than defeated.

"Why talk to me about him? You know David's my friend." My voice had grown quieter to match Duncan's.

"Isn't Sarah?"

"I don't have to choose between them. There's no need to."

Duncan threw up his hands. "All right. All right. Have it your own way."

"Do you talk to Sarah like this?" I asked, wondering how much of her mood that summer might have been due to Duncan's interference.

He shook his head. "I only encourage her to work. There'd be no point in my criticizing David to her, would there?"

"None at all," I replied, which—I supposed—was why he wanted me to do it in his stead. Again, as with Cassandra, Duncan's concern seemed part genuine, part an expression of possessive egotism, exacerbated in Sarah's case by that competitiveness David always brought out in people.

"You may think I don't like David, but that's not true. I admire him enormously," he said as if that were the same thing. "But I'm worried that he'll let Sarah sink into idleness the way she did after the other children were born. It would be such a pity. She's such a brilliant actress, you know. A truly wonderful actress. Why don't you have a word with her?" He returned to the attack. "Perhaps if she likes the play Simon gave her, you could encourage her to do it? After all, that's no skin off David's nose, is it?" Then he smiled at me, one of his totally sincere, absolutely brilliant smiles. "What a strange expression that is. Do you suppose I've been spending too much time lately in Los Angeles?"

✀ *Chapter 31* ✀

At eight the next morning, Lissie came into my room and leaned tentatively over me. "Daddy says you have to get up now," she whispered.

"Go away," I mumbled. I'd been plagued with bad dreams all night and hadn't slept well.

"We have to get an early start," she continued, undaunted.

"Why?" I asked, coming awake. Her bright little face shone into mine. She had Caroline's thick red hair pulled back and plaited into a pigtail, but her green eyes were always alight with enthusiasm. Like David, she seemed incredibly alive. Unlike him, she possessed a wonderfully forthright and sunny disposition. "Isn't she just like my mother?" David would ask, more and more often as Lissie got older.

"To have time to see everything," Lissie replied in answer to my question. "Don't you want to?" Her voice expressed the incredulity she always felt when faced with an apathetic other. It was a tone she often used with her sister, Kate, whom she loved, but didn't understand at all.

"At this moment, no," I said, as I sat up. Then I smiled at her reassuringly. "But I will, when your father gets through with me."

"We're going to the castle where Richard the Lionheart was held prisoner," she said, trying to instill in me some of her own sense of adventure.

"Did you learn about him at school?"

She shook her head. "No, Daddy told us the story. We learn American history at school."

"When do you have to be back for the new term?"

"The week after next." A worried look crossed her face, and I was immediately sorry I'd mentioned the subject. "Next week, really," she continued, "but Daddy talked Mommy into letting Kate and me stay longer. She didn't want to. I guess she misses us."

"I know she does," I said, "very much." Then, because children of divorce don't need anyone contributing generously to their guilt, I added: "But she's not lonely. There's a difference, you know. She's having a really nice summer, with all her friends. I had lunch with her before I left New York."

"Did Mommy," she began hesitantly, an unfamiliar nervousness in her voice, "did she say anything about California?"

"Like what?" I asked, cautiously.

Lissie shrugged. "I heard her and Daddy arguing, on the phone. She wants to move there. Daddy said I shouldn't worry about it. He said Mommy's changed her mind. But . . ."

Lissie had, after the first shock, coped amazingly well with her parents' divorce, accepting Sarah and Mark with a remarkable graciousness, adjusting quickly to circumstances changing so rapidly they would have sent a less innately stable child pell-mell into therapy. But the bottom line of her serenity had always seemed to be the knowledge that David was nearby and readily accessible. Lissie would adjust, I supposed, to a move to California, just as she'd adjusted to everything else she'd been faced with. But why should she have to? Caroline's desire to make a new and different life for herself was understandable, commendable even, but was it worth the cost to her children? Even the phlegmatic Kate would suffer. The only joy she seemed to get from the world came from either David or Mark. Only they kept the dark cloud fixed firmly over her head from totally enveloping her.

"Does thinking of the children ever stop David from doing what *he* wants?" Caroline had said to me while still in the first throes of excitement at the prospect of opening a business in Los Angeles. "Not on your life! It's just that he's smart enough, manipulative enough, to get Sarah and me to arrange our lives to suit him. Well, now he can arrange his to suit me. It's about time!"

"Your daddy's right," I said. "There's no point worrying about something that may never happen, or might not happen in the way you think. Even if your mother does finally decide it's best to move to California, don't forget, your father could always move there, too."

"He doesn't want to," she insisted. "He said so."

"Well, he might have to, whether he wants to or not, because of business. That's where movies are made, after all."

She cheered up at that. She was old enough, or smart enough, to realize that the combination of business and children might change David's position, where one of them alone would fail. "We spent last summer in Los Angeles," she said. "Remember? When Daddy was writing the movie."

"You had a good time, didn't you?"

She nodded. "Kate liked Disneyland." That obviously gave the state an important seal of approval. "I liked the mountains. There was snow, in July," she said, her voice full of wonder.

There was a knock at the door, and when I replied it opened and David peered in. "That's the last time I send you to wake Nikki up," he said to Lissie when he saw her sitting on the edge of my bed.

"She did her best," I replied. "I'm not easy."

"That's what I've heard," said David.

"*Pas devant*," I said, with mock severity.

"Lissie speaks fluent French. Don't you, sweetheart?"

"No, I don't," corrected Lissie. "Nikki doesn't care about Richard the Lionheart," she added.

"She will when I get through with her."

Lissie smiled gleefully. "That's what Nikki said."

Overcome as usual by Lissie's smile, he hugged her. "Enough loafing. Go and help Mrs. T with breakfast. Marie-Paule's already left. Will's driven her to the airport." She'd gone home to visit her family for the weekend. "I'd like to get out of here before noon, if possible."

"First I have to help Olivia get dressed. I promised."

As Lissie went out the door, David stared after her a moment. "I'm going to miss her when she goes. And Kate." He ran his hand through his hair. "What were you two talking about?"

"None of your business," I replied.

"She's my daughter," he wheedled.

"Private conversations are private." I pushed back the covers and stood up.

"You used to tell me everything," he said sadly.

"That's what you think. Now, go away and let me get dressed."

He eyed my body, covered more than adequately by a cotton nightshirt. "You've gained weight since you arrived."

"There's no need to be nasty just because I won't tell you what you want to know."

"It's all those dumplings you've been eating, all that Sachertorte."

"Go away," I repeated.

"You never could take criticism," he said in a superior tone which implied he could. I laughed, and so did he. Then he handed me a letter he'd been holding. "This is for you. And don't spend hours mooning over it. I really want to get going."

He left and I climbed back into the bed to read my letter. It was from Sam, postmarked Chicago, where he'd been the week before on business.

So much else had been going on, I'd hardly thought of him at all since I'd arrived in Vienna. Usually I thought of him a lot, either because I wanted to see him and couldn't, or because I could and didn't want to. I spent a lot of time trying to assess exactly how much he meant to me, how important he was to my life. Often, during those ruminations, it would begin to seem much less demanding to be married, with life settled into a thoughtless routine, than to be seesawing through a relationship with a married lover. If large clear spaces of mind were what I needed to work, perhaps marriage was the place to find them. I certainly didn't have them at that moment, cluttered as my thoughts always were with questions: Will he meet me for dinner, or won't he? Should I make an alternate plan, or just stay home if he can't? Do I really love him, or don't I? Do I want to end this relationship, or not? Still, I never once asked Sam to get a divorce; and when he once or twice broached the subject, I changed it.

He had telephoned me often while I was in London, but our last conversation had ended in a fight when I'd told him that instead of returning to New York I was flying to Vienna for a few days. Sam had none of Ned's understanding about or appreciation for David. He loathed him, and was jealous of him; and I suppose he had every right to be.

"We could finally have some time away together. Isn't that what we've been saying we want?" Sam had asked, trying to change my mind. "It would be fun." He was calling me from his office, an elegant room done in shades of beige with brass accents and Hockney lithographs. I had been there only once, and only because I had insisted: I had needed a setting to place him against. On a table opposite his desk was a lily in a clear round vase, placed there fresh every morning by his secretary.

"I'm sorry," I said, and heard the squeak of his chair as he rose in frustration and turned to look out through his blinds to the traffic passing below on Madison Avenue. He was about five feet eleven and slender, with pale blue eyes and blond hair that was by then almost completely white. He'd been a very pretty little boy (I'd seen a bar mitzvah photograph of him looking like a Botticelli angel with yarmulke), but age and arrogance had toughened his face. He exuded an aura of success that I, and a lot of women, found sexy. Since five years after his marriage, he'd had a mistress, whom he changed about every two years, I suppose at the point where she started to ask for more than he was willing to give. Until that point, he believed himself head over heels in love with her, and merely tolerant of his wife, who was characterized always as "a good woman, a caring woman, but just not for me." His wife was, however, the mother of his three children, and while they were small, he was determined not to leave her, or them. One of his grievances against David was that he had done just that, abandoned his wife and daughters, the act of a contemptible, irresponsible man. When I met Sam, his two sons were in college and his daughter was a junior in high school. In just a few more years, he'd told me, just as soon as Janie left for college, he'd be free. She'd left the year before, and Sam was still safe at home. On the other hand, our affair had lasted about two and a half years: a record.

Sometimes, when I felt guilty about his wife, I consoled myself thinking that since Sam was always going to have a mistress, his wife was much safer with me in the role than anyone else. I certainly wanted to sleep with her husband, talk to him, laugh with him, even have an occasional surreptitious weekend. But I didn't at all want to marry him.

"I don't get it," Sam had said, unable to control the frustration, the irritation, in his voice. "I thought you'd leap at the chance of going to Chicago with me."

"My idea of a good time is not hiding in a hotel room while you booze it up with your business cronies and their wives in the bar."

"It wouldn't be like that."

"What would you tell them? That I'm your sister?"

"I can't exactly see you 'hiding' either," he evaded. "I'm sure you'll find plenty to keep you occupied while I take care of business. You can walk along the shore. You like to walk. You can go to the Art Institute, look at the Impressionist collection. You can go shopping, for chrissake."

"I've been to Chicago. I haven't been to Vienna," I said quietly.

"That's not the point. The point is being with me."

"I'll be with you the week after, in New York."

"Nikki, sometimes I get the feeling you don't give a damn about me."

"That's not true."

"You'll do anything, go anywhere, for David Walton. All he has to do is hint he wants something and you run to see that he gets it."

"That's not true either."

"If he were the one asking you to come to Chicago, would you be saying no?"

"Now you're being ridiculous."

"I want you to come back."

"Don't tell me what to do, Sam. Don't pressure me."

"No one's allowed to pressure you, right? No one! Except maybe David."

"Would you leave that one alone, Sam, please? I'm a little sick of hearing it."

"Maybe you're sick of me."

"Right now, I am. Very sick."

"If that's how you feel . . ." he began, revving up for a scene of major confrontation, which I wasn't in the mood for and didn't want to have on the phone.

"I think we should end this conversation, before I say anything else we'll both be sorry for. I'll call you when I get back to New York. At your office, of course," I added sarcastically, and hung up. I could never resist goading Sam for being married, though I didn't want him any way else. I did it instinctively. Not only did the conventions of the situation seem to demand it, but Sam needed it as a proof of my love. All in all, his marriage was a very convenient scapegoat for the ambivalences in my mind, the inconsistencies in my behavior.

His letter was a flag of truce. He was prepared to forget my defection over Chicago as long as I was prepared to negotiate new rules for our relationship when I returned to New York. "We have to find ways to spend more time together," he wrote, "even at the sacrifice of your career, and my family." There was the hint that he had already discussed the possibility of divorce with his wife, which I doubted. According to my theory, after twenty-seven years of marriage, a man was unlikely to leave his wife except for someone exactly like her, but younger. I didn't have the right qualifications. Perhaps whoever came after me would.

I folded the letter, put it back into its envelope and out of my mind. I didn't want to give Sam up, but then I didn't want to give anyone up. I wanted to keep them all, on my terms. When I got to New York, I would negotiate; but until then, I didn't want to think about how much, if anything, I would be willing to sacrifice. It weakens the bargaining position to know in advance just how much you're prepared to concede.

By eleven that morning we were on our way, David driving the station wagon, Lissie navigating, Sarah and me and the children altering our seats at every stop, so that those in the back could be up front, and vice versa, David stopping every squabble with a joke or a warning. The children, despite David's being neither a stern nor a remote parent figure, usually obeyed him, which never ceased to amaze me. Doting parents are inevitably laid waste by their offspring, my mother used to claim; and I was inclined to agree. But David's children seemed no more capable than anyone else of denying him what he wanted. They either succumbed to his charm or collapsed against the brick wall of his will. Even Olivia's tantrums were quelled by one curt word from him. He could easily have been the ruin of them all, I suppose, but he wasn't. What saved them was that David did know, despite what Sarah thought, who they each were, and loved them for being it. That he saw their flaws was evident, but so too was the fact that he admired them though they weren't perfect. That gave them confidence, and that confidence enabled them to grow unfettered by the desire for revenge, the need to get back at their father either by being overly ambitious or by failing. David was, finally, able to give his children what Mr. Walton had denied him. He became the father he'd wanted and never had.

We left Vienna through softly billowing green countryside which I thought was lovely but David and Sarah dismissed as insignificant compared to the wonders I would soon see. They had returned to Austria often over the years, to ski in winter and tour in summer, so they knew the country well.

"Just wait until you see the Danube Valley," said Sarah.

"The Wachau," translated David lovingly.

It was all that they promised: a misty, meandering stretch of the Danube, flowing in a hollow between rolling granite hills topped by pine trees with long, bare trunks and an asymmetrical cap of branches, like a parade of circus clowns on stilts. Pretty villages perched above its banks, ruined castles loomed in the distance, and onion domes (a legacy of the Turkish invasion) crowned church steeples and farmhouse towers. The warm, sweet smell of manure penetrated even the closed car windows.

"And this is nothing compared to the Salzkammergut," warned David.

To Lissie's delight, we explored the castle at Dürnstein where, during the Third Crusade, Richard the Lionheart had been imprisoned by one of the Austrian dukes. They'd had a big row, explained Mark, during a siege and were sworn enemies. So when a shipwreck in the Adriatic forced Richard to travel overland, he did it warily, disguised as a peasant. "But he wasn't a very good actor," said Mark.

"He forgot to keep his head bowed," supplied Lissie, "so he was recognized and arrested."

"And he wasn't found till years later," said Kate, "by the faithful Blondel."

"He stood outside the castle, singing," added Olivia.

"Hoping Richard was inside and would recognize his voice," continued Mark.

Then all the children, including Nicholas, chimed in: "'Surely that's my old friend Blondel,' said the king, who began to sing along so Blondel would know he was there." They'd obviously heard the story many times before.

"His ransom paid for most of the buildings in the neighborhood," summed up David succinctly.

Though mostly David drove, confining his cigarette smoking to rest stops, so as to avoid a car full of sick passengers, occasionally Sarah and I would spell him. Sarah was an excellent driver, with iron nerves, totally unfazed by the narrow mountain roads that terrified David, who was afraid of heights. Mark had inherited the trait, as had Kate, and both children sat pale but uncomplaining through the most harrowing parts of the trip, mimicking their father's stoicism.

"Close your eyes if you want to," encouraged David.

"You don't," Mark pointed out.

"I'm trying to teach myself not to be afraid."

"Me, too," replied Mark.

And Kate would nod, her eyes round with terror, determined to follow her brother's lead. If the poor child even blinked, Olivia would hoot at her, "Fraidy cat," then immediately apologize at a look from David.

"Olivia, you really are a little monster, aren't you?" said Sarah, her voice disapproving.

"I'm not afraid," Olivia replied defensively.

"Me, too," Nicholas chimed in.

"Well, I am," said David in repressive tones.

"It's all right," Mark comforted, patting Kate's hand. The bond between them was so strong, they might have been twins.

We stopped at quaint villages to eat Wienerschnitzel or sausages, walked through cobbled town squares where men strolled in lederhosen and feathered caps, stood gaping at churches plain enough on the outside but inside (no matter how tiny the town) a baroque fantasy trimmed ornately in gold. We slept in white stucco *gasthausen* with balconies of worked wood and window boxes dripping pink petunias.

The farther we drove, the more picturesque it became, until—as David and Sarah had promised—in the Salzkammergut we rode out of reality into storybook illustrations of idealized villages. They perched precariously on the edge of limpid blue lakes dotted in the distance with sails, climbed steeply up winding paths lined with creamy stucco houses bedecked in flowers, ascending to churches with terraced graveyards accessible only by foot, to the towering granite massif behind that marked their outer perimeters. They were a fantasy that surpassed the wildest imaginings of Walt Disney.

"I'm tired," moaned Nicholas, confronting another steep climb.

"You're such a whiner," said Olivia derisively.

"Pretend you're superman," said David, and he and Sarah grinned as Nicholas got his second wind and spurted to the top.

There were pastries in Bad Ischl even better than the ones I'd had in Vienna, and near Hallstatt there were salt mines and ice caves and underground waterfalls to compensate the children for all the churches and ruined abbeys, though in fact for the first two days they had been interested in everything, and even remained patient when I took too long over a photograph.

"Here she goes again," Olivia would say, her voice full of pained resignation, as she saw me reaching for my camera.

"New York is bigger," said Kate. "As big as that mountain. And you can take a bus."

In Salzburg we stayed at a hotel which overlooked the river to the Old Town and the hulking presence of the Hohensalzburg Fortress. We only had the one day to explore, and the city remains a jumble of impressions: of traffic jams and crowds of tourists, of narrow streets and grand squares, the terrifying jerk of the funicular starting its steep ascent to the fortress, the clip-clop on the cobbles of the horse-drawn *Fiakers*, the smell of manure in the Domplatz, of fresh pastry in the Getreide-gasse, the rich brandy color of Mozart's violin.

The children had had enough of churches and graveyards, of palaces and statues: the sight of the house where Mozart was born failed to impress. On the other hand, the chocolate Mozartballs instantly won their hearts, though it was difficult to tell whether they preferred asking for or eating them. "Mozartballs, please," Nicholas would say as the others giggled, thrilled by the daring of it. It became their favorite term of derision.

"That's enough," Sarah said sharply, when Nicholas tried for the laugh once too often. But David was too amused to lend support, and the clowning continued. "He's more of a child than Nicholas," muttered Sarah to me, shooting David a resentful glance.

All our nerves were by then a little frayed. We'd been in too confined a space with only one another for too long. My modest apartment in New York had begun to assume in my mind the proportions of a mansion and its quiet the essence of heavenly peace. Like the children, I wanted to go home.

But David had decided that hearing a concert would be good for our souls.

"That's mad," said Sarah. "They're exhausted. They'll never sit through it."

David democratically asked the children if they wanted to go, and, faced with the choice of that or bed, they chose the concert. "It'll be good for them," said David. "They don't hear enough music."

"I'm not going," said Sarah.

I was torn. Like Sarah, I thought it an idiotic idea. However, the concert was being held in the turret room of the fortress and the appeal of that was hard to resist.

"Don't be spoilsports," encouraged David, and finally Sarah and I gave in.

The children were put down for a nap, on the theory that would avoid any potential problems, and possibly it would have, except that Simon phoned.

We were in the sitting room of the Walton suite, just about ready to leave, when the phone rang. Lissie answered and handed the receiver to David. "Daddy, it's Simon," she said, and he frowned in anticipation of a crisis.

But the problem didn't seem to be serious, just a question of cutting Louis Foch, who'd had some kind of gastric upset, from a scene in which he didn't figure too importantly to begin with. They did it in minutes, David making bold pencil notes on the script which Mark had brought him from the briefcase in the bedroom. Despite the ease of the solution, the tension never quite left David's voice, and I saw Sarah look at him curiously, wondering what could possibly be wrong. She knew nothing, I supposed, about David's strained relationship with Simon. How could he have told her when Fiona Brent was its cause?

When they'd finished, David handed the phone to Sarah. "He wants to talk to you." It was his turn to look curious.

Sarah took the receiver reluctantly, and her replies to Simon were monosyllabic and wary. I knew very well what they were talking about, though David clearly didn't. "Don't hound me, Simon," said Sarah finally, sounding extremely irritated. "I'm in no state to make any decisions now." Then Simon must have said something conciliatory, because Sarah smiled, and her goodbye when she said it was warm.

"What was that about?" asked David.

Sarah hesitated while she decided whether or not to lie. Then, casting a swift and apologetic glance at me for what might follow, she said, "Simon sent me a play to read, and he wanted to know if I'll do it after the baby is born."

"You never mentioned it to me," said David.

"Oh, didn't I?" asked Sarah. She was such a good actress I almost believed she had actually forgotten.

"You know goddam well you didn't," snapped David. "When did he send it to you?" The children shifted uneasily, dreading the quarrel that seemed inevitable.

"A few weeks ago. What difference does it make? It's not as if I've decided to do it."

"That's not the point," said David.

"If we don't leave now," I interrupted, "we're going to miss the concert. Of course," I added, "if you'd rather stay here and fight, the children and I can go on our own."

As our disgruntled group walked through the Old Town towards the funicular, it started to rain. "It's going down my neck," complained Kate.

"Whiner," sneered Olivia.

"Don't start," warned Sarah, as she adjusted Kate's collar to keep out the rain. "I couldn't bear it if you started quarreling."

We climbed into the first car, for a better view of the city, which was another mistake. As the funicular lurched forward and began its ascent at what seemed like a ninety-degree angle up the sheer rock face, David and Mark turned white and Kate threatened to be sick. I pulled her head down into my lap, ordering her to close her eyes, while David and Mark stared resolutely at the floor of the cabin and Sarah, Lissie, Nicholas, and Olivia looked out unperturbed over the darkening city.

At the top, crossing the observation terrace to the entrance, we were buffeted by wind and pelted by rain. Then came the climb up five flights of stone steps to the tower. The whole thing suddenly began to strike me as funny. What a price to pay for music! But David and Sarah weren't at all amused, nor were the children. "I'm tired," complained Nicholas, in the middle of the third flight.

"It's not much farther," said David, the enthusiasm gone from his voice. Then he reached down and swung Nicholas up into his arms. Olivia frowned.

"Not a word out of you, miss," warned her mother.

The concert room once we got there was worth the effort. It had Gothic wood carvings on the walls and coffered ceilings with gilded studs. At the far end was a raised platform on which stood four music stands and two giant candelabra. On either side were windows overlooking the illuminated towers and domes of the city. Other candelabra, their candles flickering in the slight draft, spread light from the corners of the room. An audience gathering to hear Mozart play would have been greeted by essentially the same sight.

But perhaps they would have left the children home. The modern seats were graceless folding chairs, and the unraked floor prevented all but those in front from seeing the musicians. The children kept quiet through most of the Mozart quartet, but finally Olivia began to fidget, kicking her feet against her chair, and Nicholas to whisper, asking how soon it would be over. Warnings from David and Sarah had no effect. "I'm tired," pleaded Nicholas. During the pause before the Beethoven began, Sarah—completely out of patience—grabbed both children by their arms and hauled them from the room. Nicholas let out a wail, and David got up and followed them out.

"Shall we stay?" I asked the other three.

Kate looked to Mark for a decision. "Do we have to take the funicular down?" he asked.

I shook my head. "There are steps. We can walk."

"Then I think I'd like to stay," he said.

"So would I," agreed Lissie. They were less avid to hear the rest of the concert than anxious to avoid witnessing the battle that was about to be fought. So, for that matter, was I.

By the time we got back to the hotel, it was over. Or, rather, a truce had been called. Sarah had retired to their bedroom while David waited in the sitting room for our return.

The three children looked at him warily as we entered, but David smiled at them. "Come in, come in," he said reassuringly. "All's quiet on the home front. Don't look so nervous."

"Did you and Mommy have a fight?" asked Mark.

David nodded. "But it's finished now and everything's fine. We just have bad tempers we never learned to control. Let that be a lesson to you to learn to control yours."

"I don't have a temper," said Kate.

David grinned. "Yes, you do," he said, picking her up. "It's just buried very deep, like your sense of humor." He began to tickle her, and she started to laugh. So did the rest of us, suddenly relieved to find everything back to normal. "Shhh, quiet," he cautioned. "Everyone's asleep."

As soon as he'd sent the children off to bed, with a warning to go to sleep immediately since we had to make an early start for Vienna in the morning, the strain reappeared in his face. He lit a cigarette, offered me a nightcap and when I said no, opened the well-stocked liquor cabinet, took out the whiskey bottle, poured a shot into a glass, and drank. It must have been some fight, I thought.

"I'd better get to sleep, too," I said.

He nodded and watched me walk to the door. Just before I reached it, he said: "Why do you suppose she never mentioned that play to me?"

I didn't have the energy then even to attempt to explain. Not that it would have done any good. "Don't ask me," I said. "If anybody knows, it's Sarah."

He shook his head. "If she does, she's not saying. Goodnight."

"Goodnight," I said, and left, wondering—not for the first time that evening—if Simon had deliberately meant to make trouble.

I was awakened by a loud crash from the Walton sitting room. It was followed a moment later by another. I leaped out of bed, pulled on my robe, and opened the door that led through from my room to their suite. An end table had been knocked over and a lamp lay broken on the flowered carpet. A chair was knocked on its side. Sarah was crouched on the floor, David bending over her trying to lift her to her feet. Somewhere in the background, Nicholas was crying, while the other children stood in their bedroom doors watching wide-eyed.

"I'm sorry, I'm sorry," moaned Sarah. Her speech was thick and slurred. The door of the bar was open, and on top of it stood an almost empty bottle of gin.

"Mommy fell," said David. "She'll be all right."

"Didn't mean to wake you," said Sarah, letting David help her unsteadily to her feet. "I'm fine. See?"

"Come on, kids, back to bed," I said, as David looked at me gratefully. "We still have to get up early in the morning."

"I'm sorry," repeated Sarah, leaning heavily on David as he led her back to their room.

Lissie and I were still trying to quiet Nicholas when David entered. "Go stay with Sarah for a minute," he said to me, as he took Nicholas into his arms.

"Is Mommy all right?" asked Mark.

"She's fine," replied David soothingly; then, to Nicholas: "Come on, big boy, tell Daddy the problem."

Sarah was lying on the bed, her arm over her eyes, when I entered. There were tears running down her cheeks. She moved her arm to wipe them away and saw me. She closed her eyes. "Oh God," she said.

I sat on the bed beside her and took her hand. "It's all right," I said. "David's getting the children back to bed."

"I couldn't sleep," she told me. "I just wanted a little something to make me sleep."

❧ Chapter 32 ❧

The next morning, at Sarah's instigation, we returned to Vienna by plane. No one, she pointed out, was looking forward to the drive back, so why not just deliver the car to the rental agency and arrange for another to be waiting at the airport in Vienna? When she put her mind to it, Sarah was an extremely good organizer.

We were all feeling subdued. The children were on their best behavior, Olivia hardly daring to speak, Nicholas contented as long as he was near his mother. He sat next to her on the plane and fell asleep with his head in her lap while Sarah leaned over him, stroking his face gently, running her fingers along the line of his cheek and across his mouth. She felt my eyes on her, looked up, gave me a brief smile, then returned to contemplating her son. Her face was pale and drawn with pain. David was remote, unreachable. When he had to, he spoke very quietly, very politely to everyone, including Sarah. Lissie, who sat next to him reading, from time to time glanced up from her book to look anxiously into his face. Olivia, wisely, sat quietly coloring, while Kate and Mark played Go Fish. Once, Mark got up from his seat to look at his mother. "Mommy, are you all right?" he asked.

"Fine, darling. I just have a bit of a headache."

"Mark, don't pester your mother," said David.

"He's not pestering me," replied Sarah evenly. She gave Mark a comforting smile. "I've taken a pill the doctor gave me. I'll be fine in a minute."

When we got back to the villa, Mrs. T took immediate charge of all of us. That we'd returned sooner than she'd expected in no way discombobulated her, though I saw her cast speculative glances at both David and Sarah. "Don't leave those bags here," she said to Will, who had run out to meet us as the car pulled into the drive. "Upstairs with them now, if you don't mind." Then, as Will and David did as told, she turned to Sarah. "You could do with a lie-down," she said.

"It's only a headache," replied Sarah.

"Only," she repeated. "Well, go on up to bed then, and I'll be along in a minute with your tea. I'll ring the doctor, shall I?" she asked, but Sarah shook her head, assuring her it wouldn't be necessary.

Within half an hour, she had Sarah tucked up in bed; the children, over the lunch she had prepared, regaling her and Will with tales of their adventures; and David and me on the patio with a pitcher of lemonade.

He lit a cigarette and blew a cloud of smoke. "Are you still planning to leave tomorrow?" he asked.

"Don't make it sound as if I'm running out on you."

"Will you stay until Sunday?" he asked. Before I could protest, he added, "That way you can take Lissie and Kate back with you. I know they don't mind traveling alone, and they've done it often enough, but this time I'd really prefer them to have company."

Aside from my desire to go, there was no real reason I couldn't stay another few days. My next assignment, some fashion pages for *Harper's Bazaar*, was scheduled for the following Wednesday; and nothing else was set until the end of September when I would cover the Pope's world tour for *L'Express*. I needed more than that to be able to refuse David, who was never, as Sarah had pointed out, an easy person to say no to.

He smiled in approval when I agreed, and with gratitude. "Thank you," he said. "One less thing to worry about." In that sense, David didn't take his friends for granted: he was always touchingly grateful whenever you caved in to his desires. That's what made his friendship even more dangerous.

The phone rang then. It was Simon, announced Mrs. T, for David. I went upstairs to unpack and, about an hour later, was lying on my bed, reading Ambroise Vollard's *Recollections of a Picture Dealer*, which I'd picked up at Hatchard's in London, when there was a knock at the door.

"May I come in, just for a minute?" asked Sarah. The color was back in her face, and the pained expression had faded.

"Of course. Headache better?"

"Much," she said. From outside came the sound of the children playing in the pool, and occasionally Mrs. T's voice cautioning them to be quiet. "David's gone to a script meeting."

"I thought I heard the car."

"I want to apologize," she continued, sitting in the armchair at the foot of the bed, the one in which David had sat on the day of my arrival.

"That's not necessary, Sarah. Really."

"I ruined a lovely holiday."

"It wasn't ruined."

"And I so looked forward to the trip. I wanted everyone to have such a good time."

"Everyone did. I did, certainly."

She shook her head. "When the children look back, all they'll remember is that I made a scene. That's what David will remember, too, isn't it?"

"No," I said, "what David will remember is that funicular ride to the fortress. I've never seen him look so scared."

She smiled. "He was terrified, wasn't he?" Immediately, the smile faded. "It serves him right for suggesting it. What an awful thing to do to Mark and Kate. If only we hadn't gone to that concert," she added, as if that had been the sole cause of the quarrel with David.

"If you'd ever been on vacation with my family, or with the Waltons when David and Jack were small, you'd know how easy we all got off these past few days. We used to start fighting the minute we climbed into the backseat of the car, and never stopped the whole time we were away. I don't know how our parents stood it."

What I was saying was true, but I didn't quite believe it was relevant. And I'm not sure Sarah did either. Family scenes may be inevitable, but they are not all inevitably destructive.

"I know families quarrel," she said, with a sigh. "Mine did, too, though if you had seen us arriving at church on a Sunday morning, you would never have believed it, we looked so ideal, the doctor's picture-book family. But my father had an awful temper. He made life such hell sometimes. I couldn't bear it, all that endless fighting. And yet I have such a dreadful temper myself. Strange, isn't it? And a little frightening, the thought one may turn out to be the way one most hates in the world."

"Life around here is hardly hell."

"I really couldn't bear to be like him," she said. She got up and walked to the window, and looked down at the children playing in the pool. "To do that to my children. My father was the one who fought against my going to drama school. I kept running away and getting dragged back home, until finally he gave in. My mother didn't mind at all, really. Though she didn't dare argue, I think secretly she was pleased. She died a year later, of a heart attack, which my father of course said was a broken heart, because of me. He died just before I married Duncan, of a heart attack, too, strangely enough. My brother was totally distraught. I wasn't. I think I was relieved. Isn't that awful? He was so understanding with everyone else, but nothing I did ever seemed to please him. It was bewildering, really. And exhausting." She turned and looked at me. "Sometimes I think I used up all my courage, all my energy, fighting him."

Sarah walked over to the chair again, and sat. She pushed one of the loose pillows into the small of her back. "Drinking soothes me," she said. "It keeps me calm. I try not to drink because David doesn't like it, because he doesn't think it's good for the baby. But there's no real harm in it. I do it so seldom, only when I'm very upset. And I'm not a nasty drunk."

"Everyone uses a drink sometimes, Sarah, to settle the nerves. But if that's the only way you feel you can deal with problems, it's not good. Maybe you should think of going for some kind of professional help."

"You mean see a psychiatrist?" She sounded as dubious as if I'd suggested she consult a palm reader. More so. The English tend to consider psychiatrists far more suspect than psychics. To consult the first, they seem to think, implies you're crazy, while visiting the second means merely that you're spiritual.

"Why not? It might help."

"I'm not crazy," said Sarah, predictably.

"I know you're not. But you are upset. It might be good to have someone to talk to, someone objective."

"There was a time when I thought I could tell David anything," she replied. "But I was wrong. It's not that he doesn't understand. Or that he isn't sympathetic. He is. But his solutions to my problems always seem awry. They don't seem to fit somehow. I always feel it's *his* problem he's trying to solve, and that the problem is me."

It seemed so unfair that David, who could pull me out of any doldrum I sank into, was unable to do the same for his wife. What was the point of loving someone so much, loving someone so completely, if it deprived you of the ability to be of any help? "He's not objective," I said. "He can't be."

"Of course, the problem may well be that I've stopped trusting him. Somehow I didn't seem to mind when Duncan was unfaithful. It didn't seem to have anything to do with me. I don't feel that way about David. I suppose I love him too much. I love him obsessively, I think."

"David isn't unfaithful." She looked at me sharply, wanting to believe me, and not daring to. "I wouldn't say it if I didn't know it was true," I insisted.

Finally, she shook her head. "He doesn't tell you everything, you know," she said, as Caroline might have, though totally without the concomitant anger.

"Simon is the one sleeping with Fiona Brent." I thought, if anything, that would convince her.

"Who told you that?" she asked.

"Simon did."

She thought it over for a moment. "So that's why there's been so much tension lately between him and David," she said finally. "Simon's jealous." She laughed then, as if she found the idea extremely funny.

"Well, he's wrong to be."

"We can't both be wrong," said Sarah.

I tried to explain, but soon gave it up. Nothing I said could convince her, because she wasn't ready yet to believe. She simply thought I was being extremely naive.

"I know you're trying to help," she said kindly.

"Will you at least think about seeing a therapist?"

She raised herself carefully out of the chair and stood with her right hand pressed against the hollow of her back. "I don't need one," she replied. "Really, I don't. I just need to get myself under control. And I will." She crossed to the door and opened it, then turned to smile at me. "I hope you did enjoy yourself," she said. "I'd hate to think I'd spoiled your trip."

"I did."

Her smile broadened, wiping the last traces of fatigue from her face. Sarah really had a glorious smile. "Thank you," she said, and went.

I tried to go on reading, but it was no use. My head was too full of David and Sarah to concentrate. Instead, I changed into my bathing suit and went to join the children in the pool.

Keating insists Sarah spent the whole of that summer in an alcoholic fog. She didn't. There were times I know she was sober; but she was, for the next few days certainly, always a little bit high. I never saw her drinking, but I was sure she was because she seemed so calm, too calm, and had a vague, distracted air. She spent hours in the garden, weeding and cutting. She sat in the lounge chair, *The World According to Garp* balanced on her round belly, and read. Mrs. T watched her every move with worried eyes; and so did David when he was home. Only the children didn't mind the change in her. No matter how rowdy they got, the cutting edge didn't enter her low, sweet voice when she called to them to be quiet. They pestered her to read them stories, which she did beautifully, acting out all the parts; to help make a puppet theater; to devise a play for Lissie and Kate's last night. No matter how importunate they became, Sarah never lost patience. She had herself under control.

When I called Simon to say goodbye, he invited me to the set. "I thought I was banned," I said.

"Don't be a fool, Nikki. I told you I was sorry I'd lost my temper. I meant it."

"I'd be delighted," I said.

While we were away, the company had moved from Schönbrunn to the Spanish Riding School to shoot the two scenes set there. The one in which Franz arranges an assignation with the Archduchess Sophie, his uncle's wife, had already been shot. (She was the woman with whom, according to mythology, Franz had a son, the Emperor Maxmilian of Mexico. David did not use this juicy bit of gossip in his play. He thought it extraneous.) When I arrived, they were shooting the master for the second, a complex scene which involved almost the entire cast as well as a performance by the Lippizaner horses, and Simon was using five cameras. I kept well out of the way, shooting in the inevitable breaks, trying to capture something of the mad juxtaposition of the unkempt film crew, the untidy sprawl of equipment, and the rectangular elegance of the white galleried hall, the crystal chandeliers, the beauty of the white prancing horses, against which the colorful costumes of the cast glittered like glass beads in snow.

At one point Simon saw me and beckoned me over. When I reached him, he put his arms around me and hugged. "Forgive me?" he asked.

"You know me," I replied. "I never hold a grudge. Have you patched things up with David?"

"I'm trying. You watch and tell me how I'm doing."

He was, in fact, doing very well. Duncan and David had a small vignette in the scene where Metternich sarcastically reminds Neipperg that falling in love with Marie Louise had not been part of his assignment, warning him that if he does not follow orders to get her to do what and go where she's told, his career will be over. When the time came to cover it, a disagreement arose about characterization—that is, how intimidated Neipperg should appear to be—and Simon handled it without any of the tension, any of the animosity, he had displayed towards David the last time I'd seen them together. David responded in kind, and helped matters by keeping as far away from Fiona as possible, given that they had some lines together.

On the other hand, Fiona didn't help at all. She took every opportunity she got to corner David, who used me or one of the AD's or even Duncan to fend her off. Luckily, Simon was too busy with his five cameras to notice.

"If she keeps that up," remarked Duncan sotto voce to me, "Simon's good mood isn't going to last. What the hell is she up to?"

"Troublemaking," I replied succinctly.

"I wish her husband would get here and take her in hand."

"Could he?" I asked.

"Of course, he could," replied Duncan. Then he added, with a smile, "Provided Fiona still believes a film producer is a better catch than a director or writer. Trust that girl to know what side her bread is buttered on."

"I think she's a fool."

"She's not, you know," said Duncan. "She may be a cunt, but she's no fool."

When the company wrapped for the day, Simon came over and put his arm around me. "You deserve a send-off," he said.

"A kiss on the cheek will do," I replied.

"David," he called, "what do you think about giving Nikki a going-away party?"

"Does she want one?"

"No," I said.

"Who cares what she wants?" replied Simon. "I want to have a party. My suite, tomorrow night, at seven-thirty." It was a Saturday, and Sunday was a day off.

David shook his head. "It's Kate and Lissie's last night," he said. "The party will have to be at the villa, so the kids can be there."

"You can't plan a party without asking Sarah first," I protested.

"She won't mind," said David.

"Of course she won't," agreed Simon. I stopped protesting. Having all those volatile and competitive personalities under one roof at that time seemed to me to be the height of folly; but Simon and David were determined to have a party, and I was no more than a handy excuse. "Seven-thirty at the villa," continued Simon. "That's fabulous. Sarah's so much better at arranging things than I am."

"What party?" asked Fiona, who had just joined us. She was minus her costume and wig, but still fully made-up. The contrast between her casual clothes and pancaked face seemed to emphasize her hardness, her coldness. She looked like a drag queen.

"A going-away party, for Nikki," replied Simon.

She looked at the arm he still had draped around my shoulder as if she could cheerfully amputate it. "How lovely," she said.

Simon smiled at her and said, with mock formality: "Miss Brent, are you by any chance free for dinner tonight? And, if so, would you care to join me?"

"I'd love to," said Fiona, shooting me a vengefully triumphant look.

I kissed Simon on the mouth, I couldn't help myself, and said, "Sorry I couldn't make it tonight, darling. See you tomorrow." And I linked my arm through David's.

"Bitch," said David cheerfully, as we started towards the parking lot. I smiled up at him and nodded. "It's no help to me, remember, if you cause trouble between them,"

"Helping you," I reminded him, "is not my sole purpose in life. Occasionally I reserve the right to get a little pleasure for myself."

Our plane wasn't until late Sunday, so I left the packing as usual for the last minute, and spent a stolen hour Saturday morning with the Rembrandts at the Kunsthistorisches Museum and the rest of the day helping Sarah and Mrs. T prepare for the party, while Marie-Paule, back from visiting her family, packed for Lissie and Kate, then helped rehearse the anxious children for the play they were planning to perform that evening. They had been expecting a doting audience of five or six, but as the day progressed the count for the evening grew steadily larger. Simon kept inviting anyone he ran into.

If I'd been Sarah, I would have been furious. For one thing, the timing of the party was execrable. With Lissie and Kate about to leave, the villa was the scene of some turmoil. Drawers and closets, toy chests and bookcases were turned out as the two girls tried to find and sort everything they had accumulated over the course of the summer. Then, too, they were upset at the prospect of leaving, not just because the summer was over, but because David and the others were remaining behind, even though not for very long. The other children were equally unhappy. Except for Olivia and Kate, the children were very close. To keep their minds off the imminent departure was one of the reasons Sarah had suggested they produce a play.

In any case, arranging a party with twenty-four hours' notice was not my idea of fun. But David and Simon were right: not only was Sarah not annoyed, she went along with their plans with gusto. And Mrs. T, as usual, was completely unfazed and concurred happily with every suggestion Sarah made. They drew up lists and divided chores, ordered food from favorite shops, sent Will to rent sufficient china and cutlery, David to buy the wine, and me to pick up the pastry. Sarah filled the house with flowers from the garden, supplemented by some she had bought in shops. By seven-thirty, to my amazement, everything was ready.

That night, Sarah wore a maternity dress of black chiffon cut in easy, flowing lines. Her yellow hair was piled on top of her head, and she was aglitter with diamanté jewelry: in her hair, on her ears, around her neck and wrists. She looked simple and elegant and beautiful. When David came into the hall and saw her descending the stairs, for the first time in days the worry disappeared from his eyes. He looked at her not only with the pride of possession, but with love. Was he thinking, I wondered, as I was, of that party where they'd first met? And then the guests began to arrive and the moment was gone.

About forty or fifty people came and went in the course of that evening: most of the cast, a lot of the crew, a handful of Viennese with whom either Simon or Duncan or David had become friendly. I knew comparatively few, as did Sarah. But whereas large groups of people make me want to run and hide, for Sarah they were an audience. She was at her best for them, a radiant presence, graciously dispensing hospitality.

"You look like the Milky Way," said Simon, as he kissed Sarah hello. She thanked him for the compliment, and he asked if she'd had any more thoughts about the play.

"Only that I don't want to think about it now."

"Have you read it yet, the play I sent Sarah?" he asked David.

"Not yet," replied David.

"You ought to," said Simon. "It's good. She should do it."

"I'm sure she will, if she wants to," said David.

Then Fiona arrived, and it was immediately obvious that she and Simon had quarreled. Any hope I'd had that seeing them together might convince Sarah their affair was so passionate Fiona's infidelity was unthinkable was dispelled instantly. The only passion between them at that moment was rage.

The two women greeted each other coolly, exchanged perfunctory compliments, and left each other as quickly as possible to move on to other people. They'd never liked each other, and the rivalries of that summer had deepened their aversion to such intensity they were not prepared even to give a performance as friends.

A few minutes later, Duncan arrived, followed by a large blond woman and three men. He introduced the people accompanying him to Sarah; then, to get everyone mingling, he brought the woman and one of the men over to join the group I was in, which included Milos Andrejvik and Joe Vasari. I smiled hello and moved away, but Duncan followed me and asked what was wrong. "You look like a thundercloud about to burst."

Across the room, Fiona was holding court in a circle of admirers. As David passed, she called to him and demanded he settle an argument they were having about the virtues (or lack of them) in some play currently running in the West End. Her voice was so penetrating that both Simon and Sarah, at opposite ends of the room, looked her way and frowned. David said something succinctly damning, got the laugh which he'd intended, and moved on to a safer group. I suggested to Duncan that he might, for Sarah's sake, try to keep Fiona away from David that evening, since Simon clearly wasn't going to make the effort.

"I have my own problems," replied Duncan, a note of irritation in his voice. He cast an anxious look at Ingrid, the woman he'd brought with him, who was now talking to Milos. "Deirdre's coming back tomorrow," he said.

Outside, by the pool, the children performed their play, which was of course about Richard the Lionheart and Blondel (Lissie playing the former, Mark the latter, and the others assorted dukes, peasants, and jailkeepers). It was such a delightful, such a normal few minutes that I actually began to believe the party would after all have a happy ending. Lissie made a very dashing Richard, and Mark a heroic Blondel. They pulled out all the stops. Kate, as the wicked Duke Leopold, stormed and raged with a passion she never showed in daily life. Olivia mouthed everyone's lines as they spoke them and prompted Nicholas when he forgot his.

As Marie-Paule dropped the curtain of table linen, the audience burst into applause. "Bravo," shouted Duncan, echoed immediately by Milos and Joe. "Encore," urged David, as they took their bows. Beaming, Lissie led them into Blondel's song once again, and at the end they got another round of applause.

"What sweet children," I heard Fiona say to David, next to whom she had somehow contrived to sit. A frown flickered across Sarah's face.

Fiona didn't need to say anything offensive: the sound of her voice was enough. In Sarah's ears, it was the screech of a fork against the bottom of a pot.

The children mingled with the guests for a while, ate some supper, kissed their parents goodnight, and were taken off to bed by Marie-Paule. Someone suggested music, and as the guests pushed the furniture back against the walls, David slipped a Donna Sommers cassette into the tape deck.

A little while later, I was dancing with one of the ADs, flirting a little, thinking what a pity it was that I didn't find him attractive and how nice it would be if Sam were there and shortly we could go off to bed together, when Fiona's voice penetrated the slight alcoholic fog I was in.

"Dance with me," she said, lifting her arms to David, who was standing at the side of the room watching Sarah dance with Joe Vasari.

Fiona was so pathetically obvious. How could anyone take her seriously? How could David, who probably didn't, but nevertheless began to dance with her? Or Simon, who glared at her across the head of the man he was talking to? But watching her one couldn't help wondering what she was like in bed, what she did to earn that incredibly erotic look she possessed. I knew it was absurd, but looking at her I felt sexually inadequate. Did Sarah feel the same? She had stopped dancing as soon as David had begun and stood quietly beside Joe and his boyfriend, pretending to listen to their chat, her eyes never leaving David and Fiona.

"That's it," I said to the AD. "I'm exhausted. I have to sit down."

Through the glass of the French windows, I could see Duncan outside on the patio talking to Ingrid, with whom he'd been sleeping since his wife had left for London. Ingrid was big and blond, and though not nearly so attractive and much much quieter, very reminiscent of Cassandra, which I don't suppose Duncan had (consciously) noticed. Ingrid's main attraction, David had theorized when he'd told me about the affair, was that she was over forty and could be counted on to know when a fling was just a fling, unlike the twenty-year-old script girl with whom Duncan had been flirting for weeks, who might be inclined to take the whole thing too seriously.

If so, that night presented Ingrid's golden opportunity to prove Duncan had not misjudged her character: his wife's phone call announcing her return hadn't left Duncan much time to dispose of Ingrid gently. And Duncan prided himself on being considerate.

He held her hand and looked soulfully into her eyes, his voice (I was certain) at its most mellifluous. But he was distracted for a moment as he turned to see whose footsteps it was he'd heard and frowned as Sarah and Joe Vasari crossed the patio and disappeared into the dark of the garden beyond. He looked tempted to call out to them, but was returned to the urgency of his own problem by the sound of Ingrid sniffling. While Duncan's head was turned, she had reached into her purse and extracted a handkerchief to wipe her eyes and nose. No one, no matter what age, can be counted on not to fall in love.

Slowly, the crowd began to thin. Simon came and stood over me. "Dance?" he asked, sounding a little drunk. I shook my head. Whoever I'd been talking to excused himself and left.

"Do you think you could ever have fallen in love with me?" he said.

"If I hadn't been in love with someone else at the time, probably," I replied, though I doubted it.

He shook his head morosely. "Do you know everyone I've ever been in love with has been in love with David?"

"That's not true."

"I was in love with you."

"Don't exaggerate," I said.

"Do you know I was in love with Sarah?" he asked. "A long time ago." I nodded. "No one could help being in love with Sarah. Except David. He gets one of the best women going, and what does he do?" He pointed. "That's what he does."

David and Fiona had finished dancing a long time before, and had gone their separate ways; but, somehow, there they were together, laughing. Why hadn't he kept away from her? Why? I knew he'd defend himself, saying Fiona was a guest in his house and he was only being polite. But there was more to it than that: David had finally given in to the temptation to explore the full dramatic potential of the scene.

"Simon, why don't you get someone to drive you back to the hotel?" I said. "Or, better yet, go upstairs and go to sleep."

"Come with me?" he asked.

"Happily," I said. Anything to get him away. I stood up and took his hand.

"Where's Sarah?" he said. "I want to say goodbye. Sarah!" he bellowed.

I hoped that David would ignore us, but of course he didn't. He came hurrying over, followed by Fiona. "What's the matter?" David's voice, too, was a little thickened with drink, which wasn't surprising. It only took a glass or two to make him drunk.

"Nothing," said Simon. "I'm going to bed with Nikki, but first I want to say goodnight to Sarah. Where is she?"

"You fucking bastard," said Fiona.

"You cunt," replied Simon.

"All right, that's enough," said David.

Everyone else in the room had stopped talking. Duncan came in from outside, followed by a red-eyed Ingrid.

"Simon, let's go," I urged. "Let's go upstairs." That seemed the lesser of all possible evils.

"You're bloody right it's enough," Simon replied to David, ignoring me. "More than enough. Who the bloody hell do you think you are? You think everyone in the world will bend over just so you can fuck them up the ass?"

At that point, David exploded, the anger, the resentment, he'd been suppressing for days breaking through the barrier of common sense. He swore even more fluently than Simon and ordered him out of the house. Simon swung at him, clipping David beneath the eye with his ring. Enraged, David swung back. Duncan and the two assistants jumped in, trying to separate them. Lissie crept down the stairs to see what all the noise was about, just as Will came in from the kitchen followed by Mrs. T, who got to Lissie before I could and took her back to her room. Will flew into the thick of it. He hauled Simon back, enabling Duncan and the others to get David under control. Simon's lip was split, and blood dripped from the cut beneath David's eye.

Only then did Sarah appear. She came through the patio doors hand in hand with Joe Vasari. They appeared to have had a very good time in the garden: they were much more animated than they'd been when they left, virtually glowing with good humor, and laughing at what must have been the funniest joke either had ever heard. To me, frozen for a moment in the aftermath of violence, they seemed to move with the jerky rhythms of silent-film stars. Suddenly, I knew exactly what they had been doing in the garden. I looked at David and saw that he knew, as well. He started towards her, but she saw his bleeding face and screamed. She screamed again, then turned and fled back into the dark, David following quickly after her.

"She'll be all right," said Joe. "She only did a couple of lines. She just needed something to cheer her up." He moved a couple of steps nearer to his boyfriend, who glared at him.

"Bloody hell," said Simon.

"I think you had all better go," said Mrs. T, coming back down the stairs. "If you don't mind. The party is over."

"Come on, I'll drive you back to the hotel," offered Duncan. He put an arm around Simon and started with him towards the door, asking an AD to give Ingrid a ride home. "Call me and let me know if I can do anything," he said as he passed me. I nodded.

Fiona took out a handkerchief and offered it to Simon. "Here, darling. Your lip is bleeding," she said, but he didn't even glance her way.

When they'd gone I walked over to the patio door. I could hear Sarah crying, and the sound of David's voice, deep with misery. "Why do you do it? Why? Why do you hurt yourself like this? And me? Don't you know I love you? Only you. Forever."

Los Angeles
June/July 1984

❧ *Chapter 33* ❧

If any time is the right time to be in Los Angeles, the summer of the 1984 Olympics was it.

The weather was warm and dry, and not even a smog haze hanging constantly in the air could wet-blanket the high spirits. Despite the acid attitude assumed long-distance by the New York journalists who didn't bother to cover it, the choice of things to do in dozy LA was staggering since an arts festival preceded and then ran concurrent with the games. There was theater and music, ballet and art from all over the world, most of it never seen in the United States before, and much of it wonderful.

Many of the natives, either worried by prognostications of severe traffic congestion or determined to make money by letting their homes at inflated prices, had left town, leaving the freeways and other major traffic routes eerily empty. In contrast, the usually deserted streets teemed with people who actually spoke to one another, and the polyglot murmur of voices played constantly like a catchy folksong. Banners in the iced-sherbert Olympic colors of turquoise and orange hung suspended across streets, flew from lampposts, and adorned the faces of buildings. Sculptural forms in the same colors highlighted corners and broke the perspective of broad avenues. Matching trashbins collected litter. Palm trees waved in the wind. Policemen smiled and pointed the way. Crime was down and spirits up. Everyone was gay.

Even the massacre at a suburban McDonald's or the bewildering
deaths of pedestrians run down by a crazed driver in Westwood didn't
succeed in dampening the mood. The events were too localized: they
lacked the kind of broad political significance that reverberates and
stuns. Unless you were yourself involved in some particular disaster,
some unmitigated personal sorrow, the city simply caught and held you
in its ebullient embrace.

I was awakened by the sound of a doorbell ringing. My eyes opened
slowly and saw a louvered window, a pickled-pine armoire, a series of Ed
Ruscha lithographs on a pale gray wall. For a moment I couldn't remember where I was. Then the lilac print Pierre Deux fabric of the
bedcover reminded me. I was in an exorbitantly expensive rented apartment in West Hollywood. I'd arrived the night before.

The doorbell rang again, more insistently, and I climbed out of bed,
threw on a robe, and went to open it. I looked through the Judas hole
and saw David.

"I was asleep," I said, standing grudgingly aside to let him in.

"It's three hours later in New York," he replied, as if that information
would suffice to make my aching head feel better.

"I didn't get to bed till three. Why didn't you call first? You know I
hate people showing up unannounced."

"I wanted to see you," he said, sounding not in the least repentant.
He smiled and so did I; then I put my arms around him and hugged.
We hadn't seen each other in over a month. He followed me to the
kitchen, sat at the small lacquer table, and lit a Gauloise, while I figured
out how to operate the coffeemaker. "Nice place," he said.

"It should be. It costs enough."

"I told you to stay with us." He and Sarah had exchanged their house
in London for one in the Hollywood Hills. It was big enough to accom-
modate an army, David had insisted, with a little guest house on the
property. I could see the Waltons or not as I chose.

I had avoided staying with them since Vienna. "This is more convenient for the gallery," I explained, carefully not looking at him, measur-
ing coffee into the filter and turning on the machine. As part of the arts
festival I had an exhibition of photographs, mostly of theater, film, and
art subjects, on show at the de Witt Gallery on Melrose, not too far from
La Cienaga Boulevard. "I can walk from here."

"I don't blame you," he said, which was as near as he ever got to
saying he understood. "Seen the gallery yet?"

I nodded. "Peter de Witt picked me up at the airport last night and we went right there. I couldn't wait. It's terrific, a great space. He took me to dinner at Spago's and I ate an enormous piece of chocolate cake. You were right, it's wonderful. And then we went dancing at some club. Baryshnikov was there. Oh, David, I am so excited, and so scared." I'd been in exhibitions before, twice in New York and once in Chicago, but they'd been group shows. This was my first solo, and I was hoping, I told him, that the combination of the de Witt Gallery (which had an excellent reputation) and the Olympics Festival would somehow overcome the usual dismissiveness of New York critics to shows mounted in Los Angeles.

"Don't count on it," said David carefully. And, as it turned out, justifiably. The few notices which appeared in the New York magazines and newspapers damned with faint praise, in contrast to reviews by Californian (and, in fact, European) critics, which were generally excellent. I was very hurt at the time. Like everyone, I tend to believe the worst opinions are the truest. "Anyway, reviews aren't what matter," he continued. "You can't take them seriously."

"How can you say that?" I demanded irritably, splashing some of the coffee I was pouring into David's ashtray, drowning his cigarette. He immediately lit another, as I removed the mess and dumped it down the disposal. "It was the critics who first got *you* taken seriously. Nobody paid any attention to your plays before the *New York Times* decided you were the best thing to happen to the American theater since Eugene O'Neill."

"Did that make my work any better or worse than it was?"

"Of course not."

"It's the quality of the work that's important, Nikki, not what people say about it. And there aren't many people able to judge that anyway. Maybe nobody. Maybe not even yourself."

"I don't want to be considered just a fashion photographer, just a portrait photographer. I don't want to be considered 'just' anything. I want to cross the line." He knew what line I meant: the one dividing the craftsman from the artist. "I want to be taken seriously."

"For that, you have to take yourself seriously."

David hadn't appeared at my door at eight in the morning to discuss me and my artistic future. I knew that, but I didn't care. I was too excited, too anxious about the exhibition, to be generous. And, again, David was able to put his problems on hold to pay attention to mine. "You are good," he said, more than once, in more than one way, knowing those were the words I needed to hear. And he made me believe he meant them. He did mean them. That was the fundamental blessing of his friendship, his faith.

"I know," I said, and for the moment I meant it, too.

We talked for a while, perfunctorily, about family, my brother, his father, Jack and Trudi, his sister, Claudia, and her husband, the various Walton children, filling each other in on all the month's news; but just when I thought David was about to tell me what was bothering him, he stood. "I have one more stop to make before I can get to work," he said. He was rewriting his new play that summer.

I looked at the clock on the kitchen wall. It said ten. "Oh, no," I muttered. "I have to meet de Witt at the gallery in half an hour."

"Come to dinner tonight."

"What did you want to talk to me about?" I asked.

"It can wait."

"Do you want to meet later, for lunch?"

He shook his head. "I can't. Don't worry, it wasn't important. Come for dinner tonight. That's an invitation from Sarah. She'll be hurt if you say no."

"How is she?" I asked, hoping I didn't sound as concerned as I suddenly felt.

"She's fine. Right as rain. Fit as a fiddle. Happy as a lark," he said, grinning, leaving me doubtful and worried. "Eight o'clock. Do you want directions? It's pretty hard to find."

"I'll find it," I said, with the smile he was expecting. "Don't worry."

He kissed me goodbye. "I never worry about you anymore," he said. "You're so obviously all right."

I wish I could have said the same of him.

Peter de Witt was waiting for me at the gallery when I arrived ten minutes late and out of breath.

"You walked?" he said, sounding shocked.

I could have replied that I liked to walk, that walking is the best way to learn a city, that the distance from the apartment to the gallery was less than a mile, but I didn't: when in Rome, at least pretend, is my motto. "I haven't had time yet to rent a car," I said reassuringly.

Peter was in his mid-thirties, nine or ten years younger than I, just under six feet tall, and thin to the point of gaunt. He wore high-waisted black-and-white baggy plaid trousers, a yellow T-shirt, and a white silk jacket with rolled cuffs. His dark hair was styled in GQ punk, and he sported a fashionable two-day stubble of beard. He had an erotic quality that always reminded me of Fiona Brent's. Very nice, I said to myself every time I saw him; and then, Danger, keep off. We had met months before at a party in New York, and I'd been toying with the idea of him ever since. What would it be like, I wondered, if I were to throw caution once again to the wind? It had been at least two years since I had.

Peter smiled at me, a speculative smile, I thought. "It's going to be terrific," he said ambiguously. Everything about him was ambiguous, including his sexuality: that was part of the excitement.

"Is it?" I asked, flirting a little in response.

"Oh, yes," he said. "When I make a promise, I deliver." I felt a familiar catch of excitement in my throat. "If I'm allowed."

We sorted through the photographs I had sent, in black-and-white and color, portraits mostly of international film and theater stars, dancers, painters, sculptors, trying to make some sort of preliminary final selection. And all thoughts of Peter, all thoughts of sex, receded from my mind. Only the work mattered. I was totally focused on it.

"Lunch?" suggested Peter. Startled, I looked at my watch. It was already after one. We crossed the street to a large, crowded restaurant, decorated in the same shades of gray as my rented apartment. It had large expressionist paintings on the walls to add interest, the ubiquitous *Ficus benjamina* for warmth, and bad acoustics to keep the sound level high in the hope of convincing all they were having a good time.

I was. Peter and I talked about the show, argued about the publicity, digressed into personal anecdotes, laughed at each other's stories, and kept a layer of sexual energy pulsing away, just below the surface.

"Tell me about those photographs of David Walton," said Peter, over his demitasse. We had chosen three portraits as well as some group pictures of David for the show.

"Tell you what?"

"Well, they were taken years ago, before he became famous."

"Not exactly," I corrected. "I took those long after his plays were successful. They're only about six or seven years old."

"I meant before he became a film star."

A film star. Of all the bizarre things for David to have turned out to be, and without fixing his broken nose or chipped tooth! I still wasn't used to it.

The film of *The King of Rome* had caused quite a sensation. Duncan edged Joe Vasari out and walked off with the Oscar for Best Actor; Simon Wroth for Best Director; the film for Best Film. Though he didn't win, David was nominated for Best Supporting Actor and turned into what is known as a "hot property." He had played Count Neipperg so romantically, so sexily, to so much critical acclaim, that instead of the expected offers to write movies, he got besieged with requests to star in them. Scripts came pouring in, all with leading roles for David. At first he laughed. He enjoyed acting occasionally, he always had, in small character parts, but he had no pretensions to stardom, no ambition for it. To start with. Then Steven Apsberg, a director he knew and respected, brought him a filmscript he liked, and David hesitated.

Just Until Spring had opened in Washington to mixed notices and hadn't made it to Broadway. It was too stark, too somber, I suppose. The audiences left long before Janette Riker, triumphant at the end, having survived the Montana snows by sheer force of will, is discovered by an Indian hunting party. The moment she stumbles forward to greet them is extraordinarily moving, I think: but very few of us got to see it.

Tired and disappointed, beset with problems at home, David couldn't muster the energy to start a new play. The fee offered for the part in the film was a lot: a fortune, and right then he needed all the money he could get his hands on. It was tempting, not least because here suddenly was a chance at a totally unexpected plot twist to his life.

I was having dinner with the Waltons in New York when David first broached the subject to Sarah. "You're not serious, are you?" she said. Though she had at first been indulgent about David's forays into acting, as her own career declined, she became increasingly antagonistic towards his. The Oscar nomination for *The King of Rome* had surprised her, angered her, depressed her. And now he was being offered a starring role in a film. "Of course," she had added, "if you really want to do it. If you think you *can* do it."

But that wasn't what had finally decided David to say yes. The look on Duncan's face a few days later did that: shock and rage mingled with that hope that if David did say yes, he'd fail miserably. The look lasted only a moment, to be replaced instantly with an encouraging smile. "By all means, try it," said Duncan.

"I think I will," said David.

The film was called, succinctly, *Cop!* and if it wasn't as successful as *Star Wars* at the box office, it came close. David played a Chicago policeman who falls in love with the prostitute he's manipulating to get to the city's vice king. It had just the right amount of sex and action, romance and humor, to be a major success. Giant posters with David, in a leather jacket, brandishing a gun, appeared in newspapers and magazines, on theater marquees and street posters, across the country, around the world. He was the biggest thing to happen to Japan since Chuck Norris.

His success amazed even him, and he enjoyed it. When he was offered, the next year, another film by the same director, again he said yes. That one was *Down Home*, the story of a small-town boy made good who returns to find out the truth behind his father's suicide and uncovers a long and dirty history of local corruption. For it, David got his Oscar.

He was good, amazingly good. His acting was instinctive and natural, easy and truthful. But, perhaps even more important, the camera captured all David's sexuality, his energy, intelligence, and humor. Audiences apparently wanted to spend as much time with him as his friends and acquaintances did. He became one of the "bankable" stars.

"I met him the other day. David Walton, I mean," said Peter. "At a party. He's an amazing guy."

"Amazing," I agreed.

"Have you known him a long time?"

"Quite a while," I replied.

"I'm a great admirer of his. Of his writing, as well as his acting. *The King of Rome* is a great play."

"Yes, it is," I said.

"Is he writing anything now?"

"Another play. But he doesn't talk about them," I lied, "until they're finished."

"That's smart. Very smart. And his wife. She's a real beauty. A little weird, but a beauty. Does she act, too?"

I thought of Sarah as I'd first seen her in *The Folly*, as I'd seen her in *Sky Burial*, radiant, gifted, on the threshold of a major career. "Yes," I said. "She acts."

✌ *Chapter 34* ✌

As soon as I'd finished sorting photographs with Peter, I rented the essential automobile and returned to the apartment, where I found a message on the answering machine to call Cassandra at the Bel Air. Half an hour later I was sitting with her beside the hotel pool. She was already an exquisite shade of brown. "Isn't this yummy?" she asked, her voice startling the person next to her out of his doze. He looked first annoyed and then admiring. Cassandra was wearing a bikini she had designed for herself in the Olympic colors, and it looked spectacular on her statuesque, though no longer overweight, figure. Her eyes were closed and she was oblivious to his admiration. "It was such an absolutely filthy winter in London, and with Duncan doing that dreary play, we couldn't go anywhere. I've been out here all day, every day, since we arrived."

"Where is he?" I asked.

"He said he had a fitting at the studio." Her tone was, as always in those days when she spoke of Duncan, faintly ironic. It was more self-protective than hostile, though it was not Duncan she felt the need to protect herself against, but the pity of her friends.

Duncan's marriage to Deirdre had lasted slightly less than a year. She had not accepted his infidelities graciously, and had gone off in a huff with a pop musician from whom, optimistically, she expected better. If Duncan had been stunned by Deirdre's quick exit, he had also (in Cassandra's opinion) been enormously relieved. The satisfaction at being the lover of a teenage girl had quickly ceded place to a parental frustration at Deirdre's untidiness, her carelessness, her haphazard approach to life, not to mention her taste in music. When he and Cassandra ran into each other at a theater opening a few weeks after Deirdre's departure, Duncan asked her out to dinner. A few months later they were living together, and early in 1981 they remarried. "I know I'm a fool," Cassandra had said to me a few days before the wedding, "and I know every fool of a woman throughout history has made the same excuse, but I can't help it, I love him." She had sighed and crossed her fingers. "Wish me luck. Maybe this time he can keep from behaving like a complete idiot."

That was perhaps asking too much. Duncan's affairs had continued, though in his defense let it be said that they were fewer in number and he did make a greater effort to be discreet. But while in their previous marriage Cassandra had pretended to be oblivious to Duncan's conduct, this time she let it be known she was fully informed. Knowledge was the only weapon she had to shield herself against the people who presumed to pity her. She was not a trusting and betrayed innocent, she insisted, but a sophisticated woman involved in a complex relationship. Duncan's infidelities might hurt, but that pain was the price she had to pay for the privilege of staying married to him. "In all my life," she had said, a little defensively, "I've only met one man I could actually care about. God knows *I* don't know why I care about him, but I do. And I'm not mad enough to let him get away, if there's a thing I can do to prevent it."

In any case, Cassandra believed (and it was a belief that Sarah had seemed to share) there was no malice in what Duncan did, no attempt to prove her inadequate as a wife or as a lover by fucking other women. He did it simply because it made him feel good. The hurt he caused Cassandra was regrettable but incidental. Except for that one time with Deirdre, he never got carried away, never fell in love, never made promises he wouldn't keep. And when he went home to Cassandra, he always made her feel there was no place in the world he would rather be, no woman he'd rather have with him.

"In general, I agree with you about infidelity," I'd said to her at one point. "It may not be as significant as people choose to believe it is. And jealousy is certainly a disgusting emotion. Still, don't you think having your husband actually marry someone else is maybe just a bit much?"

Cassandra had laughed. "I told you I'm a fool. What can I do?"

* * *

A waiter arrived with a hamburger she'd ordered, and placed it on the table beside Cassandra's lounge chair. She sat up, signed the tab, and took a bite of it. "You know, I don't think Duncan is being unfaithful at the moment." I looked anxiously towards our neighbor, but he was gone. There was, thankfully, no one within hearing distance of even Cassandra's powerful voice. "Are you sure you don't want some of this?" she asked. "Americans do make the loveliest hamburgers." I declined, and she took another bite. "I can always tell when he is, and it's been months now, almost a year in fact, since before he started rehearsing the Massey play in London last autumn."

"That's good," I said, hoping I didn't sound too surprised.

"Oh, I'm not sure it matters all that much," she said dismissively. Then she laughed. "Only he's home such a lot now, I've had to learn to design much faster." Somehow, amazingly, she and Duncan had evolved a relationship that, however bizarre, remained stable and close while managing not to impinge on each other's freedom or interfere with each other's work. Like Duncan's, Cassandra's career, except for that one brief period just before her divorce, had continued to flourish. She was a major success on three continents: the year before she'd opened a boutique in Japan. Do you know who *is* having an affair?" she asked, her voice loud and clear.

"Almost everyone else, I imagine."

"David," she said, watching my face for a reaction.

She got one. I sat up and glared at her. "That's ridiculous," I said.

"Hmmm," she sighed speculatively, picking up a french fry and biting into it. "I was sure you'd be among the first to know."

"If it were true, I would be." I relaxed back into the lounge.

"It is true," she replied, with a conviction so positive, I felt my own certitude crumbling away. Was that what he had wanted to talk to me about? I wondered. "And one can hardly blame him," continued Cassandra. "He's had an awful lot to put up with these past few years. He's been a veritable saint in my opinion."

Undeniably, he'd been good, better than I would ever have expected him to be. But a saint? I suppose that depended on the way you chose to apportion the blame for what had happened. No, not blame—responsibility. Were people totally accountable for their own lives, as I liked to believe, or were there mitigating factors, inescapable influences, as the social psychologists insisted? Do we all have the option of pulling up our socks and getting on with it, or are some of us so overwhelmed by circumstance we wouldn't recognize an option even if it came gift-wrapped complete with nametag?

* * *

That hysterical scene in Vienna had terrified Sarah so much that for the remainder of her pregnancy she had kept away from drugs and stayed sober. Consequently, those next few months were the most peaceful time of David and Sarah's marriage.

When the filming of *The King of Rome* ended, the Waltons returned to New York, and David began to work seriously on *Just Until Spring*. He wrote at home, in his study, at the top of their pretty Edwardian house on West 24th Street. Except for an occasional disagreement with Simon (with whom his relationship remained strained) about the editing of the film, there was nothing to pull David either physically or emotionally away, not Caroline, who had finally decided to start her own business in New York, nor Lissie and Kate, who, as Caroline grew increasingly busy, began spending more and more time at their father's home. For the moment, David's work, family, and love lives were centered in one place, and Sarah was secure and happy. At parties, they could often be seen alone in a corner, talking, laughing together, looking at each other again with trust and admiration.

But when Ben was born, Sarah went into a postpartum depression which grew steadily worse as *The King of Rome* was released and David began collecting rave notices for his performance as Neipperg. Sarah took little interest in the children, no longer even playing with them, leaving Marie-Paule, who was gradually taking over from the aging Mrs. T, increasingly more responsible for the running of the Walton household. Sarah refused to accompany David on the necessary publicity trips for the film, or to the Academy Awards in Los Angeles. She withdrew more and more into herself. When Simon asked her, as he had done repeatedly since Vienna, about doing a play in London, Sarah told him she was too happy at home with her baby to want to work.

Instead of the pleasure it had once been, visiting the house became an ordeal. It was clean and orderly, but no longer gay. I missed the flowers everywhere.

Eventually, the medication prescribed for Sarah eased the depression, but it also quickly (and with hindsight, predictably) confirmed Sarah in a cycle of drug and drink dependency. She was in and out of clinics. The cures worked for a time, and then ceased to work. Mark and Nicholas watched their mother in bewilderment, and Olivia with growing rage. Ben, when he began to talk, called Marie-Paule Mommy.

David did the best he could. He cared for the children, was alternately tender and enraged with Sarah, finished *Just Until Spring*, and —when he needed money to pay for the clinics—agreed to act in the film which was to make him famous.

After two years of watching Sarah deteriorate, Simon and Duncan again decided that all Sarah really needed was to work. They were doing a play together in London and offered Sarah the leading role. For once, David actively encouraged her to take the part: at that point he was so desperate he would have tried anything. Sarah let herself be talked into doing it, and the Waltons returned to London.

Her mood improved immediately, David wrote me, his letters full of hope. She seemed delighted to be back in London. Bouquets of bright asters cut from her now almost wild garden once again filled the house. Friends called, invitations flowed in, and Sarah insisted that they accept them all, though David protested he wanted to begin a new play, and Sarah had a strenuous rehearsal schedule to keep.

Too curious to keep away, David attended some of the rehearsals, although he knew that wasn't a good idea. But he kept his distance from both Simon and Duncan and managed to avoid arguments with either of them. Sarah was at first anxious, hesitant, uncertain about how to approach the role. But David insisted, when he phoned me, that Sarah's voice had lost none of its quality, none of its power, and that she still knew how to deliver a line. The play she was rehearsing was *The Proposal* by Hugh Mills, his historical drama about Shane O'Neill's reluctant proposal of marriage to Elizabeth I, a vain attempt to settle the Irish problem in the sixteenth century. It was overtly political, structurally complex, and brilliantly funny. Mostly due to the last, it was a big hit when it opened.

But Sarah wasn't in it. Gradually, during rehearsals, her self-confidence had seemed to increase, but just as Simon and Duncan began to pat themselves on the back for having so easily succeeded where all the clinics had failed, just as David began to pay less attention to Sarah's problems and immerse himself in his work, Sarah misjudged the amount of coke she was taking to get her through and arrived at a rehearsal so high that she performed a run-through at the dizzying pace of a Keystone Cop. With the wiliness of the true addict, she had fooled everyone—for a while.

Caught, she pleaded tension and anxiety and promised not to do it again. By the middle of the next week, she had withdrawn from the production and entered another clinic.

But that had been the turning point. For a year now, Sarah had been clean: no drugs and no alcohol. The children had begun to lose the wary look they'd worn in her presence, and the Walton marriage again seemed stable, even happy. Despite all the anger, all the resentment of the preceding years, exacerbated constantly by ugly newspaper stories about Sarah's breakdowns and David's alleged romances, the bond between them held. "There's more than enough love," David had told me, "to balance the scales."

"You'd think, wouldn't you," said Cassandra, echoing my thoughts, "that if their marriage could survive all that, it could survive anything?"

"Even if you're right," I temporized, "and David *is* having a little fling, don't you think it may be a bit soon to start predicting the end? Marriages have been known to survive infidelity," I sniped. I still wasn't convinced she was right. If nothing else, Vienna had taught me to be circumspect in my suspicions. On the other hand, life had taught me not to defend anyone's fidelity too vigorously: the odds were too much against your being right, and you looked like such a fool when proved wrong.

"Don't be sarcastic, darling. I only mentioned it because I thought you knew. Anyway, it's probably not in the least important. I'm sure David will end it as soon as Sarah's finished with the play." She was referring to the London Drama Group's production of *Macbeth* for the Olympics Festival. When his leading lady had withdrawn for some reason or other, Richard Carew—the director—had offered the part to Sarah. He had seen her, he said, do Desdamona at the Chichester Festival in the summer of 1969, and had never forgotten her.

This time, Sarah said yes with no coaxing from anyone. Even David's tentatively voiced objections to the strain of it all didn't deter her. It was time, she insisted, she got back to acting. Sarah was determined, and David conceded gracefully. The Waltons, with their usual entourage, left New York for a summer in Los Angeles.

"David has never liked Sarah to act," added Cassandra, "or she wouldn't have done so little of it since her marriage to him. Before that, Sarah was always a workaholic." There was no point protesting. Cassandra was right. Whatever Sarah's other excuses, the main reason she'd given up her career was that David had wanted her to. "But as much in favor as I am of working wives," continued Cassandra, "I really do think they should take precautions. Imagine me doing anything so daft as leaving Duncan dependent for comfort on a beautiful au pair."

"Au pair?" I said blankly.

"Au pair. Secretary. Housekeeper. Whatever it is they're calling her now. Marie-Paule. Don't tell me you really didn't know, darling? How extraordinary. I was sure you were just being discreet. Well, it really is too awful," said Cassandra, with genuine distress. "She's pregnant."

❧ Chapter 35 ❧

According to Philip Keating, David had the kind of personality that commanded attention and provoked interest, ensuring that almost nothing he did escaped notice or comment. About that, Mr. Keating is certainly right; and inevitably (in accordance with the laws of human nature), it was David's sex life that received the closest scrutiny. Gossip about it was as rampant as it was exaggerated. By Keating and other aficionados, David's lovers were deemed to be legion.

They weren't. David liked to flirt. More than that, he was interested in women. He listened to them, and understood; and they bloomed in the light thrown by his attention like flowers in the sun. But he didn't steal kisses in corners, he didn't cop feels in gardens. Unlike Duncan, he didn't find it necessary to make a pass at every woman who crossed his path, and fuck the ones who'd let him. Still, it was only a difference in degree, not in kind. David was merely more selective. When he did meet a woman he wanted, for whatever reason, he had no scruples about pursuing her. Nor did he hesitate to use sex as a weapon, for power and control, withholding or performing as necessary, employing whatever strategy best suited his long-range plans.

David was sexually active from the age of thirteen, and I'd stopped counting his lovers long before Caroline entered his life. To her, he was unfaithful from the start, and throughout their marriage he went on being unfaithful, though not nearly so often as rumored. But once

David had married Sarah, he changed: for the first time in his life he was faithful, unexpectedly, surprisingly faithful. I was sure of it, because he would have told me of any lovers. Sooner or later, he always told me everything.

I watched him expectantly, waiting for him to fall from grace. Not that I doubted his love for Sarah. I couldn't. It was too obvious, too palpable. But I thought it merely a matter of time before he succumbed to the seductiveness of novelty. Even the lesson of Vienna hadn't made me change my expectations. If he'd remained faithful there, then he wouldn't somewhere else. Eventually, he would give in to temptation.

But when Sarah was at her most depressed, at her most withdrawn, when David became a movie star and women flung themselves at him with ever-increasing fervor, still he was faithful. "We're connected," he'd said to me once, "in a place so deep I can't reach it, even to cut it off. She uses all of me. There's nothing left over for anyone else."

So when Cassandra announced David's latest supposed fling, I thought it unlikely, but certainly possible. That Marie-Paule lived in his house and took care of his children would not have deterred David, who'd dare anything to get something he wanted. In fact, the situation was so fraught with complexity, with perversity, so rife with potential for drama, that he might have found it irresistible.

And Marie-Paule, during her years with the Waltons, had changed from a plain, awkward teenager into an attractive woman. Though she had replaced her spectacles with contact lenses and got a haircut from someone who knew how to style, she'd done more than just whip off her glasses and let down her hair: she'd lost weight, exercised herself into shape, and learned to dress with flair. Not that she was now a beauty, but then David didn't require beauty in a lover. I was a prime example of that.

Still, I had seen them together recently in New York and David had treated her then with the same teasing concern he'd shown since her first day in his household. And it didn't seem likely that in just four weeks, David's avuncular fondness for his attractive au pair had been transformed into passion. And without passion, David would never risk such a great hurt to Sarah.

When I arrived at the Walton's house for dinner that night, it was Marie-Paule who opened the heavy wood door to greet me. "Nikki, 'allo," she said, her voice low-pitched and lilted with the trace of an accent too slight to seem a parody. "It was beginning to be so late, we thought maybe you got lost." We stood for a few moments in the entry hall, chatting, as I searched her face for signs of a change in status. She was twenty-one years old, but looked older, or at least more sophisticated, the way French women often do. She'd had her hair streaked blond and cut in a spiky modified punk which suited her. She'd added a second earring to her right ear, and the layered denim outfit she wore had definitely come from a shop in Beverly Hills. The changes in her all seemed that superficial, except for one. Jutting out of the denim skirt was a small round belly, about five or six months pregnant.

"They are in the back, waiting for you. It is lovely out there," she said when we'd finished discussing our astonishment at how different Los Angeles seemed this particular summer.

"I told you the house was hard to find," said David, coming into the hall through an arched doorway.

I apologized and explained that, contrary to hopes or expectations, I'd not got lost, I'd been at the Bel Air with Cassandra and had forgotten the time.

"Did she fill you in on all the gossip?" asked David.

"Yes," I replied.

He shook his head and grinned. "What a pair she and Duncan make."

"Duncan doesn't gossip. He anecdotes."

David laughed. "He talks. A lot." He put an arm around me. "Come on out." Then he turned to Marie-Paule. "We can eat anytime, now that Nikki's here," he said.

"I'll tell Mrs. T," she replied. Her face when she looked at David was transfused with adoration.

The Waltons that summer were in a rambling white stucco house with a red-tiled roof, terraced into a hillside above Hollywood. It had courtyards on several levels, each with a comfortable set of lounging chairs and clay pots full of bright flowers. There were numberless bedrooms, three sitting rooms, a soundproofed study where David worked, a guest house, and a playroom equipped with darts, table tennis, a pool table, and an assortment of video games. It was owned by an executive at Capitol Records, David explained, as he led me down two flights of tiled stairs, through a doorway, and out onto a small patio flanked by a patch of green lawn. There was a low wall rimming the yard, on top of which sat pots of scarlet geraniums. Beyond it the land dropped sharply away, and in the distance was a beautiful, if hazy, view of the San Fernando Valley. There were lemon trees and orange trees all hanging with fruit, and the smell of jasmine in the air. Out of sight, on other levels of the hillside, were a pool and tennis court.

The older Walton children, who were noisily and combatively playing croquet, paused to wave and shout hello. "Olivia, get down," called David, looking anxiously at his daughter dancing on the wall waiting for Mark to take his turn. It was Sarah who'd insisted on the house in the hills, and David was far from happy with the choice.

At the edge of the patio stood an arbor covered with delicate yellow roses, and under it sat Sarah, studying a script. Beside her on a table was a large bottle of Pelegrino, and a glass. I kissed her hello and told her she looked wonderful, which she did. Her life had done surprisingly little damage to her face. There were faint lines around her eyes and mouth and the texture of her skin had coarsened slightly, but it still had the delicate sheen of porcelain. Her hair was the same golden halo, any possible gray disguised by a careful hand. She was in her forties by then, but seemed years younger, really very little changed from when I'd first met her. Except for her eyes. The soft, melting look was gone, replaced by a watchful, anxious quality, as if on the alert for what might next go wrong.

"Well, enough, I suppose," she replied, when I asked her how the rehearsals were going. Then, in a tone of determined honesty, she added, "Bloody awful, to tell the truth." Her voice had deepened with age, and its lemon edge had sharpened. It wasn't perhaps as mellifluous as it once had been, but it was still rich, still remarkable.

One by one, between turns, the children came over to say hello. Children? Lissie was seventeen that summer, tall and lovely, with Caroline's coloring and all David's expressions. In the fall she would be starting at Yale. "We'll be finished in a minute," she said, as she kissed my cheek. "Do you mind?"

"Isn't she a knockout?" asked David, looking after her with an expression of mingled pride and awe.

"The wonderful thing about Lissie," said Sarah, whose occasional irritation with Caroline had never flowed over to her daughters, "is that she's not only beautiful and intelligent, she's *nice* without being in the least bit soft." She meant soft in the English sense of spineless. "If only I could say the same about Olivia," she added. "The boys are really so much nicer than she."

"Olivia will conquer the world," said David complacently.

"Why are the rehearsals so awful?" I asked.

"Because the director's an ineffectual idiot," supplied David before Sarah could answer. He took a Gauloise from the pack in his shirt pocket and lit it.

"He's not," defended Sarah quickly. "Richard's sweet, and sensitive.

He's very intelligent. But he doesn't believe in directing actors. He thinks we should find our own character, our own performance. It's rather pleasant to be credited with some intelligence for a change."

"Directing isn't about underrating an actor's intelligence. It's about elucidating the text, about creating form, and style. The cast should at least appear to be doing the same play."

"We will. It will just take time. It's a very interesting production," said Sarah, turning back to me. "Very simple, very spare. It's set in the first half of the eleventh century, when Macbeth actually ruled in Scotland. Before the Norman invasion, so it was all terribly primitive."

"Have you seen any of the rehearsals?" I asked David.

"No, I'm not allowed," he replied. He looked at Sarah and smiled. "I make her nervous when I watch."

"He glowers," she said lightly, returning his smile. "I know he doesn't mean to, but he glowers. He disapproves of everything, except his children. Doesn't he?" she asked, looking to me for confirmation.

"And you," he replied, his tone as teasing as hers. "I approve of you. Most of the time, anyway. And Wolfgang Puck's chocolate cake. I approve of that most of all."

We all laughed, and the moment's tension was gone.

Just as the game of croquet ended with a dispute over the final score, Marie-Paule appeared in the doorway announcing dinner, and we all trooped upstairs to a dining room that was paneled in carved wood and hung with wrought-iron chandeliers. There was a mammoth oak sideboard against the wall, and a large painted chest under the window. French doors opened onto a courtyard and a view of the Burbank hills. Flowers were everywhere: a single bird of paradise in a glass vase, arrangements of calla lilies, bouquets of peach-colored roses.

There were twelve of us at the table. Mrs. T, who was plump, and smooth-skinned, and even-tempered at close to seventy; Will, still broad and beefy and willing to do anything in the world for his employers; David; Sarah; myself. Four-year-old Ben had insisted on staying up to eat with us, so all the Walton children were present, as well as Louise Walton, Jack's daughter, who was visiting. She was Kate's and Mark's age, thirteen, and the cousins loathed each other. Or at least the younger girls did. Kate didn't tolerate easily any claim on Mark's attention, and Louise was a flirtatious little imp. Olivia, the most forceful eleven-year-old I'd ever met, thought Louise was a moaner and a coward (she had refused, I was informed confidentially, to go on Thunder Mountain at Disneyland, which was nowhere near as terrifying as the roller coaster at Knotts Berry Farm), so except for delivering stinging critiques of behavior, Olivia never spoke to her. Nicholas, at nine, thought Louise was beautiful and consequently earned his share of trouble from his two sisters. Lissie was too old for the squabbling and did what she could to make peace.

It was a big, noisy, family evening, ordinary and comfortable, the kind of evening I love.

David had taken Marie-Paule and the children to see the talk of the festival, Mnouchkine's Le Théâtre du Soleil production of *Richard II*, and they talked about it with great excitement and enthusiasm, hands and arms waving wildly, urging me to see it.

"But it's in French," I said.

"Thanks to the Lycée, and even more to Marie-Paule," replied David, "our French these days is excellent."

"All the children speak it. Even Ben," said Sarah. She smiled at Marie-Paule with pure, unsuspicious affection. And Marie-Paule beamed back, I thought hopefully, with utter devotion.

"Anyway," interjected Lissie, "it doesn't matter whether you understand the language. The images are what's important. At one point, the actors come prancing out into the arena, and you actually believe you can see the horses they're pretending to ride."

"It's spectacle," said Marie-Paule. "It's very exciting."

"It was long," said Kate.

"I liked the clown," said Nicholas. "He was my favorite."

"That was Richard the *Second*," corrected Olivia, in the scornful tone she normally used with her little brother.

"Of course, it's best to forget it's Shakespeare," said David.

"I was sorry to miss it," said Sarah, "but the rehearsal schedule is punishing. I'm so tired at night."

"We'll see it next year, in Paris," promised David, who then announced he had tickets for the Games' opening ceremony, the hottest ticket in town. The children went berserk with glee.

Even Ben shouted, but stopped suddenly. "What's a sarahmon?" he asked.

We laughed a lot that night, at remarks the children made, at stories they told, at David's clowning for their amusement.

"You're such a fool," said Sarah, tears of laughter streaming down her face. "Such a glorious fool."

The children helped clear the table, David and Will went off to play a game of pool, Sarah and I took Ben upstairs to bed. She ran a bath and put him into it, and I watched as she washed his plump round body. He was beautiful, darker than the other children, as dark as David. I felt a sudden fierce need to touch him. "Let me," I said, taking the washcloth from Sarah.

"I know," she sympathized. "They are beautiful at his age, aren't they? Wonderfully huggable." She settled herself on the hamper I had just vacated, and looked at me, curiously. "Are you so sorry you've never had children?"

"Sometimes, not always," I said, as I soaped Ben's smooth skin. He pulled away from me impatiently and reached for his toy boat. "Sometimes I can't help wondering what my life would have been like if I had." It was still a shock to realize that I no longer had a choice, that I was too old.

"And I wonder what my life would have been like if I hadn't," replied Sarah. I wrenched my eyes away from Ben to look at her. I remembered how distraught she'd been the two times she'd miscarried a child. "I love them, so much," she added quickly. "All of them. Even Lissie and Kate, though I never expected to. But when one has so many people to love, so many expectations to fulfill, it's hard to keep back anything for oneself, isn't it?"

"Yes," I agreed.

"It should have been easy for me, I suppose, with Mrs. T there from the start. But it wasn't. Perhaps it would have been for someone else, but not for me." She paused, and smiled, her eyebrow raised in an ironic quirk. "It's always seemed so odd to me that my name should be Cope, Sarah Cope, when I so clearly can't."

"Neither could I, with that. With marriage, children, all the endless, necessary, inescapable details."

"But you at least had the good sense not to arrange your life so that you felt you ought to." She sighed. "I did so want to be a good wife and mother, but I wasn't, not in any conventional sense. That made me feel such a failure when I realized it. And so guilty. And when I tried to do what I am good at, acting, I felt even guiltier, as if I were somehow abandoning David and the children."

Ben had by this time got tired of trying to sink his rubber boat, and I moved aside so that Sarah could lift him out of the water. She wrapped him in a towel and dried him, kissing his warm plump neck as she did, making him laugh. She looked up at me, flushed and happy. "It's always like this, you see. I'm contented, and then I'm not. I haven't been able to find the balance, I've seesawed between extremes of mother-stroke-wife and actress. And I've not succeeded at either, let alone both."

"You're too hard on yourself, Sarah," I said.

She shook her head. "My only hope of doing it better is if I understand what I did wrong. I disappointed my father and broke his heart. I tried so hard not to do the same to David. But one can't really make another person happy just by doing what he wants. One has to be happy oneself first. Or contented at least. Contentment is the tie that binds. Not love. It's the only river life can sail without sinking." She stopped fussing with Ben for a moment, and looked at me, smiling a little ruefully. "David says I talk an awful lot of rubbish since I got out of that last clinic."

"I don't think it's rubbish," I said.

"He doesn't either, really," replied Sarah. "He just worries when I sound as if I'm taking things too seriously."

"Mummy, tell me a story?" asked Ben, wiggling as Sarah fastened his pajama buttons. "Tell me about Donald and the dragon?"

"That's Daddy's story, darling, only he knows it. But I'll tell you another."

"What about?"

"A magic boat that can sail to the moon."

Ben nodded, then padded after her out of the bathroom. "Will you tell me two stories?" he wheedled.

She laughed. "No, you little imp. One, and then you go to sleep. You've had entirely too much your own way tonight."

I left Sarah and was guided to the playroom by the noise. David and Lissie were playing pool, the children involved in various video games, and Marie-Paule on a sofa reading *Elle*. The soundtrack from *Purple Rain*, Kate and Mark's most recent favorite movie, provided background music. Will had gone off to play poker with some friends, and Mrs. T, I was informed, had preferred the quiet of her own room.

The doorbell rang, and Marie-Paule leaped to her feet. "That is for me," she said, sounding a little embarrassed. Her face was flushed.

"Have a good time," said David, as she hurried from the room. "She has a date," he explained. "Someone on the French equestrian team. He seems nice enough, the son of some friends of her parents. She met him again last Christmas when she went home. They're talking about marriage, and not a minute too soon, you may have noticed."

A wave of relief flooded through me. "That's wonderful," I said, smiling gleefully.

"The news isn't *that* good," said David, dryly, a little surprised by my fervor. "God knows how we'll manage without her."

"He's very nice," said Lissie. "And gorgeous."

"Of course. Gorgeous is *de rigueur*," replied David, "in any romance." He took a cigarette from his pocket and lit it, as Lissie took her shot.

"I wish you'd give that up, Daddy," she said, when she'd finished. "You know how bad it is for you." Lissie was the only one who hadn't yet despaired of ever getting David to stop smoking.

"Just when I convince myself you actually did spring full-blown out of my head, up pops this streak of your mother in you," he said, evading the issue.

She sank the eight ball neatly, and David whistled in approval. "By the way," said Lissie, with as much nonchalance as she could muster, "I'll be out tomorrow night. I'm going to a party."

"Where?" asked David.

"At Stefanie's." David frowned. "Daddy, for once try to be reasonable," coaxed Lissie. "I can't stay home every night."

"I am always reasonable," replied David, "and lately you're never home."

"I'm home tonight."

"I thought we'd go to the theater tomorrow night. The Piccolo Teatro di Milano," he said, savoring the Italian, "is doing *The Tempest*. It's supposed to be wonderful."

Lissie wavered a moment, then held firm. "I've already promised Stefanie."

"She smokes dope," said David in one last-ditch effort.

"How do you know that?" asked Lissie.

"I know everything."

"Well, I won't," promised Lissie.

David turned to me and grinned. "I thought she was willful when she was four, but these days she's stubborn as hell."

"Determined," I said.

David smiled. "And this is just the beginning. Think about Kate, and Olivia."

Lissie smiled too. "I wouldn't be in your shoes for anything, Daddy."

When Sarah came in, she and I played pool against Lissie and David. To my surprise, we won. David insisted on a rematch, but I refused, saying I had to go home, and Sarah decided that it was time she and the little kids went to bed. She had an early rehearsal in the morning.

David walked me outside to my car; and before I got in, I put my arms around him. "Sometimes you all make me feel as if I've missed out on an awful lot," I said.

"If you've missed the good, you've missed the bad, too. That ought to be some consolation."

"Would it be to you?"

"I couldn't live life your way, Nikki, any more than you could live it mine."

"No, I couldn't," I agreed.

"Oh, Christ," he said, suddenly, angrily, "I've really fucked it up this time. Shit!"

Fear gripped my stomach again. "David, what's going on? You wanted to tell me something this morning. What was it?"

He kissed me and bundled me into the car. "I've got to go in and say goodnight to my kids. Can you have breakfast with me tomorrow?"

"I wish you wouldn't do stuff like this to me, David."

"Can you have breakfast?" he repeated.

"No, dammit, I can't."

"I'll call you in the morning," he said. He touched my hair through the open car window. "Or call me if you change your mind." And he went back inside, leaving me the whole night to speculate, to invent, to worry.

❧ *Chapter 36* ❧

Just before one the next day, David knocked on the gallery door. One of the assistants, a girl of about nineteen, went hurrying to open it, prepared to announce to the caller that the gallery was closed and wouldn't reopen for another few days. I watched her face change as she realized who it was standing before her: David Walton, genuine movie star, complete with chipped tooth, broken nose, and fierce, dark eyes. Her eyes glazed a little, her mouth dropped ever so slightly open.

"Is Nikki Collier here?" asked David.

"Yes," stuttered the girl, whose name, I think, was Rula. She had on ankle socks and a wide print skirt, several layers of T-shirts, and a stunning belt. Her hair stood up in maroon spikes all over her head. "Come in." Casting anxious, smiling glances over her shoulder, she led him to where Peter and I were supervising the hanging of my photographs.

David lit a cigarette, and the two men, who had already met, plunged easily into conversation. Though Peter at first kept looking curiously from David to me trying to assess the link between us, gradually his focus shifted entirely to David, where the three assistants' had been from the start. And even with David's mind clearly elsewhere, as it was at that moment in the gallery, charged energy particles seemed to emanate from him, phototropically pulling everyone into his field of force.

The conversation wasn't interesting. Compliments were exchanged about David's play, *Just Until Spring*, and an exhibition at the gallery which it happened David had seen. Questions were asked and evaded about David's next play. Then came a few kind words about the quality of the photographs and the inevitable success of my show. Still, David managed to be clever and earned a few laughs from the admiring assembly. Clearly hoping for more and better, Peter invited David and me to join him and a friend for lunch. David's refusal was accompanied by his warmest smile, and was firm though very vague, something about the two of us having prior, sacrosanct plans. It wasn't true, of course. We hadn't spoken since I'd left the Walton house the night before.

"You think he's sexy," said David as soon as Peter and his assistants had departed for their various lunch appointments, leaving me to lock up the gallery.

"Very."

"You know he'd fuck *me* if I'd let him," said David in a dispassionate tone that was meant to warn without solidifying interest.

"I worked as an assistant once to a photographer in New York, a great old guy, sexy as hell, Detto Ferrante."

"I remember."

"'What do I care,' Detto used to say, 'whether it's a man or a woman, black or yellow or white. Beauty is the only thing that interests me.'"

"Peter de Witt's sexual choices are not based on aesthetics," said David. "They're based on curiosity."

"Also my besetting sin."

"You think *he's* beautiful?" asked David, getting to the nub of the problem.

"I do. In a decadent sort of way."

"There's something about him that reminds me of Fiona Brent," said David distastefully.

"Me, too," I agreed. "But on him, I like it."

"I'd rather cuddle up with a snake."

"Don't worry, I'm only enjoying a few dirty thoughts. I'm too sensible to act out my fantasies."

"All of us act out our fantasies," said David. "But most of us choose only the safer ones, the ones we've got the courage to indulge."

He lit another cigarette and began to walk around the room, looking at the photographs. Some were hung, some were still stacked against the walls.

"You really should wait till they're all hung," I said.

"I've seen them before," he replied.

"In a show, it's the juxtapositions that matter," I told him pompously.

"Bullshit," he countered, and kept looking. "I remember when you took this," he said, referring to a portrait of Duncan Powell.

"So do I. It was a very memorable day." The black-and-white portrait was from that first photo session with Duncan and Sarah. It was the one of him relaxed in a wing chair, all easy charm and sexy affability.

"I was furious with you," reminisced David. "God, he was good-looking."

"He still is."

"Better-looking than I am?" He was only half joking.

"What's the matter? Have the endless hordes of women stopped throwing themselves at your feet?"

He laughed, and continued his slow walk around the room, blowing clouds of smoke as he went. "Where are the pictures of Sarah?" he asked, when he'd seen them all.

I hesitated a moment, then answered, "Peter doesn't think she's well enough known. This is a star-spangled show for a star-spangled event," I added ironically.

He ran a hand through his hair, a gesture of confusion. His face was suddenly bleak. "What happened to her, Nikki?"

"You," I said. Then, quickly, "No, that's not fair, or even accurate. Whenever Sarah had to make a choice, she chose you. That was her right. And ultimately no one's to blame but herself."

"I never forced her," he said.

"No," I agreed, "you didn't. Not overtly."

"How do you force someone covertly?"

"You know very well how. You're a master at it," I said. "You do it by wanting what you want so badly, by needing what you need so ostentatiously, that everyone else's needs pale in comparison, dwindle into insignificance. You don't have to ask. You're like a great river of desire that catches up everyone else's little stream and carries it towards your own mammoth sea."

"Very pretty," said David, his voice dripping with sarcasm.

"Thank you," I replied. "I've been searching for years for the right image."

We drove out along Sunset Boulevard to the ocean, stopped at a deli to buy a couple of sandwiches, and sat and ate them on the beach. The day was overcast and cool, so we didn't have much company except for the seagulls, who kept up a relentless squealing attack on the trashbins, scattering refuse all over the sand.

"Jean-Jacques Rousseau has a lot to answer for," said David, "filling people's heads with romantic twaddle about the nobility of nature. It's just as filthy as the rest of creation."

We argued awhile about the place of scavengers and the effects of polystyrene in the modern world; then, reluctant to add to the debris around us, carried our own litter back to the car for later disposal.

The wind had come up. David picked up my jacket from where I'd left it on the seat, handed it to me, and suggested a walk. "You don't have to get back right away, do you?" he asked. I didn't. Peter had a meeting that afternoon and wouldn't return to the gallery until after four. We walked down to the water and started north along the damp sand towards Malibu.

Even in the closest friendships, you have to wait for what seems the right moment to open a discussion, the moment when both friends are willing to talk.

"I'm sorry about yesterday," I said. He looked at me blankly. "I knew you wanted to tell me something, but I was so involved in my own troubles, I didn't give you a chance."

"Oh, that," said David. "I'd forgotten." Then he grinned. "Do I get an apology for your behavior last night, too?" he asked. "And why wouldn't you meet me for breakfast this morning?"

"I had to be at the gallery early. Anyway," I added, a little of my former irritation showing, "you know I can't stand it when you start being mysterious and melodramatic. I always feel as if you're trying to manipulate me."

"There was no way we could talk last night."

"I know."

"Then what did you want me to do?"

"How do I know? Anything but *hint*. Tell me in thirty seconds or less what was on your mind, I suppose, so I wouldn't have to stay awake half the night trying to figure it out."

"And what did you come up with?"

"That you're having an affair."

"Not a very original notion," David replied, but his tone was neutral. He wasn't denying it.

"Less original than you think. Cassandra told me yesterday afternoon, though I wasn't sure then I should believe her."

A dog swam up out of the water, a large stick in his mouth. He shook himself, sprinkling us with seaspray, then ran, tail wagging, to where his owner waited, and dropped the stick at his feet.

"It's true," said David.

"Oh, shit," I replied. "I was hoping I was wrong."

David cocked an eyebrow. "I thought fidelity was incidental in a relationship?"

"When I said that, I was referring to my relationships," I replied, "not yours. I don't make any promises. I don't give anyone the right to expect things of me."

"That can't be said of me, can it?"

"No."

"Did Cassandra mention any names?"

"Yes," I said, "but I know she's not right about that."

"Who does she think it is?"

"What does it matter?" I said impatiently. Then, more quietly: "Are you going to tell me?"

"Tessa Hoffmann."

I suppose any name would have surprised me. When I'd spent hours thinking about possible women the night before, none had seemed reasonable to me. None I thought of seemed to coordinate with David. None, that is, except Sarah. Eventually, I had concluded that either I was wrong, or the woman was someone I didn't yet know.

Tessa was a friend of mine. We'd done a book together, the one on Ronald Graves, the sculptor, and were planning another on Louise Nevelson. I liked Tessa. Most people liked Tessa. She was a tall, handsome rather than conventionally pretty, big-boned woman with shoulder-length brown hair and large hazel eyes. Inevitably, by every man who met her, she was described as "a great girl." She was also a talented writer. She had done a series of articles which I'd very much admired for *Esquire* several years before on the women's movement. They had established her reputation both as a notable journalist and as a reasonable and responsible apologist for the cause: she had even managed to lobby for the Equal Rights Amendment without getting called a lesbian. Her coverage of the 1980 presidential elections had solidified her position, and in 1983 she won a Pulitzer for her articles about the veterans of the Vietnam War.

Tessa was married for a long time, or what constitutes a long time these days, about twelve years, to Vic D'Amato, an actor who frequently worked in David's plays, so David had met her often, both with me and with her husband. David had flirted with her, but never seriously. It hadn't once crossed my mind that his interest in her was anything more than casual.

Early in 1984, Tessa had divorced Vic. She never told me why, just remarked cryptically that she'd had enough. I heard from others that what she found so hard to take was Vic's resentment of her success. Her marriage had been foundering for years; the Pulitzer finally sank it.

"Close your mouth," said David.

"Well, knock me over with a feather," I said. "How long has this been going on?"

"Not long. Since March. Maybe April. I ran into her at a press party in New York."

"Why?" I asked, not at all understanding. "Why now? Before, I could have understood. When Sarah was so sick, it would have made sense."

"It seemed like a good idea at the time."

"Don't joke," I snapped. "It isn't funny."

"Are you going to turn prig on me?" he asked, his voice suddenly cold.

"No," I replied. "No, of course not."

"There's no one else I can talk to about this." He wanted to go to confession, to me. He wanted absolution. He had done as much for me many times. That's what we used each other for, as a source of the infinite mercy of the God we weren't sure we believed in.

I walked away from him, up the beach a little way, and sat. David came and lay next to me. He took my hand and patted it. "Poor baby," he said. "I do demand a lot of you, don't I?"

"Are you in love with her?" I asked.

He didn't answer right away. Then, he said, "No, not in the way you mean. I love Sarah."

I sighed with relief, thinking this was going to end better than I'd feared. "Good," I said. "Then tell Tessa goodbye."

"It's not that easy."

"It could be."

"I want Tessa."

"Oh, Christ, David. Come on. You want her, you've had her. You don't have to let it ruin your life. Sarah's life." For some reason I was convinced of the impossibility of David's continuing his affair with impunity. I knew some men did. I had had affairs with men who did, Sam Graber, for example, who was by then two mistresses past me, and still married. Why did I doubt David's ability to succeed when Sam had? "This time, surely, you don't have to insist on turning a one-act play into a full-length melodrama? God, you all seemed so happy last night, the perfect family. When will I ever learn there is no such thing?" David was lying on his back, not looking at me. I leaned over him and looked down into his dark eyes.

"I'm being very careful," he said.

"Not careful enough, if Cassandra's gossiping," I reminded him.

"It doesn't matter what I do or don't do, whether I'm guilty or innocent, there's always gossip. You know that."

"And if Sarah hears it?"

"She won't. She's too wrapped up in her play." Was there a trace of bitterness in his voice? He took my hand again. "I had to tell you. But I don't want you to worry. Everything will be fine. Tessa's a great girl. She's bright and talented and funny. I need her right now. I deserve her, for all I've had to put up with. And she understands. She knows I love Sarah. And she doesn't want any more from me than I can give. She's a lot like you, Nikki. Fiercely independent. Believe me, she's not looking for either a home or a husband. Tessa won't cause any trouble."

"It's you I'm worried about," I said, "not Tessa. It's you who likes to add the drama, the excitement to life. Just for this once, David, don't."

He stood up, grabbed both my hands, and pulled me to my feet. "A little excitement," he said, "never hurt anybody."

ᵛ Chapter 37 ᵛ

Hundreds of productions were mounted that summer by local theater groups as part of the arts festival, and a few nights later, Peter took me to an evening of one-act plays, none longer than ten minutes. Two were worth seeing, an extremely funny monologue about baseball and a touching two-hander between a dying Indian chief and the warrior who was to succeed him as head of the tribe. A friend of Peter's performed the monologue.

We ate afterwards in a pretty little restaurant in Beverly Hills. It had whitewashed walls, gaily painted rush-seated chairs, a profusion of dry flowers in pottery vases, French faience dinnerware, and Cajun cooking. It was all very quaint and cozy and the noise level was happily low. I could actually hear Peter when he spoke.

We talked about my show for a while, but neither of us was particularly eager to pursue that line of conversation. Over the past few days we had said about as much as could be said on the subject, and we were both bored with it. As of late that afternoon, all the major decisions had been made, and the exhibition would either be a success or it wouldn't.

The Olympics Festival and the Games themselves came in for their share of discussion, but gradually the conversation shifted to more personal ground. Peter told me how delighted he'd been to see David and tried again to discover how long I'd known him, and, more subtly, how

well. It wasn't at all the starfucker's usual obsession Peter was displaying, that desire to share vicariously in what is perceived as another's
heightened level of existence, but a blend of several emotions. There
was that competitive element David incited almost inevitably in successful men; the interest that David's mind and personality provoked in people of no matter what gender; and an excitement that was purely sexual.
Peter was horny, for David, and for me. What he wanted at that moment, I knew, I could *feel*, was the three of us together in a bed.

I told him David and I knew each other very well indeed: we'd grown
up together, I explained. To the questions about our childhood and
David's career, I responded as briefly as I possibly could. Then, to avoid
having to discuss David for the rest of the night, I asked, "Where did you
grow up? Here in California?"

He hadn't. He'd grown up in Texas (though there wasn't much of an
accent left, only the trace of a drawl if you knew to begin with there
would be), just this side of the Mexican border. His family hadn't struck
it rich in oil, but they'd done all right in cattle ranching. They were
wealthy enough to make Peter's young life extremely comfortable.

Unlike David, Peter had few fantasies about ranching. He didn't see
it as an ideal expression of the American spirit. It all seemed a lot of
hot, smelly, hard work to him; and the only pleasure he got from it was
riding horses. He loved horses, and still rode whenever he could. "To
be out at daybreak, on horseback, riding in the hills, waiting for the sun
to come up," he told me, "is one of life's great highs."

When he was twelve he was sent north to prep school and fell in with
the arty crowd. He developed a smugly superior attitude to his family
and former friends, and became noticeably contemptuous if not of their
money, then their way of making it. "I was a real asshole," he said,
laughing. "As if one way of making money is any better than the rest."

His father ignored his contempt, or possibly didn't notice it. Only
when Peter said he wanted to go to art school in New York did Mr. de
Witt react, and then it was firmly and with conviction. Peter would go
to school where he was told or learn to manage without de Witt money.
That Peter had no desire to do. In any case, he soon realized he had no
talent, or not enough. He could draw with a certain facility, but beyond
that there seemed to be nothing, no vision, no spark of divine fire, not
even a sustaining sense of commitment.

So he went to Texas A&M, studied something appropriately agricul-
tural, played enough sports to make his daddy proud, then at the end of his
third year went traveling in Europe for the summer with a prep school
buddy and neglected to return in time for the fall semester. From then on,

he was on his own, without the comfortable cushion of the de Witt money. Though Peter still had long-term hopes for it, at that moment it was being cheerfully squandered by his brother and younger sister.

Through his friend that summer in Europe, Peter was introduced to an international art circle in Munich, Berlin, Paris, and London. He met artists, dealers, collectors. Using the little bit of money he had left, he speculated and bought, sold at a profit, and bought again. Before he knew it, he was in business. Gradually, his circle of acquaintances grew, as did his knowledge of the art world. He narrowed his interests to contemporary art and decided eventually to settle in Los Angeles. It was a wide-open city, he said, a city whose potential was only beginning to be explored, a city where anything was possible.

Sexual excitement is contagious. Though my fantasy wasn't at all Peter's, though one other was more than enough for me in bed, still I began to respond to him. As Peter talked, we exchanged sidelong glances fraught with suggestion. Our fingers touched as if by accident, our legs brushed together and drew apart. His elegant hands framed by silk cuffs, the exaggerated shoulders of his jacket, the shadow of beard on his face lent him the murky appeal of a gangster in a thirties movie. I was keenly aware I hadn't made love in well over a year. I found myself wondering how in Los Angeles people finessed the two-car handicap. In New York, in a shared taxi, nothing is easier than suggesting a nightcap at "your place or mine." Wouldn't the same suggestion made in a parking lot rub the edge off an erotic thrill?

Peter paid the bill and I followed him back through the restaurant and outside across the patio, where someone called my name and I turned to see Simon Wroth and Fiona Brent finishing dinner. Simon, as unselfconsciously rumpled as ever, was genuinely glad to see me, I think, which is more than can be said for his companion.

Though Fiona was by then long divorced, she and Simon hadn't married. No one was absolutely certain why, though the tendency was to attribute it to a persistent reluctance in Simon. "There's no doubt he's absolutely mad about her," insisted Duncan, "he just doesn't like her very much."

I introduced Peter to them both and saw that David and I had been right: he did resemble Fiona. They looked nothing at all alike, but they both had the same concupiscent expression in the eyes, the same sensual lift of the lips. For the first time since I'd met Fiona, I had some sympathy for Simon and his obsession with her.

"We got the invitation to the opening," said Simon.

"Are you coming?" I asked politely, feeling impatient to get away, to be alone again with Peter. There was a lovely knot of tension in my stomach, and my breathing was in trouble.

"Certainly," he replied. "What are friends for, if not to launch one's endeavors with a champagne toast?"

"We're so looking forward to it," added Fiona, who sounded as if she'd much prefer going to Siberia in winter. "I just hope I can get away from the set early enough to make it."

"Oh, are you working?" I asked, hoping I'd found a level of surprise that was offensive without being obvious.

Fiona shot me a deserved look of sheer loathing and then said indeed she was, in a film by a "brilliant" new director, who was working them all like "navvies" in order to finish before the Games started. (That was everyone's goal those few weeks, to finish work and get out of town before the onslaught of Olympic visitors.) Simon's eyes clouded, I thought, at the mention of the director, but I might have imagined it; though, in fact, he wasn't working and was worried about it. Then, too, he was always fiercely jealous of any man that came near Fiona. And with good reason. She had no discernible morals at all.

And my morals? Well, as I'd said to David, I made no promises. If anyone who came near me got hurt, it was without my active participation. But not many did come near anymore. In the past two or three years, I'd found fewer and fewer men attractive, and my feelings (or lack of them) were, it seemed to me, reciprocated. Was it only age and hormones? I wondered. Was Fiona having the same experience? What a relief it was, after so long, to feel desire.

Peter and I walked back to the lot behind his gallery where we'd left our cars parked. "Are you awake enough to come home with me?" he said. "I'd love to show you my house. It's spectacular." In Los Angeles, people now use houses as they once used etchings: like everything else, sex is subject to inflation.

Peter's house was tiny, a little aerie perched at the top of a hill with a view of nearby mountains and distant lights. There was an extravagant bathroom with copper fittings and a sauna; two large and uncluttered rooms with oversized chairs upholstered in gray, black lacquer tables, a carefully placed Stella, and two Diebenkorns; there were sculptures on the floor, and no plants anywhere; in one room was a bed, big and low and covered in glazed gray cotton.

He rolled a couple of joints, opened a bottle of wine, turned on the pool lights, and led me outside, into the warm night air. We sat to-

gether in the glider, barely touching, talking softly as we smoked, looking out across the pool and the bubbling Jacuzzi, beyond the potted
plants and the fruit trees and the oleander hedge, to the lights of the
city. The sweet, pervasive smell of jasmine hung in the air.

Finally, Peter bent his head towards me and we kissed, gently, experi-
mentally, with no urgency. And when he suggested we get into the
Jacuzzi, we helped each other undress with the same slow sensual appreciation. Time was moving so slowly, it seemed pointless to hurry.

The water of the Jacuzzi played with us. "Open your legs," said Peter.

All residual tension, anxiety, even apprehension drained from me. I had
never felt easier, more relaxed, in all my life. "What is in that stuff?" I
asked.

"Only good things," he replied.

I reached out a hand and stroked his face. "It will scratch," I said.

"I'll be careful."

Thinking of all the times I had heard or read that line, I smiled. Peter was
so young, he probably had no idea why. "You're so beautiful," I told him.

And then we didn't talk anymore. Words were no longer of any interest. We were totally preoccupied with sensations, the tip of a wet tongue
tracing the outline of a lip, the brush of a mouth against a neck beaded with
water, the long liquid slide of a hand approving a curve, the sensuous stroke
of fingers exploring.

It was folly, I had always believed, to make love with the people with
whom you did business. But that one time I didn't care. I didn't care at all.

If the sex wasn't the most fulfilling, the most profound, I'd ever had,
it was still a great deal of fun. What was missing in intensity and depth
was balanced by excitement and, strangely enough, good humor. One
of the ways in which Peter differed from Fiona Brent, I discovered, was
that his eroticism was neither narcissistic nor mercenary. All he wanted
from sex was pleasure, which he was as avid to give as receive.

What was remarkable in Peter was his lack of sentimentality, the absence
of guilt. He felt no compulsion to despise himself for his desires. He was
capable of passion, joy, tenderness, even (to my surprise) affection, without
needing to distort or inflate their meaning, without any attempt to make
them add up to love. There was, consequently, no possessiveness in the
aftermath of his lovemaking, no jealousy, no disgust, no desire to demean
or hurt. With me, at any rate, there was only a relaxed camaraderie. The
next day, without the discordant edge that sexual curiosity causes, with no
unfulfillable expectations of one another, we worked together even better

than we had before. And if part of me wanted something different, something more, still I understood that what I'd had was, considering what I was prepared to give, all I had a right to expect.

Peter had a lunch date, so I wandered into Beverly Hills on my own to browse through the shops, and ran into Simon in a bookstore on Little Santa Monica.

"What are you buying?" he said. His sleeves were unevenly rolled, and a portion of his shirt had escaped from his trousers. He took the books I was carrying from me to read their covers. There were a couple of paperback Anne Tylers and a large book of photographs, I think Hiram Dodd's Arizona landscapes. "They're out of stock on the book I wanted. It's probably too late anyway. If a book's really hot, film rights are sold months before publication. Is she any good?" he asked, referring to the Tylers.

"Wonderful."

"Would either make a movie, do you think?"

I laughed. "I have no idea. I haven't read them yet."

He laughed too, half rueful, half embarrassed. "This town has a one-track mind," he said, "and I'm on it. It's lovely to see you, darling. Come and have a cup of coffee. Or are you hungry? Would you like some lunch?"

I paid for the books and we went outside into the hot, hazy day, joining a throng of happily jabbering shoppers, walking past windows full of unbelievably expensive running clothes. On a corner, waiting for the light to change, were two women, plump sixtyish twins wearing identical lilac-colored polyester pantsuits and sprays of paper violets in their platinum hair. Simon looked at me and grinned. He began to hum, "Hooray for Holly-wood..."

It was late, and Nate 'n' Al's Deli had emptied. "The first time I came here," said Simon, when the hostess had seated us, "was with David." There was regret in his voice; and anger, still. I didn't say anything. "It's too bad about all that," added Simon after a moment.

"Yes," I agreed, "it is."

It was David's guilt, speculates Keating, that ended the friendship. Actually, David was hurt, not guilty. And, ruthlessly, he reduced Simon's role in his life from leading player to walk-on. The close male companionship he needed, after that summer in Vienna, he got from Rob Maxwell, his agent, and from Steven Apsberg, the director of his films.

The morning after the fight, Simon had phoned to apologize, and David, totally involved at that point with Sarah's collapse, had neither the time nor the energy to prolong the quarrel. He accepted Simon's apology and added his own perfunctory sorry. That had patched the break well enough for them to continue working more or less cordially together until *The King of Rome* was completed and released, but the trust between them was gone. All Simon's long-repressed resentment of David had risen too near the surface; and while David was rampantly competitive with everyone, among his friends he numbered only those with whom competitiveness was based on mutual respect, not on envy, or anger. In any case, the only anger David was then able to deal with was Sarah's: she exhausted his resources of compassion and diplomacy.

Simon at first tried to get their friendship back on its old footing and seemed genuinely unable to comprehend David's resistance. He'd had a little too much to drink, he protested, and he'd lost his temper. But friends quarrel, don't they? For him, the tensions of the entire summer had reduced to the aspect of one brawl. He was totally unwilling, or unable, to consider that the trouble might be both wider and deeper.

They had continued to meet socially. David and Simon had done too much business together, been friends for too many years, not to know essentially the same people. But any suggestions Simon made about follow-up lunches or dinners were evaded by David, whose regret at losing Simon's friendship was tinged with relief at no longer having any need whatsoever to associate with Fiona Brent. As soon as *The King of Rome* was finished, Fiona had left her husband, whose ventures into film producing had been spectacularly unsuccessful, to live openly with Simon and to work in the films he directed. He had made two since then. The first, *Sweet Surrender*, was successful; the second, *Journey to Jerusalem*, was not. His next one, *Bust-up*, would be the biggest success he'd ever had, but in the summer of 1984 it was still in the talking stages, and Simon was worried. He'd taken a house in Los Angeles to be on the spot for discussions, but so far the only undeniably positive result was a major role for Fiona in someone else's movie.

Simon looked up from his menu, announced he was having a bagel with cream cheese and lox, then settled back to observe me. "You look fabulous," he said. "Really, better than ever. Are you happy?"

"Reasonably," I said.

"You ought to be. Things seem to be going very well for you."

"What's happening with you?" I asked.

The waitress came, took our order, and brought us a stainless-steel pot full of coffee, while I listened as Simon told me a little about the current state of the negotiations for *Bust-up*. The tale was an ordinary one, the studio wanting someone else, Simon's agent and one of the stars pressuring for him. Since the occupants of the deli's large booths seemed to be salt-and-pepper-haired, bespectacled denizens of the film world, I suspected there were similar conversations going on at tables all around us. "It could go either way," said Simon. "What a business."

"You love it."

"When I'm on top," he admitted.

"You are on top," I said. "One unsuccessful movie does not a failure make. Anyway, it was a good film."

"Thank you, my darling." He smiled ruefully and shook his head. "Nevertheless I seem to have slid somewhat down that slippery hill. Unlike our mutual friend, who just keeps climbing from one peak to the next. Isn't it amazing, the way everything seems to go right for him?"

I thought of the anguish of those years when Sarah was ill and shook my head. "Not everything."

"Sarah's all right now," he said. "She's steady as a rock. Have you seen her?" I nodded. "With all the pain she's caused him, he's still damn lucky to have her. She worships him. I never knew a woman so besotted with a man. And after all the years together. You would have thought their passion would have been wearing a little thin by now, wouldn't you?"

"If I hadn't seen it with my own eyes," I agreed, "I never would have believed it."

"What fools women are. They inevitably love the men who are bad for them." The smile and joking voice didn't quite conceal the anger, or the bitterness.

"Men, of course, always love wisely and well. I've noticed that."

"Not me, certainly. Ask anyone." He laughed, then his face grew somber again. "But I still say Sarah made a big mistake."

"I like you, Simon. I always have. But when you start talking about David you get really boring, you know?"

"He let her waste her talent. He let her throw herself away. He saw her sacrificing everything that was best in herself for him, and he made no attempt to stop her."

"And you, if you saw Fiona doing that for you, would you stop her? Would you even notice?"

That stung. He sat back. "I apologize. I'm so fond of you I tend to forget you have a blind spot where David's concerned. Not another word on the subject. All right?"

"That's fine with me," I said, and waited for the wave of anger to recede. It would. It always did. If I lost Simon as a friend, it was going to be for my sake, not David's.

The waitress brought our lunch. I noticed James Caan in a booth across the aisle looking at me as if he remembered my face if not my name. I waved and he smiled. The year before I had photographed him for *Esquire*.

While I arranged my lox into a messy sandwich, Simon began to eat his fastidiously with a knife and fork. "When in Rome," I said.

"I lie indolently by my pool for hours every day," he responded. "That's all the acculturation I'm prepared to permit." Then, a complete non sequitur, he added, "By the way, Fiona and I are getting married." The shock must have shown clearly on my face. "It's about time, wouldn't you say?" he asked rhetorically, sounding annoyed. "After all, we've been living together for years."

I felt a rush of pity for him, not at all an appropriate response to someone's announcement of impending marriage. "I suppose that's why I'm surprised," I replied. But it wasn't. With Simon's career in decline, I couldn't imagine why Fiona had said yes.

"Fiona took some convincing, but finally she gave in," he said, in response to the unasked question. "Her experience of marriage, so far, hasn't been happy." He poured us both another cup of coffee. "There comes a point when every man wants to settle down," he continued, "when he needs to feel something in his life is secure."

If Simon's last picture had been a success, I thought, everything would be reversed: it would be Fiona pressing for marriage, and Simon trying to avoid it. And possibly succeeding, sparing himself even more pain.

But who was I to prognosticate? I had been wrong before, wrong about Duncan and Cassandra. Fiona might yet reveal sterling qualities. "I hope you'll both be very happy," I said, hoping my doubt didn't show.

Simon reached across the table and took my hand. "I'll never understand why it was that you and I never fell in love," he said, giving my fingers a fond squeeze. "I like you better than any woman I know."

"If anyone knew why people fall in love," I said, "what causes it, there would be a vaccine against it by now. Only religion makes people suffer more."

"Cynic," said Simon.

"No," I responded. "I'm a romantic. That's the problem. I believe in the power of love."

Which was why I believed Simon was right. For both their sakes, it really would have been wise of Sarah to have loved David just a little less.

❧ Chapter 38 ❧

The next night, Lissie and I drove to Pasadena to see the Alvin Ailey Dance Company, which was performing at the Civic Auditorium, one of the festival halls. Though I frequently took all the children en masse to lunch or dinner, to the movies, a play, or an occasional ballet, I always contrived to spend time alone with Lissie, without the dour presence of Kate or the roisterous ebullience of the younger Waltons.

Over the years, Lissie had changed little. Puberty hadn't radically altered her face, or her personality. Despite the mascara and lipstick, the wild mane of red hair and the subtle curves of her lean body, it wasn't hard to find the little girl who had sat on my lap, green eyes luminous, listening intently as I read to her, correcting me if I made a mistake or skipped a page, demanding I start again at the beginning as soon as I'd finished. "I think you're wrong about that," she would say when she hadn't liked a particular twist in a story's plot. "I don't think it's the baby-sitter at the door," she would emend, supplying me with a version more acceptable to herself. "I think it's a friend coming over to play. You know, like you, Nikki." She had been a child completely without artifice, totally without guile. She had been forthright and intelligent, considerate and loving. And she still is. Somehow, Lissie managed to escape relatively unscathed from Caroline and David's divorce and from all she'd had to deal with since.

We were in one of the Walton cars and Lissie was at the wheel, since she needed to practice before taking the driving test in New York when she returned. "Isn't Los Angeles wonderful this year?" she said. "Look, no traffic. It's amazing."

"Don't talk," I cautioned. "Concentrate."

She laughed. "Are you nervous?"

"I'm always nervous when someone else is driving," I temporized.

"I'm good," she said. "Daddy taught me."

"Hmmph," I muttered. David's driving was not one of the things I admired most about him.

"He's a great teacher," she defended. "He stays calm no matter what."

"No matter what?" I repeated, leaning heavily on the irony.

She laughed, again. "Well, almost."

The Pasadena Civic Auditorium is a long mission-style building, stuccoed, with a tile roof, set at the top of wide, terraced steps. During the festival, an outdoor café straddled one end of the building, and people braved the wind to eat buffet suppers of cold chicken at crowded tables. On the steps, others stood in small clusters, talking, laughing, waving at passersby, some trying to buy or sell seats. The air reverberated with the gaiety typical of the festival events I'd attended, and yet there was something distinctly different about this particular gathering. I looked around me, trying determine what. And then I realized: the crowd was rainbow-colored, an older, better-dressed version of a Pepsi commercial. For once, white faces did not predominate. There were Chinese and Japanese in the indigenous California garb of jeans and jackets, there were Indians in saris, but mostly there were Blacks— handsome black men in suits, elegant black women in hats. We were a motley and stylish gathering. We were integrated. We were a rare phenomenon, and I longed for my camera.

The company that night didn't dance as well as I'd seen them dance before, but I didn't care and neither did any one else who noticed. The applause was loud and sustained. Cheering brought the performers back for curtain call after curtain call. Lissie's green eyes flashed with excitement. "Isn't this wonderful?" she said, as she clapped her hands red with appreciation.

We stopped afterwards for a hamburger at a nearby restaurant where Lissie had eaten before with friends. These days she had a very active social life. Over the past few years, she'd spent enough summers in Los Angeles and had met enough of the children of David's business associates to have found a niche she was comfortable in. Though sexually less experienced than most of her Los Angeles friends, she had enough sophistication to carry it off. Enough something to carry it off. Like David, Lissie attracted people to her. It wasn't just her looks. She had an irrepressible enthusiasm for life, and she had style.

The restaurant had wood tables and paper placemats and movie posters on the walls, including one of Duncan in *Calypso Bay* and another of David in *Cop!*

"Kate's going to miss you next year," I said, thinking how much I would miss her, too. "You've never been apart before."

"She'll be all right," responded Lissie with her usual good sense, "As long as she's got Mark. I'm the one who's going to do all the missing. I can't imagine what it will be like to live away from everyone."

"Are you excited?"

"Oh, yes. I can't wait to get down to work." Lissie was going to major in anthropology, because, as she explained to me, it was the best excuse she could think of to travel anywhere in the world she wanted to go and learn everything she longed to know. "But I'm scared, too," she continued. "I've been in one school for so long, I'm so used to doing things one way, Yale's bound to seem strange at first." The previous spring, she had graduated, with honors, from the Lycée (all the Walton children, except Ben, who was still too young, were scattered throughout the school), which she'd attended since the age of four.

The waiter, a cute blond boy who was doing his best to attract Lissie's attention, brought our hamburgers and Cokes. "You'll do fine," I encouraged.

"Well," she agreed, "I do seem to adjust to change pretty quickly. Daddy says I take after him." She smiled. "He says we have rubber molecules programmed into our DNA and we bounce." The smile faded. "But nobody gets as miserable as Daddy when he's depressed. He's been so down these past few weeks."

"The other night he seemed fine."

"He was fine," agreed Lissie. "Having us all together, and you there. You know nothing makes him happier. And everything went just right. Even Olivia and Nicholas managed not to fight." Her eyes were suddenly shadowed. "Do you think he's worried about Sarah?"

"No," I said. "I don't think so. Sarah's been all right now, for a long time."

"Oh, yes," agreed Lissie quickly. "She's been wonderful. And even though she gets furious with the director, you can see she loves doing the play. She loves acting. I haven't seen her so"—she groped for the word—"satisfied, I guess, in a long time. Only..." She hesitated. "Only you never can tell, can you?"

The times when Sarah had seemed "cured" and had then relapsed

were too numerous to be discounted. Lissie was voicing a fear that was
everyone's, that this "cure" too could be temporary, that some unexpected provocation might at any moment push Sarah again over the
edge. It would take a long time for Sarah to regain the trust she'd lost;
perhaps she never could completely. And perhaps that was it. Perhaps
David was tired of watching and waiting for the next time to happen.
Perhaps he needed some relief from the tension.

"It must be hard for Sarah," I said, "knowing you're all just waiting for
her to fail."

"We're not," said Lissie, shocked.

"You think she might."

"Well, yes. I mean, she has before."

"You know what happens when you think you might miss a tennis
shot?"

Lissie grinned. "Nine times out of ten, I miss it. Daddy says you
can't even let the idea of failing enter your head. It sets up a field of
negative energy."

"And if you're walking a tightrope with everyone expecting you to fall,
when you yourself think you might fall?"

Her eyes filled with tears. "I love Sarah," she said. "She's always
been so kind to me. And to Kate, too. It isn't always like that, you
know, with stepmothers. What an awful word. The French say it better: *belle-mère.*" She savored the word, as her father would have.
"That's what she is, beautiful." The tears spilled over. "I really do love
her."

"Lissie, sweetheart, of course you do. It's obvious you do." She'd
taken what I'd said as an accusation rather than a warning.

"What happens if you believe, with all your heart, that something
will be all right, and then it isn't?" Her voice summoned up the
image of all the crushing disappointments she'd known, not just the
boy two years before who had preferred her best friend to her, or the
English prize she felt she'd been unfairly done out of in eighth grade,
or even discovering the golden Sarah's feet of clay. But back beyond
those, the insuperable hurt of David's leaving her when she was
small. How much she had wanted him back! How hard she had
believed he *would* come back!

"That's the only real consolation of faith," I said, "knowing you didn't
collaborate in your own ruin."

Since Lissie's permit didn't extend to driving in the dark, I drove
home. Lissie sat quietly, though uneasily, at my side. Finally, she

said, "I have a favor to ask.   My mother's arriving tomorrow." I was surprised. I'd spoken to Caroline before leaving New York and she hadn't mentioned a trip to Los Angeles. "It's a business trip," said Lissie. "It came up kind of suddenly."

When David had finally convinced her that moving to Los Angeles would be a mistake, at least for Lissie and Kate, Caroline had started a business in New York. With a friend, she had developed a line of natural cosmetics which they began to sell from a small shop in SoHo. It was no hit-or-miss, amateur operation. Caroline and Cleo had done their homework well. They raised sufficient financing privately from assorted wealthy acquaintances to make sure they were adequately capitalized. They spent heavily on market research, packaging, and advertising. I photographed their first campaign (which had as its inspiration Van Huysman's flower paintings), featuring a basket full of delicious-looking cosmetics. It all appeared very expensive but was in fact moderately priced, and soon was successful in its target market, young executive women who wouldn't dream of smoking, who jogged consistently, ate health food, and were careful about the amount of alcohol they drank.

A year later, CC Cosmetics opened a second shop at South Street, followed by another on Columbus Avenue. Caroline and Cleo resisted offers from Bloomingdale's and made no attempt to distribute through designer boutiques. They didn't have to. They were being phenomenally successful going on as they were; and, more important, Caroline and Cleo wanted to keep the line exclusive.

Caroline had mentioned the idea of opening a branch in Boston, but she'd said nothing about Los Angeles. Now, Lissie told me, an investor had offered to back four stores in California, in Los Angeles, San Francisco, San Diego, and Palm Springs. There was a lot of money at stake, and Caroline was on her way with the investor to assess the prospects for success.

"Just Caroline?" I asked, surprised. Caroline had changed since her divorce from David. No longer living in his shadow and resenting it, she had become a lot less suspicious, less sullen, and with her growing business success more self-confident. She had an easier time making and keeping friends. But though Caroline was indisputably the hardheaded business executive, and nothing was finalized without her okay, it was Cleo who was the charmer in the company, and it was usually she who handled the preliminary stages of deal-making.

"There's some sort of crisis on in New York that only Cleo can handle," said Lissie. "Anyway, the investor apparently has a thing for Mom. They decided she was the best one to come."

"And does she have a 'thing' for him?"

Lissie shrugged. "I don't know. It's hard to tell with Mom. I hope so."

"Have you met him?"

"Yes. I liked him. His name's Alex Chakiris." My eyes widened, and she nodded. "Yes. *That* Alex Chakiris."

Chakiris was just then becoming famous. His name and face had been splashed all over the New York papers and local television news, and the week before he'd been on the cover of *Time*. He'd built the Pueblo D'Oro tower on West 72nd Street in which not one apartment for sale cost under a million dollars, and his acquisition of some Hudson River property had local residents up in arms because his proposed building threatened their views. Financing a small cosmetics company seemed far out of his league. "I think it would be very good for Mom to remarry," said Lissie.

"Why?" I asked.

"I'm going off to college in the fall," said Lissie, as if explaining the obvious. "And before you know it, so will Kate. I hate to think of her being alone. Anyway, I think it's time she stopped mooning over Daddy and got on with her life. She's wasted enough time."

"Is that what you think she's been doing, mooning over your father?"

"Yes," said Lissie, with all the conviction of her years. "Not that it's Daddy's fault," she added. Her face, illuminated for a moment by a passing headlamp, shone with loyalty and testified to her belief that David was infinitely worthy of devotion. "He always encouraged her to date more, to think about getting married again." The way he encouraged Sarah to work, I thought cynically. "Mom always said he was just trying to get out of paying her alimony, but I don't think that's true. I think he really felt bad about hurting her and wanted her to be happy again."

"Aren't you at all angry with him for leaving you and Kate?" I asked, the intimate dark of the car encouraging me to pry.

She shook her head. "I guess maybe when I was little. Mom says I was very upset at the time, but I don't remember any of that. All I know is that he didn't really leave us, not Kate and me. He was always there when we needed him. And it's not his fault he fell in love with Sarah. He couldn't help himself. He hadn't been happy with Mom for a long time. And everyone deserves to take their chance at happiness, if they're lucky enough to get one," she added, parroting her father. It was amazing to me really that Lissie could sympathize so unselfishly with David's point of view.

"How does Kate feel about it?"

"I try to get her to talk, but she won't. She says she was too little when it all happened for any of it to matter to her. She fights with Mom all the time, and I'm not sure what that's about, because I always thought Mom loved her better than me. But Kate adores Daddy. And when she stops to think that if he hadn't met Sarah there'd be no Mark, she gets very upset. Feelings are so confusing, aren't they?" she asked with a bewildered shake of her head.

I agreed that they were. We exited the freeway at Laurel Canyon Boulevard, climbed through the canyon to Mulholland Drive, and turned east. For a while we drove in silence along the winding unfamiliar road. Lissie looked down into a deep hollow between the hills crowned with houses. "Look," she said, "we're above the clouds." I looked quickly and saw a patch of gray hovering a few feet below us. It was, for some reason, an eerie sensation. "Daddy just hates driving along here," she said. "He usually lets Sarah do it."

"You're wrong about your mother," I told her. "She hasn't been mooning over your father, or wasting her life. She did for a while, of course, but she stopped that a long time ago."

"Then why hasn't she ever married again?" asked Lissie, delivering her one bit of evidence as a question.

"Because she hasn't met anyone she wants to marry. Or because she's happier being unmarried. Who knows? I mean, does she really seem miserable to you?"

"No," said Lissie after a moment's reflection.

"When I first met your mother, she oozed unhappiness from every pore. And the longer she stayed married to your father, the worse it got. It was nothing he did, particularly. I'm not trying to blame him. But whatever the reasons, just being with him made her wretched. She resented him for everything he was, everything he did. Nothing about him gave her any pleasure at all. And her misery choked him. Living together was awful, for both of them. Yet, I really believe, if he hadn't met Sarah, he'd still be married to her. Leaving you was the hardest thing he's ever had to do."

"Why did they ever get married?" asked Lissie.

"As your father would say, it seemed like a good idea at the time. But it wasn't. Divorcing her was the best thing he ever did for your mother. It helped her make a success of her life. I really don't think you have to worry about her, Lissie."

Lissie shook her head. "It's hard to know. She won't talk about things. She's like Kate."

"What favor did you want to ask?" We were already pulling into the Walton drive.

She hesitated a moment and then said, "It's about Mom. Will you ask her to your show? We're all going, and I'd hate her to feel left out."

"Of course I'll ask her. If I'd known she was going to be here, I'd already have sent an invitation. But why did you think that would be a problem?"

"She didn't come to the one in New York."

"She had an invitation," I said.

"Oh, I didn't know." She thought a moment. "Maybe she doesn't like to be where Daddy and Sarah are. Maybe that's why she didn't come," she said.

"Yes," I agreed. "Or maybe she was just busy."

Lissie smiled. "Daddy says I have a flair for melodrama."

"Bring your boyfriend, if you like," I told her. She was dating the son of a film company executive. He was thin and dark and rather homely, but he read poetry and had heard of Claude Lévi-Strauss, both very seductive qualities to Lissie. David, who had been prepared to disapprove of any boy Lissie brought home, actually liked him, probably because he didn't seem much of a sexual threat, although David above all should have understood that intelligence to some women is as great an aphrodisiac as power.

"I will," said Lissie. "That will be fun."

And her mother will bring Alex Chakiris, I thought. I had no doubts whatsoever that Caroline this time would appear at my show, and with her more than eligible suitor. I had meant every word I'd said to Lissie: it had been a long time since Caroline had wasted energy resenting David, nor did she still crave revenge. But what woman could resist showing off Chakiris to an ex-husband, especially an ex-husband with an ego the size of David's? I felt my old nemesis curiosity creeping up on me. If I had any sense, I would probably not send Caroline an invitation. But not only would that be rude, it would deprive me of the pleasure of seeing what would happen.

"Yes," I agreed with Lissie. "A lot of fun."

❧ *Chapter 39* ❧

Of course, Tessa Hoffmann phoned and suggested we meet. I say "of course" because, once David told her I knew they were lovers, it was inevitable that she would want to see me. Mistresses like, overtly or otherwise, to win as many friends in the wife's camp as possible. It makes them feel less isolated, less hopeless, less culpable.

"I didn't know you were in Los Angeles," I said. David had neglected to give me that piece of information, and I had assumed she was safely at home in New York.

"Oh, yes," she said brightly, "I'm doing a piece on the festival for *Esquire*. I spoke to Ned last week," she added. "Did he tell you?"

"No," I replied. "We haven't talked since I got here."

"I was doing an article on the Senate Foreign Relations Committee, so I called him. I thought he could give me some good inside stuff. He wasn't a lot of help."

"He's out of politics, and he intends to stay out," I told her. Ned's wife, Mary, had died suddenly of a cerebral hemorrhage three years before. Her death had shattered him, though perhaps not with the wholly destructive consequences people imagined. When he had emerged from the numbing grief and had begun to pick up the shards of his life, Ned had realized he was no longer interested in politics. His desire for the power and the glamour of national office was gone, along with the conviction that he might actually accomplish some good. He had come to believe that elected officials were inevitably in thrall to special-interest groups and that those interests would always prevail over the general welfare of the people. Believing that, he had found it impossible to continue making the sacrifices of time and money, energy and privacy that a political career requires. Mary's death, as emotional cataclysms frequently do, made Ned reexamine his life. He resigned from the Senate and returned to private practice, to the kinds of criminal and civil liberties' cases that had made his reputation before; but he limited his case load and spent as much time as possible with his sons. What he wanted more than anything was for them to grow up whole and sane, even if the world which they were to inherit would be fragmentary and mad.

"A pity about that," said Tessa. "I had thought Ned would go far in politics. He had a lot to offer."

"He went as far as he wanted," I replied.

"He told me he'd be out here in a few days," she added in that benign tone of voice journalists frequently use when they're hoping there's more to a story than is obvious. In this case, her interest was purely personal. Ned's life now was hardly of interest to the public.

But habits die hard, and I had learned over the years, when he was embroiled in politics up to his neck, to speak of Ned discreetly. "Yes, so I understand," I said, noncommittally, though there was no reason not to admit Ned was coming to see my show. He was, as Tessa knew, one of my best friends.

The preliminaries out of the way, Tessa got around to the real purpose of her call: she suggested we have lunch. It was a suggestion she would have made any time, in any city where we happened to find ourselves, and normally I would have said yes without hesitation. This time I didn't want to. I had no desire to see Tessa. We would have to meet eventually, if only to discuss canceling the book we were planning to do together; but just then, I didn't want to hear how much in love with David she was, how wonderful she thought him, how she'd suffer if he left her. I didn't want to be questioned about his marriage, asked for information about Sarah. I didn't even want to hear that her affair with David was nothing more than a casual fling, an exciting pastime, a stopgap until something more serious and permanent happened along, or something equally short-term but interesting should crop up. And, of course, that's all it might have been for Tessa, for both of them, a diversion. Affairs, as I knew from my own experience, were not necessarily either important or destructive. They could just as easily be meaningless and dull.

But, either way, I didn't want to know. I didn't want to face Sarah the next time having given my imprimatur to Tessa and David. That's how my meeting with Tessa would be interpreted, I knew, as an acceptance of her role in David's life, an acceptance that promised the loyalty of silence, if not of active collusion. My reluctance wasn't based on moral prinicple: after all, years before I had met Sarah in essentially the same circumstances. It was purely an emotional response. I loved Sarah in a way I never had, never would, be able to love Caroline. I was Sarah's friend, and she trusted me. I would do nothing, actively, to hurt her, not even to please David. I told Tesssa I really didn't have the time.

"If I promise not to talk about David, could you make the time?" she coaxed. Tessa is nothing if not smart.

"Sorry, Tessa. It's impossible. I'm up to my ears in work."

"Okay," she replied. "Too bad. Then I'll see you at the show. Bye," she said, and hung up.

"Shit," I muttered as I replaced the receiver. "Shit."

David and I had arranged to go to the Getty Museum at Malibu, which I'd never seen. At two-thirty that afternoon, he knocked on the gallery door. While I combed my hair and hastily applied lipstick, David flirted with Rula, the assistant, who gazed at him with a seductive hopefulness as she replied fliply to his teasing. Outside, Mark, Kate, Olivia, and cousin Jane waited impatiently beside the car, a shiny new Jaguar. "A thoroughbred," David had asserted quixotically when he bought it despite dire warnings. "All heart. It needs pampering, but it will give you all it's got in the end run."

"Daddy, do hurry," called Olivia. "Or we'll never get there."

Sarah was rehearsing, Marie-Paule was at home with the two younger boys, and Lissie was somewhere with her boyfriend, "reading poetry together in the UCLA Sculpture Garden, no doubt," said David, his voice combining pride in Lissie's intellectual bent with regret that she was moving out of his grasp.

"He's such a toad," said Olivia.

"He beat Lissie at tennis," mediated Mark. "And that's not easy."

"She let him," returned Olivia. "She wanted him to like her."

"If he beat Lissie," corrected David, "he did it fair and square. No child of mine takes a dive, not for love or money."

"I like him," offered cousin Jane, only to receive a look of withering scorn from Olivia.

"Her last boyfriend was taller," added Kate, whose present never quite measured up to what was past or absent.

As the kids were climbing back into the car, Peter—returning from his lunch at a restaurant across the street—walked over to say hello. That is, he said hello to David. The children he ignored. He wore a turquoise T-shirt, yellow slacks, and a beige silk jacket with enormous shoulders. His hair was pomaded into a David Bowie. Mark looked at him in wonder, Olivia in obvious disapproval.

When I say Peter was fascinated by David, I don't mean that there was anything overtly sexual in his behavior, or that he in any way toa-died or gushed. His words were frequently flattering, but he rarely re-sorted to hyperbole, and there was nothing sycophantic in his manner. With David, as with everyone, he was cool, even a bit ironic, as if aware that sophistication and admiration made strange bedfellows. Yet the air around us pulsated with disturbing currents. Again, I felt that Peter's interest in David was as much erotic as intellectual. And, again, I found that more intriguing than distasteful.

Finally, Peter turned to me. "Everything under control?" he asked.

"I changed the angle on one of the lights," I told him. Then I grinned. "You could try to guess which one." We'd had a small argu-ment on the subject the day before. "If you do, I'll concede defeat."

"I'll guess," he said, laughing as he turned to look at David. "Is she always so stubborn?"

"Righteous," said David.

"Right," I corrected.

"Dinner tonight?" asked Peter, as he started away towards the gallery.

"Sorry," I said, shaking my head. "I have to meet a friend at the air-port."

Peter waved, then disappeared through the gallery's large gray double door. I strapped my seat belt on and looked up to find David looking at me knowingly. "Yes," I admitted.

"Yes, what?" asked Olivia.

"I thought you had a rule about mixing business and pleasure."

"We all have rules," I said, "which we all seem to break when it suits us. This suits me."

"I don't approve," said David, as he steered the car out of the park-ing lot.

I shrugged. "At least nobody's at risk but me," I said pointedly.

"Do you know the way, Daddy?" asked Olivia.

"Certainly," said David, convincing no one, though in fact this time he did. He headed up to Sunset and turned west towards the ocean.

"Can we stop to eat?" asked Mark, who was suddenly always hungry.

"Again?" said David; then, conceding, "At the Getty. There's a café."

"The food won't be any good," said Kate. "It never is at museums."

* * *

There is something unreal, even surreal, about the Getty Museum. For one thing, it looks as if it were constructed entirely out of papier-mâché, and I found it essential to touch one of the columns to convince myself it was indeed made of something as substantial as stone. And then it is extremely disconcerting to find a brightly colored Roman villa, perfectly reconstructed to look too new, perched on top a California hill, overlooking the Pacific Ocean. On a clear day, apparently, one can see Catalina Island. Those days are rare and occur mostly in January. Through the nebulous July sunshine, I saw only the sea.

David looked at the villa and laughed. "Shhh, Daddy," reproved Kate. "Everybody's looking."

"What's so funny?" asked Jane.

"It's not funny," he said. "It's wonderful. Like Disneyland. I love it here."

The Roman collection was interesting, and the decorative-art collection, but few of the paintings were first-rate, though I did like one of the Rembrandts very much. "He reminds me of someone," I said to David, pointing to a portrait that looked so modern to me it might have been painted early in this century. "Who?"

"T. S. Eliot," replied David, without hesitating.

"This is boring," said Olivia. "Can we go yet?"

Of all the new acquisitions—including the Cézanne and the Degas—only Goya's *Marquesa de Santiago* was remarkable. "Definitely worth the trip," said David.

We got sandwiches and cakes and sat outside on the patio to eat, David attracting curious glances from passersby and signing autographs for two young girls brave enough to approach him. The children were delighted: it was only at those moments they remembered their father was a movie star.

Afterwards, stopping several times to ask directions as David got hopelessly lost, we took the children to a water slide somewhere in the San Fernando Valley. That had been the bribe which assured their good behavior at the Getty.

I declined David's offer of a turn and sat instead in the bleachers and watched terrified as hordes of youngsters sped down high, narrow, tortuous polystyrene channels and plunged into a pool of water from which they emerged shrieking and gasping for breath. David returned with containers of coffee, handed one to me, and sat.

"Nothing would get me to try it," I said.

"It's not as bad as it looks."

I turned to him in amazement. "You did it? Someone must have bet you a helluva lot of money."

"Duncan," he admitted. "We raced from the top, and I beat him. It wasn't as bad as I thought it would be. The sides of the channels are high enough to keep you from feeling exposed. It's not like a roller coaster, or even"—he smiled—"the funicular in Salzburg. By the way," he continued, "Tessa's upset you won't see her."

"Tough," I said.

"Would it be so hard for you just to have lunch with her?"

"Yes. It would."

"You're old friends."

"Are you going to make an issue of this, David?" I asked, my irritation showing. "Are you going to turn this into a test of loyalty?"

"Isn't that what you're doing?"

"I'm doing what I feel comfortable doing. I don't want to have to choose this time. All right? Don't make me choose."

"All right."

"And I don't want her coming to my opening."

"I didn't know she was," he said, sounding genuinely surprised.

"I don't want her there," I repeated. I didn't look at him. I couldn't. There was more than anger in my eyes. There was resentment, disapproval, even contempt. I didn't want him to see it.

"All right," he said, "I'll talk to her."

❧ *Chapter 40* ❧

By the time I got to the airport, Ned had collected his luggage and was waiting for me outside. I honked twice, pulled over to the curb, and got out as he saw me and walked towards the car. "Been waiting long?"

He shook his head. "Perfect timing," he said, as he dropped his bags to hug me.

Ned's slight body hadn't thickened with the years. If anything, due to overwork and haphazard eating, he was thinner than when I'd met him. But his body had lost muscle tone, since he rarely got around to exercising; and, in contrast to David's and mine, which still had only a highlighting of gray, Ned's curly hair was completely white. That night he looked particularly tired, with circles under his eyes, the skin taut around his eyes and mouth, the color drained from his face by the harsh airport lights. He badly needed a few days in the sun.

"We took the kids to a water slide," I explained, as I opened the trunk to let him stow his bags inside. "And David got lost getting back from the Valley. It took forever."

Ned frowned. "Leo hurt himself, cut his eye, on a slide last year." Leo is his elder son.

"It's really too bad the boys couldn't come with you," I said, as I got behind the wheel of the car, strapped myself in, and started the engine. The children had long been promised to Mary's parents for the week, and it would have cost Ned his life to change plans. They were on a houseboat cruising the Colorado River. "Los Angeles may never be this interesting again."

"We'll come back for some of the games," replied Ned, not one to be daunted by the prospect of no tickets and no place to stay. "How's David?" he asked, strapping himself into the seat. "Working hard?"

"He's fine. He's revising the Howard Carter play." In addition to everything else he was up to that summer, David was working feverishly to complete *The Diviner*, his play about Carter's discovery of Tutankhamen's tomb. It had started to worry him that, preoccupied with both Sarah's breakdowns and his acting career, he had written nothing since the failure of *Just Until Spring*. A production of *The Diviner* was scheduled for winter at the Village Globe, and David was determined to meet the date.

It didn't open, actually, until the winter of 1986, and everything had changed so much by then that Simon Wroth directed. It's a wonderful play, lyrical and strong, about the nature of genius, about the power of imagination, about instinct and determination. It ran only six months at the Globe, but there have since been productions throughout the United States, in Germany, Italy, Norway, Sweden. The London production is set for the spring of 1989.

"And Sarah?" asked Ned.

"Rehearsing. Loving every minute of it."

"I was away somewhere, Washington maybe, when she did that play in New York. I've never seen her onstage."

The image of Sarah making her entrance in *Sky Burial*, the first time I'd ever seen her, flickered in my mind like a sequence in a home movie. "She's wonderful," I said. "She'll knock your socks off." Sarah's talent might be rusty from lack of use, it might be a bit battered from years of drinking and drug-taking, but it was a big talent. Wouldn't it shine through no matter what?

"It's such an ugly city," said Ned, assessing the landscape edging the San Diego Freeway, a colorless stretch of shopping malls and banks, filling stations and fast-food stores, and in the distance the MGM water tower.

"Parts of it are beautiful. Bel Air is like fairyland, Swiss chalet next to French chateau next to Spanish finca . . . everybody gets a chance to live their fantasy. And some of the new buildings downtown are wonderful."

"You're joking," he said incredulously, his voice expressing the contempt most New Yorkers insist on having for Los Angeles.

"Snob," I said.

* * *

When I'd suggested to Ned that he stay with me, he'd immediately said yes. Now that he was out of politics, and Mary couldn't misunderstand, it had seemed silly for him to pay an exorbitant hotel rate when I had an extra bedroom. Neither of us cared what anyone thought, with the exception of his sons, and they weren't apt to disapprove. Over the years, Leo and Frank Conti had seen me at too many family dinners, family picnics, too many weddings and funerals, not to mention political rallies, to question my place in the Conti scheme of things. They were used to the idea of me. And since Ned and the boys had come to stay for a few weeks the summer before at the house I'd bought in Martha's Vineyard, my standing as their father's pal had been confirmed and approved by both. Our relationship seemed to be so incontrovertibly platonic that the boys in fact had nothing to object to, no threat to their mother to repel. They swam and played, ate and read, grew brown and slept. There were few quarrels, and none that reached the level of open warfare. It was the most tranquil time they had all spent together since Mary's death.

I opened a bottle of white wine, made us each a spritzer, and carried them into the bedroom where Ned was unpacking. I put his on a bedside table, then sprawled in an armchair to watch him.

"This is a great place. Whose is it?" he asked. The room had a gray carpet, black lacquer furniture, and fabric in a subdued plaid of black and gray and white on the bed, the windows, and the chairs.

"An unsuccessful film producer's, I understand."

"Unsuccessful?" He whistled.

I nodded. "He's in Europe, trying to raise money."

"What do the successful live like?"

"Wait until you see the house David and Sarah are in." I studied his face for a moment. Even in the softer light from the bedside lamps, it still looked tired and strained. "You look exhausted," I said.

"It's been a rough week."

"Work? Or the boys?"

Both boys had always been wild. There was no meanness in them, but a combination of stubbornness, hot temper, and high spirits made them difficult to handle. With Ned away so much, in Washington, most of the burden of managing the children had fallen to Mary. She did it well, keeping them more or less under control, for which the boys both resented and loved her. They reacted to her death with rage. Leo was in almost constant trouble at school for fighting. There were weeks when he was never to be seen without a cut or a bruise on his face. Ned, who never completely lost his sense of humor, said Leo's body took so much abuse it frequently looked tie-dyed. He was eight years old at the time.

Frank was six and should have been less of a problem but wasn't. He provoked fights with his brother, smashed his own and Leo's toys, refused to do anything he was told without a temper tantrum first, and once pulled a kitchen knife on the housekeeper who was insisting he eat the dinner she had prepared instead of the hot dog he was demanding. Frank had also suffered from terrible nightmares in which he was pursued by red-eyed monsters in black cloaks, brandishing swords and riding dragons. He would awaken in the middle of the night screaming and dripping with sweat. When I told Ned about the tinfoil sword that David had once given Nicholas to fight dragons, he looked at me as if I were mad. He had a serious problem and I was being whimsical, he thought. But I wasn't. Something had cured Nicholas of his nightmares, and the sword seemed as likely a candidate to me as the passage of time.

Instead, Ned had resigned from the Senate and had taken himself and the boys to a family guidance counselor. That, too, had seemed to work. Frank got to eat a lot of hot dogs but his nightmares stopped and he rarely resorted anymore to tantrums. And Leo was learning to control his temper in volatile situations. A few weeks before, during a Little League game, instead of immediately trying to beat the shit out of the pitcher who hit him three times with wild balls, Leo had accepted the pitcher's halfhearted apology with a big smile and a soft warning that if it happened again he'd kill him. For Leo, that was restraint indeed.

"Not the boys," replied Ned. "They've been great. Well, maybe not great." He smiled. "But controllable. If I look bad, it's thanks to Eddie Conlon." Conlon was a nineteen-year-old accused of raping three Sarah Lawrence undergraduates. His father owned a butcher shop in Rye where Ned lived. His mother had died when he was five. "He's guilty."

For a moment, I was too stunned to reply. Although Ned hadn't known the family before the arrest, he had liked Eddie Sr. immediately upon meeting him, and he had liked Eddie Jr. too. Given Ned's history with his own boys, the Conlons' assertion that Eddie was wild but not bad had won his instant sympathy; and since the evidence against Eddie was circumstantial, Ned has taken the case.

"What are you going to do?" I asked.

"Someone has to defend rapists," he said. "And child molesters. And murderers."

"Why?"

"It's the American way."

"It doesn't have to be you."

"I think it's time for me to get out of criminal law. I don't have the stomach for it anymore. I made a big mistake going back into it after Mary died. It was what I knew, it seemed a way for me to go on fulfilling some kind of public responsibility, but it was a mistake. Real estate conveyancing, that's what I should have done." He threw his socks in to a drawer of the black lacquer dresser and slammed it shut. "He seemed like such a nice kid. God, would you listen to me? At my age, suckered by innocent blue eyes and a wide smile."

"Will he plead guilty?"

"I told him he'd have to, or I'm off the case. It's going to break his father's heart."

"What will? The knowledge that his son raped three girls, or that he has to go to prison for it? And not for very long, I'd like to point out. How much time will Eddie actually serve? Five years? Seven?"

"Whatever it is, it won't be as much as Eddie deserves. But it's a high price for Mr. Conlon to have to pay. He's a nice man, a decent man, and he did the best he could raising Eddie. If he made mistakes, they were human ones, the kinds all parents make. The only thing he's really to blame for is not being smart enough to recognize he had a psychopath for a son." There are some crimes for which Ned holds society totally responsible; but there are others, like the Conlon rapes, where he sees only individual, criminal responsibility. "Eddie said he'd tell his father. I just hope to Christ he doesn't make me do it."

He looked so sad, so tired, I got up and went to put my arms around him. "It's not your fault he's guilty," I said. "Don't take it so hard."

He hugged me, then grinned. "You know me. I'm always upset when somebody makes me look like a fool. And Eddie Conlon's been doing that for months."

"You're not psychic. Stop kicking yourself. Forget all about the Conlons for the next few days and relax, okay? You need a suntan. You look awful."

"Thanks," he said, and kissed my cheek.

The phone rang and I extricated myself from his arms, picked up my spritzer, and went into the living room to answer it.

It was Peter, to tell me about some Japanese dance company he'd seen that evening, and to ask if I was sure I couldn't get away. "Sorry," I said, just as Ned came into the room, "I really can't." As we finished the conversation, Ned freshened the spritzers and handed me one as I replaced the receiver. He sat in the el of the sofa, at my feet.

"If you want to go out, go ahead. I'm wiped. I'll be going to bed in a few minutes anyway."

"I don't want to go out. That was Peter de Witt."

"The gallery owner?"

I nodded. "I'll see him in the morning." Though over the years I had of course mentioned other lovers to Ned, had sometimes even admitted to being upset and confused, I had always avoided burdening him with the obsessive details of my affairs or using his shoulder to cry on. It wouldn't have seemed right. It would have been in bad taste. But my reluctance to tell him just then about Peter went beyond that. It wasn't a relationship I could easily defend; and while disapproval from David was like disapproval from my other self, my alter ego, criticism and understanding mixed in acceptable proportions, from Ned—who was the best person I knew, the most honest, loyal, thoroughly virtuous person—it came with a bewildered incomprehension I found painful.

"How is the show looking?" he asked.

"Pretty good," I replied, my enthusiasm obvious beneath the deprecating words.

"I've never seen you like this before, Nikki, so . . . expectant."

I suppose I hadn't been, not even when waiting for a book to come out. I'd done lots of books by then, on potters, on artists, on sculptors. I'd done a book on the ruins of Turkey, and the new architecture of Japan. I'd done photo essays on China for *Life*, and Tibet for *The Smithsonian*. Except for the fashion photographs, which paid my rent, I never took an assignment simply because of the money it would earn me. I took the ones that appealed to my sense of adventure, that provided the greatest artistic license, the ones where I had a chance to experiment and explore, to climb or to delve. Sometimes I made bad choices, like the film I produced and directed about a Huston ballet school, but I prided myself on always having made them for the right reasons. When I took a bad photograph, which was too often, always it was because I had been trying for something better than I'd ever done before.

For years I'd been numbered among the top commercial photographers. I'd long ago achieved financial success. And while I would never claim that was unimportant to me, or that I didn't enjoy it, or that I would give it up without a thought, still it had never been my goal. In my mind, always, hung the work of my "role models"—Cameron, Adams, Morath, Cartier-Bresson, Bourke-White, Penn, and others, so many fine pictures, by so many painstaking artists. The kind of success I wanted was first of all to do such good work, and then to be acknowledged as doing it. David could insist that only the first was important, that the second was incidental, even trivial. He could sneer at the idea of acceptance, but he sneered from a secure position. Not only had he achieved fame, but his talent was undisputed. My terror still was being dismissed as a hack.

"The de Witt gallery has a reputation," I said in answer to Ned. "It throws the kind of light that will make people see my work differently."

"Your work still matters so much to you?" he said, bemused, now that his mattered so little.

"It's all I've got."

"All you wanted to have," he amended.

"That's true. More or less."

He stretched out his hand and touched my bare foot. He stroked my ankle. "Do you ever have any regrets?"

"Of course," I said, a little defensively. "Don't you?"

He laughed. "If you only knew how many."

"I look around now," I confessed, my defensiveness giving way to my need for honesty, "and see so many women who somehow managed to get it all, successful careers, caring husbands, sane children, and I feel furious. I feel cheated."

"You could have had it all," he said. "There was no reason why you couldn't have had anything you wanted."

I shook my head. "Maybe it was just bad luck, but I never met a man, even you, I could trust not to get in my way. I never loved one whose wishes I thought I could ignore."

"Everyone is egocentric. All of us, men and women, have to fight for what we want."

"I didn't want to fight," I said. "Not all the time, not with someone I loved. I wasn't brave enough, or strong enough. I wasn't anywhere near ruthless enough to win. And I knew it. Love is a weapon I'm defenseless against." He began to protest, but I stopped him. "If I had married, if I'd had children, I would probably have torn myself apart the way Sarah's done, trying to give them what I thought they wanted, what I thought they needed. I'd have lost myself the way she did."

"I thought you said she was all right," interjected Ned.

"She is, I think. Now. But look at the price she had to pay."

"She's got David and the children. Maybe that's compensation enough for whatever else she might have had. Ultimately, most of us are grateful if what we've got at the end is some human comfort, some warmth, some love." He closed his eyes, his hand lying still on my leg. "We all end up with so little, Nikki, so much less than we expected, so much less than we need." Finally, his eyes opened and he turned his head to look at me. "Nikki, please, sleep with me tonight. I'm not asking you to make love, just to hold me. I need you to hold me. I feel so unbearably alone." Then, before I could answer, he added angrily, "Christ, I knew it was a mistake to stay here. I knew I should have gone to a hotel."

I got up and moved down to the el of the couch where he was lying and stretched out next to him. "It's all right," I said. I put my arms around him and held on.

✣ *Chapter 41* ✣

I was in the kitchen making coffee when the phone rang. It was Cassandra.

"Nikki, darling, could you come over right away?" Her voice was so faint, I could barely hear her. "I really do need to talk to someone."

"Are you all right?"

"Yes . . . no. No, I feel wretched. Oh, God, I feel bloody awful."

She sounded so unlike herself I was suddenly frightened. "Cassandra, you haven't taken anything, have you?"

"No, I haven't." She caught her breath in a sob. "Though God knows I'd like to. I'd like to go to sleep and not have to think anymore. Would you come? Please, darling? I do need to talk to you."

"I'll put on some clothes and be right over. I'll get there as soon as I can."

"Bless you," she said, and I could hear her beginning to cry as she replaced the receiver.

Ned's arms went around me and I felt a kiss on the back of my neck. "Good morning," he said. I turned in his arms and kissed him. He had put on running shorts and a T-shirt, and his thick, curly hair was all awry. His face had lost some of its gray and haggard look.

"Well, you look as lot better this morning," I said.

"Thank you," he replied.

"Don't mention it." I grinned. "Anything for a friend." We had, after all, made love. Wrapped together in the darkness, two people who cared so much for each other, it had seemed the right, the necessary thing to do. It had been, surprisingly, wonderful. I kissed him again. "I have to go out. That was Cassandra. She asked me to go over to see her. She sounds awful."

We had planned to spend the day together, but he said nothing, except "I don't know why she stays with that bastard." Like me, Ned assumed that Cassandra had discovered another of Duncan's affairs.

I'd already showered, so I slipped into one of the sundresses I had wheedled out of Cassandra the last time I'd seen her, put on a pair of sandals, twisted my hair on top of my head, and fastened it with a big turquoise clip.

"You're not going out looking like that," said Ned, in tones very reminiscent of my mother's, gazing with undisguised horror first at the dress, which seemed to be made of Olympic-colored rags stitched haphazardly together, then at my hair, which resembled a storm-ravaged bird's nest.

"It's the height of fashion," I said. "I'll call as soon as I know what's going on. But don't wait in for me. Go get some sun. You need it."

It was another hot and hazy day, but the grand houses lining the broad, tree-lined expanse of Sunset Boulevard, from the Strip to the Bel Air gate, looked as impervious to problems of smog and humidity as their luxurious green lawns to brown spot and weeds. I thought resentfully how much more I'd rather be driving to the ocean with Ned than on my way to see Cassandra to hear about yet another of Duncan's seemingly endless peccadilloes. If she couldn't deal with them, she shouldn't have remarried him, I told myself, and resolved to stay only long enough to remind her of that fact and calm her down. I turned into Bel Air, found my way to the hotel, handed my humble rented Toyota over to the valet, crossed the little bridge, walked through the gardens, along the stone paths, to the Powells' bungalow, and knocked on the door.

Cassandra opened it. Her eyes were red and swollen from crying. She was still in a bathrobe. On a table lay her breakfast, untouched except for the coffee.

"You look lovely," she said, ushering me in. "The dress suits you. Would you like some breakfast?"

"Just some coffee, please."

She poured me a cup and then retreated to the couch, where she huddled in a corner. Though Cassandra was large, and generally formidable, she gave the appearance suddenly of someone very frail and vulnerable. "Thank you for coming," she said.

"Where's Duncan? Filming?"

"Playing golf. With David. Golf!" she repeated, in amazed tones, shaking her head in disbelief. "He says he wants everything to go on as normal. The idiot! The dolt! Oh, God, Nikki, what on earth am I going to do?"

"What's happened?" I asked. I sat in the armchair facing her.

She looked at me a moment, not quite comprehending the fact that I didn't know. Then, almost matter-of-factly, she said, "Duncan's dying. He's got cancer." I had expected to hear something so completely different, I couldn't at first quite believe I'd heard her right. "He's got—" Her voice caught. "Three months, six months at the very most."

"Oh God, no." I was filled with dread, with horror, but most of all with disbelief.

"Oh, Nikki, isn't it awful? Isn't it bloody, fucking awful?" I got up and went to her, and put my arms around her. She clung to me. "I'm sorry to do this to you. Really, I am, but I can't with Duncan, you know. What use would I be to him if I went all to pieces? But I had to talk to someone, someone who would let me rant and rave and scream. That's all I want to do, scream! Oh God," she wailed. She cried into my shoulder for a few minutes, then lifted her head and said, "Isn't it absurd that this should happen now, when finally everything is so lovely? We've really been so completely happy these past few months. Life is so awful, isn't it, so completely rotten?"

"When did you find out?" I asked.

"Late yesterday afternoon. I walked in when Duncan was on the phone with his doctor. He was getting the results of some tests. He would never have told me if I hadn't overheard. The bastard! He said he didn't want to upset me unnecessarily. Unnecessarily! Have you ever heard anything so amazingly stupid in your life?"

Slowly, disjointedly, she told me what she had learned from Duncan the night before. I listened as attentively as I could; but, distracting me, like a deranged mantra, the words "Duncan is dying, Duncan is dying" kept repeating over and over in my head. It was, as Cassandra had said, bloody, fucking awful. He was fifty-five years old.

The preceding winter, just before the Massey play started rehearsing, Duncan had felt tired, unusually tired. When a trip to Majorca and two weeks of golf didn't help, he went to his doctor for some vitamin shots and was instead checked into a hospital for tests. It was discovered then that he had cancer of the liver. It was inoperable. Chemotherapy might retard its spread, but not for long, and at a cost Duncan wasn't willing to pay. He decided he'd rather live out his remaining months in as normal a way as possible, eating what he liked and keeping all his hair. He also decided he didn't want Cassandra, or anyone else, to know for as long as it was possible to keep his illness secret. The unhappy eyes of his wife, the sympathetic eyes of his friends on him constantly, would be too hard to bear. He was sure he would collapse under the combined weight of their grief.

Having the play to do immediately, and a film set for right after, helped Duncan to keep up the charade of normalcy. It helped him forget it was a charade. Throwing himself into his work, living as he had always lived, he found it possible to forget he was soon going to die.

"He fooled me completely," said Cassandra. "I never suspected for a moment. Isn't that incredible, to be living with someone, sleeping with him, and never even to suspect he's hiding something so awful? And I thought I knew him so well. I thought he could never fool me again." She smiled for a moment, a faint smile gone almost before I recognized it. "He really is such an awfully good actor."

When Cassandra had entered the bungalow the night before, Duncan had been sitting on the couch, the phone pressed against his ear, one hand over his eyes. "How much longer?" he had asked, sounding unbearably tired. "I understand it's impossible to say precisely," he continued after a minute, irritated, taking his hand away from his eyes, "but you must have some idea." Then he saw Cassandra. She was standing in the doorway, face white, eyes wide with terror. There was no way to be certain what he'd been talking about, but she knew, she knew by the knot in her chest, the queasy feeling in the pit of her stomach, that it was something terrible, something irrevocable. Duncan ended his conversation abruptly and went to her, taking her in his arms. At first he tried to deny everything, but Cassandra kept pleading with him to tell her the truth. Nothing he told her, she said to him, could possibly be as bad as what she was imagining. But she'd been wrong. It was worse, far worse.

Cassandra at first had raged at him for concealing his illness from her; then, overcome with guilt and grief, had begged him to forgive her for making a scene when he was so ill, so upset. Duncan, shaken by the latest report from the doctor and by the wildness of Cassandra's outburst, kept trying to comfort her, apologizing for not having found a way to break the news to her more gently. They sat talking about their present and what was left of their future, more and more quietly and sanely, late into the night, until Cassandra noticed how fatigued Duncan was looking and insisted he go to bed. She got in beside him, holding his hand until he dropped off to sleep and turned away from her. She lay there all night, the tears running silently down her face, afraid to cry out for fear of waking him.

"And this morning he got up, told me I was a good girl, and that he loved me very much. Then he left to keep his golf date with David. He wants life to go on as if everything were normal. Normal!" she repeated. "He wants us both to behave the way we always have." She took another Kleenex from the box at her side and wiped at her eyes. "I don't know if I can."

"Of course you can't," I said. "Not exactly the same." What I didn't point out to Cassandra, because it would have served no useful purpose, was how far from normal Duncan's own behavior had been over the past year. That surprising lack of women Cassandra had noticed, was that due simply to fatigue, I wondered, or was he trying, as he said, to make those last few months as happy as possible for his wife? Could even Duncan know for sure? "You can't pretend everything's all right. You can't deny what's going to happen. But you also can't let it ruin the time Duncan has left, the time you have left together."

"I know. I know. I told myself that all night. God, I love him," she said. "I know I can live without him, I know because I did it for years. But I don't want to. I really don't want to."

She looked so exhausted that I insisted finally she go into the bedroom and lie down. I sat with her, listening to fragments of heartbroken sentences, until she fell asleep.

As I walked back along the path to the hotel entrance, I saw Duncan approaching. He had lost weight in the months since I'd last seen him, but otherwise looked tan and handsome and healthy. If I hadn't known, I would never have suspected that a dying man was walking towards me.

He saw me and waved. "Nikki, hello. Darling, how lovely to see you," he said, kissing me on both cheeks. "I've been playing golf with David. I won."

"Not by much, I hope, or he'll be unbearable at dinner tonight."

"By enough to make me feel good. Have you seen Cassandra?"

"Yes," I said. "She's just gone to sleep."

He studied my face for a moment, then he said, "She's told you."

"Yes. She was afraid she'd go to pieces on you again if she didn't talk to someone."

"She's a good girl."

"Duncan, I'm sorry," I said feebly.

"I know. So am I." He took my arm. "Come and have a drink with me. On the patio. We'll let Cassandra sleep for a while."

I thought of Ned and hesitated a moment, but only for a moment. "I'd love to," I said. "Just let me call Ned, so he'll know where I am."

Ned wasn't in when I phoned, so I left a message on the machine and went to join Duncan on the patio. Sitting at a white wrought-iron table, backed by walls hung with scarlet bougainvillea, surrounded by tubs of impatience in bright summer colors, he reminded me of so many magazine ads I'd shot, hawking liquor or cologne or watches, where the quality of the goods is irrevocably bound to the looks, the glamour, the aura of unassailable power conveyed by the male model. Illusion and reality, Duncan was a master at blurring the edges.

As I sat, the waiter arrived with our drinks. "Cheers," said Duncan, raising his glass in a salute.

"Cheers." It was only eleven forty-five, but like Duncan, I was drinking whiskey. I needed it.

"How is Ned?"

"Fine."

"That was a terrible thing, his wife's death. The shock of it. He must have taken it very hard."

"Yes," I said, "he did."

"He's over it by now, I hope."

"I wouldn't say over it, exactly. But he is trying to get on with his life."

He took another sip of whiskey. "Cassandra will be all right, once she gets used to the idea."

"Yes," I said. "She won't fall apart on you. She's determined not to, and when Cassandra makes a decision, you know what she's like."

He smiled, but the smile faded quickly. "I should have told her earlier, I suppose, but . . . well, I didn't want her grieving any longer than necessary. Once I finish this picture, we'll do some of the things we've been talking about for years. Cassandra's always wanted to go to Tibet. I thought perhaps we might do that."

"You don't want to exhaust yourself, Duncan. I don't think Cassandra will care where she is or what she's doing, as long as she's with you."

"Oh, I've got a few months yet before I have to take to my bed. I'm feeling marvelous, really. How do I look?"

"Terrific," I said. Even his voice seemed as rich and thick and delicious as ever. "Duncan, I have to tell you, I think you're being wonderful. To Cassandra. In general, just wonderful." And I never would have thought you had it in you, I added to myself. "I don't know how you managed all these months, on your own."

"I was terrified a lot of the time, believe me, and angry, but ultimately, well, I've cheated a lot in my life to get what I've wanted, but there's no cheating death, is there?"

"No," I said, looking at his handsome face, thinking what a pity, what an outrage, what an obscenity is death.

There was no fear in Duncan's eyes now, or anger, only sadness.

"You've always considered me a bit of a shit, haven't you?" he asked, his face for the first time lighting up in that charming smile I had always found irresistible.

"Yes," I admitted. "But I liked you anyway."

"Well, I have been an awful shit, a real sod, to a lot of people, but Cassandra especially. I hope I can make some of that up to her now, in the time left."

"Cassandra," I replied, not quite managing to keep the disapproval out of my voice, "seems to forgive you for whatever you do even before you do it. She's not holding any grudges."

"She's a good girl," he repeated, not noticing the note of criticism in my voice. "And I do love her, you know."

"Yes," I said. It had taken me a long time to understand that, but finally I did.

The waiter arrived with another round of drinks Duncan had ordered. "I'm going to give this up soon," he said. "Listen, you won't mention this to David, will you, or Sarah? I don't want them to know, not yet, Sarah especially."

"Of course I won't," I reassured him. "But I think Sarah ought to be told, soon."

"Yes, I know. I won't leave it too much longer. But I don't think now is a good time to break the news to her, not when she's in rehearsal. She's got enough strain to deal with at the moment." No time would be a good time to tell Sarah: she still considered Duncan her best friend. "And David's so rudely healthy, I can't bear the thought of admitting to him I'm not. It seems an awful defeat somehow. I know it's silly, but I do want to put off telling him as long as possible."

We finished our drinks, and Duncan walked with me to the hotel entrance and, like the gentleman he was, gave the valet my parking ticket and tipped him. When the car came, he put his arms around me. "You're the only woman who's ever said no to me that I've managed to like," he said, hugging me.

"I think that may be the nicest compliment I've ever had."

He kissed me on both cheeks and I got into the car. When I'd started the engine, I turned back to wave at him, then drove quickly away before he could see I was crying.

❧ *Chapter 42* ❧

When I got to the apartment, Ned was home, his skin tinged copper by his few hours in the sun.

"Was it nice at the beach?" I asked.

"I sat by the pool for a while, and read. What's wrong?"

I started to tell him and began to cry again. "I've had two glasses of whiskey, with Duncan. They've made me maudlin." Ned pulled me into his arms and held me as I choked out the news. "I didn't even know I liked him this much," I said.

I hadn't had a thing to eat all day, so Ned made a tuna salad and when I'd had that and was feeling better I left for the gallery to see Peter, who'd phoned again while I was out to remind me that the exhibition programs were due in that afternoon. Apparently he'd got Ned and not the answering machine.

"They're fine," I said, when I finished looking at the programs. If I'd wanted to be picky, I could have found fault with the color balance in one of the reproduced photographs, but it didn't seem important just then.

"Are you all right?" He slid his hand knowingly up my arm.

"Fine. Why?"

"Well, for one thing, the color balance is off in that reproduction. I thought you'd scream."

"No one will notice, except you and me."

"And you're looking pale." He dropped his hand. "You haven't had a quarrel with your friend, have you?" There was only curiosity in his voice, not a hint of jealousy.

"No quarrel. I had some bad news this morning, but I'll be all right."

"Do you want to leave all this and go across the street for a drink?"

I laughed and shook my head. "A drink is the last thing I need. I had two this morning and they're part of my problem at the moment."

"Poor Nikki," he said. I was aware suddenly that, for the first time ever since I'd met him, I was looking at him without one spark of sexual interest, without one tingle of lust anywhere in my body. It wasn't the fact of my having made love the night before, or even that it was Ned I'd made love to. It was Death brushing so near. Suddenly I was acutely aware of who was important in my life and who wasn't, who mattered and how much. Peter didn't, at least not a lot, not enough. The idea of Death makes you hunger for significance. It stirs up unfulfillable longings for permanence. It makes you reassess your life, gets you to roll up your sleeves and start sorting through the bric-a-brac you've collected, separating out the second-rate, the shabby, the irreparable, the useless, in the hope that when you've thrown away all the trash there will be room to fit something of lasting value.

For most people, the impulse doesn't last long. I didn't think mine would. But by the time it passed, Peter would be long gone to his other amusements. I kissed his cheek. "Thanks," I said.

"It's been fun."

I nodded. That was our only goodbye.

Before I left the gallery, I checked the RSVP list again. Caroline Walton had phoned that morning to say she was definitely coming, and with a guest. From Tessa Hoffmann there was, as yet, no response.

As the day passed and the gloom refused to lift, I began to dread the scheduled dinner with David and Sarah. Ned suggested canceling it, but the prospect of an inquisition by David about why seemed more daunting than brazening through a meal. Anyway, I thought company might distract me.

We met at a steak house downtown, a large, dark, rambling place with bare wood tables stained mahogany, comfortable seats, and early photographs of a bleak and arid Los Angeles on its walls. Despite its size, the restaurant managed to be intimate, quiet, and reasonably priced. It was one of David's favorites.

The food was plain and hearty: baked potato skins, french fries, onion rings, steaks, grilled chicken, bottles of ketchup and Worcestershire sauce, two kinds of mustard, and relish. The wine was an excellent California cabernet sauvignon, but I limited myself to a glass, and Sarah drank only water.

She did most of the talking. Preoccupied as she was with her first stage role in years, she spoke mostly about that, poking fun at herself for doing it. "I do sound like an actor, don't I? Me, me, me, me, me. Shall I shut up?" But we egged her on with questions. At least Ned did. He was—as usual—unabashedly mesmerized by the translucent sheen of Sarah's face, the softness of her chocolate eyes, the rasping sweetness of her voice.

David was unusually quiet. For someone whose most remarkable quality was his ability to be present, absolutely, wherever he was, he seemed that night to be a great distance away. Though he was sitting next to Sarah on the banquette, his arm didn't stray to her shoulder as it once would automatically have done, his hand didn't rest on her neck, or his fingers in her hair. He listened, he responded, he even made one or two wry comments, yet appeared somehow remote, and watchful, like one of those fictional private detectives paid to mingle with the guests. What was he on the lookout for, I wondered, something in Sarah, or in himself, some word or gesture that might provide the clue to what would happen next?

Sarah told anecdotes, recounted gossip, confessed to nervousness with the opening just three nights away. With a pointed look at David, she praised Richard Carew, her director. "His approach is so gentle, I found it quite unnerving at first. I'm rather used to having very opinionated men around, men determined to have their own way."

"She's referring to Nicholas and Ben, of course," said David, with a grin, feeling neither chastened nor contrite.

"It was a marvelous experience to find my own way to the character," continued Sarah, "without having to fight someone else's preconceived ideas all the time. Whatever David thinks of him, I couldn't have had a better director than Richard to work with right now. He's exactly what I needed. He's helped me get my confidence back."

"If that's true," said David. "I'll strew his path with roses on opening night. And I'll eat my words." He touched her hand, briefly. "I'm rooting for you."

She smiled at him, her brief flash of animosity gone. "I know." Then she turned her attention back to Ned and me. "He didn't want me to do it," she said.

"I was afraid," confessed David, with no attempt to dissemble. "I thought the strain would be too much for you."

"So was I. I still am."

"You're doing great," he said.

"What do you do to 'find' a character?" asked Ned.

"That depends on the play," replied Sarah. "This time, I've been reading everything on the subject I could get my hands on: the Anglo-Saxon Chronicles; descriptions of daily life in Saxon England; the memoirs of actresses who've played the part, like Siddons and Terry and Bernhardt. I thought for a while I'd never find the key. I was in despair, wasn't I, darling?" she said, turning to David.

David looked at Ned and smiled. "I bet you thought it was just a question of getting up and saying the lines."

"Just about," admitted Ned. "And you 'found' it?"

She nodded. "Lady Macbeth was the granddaughter of a king. Her claim to the Scottish throne was better than her husband's. Better than Duncan's. If it hadn't been for the law of primogeniture, if it hadn't been for her *sex*, she might have ruled in her own right. When I read that, suddenly I understood her. I understood her ambition, her frustration, her rage."

As I sat there, watching her, listening to her talk, alive with interest, radiant with hope and confidence, the times I had seen her with dark circles rimming eyes glazed with narcotics, her yellow hair matted by neglect, rage shrilling her voice, all those times seemed suddenly improbable, as if I'd dreamed them, as if that Sarah had been only a creature in one of my nightmares wearing the distorted face of someone I love.

Before the coffee came, Sarah and I made a sortie to the bathroom. "Ned is still one of my favorite people, you know. I think he's splendid," she said, as we stood combing our hair, checking our eye shadow, reapplying our lipstick.

"The feeling is mutual."

She looked at my face in the mirror. "Nikki, you are all right, aren't you?"

"Yes. Why?"

"You haven't quarreled with Ned?"

"No, I haven't. Not yet, at any rate. Really, everything's fine." As I said it, the full force of what was happening to Duncan hit me again and my face paled.

Sarah looked at me with concern. "I don't want to pry, but you've been so quiet all night."

"You haven't given me much of a chance to talk," I said.

"That's true enough," she admitted, her face relaxing into a smile. "I have gone on a bit. Still . . . it's not the exhibition, is it? Are you worried about that?"

"Not worried, exactly. A few first-night jitters, that's all." It was true enough, and as good a red herring as any. "I want it to be a success. And the silly thing is, if it's a failure, no one really will notice but me and the three other people who read gallery reviews. It's not like a play where every success and failure is so public. I don't think I could stand that."

"One can't think about reviews. It's death. All the energy, all the concentration, has to be focused on the work. David taught me that. He reads his notices, of course, then argues until he's convinced himself he's right. Duncan's devastated by bad reviews, poor darling. Have you seen him?" she asked, as she stroked fine, translucent powder across her perfect nose.

"Yes," I said. "This morning." It seemed like a hundred years before. "I stopped by to see Cassandra."

"He's looking a bit tired, too. Didn't you think?"

"No," I said. "I thought he looked wonderful."

She shook her head. "I gather this film he's been doing has been very demanding. He and Lottie just don't get on, and it's been an awful strain."

She was referring to Lottie Hagen, who had just that year emerged as one of Hollywood's brightest new stars, the leading actress of her generation, a "great" actress according to many, with her picture on the cover of *Time* to prove it. With all of two successful films behind her, Lottie was inclined both to believe the publicity and to doubt it, alternating between intractable arrogance and paranoid confusion. Duncan, whose patience dealing with young megalomaniacs had worn thin over the years, found her insufferable.

"When the filming's over, I hope Cassandra can talk him into a nice long holiday," said Sarah. "He needs one."

"Cassandra won't have to try very hard," I said, as I led the way through the door, back into the restaurant. "He was talking today about wanting to go to Tibet."

"Really?" said Sarah, sounding surprised. "How odd. I shouldn't think there's a golf course in Tibet." She smiled. "Duncan loathes traveling. I used to have to badger him mercilessly to go anywhere." Then concern crept back into her voice. "He must be even more fed up than I thought. I think I'd better ring him tomorrow. It's amazing, isn't it, how much I care about that man, after all this time?"

"What man?" said David, as we reached the table.

"Duncan," replied Sarah.

A frown flitted across David's face. "He beat me at golf today."

Ned laughed. "You must have made his day."

"He did," I confirmed. "I saw Duncan at the hotel just afterwards. He was glowing with triumph."

"I'll whip his ass next time. Want to play tomorrow?" asked David.

Ned shook his head. "Not on your life. I haven't had a club in my hand in months. You'd pulverize me."

"I thought you were writing," I said.

"Rewriting," corrected David. "Mornings, from six until noon."

"He's never home," said Sarah.

"How would you know?" asked David, his tone light. "You're always rehearsing."

"I telephone," said Sarah, with a lightness to match his own, "and ask."

As we walked across the parking lot towards the valet, Ned and Sarah a little in advance, I slowed my pace so that David and I dropped farther back, out of earshot.

"I haven't had a refusal, yet," I said. "Have you talked to Tessa?"

"Yes. Don't worry." He sounded annoyed.

"You're the one who ought to be worried. By the way, Caroline will be there."

"Where?" asked Sarah, who'd stopped to wait for us.

"At my opening," I said.

"Christ," said David. "That's all I need."

"Why shouldn't she be there?" said Sarah, at her most reasonable. "She's a friend of Nikki's. And all our trouble was a long time ago. Such a long time ago, wasn't it?"

The valet brought our cars, we said goodnight, and I watched as Sarah got behind the wheel to drive.

"Sarah's changed," said Ned. "She seemed more sure of herself than I've seen her in years. Maybe ever. More confident, more..." He searched for the word. "Self-aware. She doesn't seem so dependent on David, somehow. This time she's going to make it."

"Yes," I said, not sounding or feeling totally convinced. "This time she's got a fighting chance."

༄ *Chapter 43* ༄

Once the guests started to arrive, the gallery, which seemed cavernous when inhabited only by Peter, his staff, and myself, shrank slowly to the dimensions of a New York subway car at rush hour.

"Quite a turnout," gloated Peter, glorying in his ability to pull in a crowd. That's how he perceived it, his ability, not my photographs. And he was right. Except for my friends, everyone was there because Peter's reputation demanded attention be paid to whatever he deemed worthy.

"No one can see the pictures," I replied.

"It doesn't matter," he said. "They only come to look at each other. And they'll buy if someone else does."

They were well worth looking at, I thought. No one seemed to be wearing anything so humble as clothes. They came in costume. Women wore oversized men's jackets above baggy clown pants or mini-skirted dresses with strategically placed cutouts and erratic hems. Men sported soft linen suits in sherbet colors or studded leather jackets with skin-tight jeans. They sparkled with sequins on their shirtfronts, with jeweled belts girdling their waists, with heavy crystalline beads encircling their necks, and on their lapels an array of large glass pins that caught the light. Hair, carefully arranged to seem disordered, came in shades of yellow, orange, magenta, any color so long as it didn't appear too natural. The fashion of the streets, which had started in protest or necessity, had been glamorized and accepted, its message parodied and rendered meaningless.

Peter introduced me to a middle-aged couple whose surname I had seen on at least one bank somewhere in the city. He was a large, square-jawed man dressed in a fringed buckskin jacket, with a string tie and cowboy boots. She was a diminutive blonde with perfectly manufactured features, wearing a nip-waisted spangled suit with exaggerated shoulders and the largest diamond ring I had ever seen. I remembered the joke about the Plotnik curse and smiled as she said, "Your pictures are gorgeous. So evocative. I love that one of Duncan Powell. He looks so young, it must have been taken ages ago."

"In 1970." She was referring to the one of Duncan in the wing chair at the Hampstead house.

"I had such a crush on him when I was a teenager," she exaggerated. In 1970, she would have been somewhere in her mid-twenties.

She wore a heady perfume that could not totally disguise the odor of money that clung to her. If I introduced her to Duncan, would she be more inclined to buy? I wondered. And then reminded myself that selling was not the point of the show, at least not for me. I had enough money. Let her find Duncan on her own.

I excused myself and joined Sarah, who was standing nearby, studying Duncan's portrait. "What a long time ago it seems, doesn't it?" she said when she saw me. "Another lifetime. It's smashing. They're all smashing."

"It's too crowded, really, to see."

"I'll be back for another look," she said. "You really are awfully good, Nikki. I mean, I've always thought you were, but seeing your photographs like this, together, as a body of work, they're very impressive. They have a kind of elegance—of form, not of content. A lyrical quality."

"Thank you," I said, more pleased by her praise than I would have imagined. It was an opinion not formed in her mind, but somewhere deeper, in that sphere that made her judgment of his plays so valuable to David, or created a character in performance both real and compelling.

"There's one of David I've never seen before. It's beautiful. I'd like to have it. There's someone around taking orders, isn't there? Oh, yes, I see, over there by the bar."

"I'll take care of it," I said.

"No, you mustn't. Really. I want to pay."

"Sarah . . ." I began, but she interrupted.

"There aren't any photographs of me," she said, making it sound merely an observation.

"No," I said. I hadn't thought she would mention it, and I searched frantically for an acceptable reply.

She put her hand on my arm. "That's all right. I shouldn't have put you on the spot. It was awful of me. I do understand, really I do."

"The space was so limited," I said feebly.

"And who would have recognized me?" she added. "That's not your fault. I've no one to blame for that but myself. Really, forget I said anything. I shouldn't have."

"Two of my favorite ladies," said Simon, coming up between us, kissing each of our cheeks in turn. "Hello." Only Simon, in that crowd of wrinkled linen and disordered hair, could have managed to seem as if he'd overdone the rumpled look.

"Simon, darling, oh it's good to see you," said Sarah. "I didn't know you'd be here." She looked at me accusingly. "What a wonderful surprise."

"It's an excellent show, Nikki. The pictures are super. I love that one of David and me at the Vienna Riding School. I'd forgotten all about it."

"There's a girl, near the bar, taking orders," said Sarah helpfully, "if you want a copy."

"Where's Fiona?" I asked, out of politeness, not interest.

"Over there somewhere," replied Simon, gesturing vaguely to the opposite side of the room. I looked and saw her talking with seductive intensity to a pudgy young man in a smartly cut Italian suit. She was wearing a pale yellow doeskin tunic with a cutout design that reminded me strongly of Emmentaler cheese. "She's talking to Jeff Kaplan."

"I know Jeff Kaplan," said Sarah, her face as she watched Fiona arranged carefully to show nothing. "He's just bought the rights to the Hester Stanhope biography. God, how I'd love to play that part."

A waiter passed by with a tray of glasses filled with champagne. Simon took one, offered it to me, then Sarah, and kept it himself when we both refused.

"I need a clear head to deal with my public," I said, excusing myself to join Peter, who had just beckoned to me.

"Have you said hello to David yet?" I heard Sarah ask as I walked away.

"I didn't see him."

"Oh, Simon, really, this is all so silly."

* * *

Peter introduced me to Drew Mather, a critic from one of the Los Angeles newspapers, with whom I spent a depressing few minutes in conversation. He was a tall, pale man with protuberant eyes whose lids blinked rapidly and disconcertingly, and he did nothing at all to conceal from me the fact that he disliked my pictures. They were too pretty for him, too slick, he hinted. None of them possessed the depth, the insight, the humanity of a photograph by Diane Arbus, he implied. What was the camera for if not to reveal human nature? And human nature revealed is not elegant, not stylish, certainly not pretty.

Every word cut. The fact that Peter and I had decided to show only limited areas of my work became irrelevant. The photographs I had taken that might come closer to Drew Mather's standard of excellence, the only photographs which suddenly seemed to me to matter, were stacked in the back of the gallery, or in my apartment in New York. I had nothing at hand with which to defend myself against the accusation I most dreaded, that my work was shallow, that it was frivolous. I didn't even have, at that moment, a belief in my own ability. I couldn't reply, as I might have if the criticism hadn't been directed at me, paralyzing my mind, that excellence is not simply a matter of content, but of form; that a photograph of a fashion model is not intrinsically inferior to one of a starving African child or a New York bag lady, anymore than Cézanne's *Still Life with Apples* is inferior to Grünewald's *Deposition of Christ from the Cross*, or Manet's *Olympia* to a Fra Angelico Madonna.

But even if I had argued, he would only have nodded condescendingly and acknowledged the merit of work by Beaton or Penn, of Parkinson or Avedon, yet somehow manage to convey the clear impression that even in that arena my work was judged and found lacking.

So I was nodding my head in acceptance, virtually encouraging Mr. Mather to be more brutal, about to supply him with my own damning verdict of my work, when David took my elbow. "Excuse me, Nikki, sorry to interrupt, but Hugh Widdimer of the *New York Times* just asked to meet you. He says he's been an admirer of your work for years. You don't mind if I borrow her for a few minutes, do you?" he asked, directing a sincere and friendly gaze at the astonished critic.

"Not at all," said Mather, whose eyelids had started to blink even more quickly.

"So nice to meet you, Mr. Mather," I cooed, as I left in David's wake. Then, as soon as we were out of earshot, "Thank you for the rescue. Where's Widdimer?"

"He's here somewhere," replied David, gesturing with his champagne glass. "I'm sure I saw him."

"You weren't talking to him?"

"You're not going to get mad because I lied?" said David, grinning.

Finally I understood. "You overheard what that jerk was saying to me."

"Just that little bit at the end," admitted David. "Don't worry. You should get a very nice review from that asshole now."

"Not if he reads a lousy one in Widdimer's column first."

"No way. He'll rush to beat Widdimer into print, then he won't be able to retract. It'll serve him right," said David, "for being such a pretentious prick. And what makes you so sure Widdimer won't give you a glowing review?" he asked, his voice suddenly stern.

"There was a lot of truth in what that idiot Mather said." I sounded sickeningly full of self-doubt and self-pity.

"He's full of shit," replied David.

I grabbed a glass of champagne from a passing waiter and David introduced me to Widdimer, who did happen to like my photographs (though he didn't bother to say so later in print). That cheered me up, but didn't completely wipe out the pain of the emotional beating I'd just received. It is one of life's great inequities that kind words can't soothe an ego nearly so fast as critical ones can do it damage.

As I spoke to Widdimer, I saw Fiona Brent exchange a few (and judging from the faces) barely polite words with Sarah, then a few minutes later receive a brief kiss on the cheek and a cool smile from David, who, duty done, beat a hasty retreat. When her path brought her close to me, I stopped her and introduced her to Widdimer, as a thank you for his praise. He, too, had been eyeing Fiona as we talked, and though I thought a man as sensitive and intelligent as he ought to have better taste in women, I didn't see the harm in allowing him a few minutes of sexual titillation. He wasn't important enough for Fiona to take seriously. Not that Hugh Widdimer received that message. Fiona's smile offered him myriad unspeakable pleasures as soon as they could find a way to be alone.

"The *New York Times*," said Fiona, sounding awed. "You haven't come all this way just to see Nikki's show? Not that it isn't a smashing show," she added quickly. "I'm very impressed, darling." She tried hard to smile as if she liked me, but her thespian abilities didn't extend that far.

"I'm here on vacation, in fact," replied Widdimer.

"The *Times* hasn't sent anyone to cover the festival, has it?" I asked.

"No, uh, I don't think so," he replied, an edge of embarrassment in his voice.

"A pity," I said. "There's been a lot of good stuff happening."

"So I hear. I intend to see as much as I can." He turned his attention back to Fiona. "Are you doing anything I should rush to get a ticket for?"

She smiled graciously. "No. Actually, I'm doing a film at the minute."

"A film? Really. How interesting."

Their conversation launched, I looked around the room to see where I should go next. Peter had returned to Mather, the critic. David, finally, was talking to Simon, and though neither looked relaxed, they both seemed to be trying hard to seem like friends. Sarah was with Duncan, whom I hadn't seen arrive. Again, I was struck with how healthy he looked, and marveled at Sarah's perception. She was looking at him anxiously, and he was laughing at her, doing his best to put her at ease.

Cassandra was the one who looked ill. Despite the careful application of makeup, her skin under her tan seemed sallow, there were dark circles under her eyes, and her mouth was pinched with strain. She was talking to Ned, who must have felt me watching and looked up to smile. My stomach flipflopped, as it used to when I first met him. Not again, I prayed, to no one in particular.

My life was so neat at the moment, so orderly. I had everything under control. I earned a lot of money, and I spent it in ways I enjoyed, asking no one for permission, not even the accountant who occasionally advised caution and was ignored. I lavished it on my family, my friends, and myself. I owned the same apartment in Manhattan I'd always had, plus a house in Martha's Vineyard. Both were full of the crafts I'd collected over the years, the antique quilts, Shaker furniture, hand-loomed rugs, the Sung bowls, the Lucie Rie vases, that added texture, color, perhaps even form to my life. I lived well and traveled well. I knew interesting poeple and did interesting things. My acquaintances were amusing and kept me entertained, my friends prevented loneliness from ever striking too deep. And at the core of my life was a small group of people who gave me all the emotional sustenance I seemed to need. I had David, always, my lodestar and my punching bag; Lissie and the other Walton children, who looked on me, I supposed, as a reliably doting aunt; Cassandra, whose affection I found surprising and touching and who awakened in me a protective tenderness all out of proportion to her large size and obvious efficiency; I had my brother and his family, into whose bosom I retreated when I felt the need for roots, for constancy, for affection that wasn't earned, but owed; and I had Ned, whose love for me over the years might have changed in kind, but never in depth. And if I wanted more sometimes, if I wanted to do better work, achieve more success, lead a richer and more interesting life, well, who didn't? If I sometimes longed to have a love affair to rival Tristan and Iseult's in fervor, I knew always I wanted it only if the cost wasn't too high. And I knew, as well, that Ned came with a very expensive emotional price tag attached. Everyone did.

I started across the room towards Ned and Cassandra but was stopped by a hand on my arm. "Will you introduce me to Duncan Powell?" asked Peter.

"Certainly," I said, changing direction. "You were just talking to Drew Mather?" Peter nodded. "And?"

Peter smiled. "He said your photographs are very interesting. He thinks they have an elegant surface which, I quote, emphasizes rather than disguises their depth, especially in the portraits. Isn't that what he said to you?"

"Not exactly." I grinned. We were waylaid en route by people wanting to talk to Peter or to meet me, but finally we managed to reach our goal.

"I envy you," Sarah was saying to Duncan, as Peter and I approached them. "It's been ages since David and I have been anywhere interesting." Duncan must have succeeded in reassuring her about his state of mind and body, because Sarah was looking far more relaxed.

"Hello, you two," I said, kissing Duncan. "There's someone I'd like you to meet. Sarah Cope, you know. Duncan Powell, Peter de Witt, owner of this establishment."

There were smiles and hellos, and something from Peter about how long he'd been wanting to meet Duncan, what an admirer he was of Duncan's films, et cetera. And then, finally, Peter turned his attention to Sarah. From polite attention, his look changed to that expression of appreciative homage I'd seen him bestow on a painting he liked or a piece of sculpture he wanted to buy. He had a collector's trained eye for beauty, and the faint lines in Sarah's face disturbed him no more than Venus de Milo's missing arm would have done.

"This is the most delightful space," said Sarah, her voice heavy and sweet and completely beguiling. "I've been here before, several times over the years. You really do the most interesting exhibitions. And, of course, you've shown Nikki's pictures off to perfection. Hasn't he, Duncan?"

Peter had hold of her hand. "You're Sarah Walton," he said. "For a minute I couldn't remember where we'd met. It was at a dinner party, a few months ago."

"Cope," said Sarah, with the slightest of edges to her voice. "Sarah Cope." I didn't look at Duncan, but I knew he was smiling.

"Oh, yes," said Peter, not quite understanding, "Of course. I saw some photos of you that Nikki took. They were beautiful."

Sarah tensed slightly and her eyes flickered quickly, inadvertently, to the photographs lining the walls; but her smile didn't falter and, her voice now richly inscrutable, she said only, "Did you think so? I must confess I always liked them."

"Sarah," I interrupted, "Caroline's just come in. Shall we go say hello?" I had just, gratefully, seen her enter the gallery. She was flanked by Lissie and her boyfriend on one side, and on the other by a dark-haired man about an inch shorter than she, stocky, with an air of restless energy and eyes that seemed to absorb everything.

Sarah looked at me blankly for a moment, then said, "Oh, yes, certainly." She excused herself, giving Peter a glorious smile, and we left him and Duncan to continue their conversation. "Really, Nikki," she said, sounding annoyed, "I am perfectly able to deal with the fact that neither my name nor my face are recognizable to anyone anymore. You don't have to protect me from reality."

"I'm sorry," I said. "I got the impression you were annoyed."

"Only for a minute," she admitted. "Who's the man with Caroline?" she asked, stopping to take a glass of Perrier from a passing waiter.

"Alex Chakiris," I said, helping myself to more champagne; and as I did, David—who was now talking to someone I didn't know—looked up and saw them. His mouth dropped open, very slightly and only for a second or two, but long enough for Caroline to notice. She smiled, brilliantly.

"*The* Alex Chakiris?" asked Sarah.

"Oh, yes," I said, "the very same."

David, Sarah, and I converged on Caroline, and she performed the necessary introductions easily and with pleasure. I had never seen her look so beautiful, or seem so expansive. The expression of petulant discontent had long been gone from her face, but that night, for the first time, I noticed no trace of suspicion, no wariness, no expectation of disaster.

"You look sensational," said David.

"Thank you," she replied. She had arrived only that afternoon, so neither David nor I had seen her yet, though Lissie had driven Kate to her hotel for a brief visit.

Sarah and she shook hands and made—for the first time since the divorce—polite, even affable conversation. They had, occasionally, met at school events, like Kate's dance recitals or Lissie's graduation from the Lycée a few weeks before, but their encounters had always been brief and cool, which is why Sarah had been surprised when I suggested she do something so overtly friendly as cross a crowded room deliberately to say hello.

David's early attempts to get Caroline and Sarah's relationship onto a cordial, if not friendly, basis had failed miserably. His efforts to weld both sets of mothers and children into one rather bizarre family unit ended in disasters similar to that awful Christmas of 1971 when he'd nearly lost both Caroline and Sarah. Caroline at first refused point-blank to cooperate. As far as she was concerned, Sarah was the enemy. Sarah, then, with the largess of the victor, was willing to make some effort to overcome Caroline's hostility. But as Caroline's resistance weakened, Sarah's problems increased. That evening, at the gallery, was the first time both women had been prepared simultaneously to bury the hatchet. It had taken fourteen years.

Lissie introduced me to her boyfriend, Steven, a shy young man, handsome behind his glasses. "Thank you," she said.

"For inviting your mother? Don't be silly. She's always welcome. Anyway, I wouldn't have missed this moment for anything. I've never seen her looking so happy."

"She's walking on air," agreed Lissie.

And why shouldn't she be? Her business had brought her success and with it not only financial but psychological security. Nearby was one of her daughters, grown into a lovely young woman, intelligent and gener- ous and loving, the sort of daughter to make any mother's heart swell with pride. At her side, obviously in love with her, was a man who ranked high on the world's list of eligible and desirable men, a man who was rumored to have admirable qualities in excess of his money. Talk- ing with her was the woman who had once been her archrival, now middle-aged, having lost, along the years of drink and drug dependency, the glamour, the success, the calm assurance that had made her once seem invulnerable. And, perhaps best of all, looking on, eyeing her with frank appreciation, with surprised admiration, was her former hus- band, the man she had once accused of having ruined her life, the man who may indeed have saved it by leaving her.

Tomorrow, it was possible Caroline might wake up and find she did not at all have the life she wanted. The way homesickness can signal the end of a longed-for trip, or an attack of wanderlust upset the peace at home, the way you can yearn for snow in August, or for the sea when high in the Alps, one day soon Caroline might discover her life lacking something or other previously irrelevant but suddenly essential. But for that moment, brief as it might be, Caroline was a woman with everything.

"Do you play golf?" David asked Alex Chakiris. After circling each other warily for a few minutes, like two tomcats or two buck deer deciding whether or not a fight for supremacy was demanded, the men had decided they actually liked each other. Which didn't mean they were prepared to forgo entirely the pleasures of competition, just that they were willing to keep them within reasonable and friendly bounds.

"Yes," said Alex, "when I have time. In fact, I'm a member at the Brentwood Country Club. What do you say we get together and play one of these days, while I'm here?" His accent was pure New York. I had been expecting, I realized, something akin to Zorba the Greek.

"I'd love to," replied David. "I'll call you. Where are you staying?"

"We're staying," said Alex, leaning with slight emphasis on the first word, "at the Beverly Wilshire."

Caroline made a face. "It's unbelievably noisy," she said. "By the way, we'd like Kate to join us there for a few days . . ."

"If you can tear her away from Mark, that's fine with me," said David graciously, though it wasn't. He hated it when either Kate's or Lissie's allotted time with him was shortened in any way. If he hadn't counted on Kate's refusal, he would have immediately said no.

"They're potty about each other," explained Sarah to Alex, who turned on her a smile full of appreciation. He might be besotted with Caroline, but he wasn't impervious to the charms of other women. "Mark and Kate, they're as close as twins, really. It's lovely."

"We should all have dinner together one of these nights," said Alex. "I'd like to meet the rest of the children."

We all looked, unwittingly, at Caroline to see how she would react to the suggestion. She smiled. "Sure," she said, "why not? It sounds like fun. I hardly know the little kids."

The conversation continued inconsequentially on for a moment. Then Lissie and her boyfriend drifted off to look at the photographs, and Caroline and Alex were about to join them when Tessa Hoffmann made her entrance. She stood on the threshold, dwarfed by the gallery's large double doors, glancing casually around, as if trying to decide if there was anyone present who could save her from death by boredom. It was a pose. Tessa was never bored. And at that moment, she was undoubtedly terrified.

I looked at David and caught him just when he, too, noted Tessa's arrival. If my face displayed annoyance, fury flashed across David's. Unfortunately, Sarah happened to glance at him just then and, startled by his fleeting look of rage, turned to see what had caused it. If Tessa hadn't chosen to wave hello, Sarah might never have known. But Tessa smiled and waved and started across the room towards us, focusing Sarah's attention. Sarah stared at her for a moment, clearly puzzled, then turned again to look at David, and at me. His face by then was studiously nonchalant, and mine had arranged itself into a facsimile of friendly welcome, so all might still have been well, except that Caroline had noticed everything, and understood it all. She said nothing, but her smile was so knowing, so full of pity, that Sarah instantly read its message. Her face paled and fear flickered in her eyes.

"Excuse us," said Caroline, "the crowd's thinning. We might actually be able to see the photographs now." And she led Alex away.

"Hello, Nikki," said Tessa, extending her hand.

"What a surprise," I said, which at least was sincere. "I wasn't expecting you."

"Oh, I wouldn't have missed your opening for anything."

"You all know each other, don't you?" I said.

"Of course," said Sarah. "Hello, Tessa." Her voice sounded thin and strained.

"Nice to see you again," said David politely. He put an arm around Sarah. "You said you wanted to talk to Jeff Kaplan before he left. I see him heading for the door."

"Oh, yes, yes I do. Excuse me, won't you?" she said.

"Bye, Tessa," said David, as he took Sarah's hand and led her off in pursuit of the film producer Kaplan's chubby, retreating figure.

Tessa watched them for a moment, then turned back to me. "Goddam him," she said.

"What did you expect? Didn't he tell you not to come?"

"He has no right to tell me anything," she snapped. "I can go anywhere I goddam please." She took a deep breath. "I guess I hoped he'd be glad to see me. I guess I hoped when he saw us together he'd realize it was me he couldn't live without."

"You're a fool," I said.

"You think I don't know it?" Then, ruefully, "God, he'll make me pay for this. Well, as long as I'm here, I might as well look at your photographs. I promise to write something nice about them."

"There are some people here you know, I think. Hugh Widdimer?" She nodded. "Just, for chrissake, keep away from David."

"If only I could," she said. Her eyes were full of tears.

After that, I drank more and more champagne, and my mood got progressively more ebullient. The awful Drew Mather left, and everyone else seemed to love my pictures. In the morning, I would have to separate the wheat from the chaff, but for the moment I was determined to enjoy the flattery.

"I don't suppose I can talk you into coming home with me tonight," said Peter.

"I can't," I said.

"You're in love," he said, "and not with me." Again, there was not the least hint of possessiveness or jealousy in his voice. I decided I liked him a lot.

"I hope not," I said.

"You're coming to dinner afterwards, though, aren't you? I've reserved a table across the street."

"If you promise everyone will go on saying nice things to me."

"I promise," he said, and turned away to say goodbye to the man in the string tie and cowboy boots.

Cassandra came up and put her arms around me. "You're not about to do something you'll regret, are you?" she said, looking over my shoulder at Peter.

"Shush," I cautioned. Ned was standing nearby with Simon and Fiona and I didn't want any of that group to hear anything Cassandra might insinuate.

"I worry about you."

"Don't," I said. "I'm fine. Just take care of yourself. And Duncan. All right?" I hugged her. "I love you."

"I'm relying on that. It's been a wonderful night, Nikki. A wonderful exhibition. I can't tell you how proud I feel. Now I'd better take Duncan home. He looks exhausted."

So did Sarah. As soon as he could without its seeming too pointed, David suggested to her they leave. He hadn't so much as looked at Tessa since he'd said goodbye to her.

"You don't mind, do you, darling," asked Sarah, "if we don't join you for dinner?" Peter had invited them. "I'm feeling a little tired, and we have our tech tomorrow."

"I'm glad you were here," I said. "I love you both very much."

"She's drunk," said David.

"Plotzed," I agreed, "but I mean it."

"I'll call you in the morning," he said, "to see how your head feels."

"One way or another, it'll feel big," I assured him. Sarah tried to smile, but didn't quite succeed. There was so much I wanted to say to her then, to tell her not to worry, to assure her Tessa didn't matter, to tell her that even David didn't matter, that nothing mattered, except that she not lose control. But of course I couldn't. "I'll see you at your opening," I said.

David put his arm around her waist. "Come on, baby," he said tenderly, "Let's go home." She didn't pull away. Numbly, she let him lead her towards the door.

Tessa, trying to appear as if she weren't, watched them go. A few minutes later she came over to me to say goodbye. "I'm leaving for New York in the morning." I looked surprised. "I just made up my mind. Call me when you get back."

"All right," I said. She was an old friend, and very unhappy.

I said goodbye to people I knew and people I didn't. I promised to have lunch alone with Caroline, and dinner with her and Alex. I listened to Lissie's lecture that I was not, under any circumstances, allowed to drive that night. And, in a moment of champagne bonhomie, I agreed to spend an evening with Simon and Fiona. Gradually, the room cleared. Ned came and put his arms around me. "Happy?"

I pushed everything but the thought of Ned and my show out of my mind. I let the champagne lift and carry me. "Yes," I said. "Yes. Very happy."

ஃ *Chapter 44* ஃ

When I finally awoke, my head predictably aching, and made my way cautiously into the kitchen, I found Ned sitting at the table, drinking coffee, staring into space, ignoring the newspaper in front of him. Which was odd because the headline read "Ferraro for VP" and she was a good friend of his. I would have expected more enthusiasm. I poured myself a mug of coffee and sat opposite.

"I've been thinking," said Ned. "And I want you to think, too, before you say no. I think we should get married."

"All right," I said.

"Good. Take as long as you need to make up your mind. God knows, at this point in our lives, there's no hurry."

"All right," I repeated. "I'll marry you."

Amazement is not too strong a word for the look that appeared suddenly on Ned's face. "You're agreeing? You're saying yes? You'll marry me?"

"Did you ask only because you were sure I'd say no?"

"Don't be ridiculous."

"Then, yes, I'm saying yes." My reply surprised me, I think, as much as it did Ned. It hadn't occurred to me he'd ask, so I hadn't given any thought to an answer. He gave a shout which hurt my head, and came around the table to kiss me. "I love you," I said.

"I certainly hope so," he replied, and kissed me again.

We spent the next several hours talking. We made decisions about when to tell the boys, when to tell his family, and mine, when actually to do the deed. And where.

"Do you want a church wedding?" he asked.

"Yes, I think I do, if we can find one we both approve of." I do like churches and church rites—if they're beautiful. I laughed. "Oh, God. Can you imagine my brother's face when I tell him not only am I getting married, I'm getting married in church? He'll never believe it."

"Neither can I. I can't believe any of this." Ned sounded as close to bewildered as I'd ever heard him.

"I suppose it's because Duncan's dying," I said.

Ned didn't understand. Nor did I clearly. All I knew was that the nearness of Death had made me greedy. Every pleasure ever delayed, every satisfaction postponed, for whatever reason, suddenly demanded gratification. I wanted not only to hold on to everything I had, but to get more.

"These past few days," I said to Ned, "I've been thinking about my life, studying it, knowing I had to make it better, not certain how to do it. You've given me a way." The nearness of Death had made me want a man to love, a man who'd love me. It had made me realize I wanted a sex life based on tenderness, not excitement, on fulfillment, not the relentless quest for orgasm. I wanted sex booted out of the Olympic Games and reinstated as an act of love.

I was forty-four years old and in all my life so far had loved and desired, liked and respected only one man—Ned. Was it likely I would soon find another, if I were to let him go again? And I was suddenly no longer willing to do that. Measured against Death, my fears seemed petty. They seemed cowardly. The nearness of Death had made me brave.

How lucky I am, I thought, to get a second chance when I'm ready for it.

But the longer we spoke, the stronger became the note of irritation, of anger, in Ned's voice. He was angry at me for all the years together we would never have, all the years that had been wasted due entirely to my invincible stubbornness, my downright stupidity. It was an unreasonable anger, and he knew it, but that didn't make it any less real.

"I don't regret a moment I spent with Mary," he said. "You know that. I loved her. I still love her. And my boys, I could never regret them. But when I think about you, about what you've missed all these years, about what we've missed not being together." He was not prepared, at that moment, to admit the impossibility of following both diverging paths in Robert Frost's wood.

"And if we had somehow managed to marry each other fifteen years ago, we'd be sitting here now with a whole list of other regrets. No, sorry, we wouldn't be sitting here now, or at least not with each other. We'd be divorced and not speaking, and complaining about our unsatisfactory lives to somebody else. We couldn't have married each other then. I'm glad we didn't. We would have made each other miserable."

But Ned was a different man from the one he'd been fifteen years before. Life had modified his ambitions and his needs, it had eased the stringency of his rules.

And I was a different woman. Though a familiar icy knot gripped my stomach at the thought of marrying Ned (and now there was not only Ned to deal with but his sons), I knew it was no longer relevant. For good or ill, I had become so much me, so totally and completely myself, love could no longer cause me to lose my soul. I would not get swept away, to oblivion, any more than Cassandra had.

"You didn't trust me enough," said Ned. "That was your problem. And you didn't trust yourself. I was more flexible than you gave me credit for being, and you were much stronger."

Was I? Perhaps. We would never know. "Are we going to go on fighting indefinitely?" I asked. "Except for a subtle change in subject matter, this is beginning to seem too much like old times to me."

Ned laughed. "Okay, you're right. No more raking up the past," he promised. "It's a waste of time." He kissed me. "I'm glad you're going to marry me. I really do love you. A lot."

That afternoon, Ned went to do some shopping for his boys, and I stopped by the gallery for a while, then went up to the Walton house to see David as we'd arranged on the phone earlier.

Mrs. T opened the door and admitted me into an unusually silent house. Miss Cope was at rehearsal, she explained, Lissie and Kate were with their mother, and Marie-Paule, with the Walton factotum, Will, had taken the other children to Magic Mountain for the afternoon. Disneyland had been suggested, but Kate had looked so miserable, that trip was postponed for a day she could go. "Not that she enjoys herself at Disneyland," sniffed Mrs. T. "The last time she was there she thought it too hot and crowded by half." Mrs. T looked tired, worried. She took the vase of dying flowers from the table in the hall and started in the direction of the kitchen. "I've some fresh scones for tea," she said, "so mind you stay."

I followed her directions through the house and down the hillside to the pool, where David was waiting for me. He was lying on a lounge, head covered by a cap, his brown body glistening with suntan oil, smoking a cigarette, making pencil notes on a typescript. Since he'd begun acting, he had become even more compulsive about exercise, and there wasn't a spare ounce of flesh on him. He looked lean and bronze, handsome and fit, his chest and arms and thighs firmly muscled.

"It isn't fair," I said, "that men don't have cellulite."

"You should exercise more, instead of bitching," he replied.

"I exercise. I diet. It's a losing battle."

"Life is a losing battle."

"May I quote you on that?"

"Oh shut up. And sit down. There's some lemonade in the thermos. Let me just finish reading this scene. It's the one where Carter finds Tut's tomb."

David returned to his typescript, and I picked up the ashtray overflowing with butts and emptied it into a nearby trashbin, brought it back, poured myself some lemonade, and sat. He made a few final notes, put the pages in their folder, and dropped it onto the brick floor of the terrace.

"Pretty good," he said. "This play might actually have a run." Then he really looked at me. "What's up? Wait, don't tell me. I know. You're going to marry Ned." He said it with absolute certainty, and when he saw the stunned look of affirmation on my face, he grinned like a smug magician at a children's party pulling a pigeon from his sleeve. "It's about time," he said.

"It wasn't possible before."

"Only because you're a coward, never willing to fight any battle you don't know in advance you can win. What makes you so sure now you can?"

"I don't think that's true," I protested, avoiding the question. "I'm not a coward. I just know my limitations." But I could see how indistinguishable my caution was from cowardice to someone like David who followed without thought the flow of his desires.

He reached over and took my hand. "I don't want to argue. I'm happy for you, Nikki, if you're happy."

"I may be happy, but you're not," I said. "What happened last night?"

"You tell me. How did Sarah know?"

"She took one look at your face. Then at Caroline's. Caroline knew immediately, too."

"Oh shit," said David. He stood up. "I need a drink. Do you want something?"

"I'll stick with lemonade, thank you. My head hurts enough as it is."

"I'll be right back."

I looked at the clean blue water of the pool and wished I had brought my bathing suit with me. It was hot sitting in the sun, and the cotton of my dress had begun to stick to my back and thighs. The terrace was edged by a wall overgrown with marmalade bougainvillea. There were pots of pink and green cymbidium in the shade of a tall tree. A hummingbird flitted past and stopped to drink from one of the red hibiscus growing profusely nearby. Overhead buzzed a pair of orange dragonflies making passes at the water like fighter pilots at a target. It was all very idyllic. I breathed slowly and deeply, trying to rid myself of the anxious feeling gathering in my chest.

David returned carrying a tray with whiskey, water, and ice. "Sure you won't have one?" he asked as he fixed himself a drink. He never drank much, and rarely whiskey. He was very upset. "Tessa's left for New York."

"She told me last night she was going."

"I phoned her hotel this morning, as soon as Sarah left for rehearsal. She'd checked out already." He took another gulp of whiskey. "It's over, all over."

"That seems to be Tessa's opinion, too," I said. It wasn't mine. Love affairs (or marriages for that matter) rarely die quickly and well; their demise tends to be lingering and painful, causing the maximum amount of grief for all concerned parties.

"Why did she do it? Why did she come?" There was anger in David's voice, as well as pain. "I told her not to."

"You know perfectly well why."

"I never lied to her. I told her I'd never leave Sarah."

"Have you ever known a woman to believe a man when he's said that," I countered, my voice dripping with sarcasm, "unless it was a man she didn't want?"

"I never said I loved her."

"Do you?"

He shrugged. "Maybe I'm in love with the serenity of being with a woman I don't expect to go to pieces at any moment right in front of my eyes."

"Sarah's been fine for a long time," I said defensively.

"And she'll go on being fine, until the next time."

Sarah had driven home the night before. She had driven fast, David told me, too fast, the tires of the Jaguar screeching as the car took the sharp curves of Mulholland Drive. David had gritted his teeth, ignored the dizziness he felt looking out at the hillside falling sharply away into the dark of the canyon, and said nothing. He could feel the anger seething inside her and wanted to wait for the relative safety of home and their bedroom before confronting it.

At first she denied anything was wrong; then, suddenly, she changed her tack. "No, dammit," she had said, "it was denying how I felt all those years that made me sick. I'm not going to start doing it again. You're fucking that woman, aren't you? You're fucking her, and I'm furious. You're fucking her, and if I had a gun in my hand at this moment, I'd empty it into you. Right now, I hate you. You make me sick."

David told Sarah it wasn't true. He told her she was imagining things. "I couldn't tell her the truth," he said.

Sarah hadn't believed him. The more he denied, the more she raged. "You want me to doubt my own senses, don't you?" she had asked. "You want to push me over the edge again, so you can be free. You can't. I'm well now, and I'm going to stay well."

He told her to stop being melodramatic, and she slapped him. He reached for her, but she backed away, picked up a vase of flowers she had spent half an hour arranging earlier that day, and hurled it at him. It missed and fell to the floor with a splintering crash. He grabbed her right arm, but with her left she picked up a crystal ashtray from a table and slammed it into the side of his head. He felt the hot seep of oozing blood. He felt he wanted to strangle her. They went at each other like street fighters and fell in a heap to the Spanish-tiled floor.

David took off the cap he was wearing and showed me his bandaged temple. "Three stitches," he said.

The noise had awakened Olivia. She stood in the doorway, her eyes wide with horror, watching them writhe on the floor. "Stop it," she had said, in perfect imitation of Sarah. "Stop it this instant." They did. David scrambled to his feet, went to his daughter, and picked her up in his arms. "You're bleeding," she said.

"I slipped," he lied, "and cut my head. Mommy was trying to help me up when she fell, too. Then we just got silly and started wrestling."

"Have you been drinking?" she asked suspiciously.

"Not a drop. Neither of us. We're as sober as judges."

While David went into the bathroom to wipe some of the blood from his head and apply a temporary bandage, Sarah talked quietly to her daughter, apologizing for frightening her, then took her back to her bed and stayed with her until she fell asleep. When she returned, she stood in the doorway of the bathroom and watched him, her eyes bright with unshed tears. "Are you hurt badly?" she asked, and when he showed her the wound, which wouldn't stop bleeding, volunteered to drive him to the hospital for the stitches he needed. She was appalled by her behavior and penitent. "I get so angry, I don't think. I don't know what I'm saying, what I'm doing." All the fight had gone out of her.

"I told her I loved her," he said to me, staring straight ahead at the dragonflies skimming over the surface of the pool. "I told her I had from the first moment I saw her. I told her I always would. I told her that if ever I did something stupid, something destructive, it was only an attempt to escape that one unalterable fact." He looked at me then, and smiled bleakly, his eyes full of anguish. "Do you know what she said to me? She said the two worst things that had ever happened to either of us was falling in love and staying in love." He took another sip of whiskey, leaned back in the lounge, and closed his eyes. "She said those two things had ruined our lives."

❧ *Chapter 45* ❧

Macbeth was being presented on the UCLA campus, at Royce Hall, which had just been refurbished in time for the Olympic Arts Festival. A few weeks earlier the Royal Shakespeare Company had appeared there with much-lauded productions of *Cyrano* and *Much Ado*. Sarah and other members of the company were a little apprehensive about following in their wake. The director wasn't. He had no doubt his production would come off brilliantly in comparison.

It was a warm summer evening, and UCLA shone with the combined glow of the setting sun and the high spirits of the crowds attending festival events at various campus sites. The turquoise-and-orange Olympic banners waved gaily in the breeze blowing in fresh from the ocean. Everywhere were smiling faces in every conceivable hue of human skin and the happy sound of polyglot chatter.

On the loggia in front of Royce Hall, coffee and cake were being sold. Ned and I stopped to get some and met Lissie and her boyfriend, the lanky Steven, doing the same. He smiled shyly, while she kissed me and hugged Ned. "Daddy told me you're getting married," she said. "I'm so glad. Am I invited to the wedding? I hope I am." Ned and I assured her we wouldn't dream of getting married without her, and all the Walton brood. Lissie pointed to the corner of the loggia. "They're all over there," she said. 'Daddy, Marie-Paule, Mrs. T, and the little kids."

Ben had been left at home with Will, but the other children stood clustered around David, eight-year-old Nicholas, for whom the theater was a rarer treat, looking ready to explode with excitement. "Mommy's in a play," he announced when he saw me.

"She knows that, you dolt," said Olivia. "Why do you think she's here?"

"That will do, miss," said Mrs. T to Olivia, with an admonishing glance, before pulling me into a motherly embrace. "What a lovely bit of news," she said. "All the best to you both."

Ned and I smiled self-consciously as the children jumped up and down demonstrating their enthusiasm for the idea and Marie-Paule shyly added her congratulations. There was a young man with her, the Olympic athlete she was about to marry. "I hear congratulations are in order for you, too," I said. She glowed as she introduced Ned and me to her fiancé, Claude. What a way she had come from the homely, awkward teenager she had been.

"Okay, everybody, that's enough," said David. "You know how Nikki hates fuss. She'll change her mind if you're not careful." He extended a hand to Ned. "Congratulations," he said, "and good luck."

"Do you know the legend about this play?" asked Mark, his voice quivering with glee; and when Ned and I confessed we didn't, he began to regale us with tales of the ill luck that had plagued various productions of *Macbeth*.

"Someone got killed once, onstage," said Kate.

"Stabbed in a fight scene," elaborated Mark, enjoying himself. "Right through the heart."

A warning bell sounded in the distance, and as we all started inside, I dropped back for a word with David as Mark enthusiastically continued his chronicle of disaster.

"Is everything all right?" I asked. The bandage over David's cut had been replaced by a smaller piece of white tape. His face looked haggard from tension and lack of sleep.

He shrugged. "Sarah took Ben to the hairdresser with her this afternoon and left him there. She forgot all about him. Marie-Paule had to go pick him up."

"She wasn't high?"

"She said she was just worrying so much about the opening, he slipped her mind." His voice expressed all the incredulity I felt. "Can you believe it? He just slipped her mind."

"That's why," said Mark, "actors won't say the name. They call it 'The Scottish play' instead. And if they forget, they turn around three times right away to the left to ward off the evil."

"Daddy says '*Macbeth*' all the time," contradicted Olivia.

"He's not an actor, idiot," said Nicholas scornfully, enjoying his chance to get back at his sister.

"I hope nothing happens tonight," said Kate, with a shudder, as Olivia pinched her cousin, Louise, and David stepped between the two girls to keep peace.

To Mark's regret, no one got run through to his death that night, though there were at least two actors I wouldn't have been sorry to see go that way, or any way. Not that the quality of the performances was the major problem. As David had predicted it would, the play lacked clarity and coherence. Whatever its cause (David during intermission posited stupidity, others inexperience), Richard Carew's failure to control the actors, his inability to shape their creative impulses into a form that could both entertain the audience and reveal the play, resulted not only in muddled characterizations, but in an array of acting styles that was bewildering to behold. Lady Macduff, for example, was straight out of a Victorian melodrama, while Banquo might recently have escaped from a revival of *West Side Story*. There seemed to be several productions of *Macbeth* taking place on the same stage at the same time.

All of which was a pity, because under the confusion it was possible to see what it was that had excited Sarah about the production and had made her believe in its success. There were the seeds of something exciting, a boldness of vision and a palpable raw energy that exactly suited the temper of the play. The minimal sets were both bleak and grand, the costumes sumptuous yet coarse. By a few impressionistic strokes, the eleventh century was conjured with a force rarely felt even in films. This is a chaotic and bloody time, they said, it must be hell to be alive.

Even some of the performances hinted at what might have been achieved had the director been talented enough, or strong enough, or clear-sighted enough. Liam McCarthy, who played Macbeth, and Jeremy Rogers, who played MacDuff, were both excellent, as were others whose names I've forgotten. But it was Sarah who stole the show. She was incandescent that night, illuminating every scene she was in. And her voice had never been better, its richness heightened by power and passion.

Sarah's Lady Macbeth was no monster, no scheming shrew. She was regal and ardent, intelligent and determined, a woman capable of boldly courageous action who took the only way open to her to get what she believed rightfully hers. Malcolm would never have tricked her with his moving wood, nor terrified her into folly. Her only weakness was her conscience, an essentially feminine conscience, one that forced upon her the (literally) maddening realization that power seized ruthlessly is as essentially self-destructive as no power at all.

Her performance was breathtaking, heartbreaking. During the sleep-walking scene, I cried, the way I can't help doing when witnessing a moment of supreme achievement, when looking at an Ansel Adams landscape or Vermeer's *Young Girl in a Turban*, for example, or watching Baryshnikov in a pirouette lift from the stage like an ascendant helicopter.

At the curtain call, when Sarah came forward to take her bow to one or two scattered bravos, I felt anger flooding through me, anger for all the years of waste, the years when Sarah should have been at work cutting and polishing her talent to shine like the jewel it was and instead had let herself languish in confusion and pain. But anger at whom? At Sarah? Was she any more to blame for being a product of her time, at the mercy of her worst instincts, than was Lady Macbeth? I searched for pity and found some; but the anger remained.

"I'd almost forgotten how good she is," said David as we left the auditorium, surrounded by unusually subdued children. His voice held admiration and tenderness and awe. I wanted to slap him. To Sarah, David's lack of encouragement, his passive discouragement, had been as lethal to her work, perhaps more lethal, than outright opposition. His air of pained resignation when she did accept a part, his relieved gratitude when she didn't, were as effective in housebreaking Sarah as the withholding-and-reward system of training dogs. If only David had been an obviously oppressive husband, or one as stupidly patronizing as Helmer in *A Doll's House*, Sarah might have realized at some point how absolutely essential it was to rebel. If only she'd been able to direct the fury of her frustration at him, instead of herself. If only she hadn't loved him so much, if only he hadn't been so well worth loving, the bastard. If...

"God," muttered Ned, still caught up in the magic of Sarah's performance, "she's fantastic."

"What's the matter?" asked David, who, looking around to see that all the children were gathered, happened to see my face. "You look ready to kill."

"Nothing," I replied.

Cassandra and Duncan had been in the audience, as well as Simon and Fiona, and we all headed backstage to see Sarah.

"Why can't you just phone her tomorrow, or send a note?" I heard Fiona moan to Simon. "It was bloody awful."

"That's why," said Simon patiently, running a hand through his already untidy hair. "She'll think I hated her, and she was brilliant."

"She was all right, I suppose," conceded Fiona grudgingly.

"What a cow," whispered Cassandra, loud enough to cause Simon to flinch. "Did you hear he's actually going to marry the bitch?"

"Darling, do you think you could lower your voice to a bellow?" encouraged Duncan, putting his arm around Cassandra's shoulders. There weren't many men large enough to do that comfortably. "Simon's gone all red around the ears."

"Good. Maybe if he hears enough unpleasantness, he'll change his mind."

"Hear it? He lives with it," I said.

"This way," said David, as we followed him outside and along the loggia towards the stage entrance.

Simon was ignoring Fiona and trying to reestablish his relationship with the Walton children, whom he'd not seen in a long while. Fiona put her hand on David's arm. "Did Simon tell you we're getting married?" she asked.

"Congratulations," said David, ambiguously and without enthusiasm.

Not able to ask about his health, Ned asked Duncan instead how filming was going.

"Almost over," said Duncan. "Three days to go. Thank God. This one's been a nightmare."

"We're doing fine," said Cassandra to me, in as low a voice as she could manage. "Or, rather, Duncan's doing splendidly, and I'm muddling along as best I can." Then she linked her arm through mine. "Forgive me if I'm being unspeakably nosy, but are you and Ned, as they say, an item once again?"

"We're getting married," I confessed.

She looked at me in amazement. "You aren't."

"I didn't take a vow of celibacy, you know. I was just waiting for the right man to come along at the right time. I guess he finally did."

"I'll never understand you."

"Aren't you going to congratulate me?"

"I'm too shocked," she said. "Give me a minute to get used to the idea."

There were flower arrangements on the floor of Sarah's tiny dressing room, and cards and telegrams taped up on the walls and mirror. She was out of her costume but still in makeup when we poured in murmuring our congratulations. Her eyes sought David's instantly. He smiled at her in approval, but the tension didn't leave her face. She looked drained, exhausted.

"You were beautiful, Mommy," said Nicholas.

"Thank you, darling."

"You were excellent," added Olivia, emphatically. "Brilliant."

The children one by one laid accolades at her feet, even Kate mustering a few shy, unfamiliar words of praise, then Mrs. T hugged her and Marie-Paule said how glad she was finally to have seen Sarah onstage. Claude, the Olympic athlete, said he'd been enchanted. For once, the word didn't seem excessive to me.

David opened a bottle of wine and glasses were handed around, while Marie-Paule poured soft drinks for the children. Sarah refused both and asked David for some Pelegrino instead.

"You've never been better," said Duncan. "It's hard to believe you haven't been on a stage in ages."

"Do you mean that?" asked Sarah anxiously.

"You were bloody marvelous," said Cassandra.

"Breathtaking," confirmed Simon, who began to elaborate the high points of Sarah's performance. "The assurance you have, it's as if you've been playing the part for years."

"The direction was quite astounding, too," said Fiona, causing Duncan to jump in again and change the course of conversation, smoothly as only he could, telling an anecdote of a long-ago production of *Macbeth* he'd been in when, to Mark's delight, the actor playing Duncan died of a heart attack backstage just before his final scene.

Everyone else carefully avoided mentioning the production, and Sarah asked no one's opinion of it, but the endless compliments about her own performance didn't seem really either to please or to convince her. She'd left her assurance onstage. She kept returning anxiously to her study of David's face.

Mrs. T, soon tired of playing referee to Olivia and Louise, left first, taking the children home to bed, accompanied by Marie-Paule and her athlete. Simon, after trying a couple of times, failed again to get past David's guard, realized the moment would not come that night, and took an obviously impatient Fiona away. Then Lissie and Steven said goodbye.

"Are you coming to dinner?" asked David. The cast and production staff and assorted friends were going on to Spago to celebrate.

"Would you mind if we didn't?" asked Lissie. "There's a party at Stefanie's."

"Another?" said David.

But Sarah shook her head. "Of course not, darling. Go, and have a good time."

Lissie kissed her. "You really were wonderful," she said. Then she kissed her father. "Bye, Daddy. See you later."

"Drive carefully. And don't get home too late."

Lissie nodded, waved, and went out, followed by her boyfriend.

David looked after her regretfully. "I'm no good being a father to anyone over the age of fourteen," he said. "I worry too much."

As soon as they were gone, Sarah asked the rest of us to join them, but we refused; Duncan and Cassandra presumably because Duncan was tired, Ned and I because we wanted to be alone.

"Thank you for coming," said Sarah.

"I'm glad I did. I'm so glad I got to see you. I'll remember this performance all my life," I said.

"I'll call you in the morning," said David to me, as he always did.

Their voices followed us out into the corridor. "It was ghastly, wasn't it?" asked Sarah.

"It was. You weren't," replied David. "Nicholas was right, you were beautiful."

Then Sarah began to cry. "Don't touch me. Please, don't touch me. I can't bear it. Oh God, it's all too much for me. Everything's too much for me."

We all looked at one another and away again. There was nothing to say.

I was expecting to hear the next day that the dinner at Spago had been a fiasco, that the tension between David and Sarah had erupted again into violence, that Sarah had been reduced to flinging plates and David to dragging her protesting from the restaurant. It wouldn't have been the first time.

But the dinner went well. People who were there told me they'd noticed no strain. David and Sarah had sat at opposite ends of the table and seemed to be enjoying themselves. David clowned for an appreciative audience and, since he was drinking, ended up arm-wrestling with Liam McCarthy, who'd played Macbeth. Sarah drank only mineral water but was flirting and laughing as if she were high. The director, Richard Carew, who had fallen a little in love with her over the weeks of rehearsal, told me later he had never seen Sarah so vital, so gay. Both she and David seemed reluctant for the party to end and were among the last to leave the restaurant.

Though I know her uncertainty about her talent, about her career, was only part of the problem, still I wonder sometimes how things might have turned out if somehow, the way I've seen it happen in numberless films, Sarah had been able to read the reviews of the play before leaving the restaurant. Over the next few days, the production was universally panned, but Sarah's notices were superb: riveting, spellbinding, magical, radiant, powerful, were some of the adjectives used. And Jeff Kaplan, I learned through Duncan, had seen her and decided only she could play Hester Stanhope in his film. He sent a script around to her agent in the morning. But, of course, it was too late.

The quarrel, if there was a quarrel, happened in the car on the way home. Sarah was, as usual, driving.

My phone rang at about two in the morning. It was Lissie at the other end of the line. She was crying.

"Sweetheart, what's wrong? Are you all right?" I could feel the panic rising in me.

"It's Daddy. And Sarah. There's been an accident."

"They're all right," I said, the words more an order than a question. Please God, I prayed, let them be all right.

"They're dead." Lissie's voice rose to a wail. "Oh God, Nikki, Daddy's dead."

As I got out of bed, Ned watched me dumbly, wanting to help and knowing he couldn't, remembering from Mary's death that nothing could. I went into the bathroom, locked the door, turned on the shower, and screamed, hoping Ned wouldn't be able to hear. The pain cut me like a knife, seared me like a flame, emptied me and filled me. Never, I thought, never, never, never, never, never. The word reverberated in my head with the hollow sound of loss. From my stomach, the pain rose and filled my chest, exploded through my throat and out my mouth. I screamed again. Ned pounded on the door. "Nikki, stop it," he said. "Don't do this to yourself. Stop it."

"I can't," I sobbed. "I can't stop. Not yet." Maybe not ever, I thought.

New York
October 1987

❧ Chapter 46 ❧

That was over three years ago, and minute by minute, hour by hour, day by day, slowly, inevitably, the sharp pain of grief has faded to a dull ache at the edge of my mind. The newspaper stories, the magazine articles, which reveled for months in the details of the death, flagging interest revived first by the release on cassette of Sarah's early films and later by the successful production of David's last play, finally faded away, giving those of us who were devastated by their deaths a respite from the shock of confronting their smiling faces at the newsstand or pushed through the mailslot onto the hall floor. Now only occasionally do the images come to provoke fresh explosions of anguish, such simple images usually: David at a dinner table promising Sarah a trip to Paris in the spring, Sarah at the gallery promising to return for another look at my photographs, David at Royce Hall that last night promising to call me in the morning—images of so many promises unfulfilled, terrifying reminders of how quickly, simply, and with utter finality we can be deprived of what we most love; how uncertain the path is to the future, and how dangerous, how suddenly it can lead even the most wary traveler over the edge into eternity.

And then Mr. Keating's biography of the Waltons arrived.

* * *

Over Mrs. T's objections, and mine, Lissie insisted on going to iden-
tify David's and Sarah's bodies. Ned and I went with her. The three of
us stood in that cold, bleak room, in the middle of a black and awful
night, for the moment too numbed by horror to cry. Lissie held tightly
to my hand and said to the police officer, "Yes, yes. That's them."
They were bruised and broken. They were cold and lifeless. They were
David and Sarah. Gone was the small flicker of hope we all had nursed
until that moment that some terrible mistake had been made. Both had
died instantly, or near enough, we'd been told. "Yes," Lissie said, "that's
them."

We sat silently in the car on the way back to the Walton house,
rewriting the night in our minds, as if we still had the power somehow to
change the ending. If only, we all thought. If only...

Lissie insisted, too, the next morning, on being the one to tell her
sisters and brothers. Ben sat on my lap, straining forward against my
arms, listening intently to her as she talked, trying to understand why
Nicholas and Olivia, Mark and Kate, and even Lissie had started to cry.
"Yes," he said finally, his voice breaking into a wail, "but when are they
coming back?"

Jack took care of all the funeral arrangements and left Mrs. T and me
to deal with the children. I had flown back with them from Los Angeles
and had moved into the Walton house to be with them until plans for
their future were made. It only struck me as odd afterwards that no one
questioned my right to be there.

David and Sarah were buried in a cemetery in Valhalla, New York,
for no other reason than that it was near Jack's house. The name, I
knew, would have appealed to David. He would have liked the idea of
going to a warrior's heaven.

Only family and close friends attended the funeral. Mr. Walton stood
pale and suddenly very old, dry-eyed throughout the service. Occasionally I saw his lips move and wondered if he was thanking God that it was
David and not Jack lying there, and realized that only my guilty conscience made me think it: I would gladly have traded Jack for David; in
an instant, with no hesitation, I would have traded Jack for his brother.
And who else? I wondered, looking around me at all those people I
cared for. Who else, if I'd had the power to choose?

Jack, flanked by his wife and children, looked bewildered, bereaved.
So did my brother, Mike, who was there with his wife and sons. Claudia, David's sister, was white-faced and trembling, oblivious to her husband and children. Sarah's brother, exhausted from the plane trip,
seemed crushed with grief.

Caroline came, and no one, not even I, thought it strange that she stood, like the bereaved widow rather than the ex-wife, close to Mr. Walton, Lissie and Kate on either side of her. Like her former father-in-law, she was composed and dry-eyed throughout, her only concern to comfort her daughters, especially Kate, who sobbed and clung desperately to Mark's hand. For once, Mark ignored her. He saw only the two coffins. Tears ran down his face, and down Olivia's, and down Nicholas's chubby cheeks. Ben held tight to my hand, still not certain what was happening.

Cassandra and Duncan were there, and Ned, of course, a dazed Mrs. T, Marie-Paule looking lost, and friends of Jack's I didn't know.

A few days later there was as memorial service at a church in Manhattan. Jack spoke, as did Rob Maxwell, and other people David had worked with over the years. Sarah's brother broke down in the middle of a reminiscence. Duncan spoke, too, and Lissie. Billy Siedler, a friend of David's, read a poem, in tribute he said to Sarah and David's love for each other:

> I have known your face from the first day;
> My soul has known yours forever.
> And if this time
> We fed each other bitter fruit,
> Still I hope for next time
> And another place.

Jack asked if I would say something, but I refused. I blamed both David and Sarah for dying, and didn't think fury made a suitable text for a memorial. In any case, I was incapable of sustained speaking. I lapsed into either silence or tears.

The day after the service, Mr. Walton called and insisted on having lunch. I was trying desperately to pick up the threads of my work life and asked for a rain check, but he was so insistent I eventually had to say yes. We met at the Ginger Man.

David's lawyer had phoned him, Mr. Walton explained as soon as the drinks were ordered, and though he didn't as yet know the full contents of David's will, he thought he'd better tell me as soon as possible what he did know, since it concerned me. I'd been left custody of David and Sarah's four children and named executor of Lissie and Kate's share of the estate.

I felt another wave of fury washing over me. The bastard, I thought, he didn't even ask.

Mr. Walton said that in his opinion David had acted in his usual thoughtless and selfish way, burdening me with his children when I had no legal or moral responsibility for them. He assured me that the Walton family were more than willing to do their duty; that his own home was open to them, as was Jack's, and Claudia's; that there were certain legal formalities I would have to follow, but other than that I needn't concern myself with the children at all.

I saw David sitting by the pool that last afternoon we spent together. He was looking at me disapprovingly. "Only because you're a coward," he said. "You never fight any battle you're not sure you can win."

I stayed in the Walton house, moving my own things into it gradually; and when Ned and I married a few months later, he and his boys moved in as well. Mrs. T has stayed with us, though Marie-Paule left as planned to marry her handsome athlete, and has been replaced by a feisty, handsome Guatemalan named Carmen. People advised us to buy a new house, to start fresh, but neither Ned nor I wanted to do that. For a moment we toyed with the idea of my moving the Waltons into Ned's house in Rye, but then Ned and I began to laugh ourselves silly at the thought of me in the suburbs, and the die was cast. Since we were keeping Ned and Mary's cottage on Narragansett Bay, with all its happy memories, his boys protested only minimally at the decision. In fact, they were excited at the prospect of living in Manhattan.

There's a difference between living morosely in the past and incorporating that past lovingly into the present. The latter is what Ned and I have attempted to do, and I think, for the most part, we've succeeded. The houses in which we live are not shrines, but homes that seem by now to belong equally to David and Sarah, Ned and Mary, the children and me. Ned and I don't want to forget the people we love, and we don't want the children to forget them either, not ever.

We sold my West End Avenue apartment, but I've rented a studio and kept the house on Martha's Vineyard. I need them as psychological safety nets. Although I love, perhaps love desperately, all the people around me, still I'm not used to living in such close proximity to others. I'm not used to dealing with the demands those others inevitably make on time and energy. I am, on the simplest level, not used to all the noise. It's hard for me, and often I need to escape to my studio, or to Martha's Vineyard for a quiet weekend on my own. And, of course, I continue to work, and to travel. In a few weeks, after my show at the Modern closes, I'll be leaving for Paris to direct a short film there for PBS. But the truth is, I enjoy travel more these days when Ned or the children or both are with me.

It hasn't been easy for Ned either. He kept on with his defense work even after Eddie Conlon was convicted, but it wears him out. He's been known to make his own escape to Narragansett, to the Vineyard, to anywhere when he's had enough. But so far, amazingly, this peculiar marriage with its strange conglomerate family has worked.

Lissie has been an enormous help. Over our protests, she didn't go to Yale that autumn, but stayed in Manhattan and attended Columbia. Not only did her sisters and brothers need her, she claimed, but she needed them. She was right. Not even Mark could comfort Kate for David's loss. She clung to Lissie to ease her pain. All the children did.

Lissie's starting to date again, finally, though now, of course, in addition to all her other problems, she has to contend with AIDS, which this past year has surfaced to terrorize the world. We've had long talks with her about that, and with Mark and Kate, who are beginning to wade slowly into the adolescent social stream, along with Ned's oldest boy. Though we worry (perhaps a little too much) about drink and drugs, so far we haven't had a problem. Olivia's rages are down to manageable proportions, and Nicholas's recurrent nightmares are less frequent, and his marks at school are improving. The sad, bewildered look is almost gone from the Waltons' faces. There's laughter in the house once again.

Caroline took David's death much harder than I would have expected. "He was my youth," she told me, "and the father of my children. He's irreplaceable." She spent much more time with Kate the year after David's death than she had since she'd started her business, and never took her daughter anywhere that Mark and sometimes Olivia were not invited as well. She never did marry Alex Chakiris. Despite the success of her business and her ability to meet the social demands that made of her, she remained a shy, solitary person, comfortable only with a few, carefully chosen friends. Alex's life-style was too fast for her. She was sad but not heartbroken when her love affair with him ended. Now she's dating someone who designs computers. As happy as Caroline is capable of being, she is, I think.

Simon and Fiona did marry. And divorce. The sexual attraction was gone even before the marriage, he confessed later; but his career, and with it his ego, were then at such all-time lows that his relationship to Fiona gained significance in contrast: she was the only thing left him from his days of glory. But once he started directing again, Simon's emotional dependency on Fiona lessened, and when *Bust-up* was released and was an enormous hit, followed quickly by the success of *The Diviner*, David's play, he was able finally to let go (or, depending on your point of view, get rid) of her. Fiona took the breakup of this marriage hard. Though she was having an affair with a well-known cameraman when it ended, she was by then over forty and frightened, not certain she could get her lover to leave his wife, and even less optimistic about her ability to replace him should she fail. In fact, she's done fine. She's living with an actor now, the star of a hit television series, a man ten years her junior. Her face is older, but no less sexually promising than before.

Simon is filming on Long Island at the moment, and I had lunch with him last week. He grieves for Sarah, but it is David he misses desperately. Simon may have resented David and envied him, but he loved him all the same. He is bitterly regretful that he didn't manage to patch the friendship before David died. "I thought there was time," he said to me, tears clouding in his eyes. "I never dreamed there wouldn't be time."

Time ran out for Duncan, too, last year. Sarah's death shocked and angered and wounded him. It was only by the most incredible effort of will that he was able to give to Cassandra those last few months of happiness he had promised. They traveled to Tibet, to China, Thailand, and Nepal, before going back to London. Duncan entered a hospital soon after and died without ever returning to their home.

Most of Cassandra's mourning took place in the long months she watched Duncan die. Afterwards, she plunged back into work and last week was in New York with a new collection that got raves from everyone but the London *Times*.

We had tea at the Plaza. "I miss his voice," she told me, "his beautiful voice. Sometimes, going into the house, I think I can hear it, sounding deep and sexy and so very much alive. I think I hear him calling to me. Isn't that absurd?"

No. Sometimes I hear David's voice, not saying anything profound, mostly just repeating those same sentences I had heard from him over and over again for so much of my life. "Come on, Nikki. There's nothing to be afraid of. Who cares what those idiots think? Believe in yourself. You can't do anything if you don't believe in yourself. Don't be such a coward, Nikki. Try."

If only he could have been for Sarah what he was for me, my best friend. If only she could have loved him yet somehow kept her distance, as I did.

The newspapers at the time of David's and Sarah's deaths hinted at suicide, and murder. This awful biography I've just read insists it was. Loath as I am to agree with him about anything, Mr. Keating is right.

Whether or not Sarah's plunge off Mulholland Drive was deliberate, whether or not David provoked her to it, David and Sarah Walton undeniably destroyed each other's lives. They shattered each other's peace, stole each other's contentment, wrecked every chance of satisfaction, demolished all hope of happiness. During the years of their marriage, they killed each other slowly, in countless painful ways. But they didn't do it cheaply, sensationally, meanly, as the Keating biography implies. They did it without malice, without understanding how, or why. They did it grandly. They did it for what they believed was love.